# THE FALLEN AVIAN

## XOCHIL AMÉRICA

# TABLE OF CONTENTS

THE AERIDOME
PIETRO'S PALACE
A V A L O N
ROAD TO PARADISE
THE COLOSSAL FOREST
WAY TO COLOSSAL VILLAGES
BLADE'S PEAK
(MURMURATION SITE)
LEGEND
MURMURATION FLIGHT PATH
RIVER OF SERENDIPITY
COLOSSAL TREE
HEARTWOOD UNDERSTORY
POINT OF INTEREST
WAY TO WIGEON'S WALK
THE KINGDOM OF AVALON
(THE UPPER REALM)

DESERT OF DAVEED
KOLI KANYONS
KINGDOM OF ALAZAR
THE MOUNTAINS OF ALAZAR
HERE LIES THE WINGED MAN
THE EASTLANDS
THE LONG FINGER
KROTOA
NORTHERN PLAINS OF NADIIR
THE WESTERN COVES
KRICKET PENCE
THE GREAT ISTHMUS OF NADIIR
EMERY FOREST
SOUTHERN WIGEONIC TRIBES
WICK'S TOWN
MOUNT SULFUR
KROW'S FOOT
NADIIR
(THE LOWER REALM)
LEGEND
POINT OF INTEREST
LANDING SITE
HARBOR
DRAGON'S LAIR
HEROINE'S QUEST
THE EYE OF NADIIR

*To my mother, who is dearest to me.*
*And to those afraid of taking their leap of faith—don't think. Fly.*

# PART I
## THE FALL

# Chapter One

Helena Nightingale hardly took herself for a night owl, but it was the eve of the Murmuration, and who was she to miss out on the most anticipated night of the year? *Dance at sundown, soar at dawn*—that was the phrase dominating the streets of Avalon earlier in the day. Now, Helena stood before a great mirror, half-dressed, and admired the broad, stunning pair of wings sprouting from her back; they were as grey and reflective as a storm cloud, and the underparts of her feathers were borderline coal black, yet they were silken to the touch. These wings were Helena's pride and joy; she took great care in preening them and applying the best wax she could afford to keep them glimmering like knives.

Tonight, Helena had two snug braids restraining her silky, dark hair, starting from the crown of her head and running down the nape of her neck—she hated the concept of loose hair, especially as it pertained to flight, where it had a habit of getting in the way. For clothing, Helena chose a staple of Avalonian fashion: she reached for a tiny, dark mass on her counter, a curious little thing known as a *utilitarian ball*, or *U-ball* for short. It had a gooey, almost rubbery texture, and in squishing it between her thumb and index finger—*Zip!* It spread over her body and around the stems of her wings until she was covered in a fine, navy-colored suit. Designed by the greatest engineers of her time, this suit offered Helena minimal flight resistance, thermal insulation, as well as a salute to fashionable modernity.

Helena crept through the halls of her house, careful not to rouse her father from his slumber. The crack of his bedroom door revealed his familiar face soothed by the caress of sleep. *See you in a few hours*, Helena thought, before she snuck her way through and out of the house.

The Nightingale residence was just one of the few treehouses lodged upon Heartwood Understory, a great Redwood said to be thousands of years old, just like the countless others that made up the natural wonder that was the Colossal Forest. Together, these ancient giants housed hundreds of families upon their bridge-like boughs and formed a landmark that could be seen from kingdoms across the Upper Realm. Once outside, Helena surveyed the giant wooden bough sustaining their treehouse, which lay ahead of her like a runway. She burst into a sprint across it, spread her large wings, and leapt off the edge of the bough and into the night air! Tonight, Helena would fly north of the Colossal Forest and up towards Avalon.

The Kingdom of Avalon, known to many as the Silver Empire, sat along the highest provinces of the great and towering Mountains of Ava, which were rich in ore and minerals. It would take weeks for someone without wings to trek up the stark and dangerous roads leading to the sky-scraping kingdom—that is, if they didn't slip and fall thousands of feet to their death first! For someone like Helena, however, it was only an hour's flight up and through the misty mountains.

There was a slight chill in the air as Helena navigated through the outermost parts of the kingdom—mostly mountains and hills shrouded in a thick, indiscernible haze. As Helena ascended, the mist dissipated, casting her into an empire amongst the stars, where castles and palaces—as if carved by some divine hand—melted in relief along the majestic mountainsides. Smaller dwellings and cottages resided in alcoves amidst the rocky ledges, with crystal-blue mountain springs gushing from underneath. Helena savored this breathtaking scenery and rode the steady breeze, her wings lax and stretched, occasionally dipping and running along a tiled rooftop before somersaulting back into the air. It was in the heart of Avalon that she overheard the news that tonight's great roost would be held at Pietro's Palace.

*Roosts* were spontaneous celebrations that boasted all manner of fun to fire the imagination; from bonfires to barnstorming, nobody was ever sure what to expect from one, or when or where the next one would take place. Helena had attended a few in her lifetime...she knew, however, that tonight's roost would be one of a kind—she expected nothing less on the eve of the Murmuration!

Pietro's Palace was a fine establishment with pleasant archways, aromatic gardens, and a courtyard nestled beneath the starlit skies. Here, hummingbirds fenced over flora, bubbling grapes spilled from baskets, and marble-white fountains spewed a viscous amber liquid called *nectar*—or liquid gold, as some liked to call the exotic and luxurious drink imported from the southern lands of Hummeria. It was abundantly clear that this roost coursed with the moneyed blood of wealthy patrons, and while it was nice in its splendor, it disappointed Helena that there would be little tolerance for backwards somersaults or loop-de-loops at this formal establishment...

Laughter and the sweet scent of flowers filled the air, and cheeky adolescents dipped in and out of the courtyard in blithe spirits. Each of them possessed a pair of sprightly wings that varied in shades and patterns, but never deviated too much from the lustrous color of silver. Their feathers were of a quality to fill pillowcases: silken and shivery, puffing with every chilly gust of wind. These people who could fly were collectively known as *Avians,* and their wings contained a degree of magical essence that remained hidden to the untrained eye.

Tonight, these aves gathered to celebrate the conclusion of a bitter winter and welcome the beginning of a warm and prosperous spring. This event, occurring at the break of dawn, was known as the Murmuration. As a matter of fact, this year would be Helena's first time actively participating in it, and *not* simply observing it from afar like she had the last fourteen years of her life! Having just turned fifteen, Helena was finally ready to cross this milestone off her list once and for all.

"Look," someone whispered, "there's the Matcher!"

All eyes gravitated towards the one person in the courtyard wearing a gleaming set of iron armor that caught as much light as his silver wings. It was impossible to overlook Ser Ulyxes Cazador, or Yulix, as Helena called him: a knight who well embodied the spirit of the eagle. His eyes were a striking amber, and his broad wings dwarfed every other pair nearby. Such a dignified disposition could only ever pair with the title of Matcher; on this special occasion, Yulix would have the honor to initiate, or "spark," the beginning of the Murmuration—a privilege bestowed by none other than the king of Avalon himself!

"Greetings, Matcher," Helena said with a smirk as soon as they collided. She took in his glamorous appearance and joked, "I nearly missed you in that get-up!"

"Subtlety has never been my strong suit," he said, puffing his wings pompously before shooting a disapproving look her way. "Nor have roosting and revelry been yours! This is no place for a girl your age. I thought we agreed you would spend the night at home, Lena."

His reproving undertone plucked at Helena. "And risk waking up late for the Murmuration? I would end up at the back of the flock, with all the stragglers—no thanks! Lighten up, old friend; it's the eve of the Murmuration!"

"I only wish for you to have good judgment today, that is all."

She snorted. "When have you ever seen me in the air without it?"

"Your skills in the air are exceptional, Lena—but you are still wet behind the ears! A well-honed ave knows that flying requires a sharp and agile mind...exhaustion dulls the senses and provides a feeding ground for poor decisions."

Helena rolled her eyes. "I don't need your sermons tonight, Yulix..."

"Soon, it won't be mine you will have to endure," he said, a smile creeping on his lips. "Does your *father* know you're out this late?"

Helena huffed and crossed her arms. "I'll have you know it's *because* of him that I'm standing before you tonight! When the flock makes its way to the Murmuration site, I want to be the *first* person he sees."

Yulix's gaze softened. Perhaps he realized he was being a bit too harsh on Helena—after all, he knew how much she loved her father.

"Suit yourself," he said at last. "But if I see you dozing off in the air, I won't bother warning you when you're inbound for a tree!"

"If that's what it takes to wake me up," she muttered, stifling a yawn. "You've bigger responsibilities, Yulix, than worrying about a girl's beauty sleep!"

"Is that so?"

"Well, for starters, the king handpicked you to be Matcher this year. Which is not only a marvel in and of itself, but also an indicator that you're inches from becoming a member of the King's Guard!"

The King's Guard was an elite squadron of seven knights that served King Haeron IV of Avalon. In taking the oath of fealty to the king, these powerful individuals swore to act as the king's protectors and closest advisors. Yulix had dedicated most of his early life to such endeavors, starting as a squire at just ten years old and earning knighthood at fifteen. Of knights there were many, but few aspired to the higher road of becoming a member of the King's Guard...and even fewer ever achieved it. Yulix, however, was an overachiever and such a feat almost certainly lay within his future.

"Please, Lena," he said, rolling his eyes, yet failing to conceal his smile. "I must yet present one more instance of valor and heroism to the royal council before I officially qualify for the King's Guard, and even then, I'm not guaranteed a spot...still, the Captain of the King's Guard did mention I would be the youngest initiated in seventy-five years," he admitted sheepishly.

"I imagine so, at only eighteen! Soon, my good friend, you'll be in the king's court, hovering around those upper-class snobs, dressed from head to toe in lustrous, golden armor, indulging yourself with the finest nectar the world has to offer, forgetting us common folk..." She trailed off wistfully, suddenly aware of how sad it all made her feel.

Yulix smiled somberly and took her hand.

"None of that could ever compare to the times I spent soaring with you, Lena. I will cherish those memories all my life."

With the scent of change in the air, it certainly felt like the beginning of a goodbye.

"Enough," she said, changing the subject. "Let's dance, shall we?"

Time slipped from their fingers as the two aves kicked their feet to the cadence of the drums, which breathed life into the crowds like a beating heart. Helena twirled her wings as she spun round and round to the lively music, though she found herself disconcerted after another ave rudely brushed past her and, with a careless wing, *thumped* Helena in the back of the head! Yulix also took a moment to regard the curious sight, and they stared after the impudent ave as Helena rubbed the back of her head and scowled.

What set this ave apart? For one thing, her wings were white and much, much more refined compared to Helena and Yulix's coarse, sterling-grey feathers. But this compared little to what was arguably her kind's most distinguishing feature: button-black eyes and an unsettling, fixed gaze that required her to move her entire head to focus on any single thing. Two more aves just like her, each with wings as white as snow, trailed behind her as they dreamily made their way out of the courtyard.

Nocturnal avians were a curious group of people, indeed. They were nowhere to be found when the sun shone brightest, yet came alive when amber rays turned to moonlight, and the forests fell to a still hush. They originated from the regions of Nocturnia, a wintery and isolated wasteland in the Northeast where they saw little contact from *Diurnals*—aves like Helena, who were most active during the day and slept during the night. Aside from their macabre appearance, they were famous for their wanderlust, as they often strayed from home and roamed the streets of Avalon at night.

In truth, Helena knew little about the Nocturnal way of life, only that they were not allowed to linger past dawn. Naturally, the dissonance between their lifestyles laid a divide between Diurnals and Nocturnals; they hardly ever associated with one another, which is why it piqued Helena's interest to see a group of Nocturnal avians attending an event which was largely centered around the arrival of daybreak.

"What are Nocturnals doing at a place like this?" she wondered aloud.

Yulix's hooded eyes followed the white-winged aves uneasily. "They're leaving, that's what matters. You know what that means."

"It's nearly dawn," she said with a firm nod. The Murmuration Ceremony would shortly begin. She could not help but ask, "Do you ever wonder what it's like to live at night like it was day?"

"I'd lead a hundred different lives before I ever considered living in darkness," he replied, and gulped the last of the remaining nectar in his glass. Helena then snatched it from his hand.

"Easy up, *Matcher!* I doubt I'll be the one having difficulty flying to-day—your cheeks are red as apples!"

He gave a sheepish smile. "Speaking of apples—have you tried the fruit bar?"

"You know I stay away. I hate flying on a full stomach..."

"You've always had the appetite of a bird...come! You must try the dragon fruit—it is in season, and its flesh is ripe and sweet!"

Helena joined Yulix in sampling an endless selection of fruits, seeds, and finger sandwiches at the fancy fruit bar, where she helped herself to a firm and juicy grape; it burst across her tongue in welcomed tartness. Meanwhile, Yulix plunged his long fingers into a dune of salted sunflower seeds and sprinkled a generous pinch into his mouth. As they delighted in these small pleasures, they couldn't help but overhear one blabbering exchange nearby.

Helena recognized Jamie Moore from the Colossal Villages—a stout, pig-nosed young man—but not the lanky boy beside him, who appeared to have had one too many glasses of nectar. He stumbled stupidly over his own feathers as he sang at the top of his lungs:

"…It's time! It's time! Time for da Murmurashun!"

"Not yet, Mikey!" Jamie exclaimed with a bellyful of laughter. "With the state you're in, I reckon the rest of us will be heading down to Blade's Peak while you'll be flying home to the goats!"

"Plade's Beak? That ol' cliff?"

"*Blade's Peak,*" Jamie enunciated. "That's where the Murmuration will start, you helpless nut! It's got a lake as big as an ocean, which is perfect for the ceremony…but you won't catch me within a mile of that place at night!"

Mikey didn't catch the meaning of this last part—he gave Jamie a pitiful, blank look and a few dumb blinks.

"It's fair to be drunk, Mikey, but not clueless! Haven't you heard? People are going missing by the tens! Just yesterday, I was talking to my pops, who knows a guy in on the case—most of 'em disappearing are kids, and when they send the hounds to look for 'em, all their trails lead past the Colossal Villages and end at Blade's."

*The Colossal Villages,* Helena thought wildly. That was her home!

Mikey gave a heavy blow of the lips. "Reckon they drowned…Oh! What if I dive into the lake and see a dead body? Their faces swell like pufferfish, I hear!"

"That's the thing, Mikey—they can't find the bodies. Weird, isn't it? You want to hear something scarier?" He beckoned Mikey to come closer and spoke just loudly enough for Helena to catch it. "My dad thinks the people behind the 'nappings are sacrificing them in the name of the Fallen Avian."

Helena stirred uncomfortably at these words. A *fallen avian* was another name for an exile, or an avian who was expelled from Avalon into the netherworld of Nadiir, never to be seen again. Such a thing was uncommon nowadays, but it was still taboo to talk about it in open spaces—especially in such formal settings as these! Nevertheless, Helena continued listening...

"My great uncle was a fallen avian," Mikey said, sobering up at the thought. "Banished by the Crown for treason, he was. Me mom doesn't like to talk about it. Says it's a black stain on the family name..."

"But I'm not talking about your disgraced uncle, Mikey, or just any fallen avian." There was a mad look in Jamie's piercing blue eyes. "I'm talking about *The* Fallen Avian. As in, the first ave to have been exiled from Avalon."

Helena shot a look of confusion at Yulix, who did not meet her eyes and continued listening intently.

Mikey blinked stupidly. "I'd almost forgotten 'bout that cursed story..."

"It happened so long ago, I reckon most people have...but there are some who look to the Fallen Avian as a symbol of hope. People who resent the Crown for sending their loved ones into exile...listen, all I'm saying is, at night, avoid that lake like the plague."

Left with a sour taste in her mouth, Helena turned to Yulix.

"I can't say I've heard the story of the Fallen Avian before—have you?"

Yulix replied instantly. "I've little use for myths and legends...what's more important to me is your safety. You must take great care not to stay out too late, Lena, or to fly alone, given the rumors circulating around the kingdom. I say this especially because you spend so much time over at Blade's Peak."

He was right—Helena lived less than a mile from Blade's Peak and often flew over its great lake for hours at a time. The thought of it becoming the hub of some nefarious scheme made her feathers prickle with unease. Where were those missing children going...and who was the Fallen Avian? Helena could not quell the brewing uneasiness in her stomach...

Yulix saw the hour on the clock and straightened himself before diving into the tumbling crowds. Approaching one young man, he whispered in his ear. Eyes widening, he ran over to a friend, who hurried to another friend, who shot off towards two others—until a series of murmurs trickled throughout the room. This process was known as a *ripple*: a common way for information to spread quickly in large avian crowds. Earlier in the day, they'd been informed tonight's ripple would be denoted by a single code word which would indicate the Murmuration was soon to begin. In seconds, it reached Helena's ear:

"*Autumnus.*" As it spread, so did a collective silence.

"Morning, aves." Yulix leapt onto the stage, his silver feathers twinkling under the limelight.

"*Morning?*" Mikey cried, rubbing his eyes incredulously. It seemed time had gotten away from him!

"You be sure to fly at the back of the flock and stay there," Yulix said to him, to shouts of approving laughter.

"We've only moments before dawn. I see the anxious faces amidst these crowds...but I assure you the ceremony will feel as natural as the stretch of a lung. Murmurating is not just a method—it is an instinct which we have inherited from our Avalonian ancestors. When they first stepped foot onto the Great Valleys of Ava nearly four hundred years ago, they battled against warring tribes and predators who posed a significant threat to their villages. Our people, however, had a secret weapon in their midst: the *Avian Murmuration!* It was the spontaneous flocking of avians meant to outwit a single enemy. Alone, an ave could not defend themselves against these dangers, but in flocks of hundreds—or even thousands—even their greatest foes could not stand a chance!

"Over time, the Murmuration outgrew its defensive purpose and evolved into one of our most sacred ceremonies. Today, we use it to celebrate the coming of spring—a season of rebirth, renewal, and rejoicing! The Murmuration also functions as a symbolic rite of communion, as well. Gather closely, aves, for the greatest threat we face now is solitude in a world meant for fellowship. As you fly out there amongst your peers, relish the true magic of the Murmuration, but keep one thought in mind: *only in numbers do we prevail.*"

A strange, lonely feeling bloomed in Helena's stomach as she watched friends, family, and lovers embrace one another as she stood alone. She tried not to let this bother her, instead fixing her eyes upon her childhood friend who stood upon the stage and raised a glass to the crowd.

"To my fellow aves in this room," Yulix said, "and to new beginnings!"

His gaze had just met Helena's when a soft gradient of light bloomed in the eastern horizon.

Dawn had arrived.

*"It's time!"*

# Chapter Two

Excitement swept the courtyard as a periwinkle halo in the distance chased the darkness away. Hundreds of whooping avians poured out into the streets of Avalon, spreading their wings and taking off to join the mass flock that now eclipsed the entire city. A powerful gale overcame the streets, cool and invigorating, and the calamitous sound of a thousand avians thrusting their wings at once roused countless others from their slumber. Those who could join did so, and those who could not marveled from their windows and balconies. Yulix secured himself at the head of these masses, leading the event, and Helena was not far behind.

The mass flock glimmered like the blades of a thousand knives as it hurtled its way through the city of Avalon, flying to and around the King's castle—*the Aeriodome*. The magnificent palace sat perched atop the tallest recorded mountain known to avian kind, overlooking both the kingdom and the world. King Haeron IV, laden with age and sickness, would not be attending the ceremony in person this year. Nevertheless, he sat upon his highest balcony alongside his Queen and basked in the awesome sight of thousands of his subjects rejoicing in honor of spring come again!

The flock set off on a course due south, following the River of Serendipity, down past the Mountains of Ava, and into the Colossal Forest. Families stumbled out of their treehouses to marvel at the flock, cheering and whistling as it passed. Many aves leapt off their home trees to join the Murmurating crowd, while children—who hadn't yet earned their wings—ran around giggling with their arms extended, pretending they were joining in on the fun.

Then came the moment Helena had been waiting for as the flock approached Heartwood Understory. From her treehouse, a wingless man burst out its front door, waving his arms frantically as he saw Helena at the forefront of the flock passing his home. Raphael Nightingale had never been prouder of his daughter than he was that day.

At last, they arrived at the Murmuration site; Blade's Peak was a towering cliff that projected obnoxiously over the waters of a great lake like the lower half of a bird's beak. Helena was one of the first to make her landing run at the top of the cliff, before a lake as vast as an ocean; its waves crashed ferociously against the sides of the cliff. Closing her eyes, Helena briefly wallowed in the feeling of the cool breeze pushing against her wings, swaying her back and forth, before turning to Yulix, who landed just behind her.

Helena was not so oblivious as to miss the profound crease between his brows; it was not like Yulix to be so troubled, but when questioned about it, he seemed reluctant to admit anything was wrong.

"You've been sulking all night," she told him half bitterly. "Pre-Matching nerves?"

He scowled. "Please! I'm not worried about messing up the ceremony..."

Yulix leaned his head over the edge of the cliff. Helena did the same. Together, they took a long look at the stirring waves below, which smacked the lower cliffside in jarring *CLAPS!* It was at least a hundred-foot fall.

"...Hitting water from these heights is like hitting concrete," he said.

It was nothing compared to the heights Helena had just flown, but oddly enough, the sight made her dizzy. She placed a hand on Yulix's arm to steady herself and sent him a quizzical look.

"Are you trying to make me nervous?" she asked.

Ignoring her question, he whispered, "You've mastered the aerial dive, correct?"

There it was—his utmost concern revealed. Helena gasped loudly, prompting some curious looks from others nearby. *That's what you're so worried about? You think I'll miscalculate my dive?*

Every Murmuration ceremony concluded with a solid, collective dive into the lake, and it was probably the most thrilling aspect of the entire ceremony. It would not be the first time Helena attempted an aerial dive into water, but for some reason Yulix suspected she wouldn't be able to pull it off!

"Lower your voice! I don't think, I fear. It's why I wanted you fully rested, Helena...there's always some novice who miscalculates..."

*"Novice?"*

"Oh, relax! I'm trying to caution you. It's important you dive correctly, or there could be deadly consequences. You've refreshed your mind on the Aerial Plunge-Dive Maneuver like I asked of you? Know it like the back of your hand?"

She crossed her arms, thoroughly affronted. "I'm confident I could do it in my sleep!"

"Then I expect to see you alive when I resurface."

Without a doubt, diving was one of the most rewarding aspects of the avian experience. It often made for a fun skill to show off to one's family and friends. However, there was a process one had to follow in order to pull off the stunt successfully, otherwise what was thrilling could quickly become lethal...

The *Aerial Plunge-Dive Maneuver* was the safest, most effective technique which allowed an avian to reach remarkable depths from equally remarkable heights. To achieve it, the ave must straighten their body from head to toe while flattening and extending their wings behind them. In doing this, the ave approximated their body to an arrow, allowing them to penetrate the water with as little resistance as possible. Still, it was a high-risk maneuver, one where precision drew the line between life and death...

The *penultimate moment*—or what most aves would simply refer to as the *"sweet spot"*—was that brief point in time, just before the avian penetrated the water, in which they must brace themselves, adhere to formation, and hope for the best. Should the ave hesitate in this golden window of opportunity for even a fraction of a second, the force they'd meet when hitting the water would be enough to shatter every bone in their body—let alone their wings! It appeared, however, that through some biological design, most avians inherited an instinctual knack for executing the plunge-dive flawlessly. For someone like Helena, the chances of missing the sweet spot and breaking her neck were extremely low, and the chance of death was highly unlikely.

Her exchange with Yulix, however, left Helena dealing with lingering feelings of doubt. In truth, she had hardly put much thought into her ceremonial dive these last few days. Perhaps she could've taken the time to refresh her memory on the topic, but in her experience, it took a lot more than theory to master any technique or maneuver in the air. True success in flight, Helena had found, was achieved through the art of risk taking; much like the leap of faith you took when learning how to fly for the first time, you must trust that instinct will carry you away to victory, otherwise it would be a long and terrifying fall to your death! Ultimately, Helena assured herself that it would not take much to execute a proper dive, and trusted that her sharp instincts would guide her in pulling off the maneuver...

Still, there was always that slim chance that something could go wrong. As Helena took one last look at the waters beneath her, each wave slapping harshly against the cliffside, a terrible feeling of foreboding rumbled inside her.

In the short time remaining until sunrise, the chattering aves linked arms and danced their hearts away. When the time came, Yulix made little effort to garner everyone's attention as Matcher; he stretched his long, silver wings open and revealed a stunning set of gilded feathers across his wingspan. Each golden feather was a medal of honor symbolizing an act of courage or heroism—one needed a minimum of seven to qualify for the Knights' Guard, which could take most Knights a lifetime to achieve. At just eighteen years of age, Yulix boasted three golden feathers inside of each wing, totaling six.

Because he knew better than to give a long, drawn-out speech to an anxious, pre-Murmurating crowd, Yulix kept his words short, sweet, and profound.

"At sun's arrival, the Murmuration will commence. Don't think. Fly."

His words rippled across the crowd. Helena looked at him with all the admiration in her bones, grateful he would be the one to spark her first Murmuration. Today, they would soar the skies together and rejoice in the wake of a new beginning.

"Fly free, aves, and never forget: *in numbers, we prevail!*"

As one, a united voice echoed back to him, *"In numbers, we prevail."*

The sun peaked over the horizon, slowly at first, as if shy to greet its admirers. Sunrise.

It was time for the Murmuration to start. The Matcher released a galvanic howl before sprinting and leaping off the edge of the cliff. This ignited the crowd behind him; thousands of aves, Helena among them, followed his lead in spreading their wings and launching themselves off the edge. Helena lingered in the air, basking in the thrill of the fall before the wind caught under her wings and swept her up and away!

Helena naturally fixed herself within a circle of six other aves who, like her, were set to follow the simple yet taxing guidelines to Murmurating: in a seven-count flock—which is considered the smallest subdivision in any given Murmuration—every ave was to follow the headbird at the center. If the headbird flew upwards, you followed; if they made a sharp turn, you could not hesitate to do the same! It was essential that no member of the flock stray too far, for doing so would ruin the integrity of your inner circle, and the formation would instantly collapse...

For Helena, the only thing remotely visible were the six other avians in her immediate flock; the thousands of others around her were only a blurry, deafening backdrop. Rushing wind cut like razors against Helena's face and gravity pressed hard on her skull as she and her flock maneuvered through the air, soaring upwards, downwards, left and right, pivoting and even flying topsy-turvy! Her wings bent and twisted behind her, skillfully responding to every shift in the wind. The sun shone brightly overhead; beams of light weaved themselves into the fabric of the teeming Murmuration. The pressing gales howled past Helena's ears and swept away the beads of sweat gathering upon her forehead. There was one surreal moment when she teetered just above the surface of the lake, catching one full glimpse of its mighty blue waters glimmering with the sun's rays, before being swallowed once again by the mass flock.

There was an unspoken magic to the Murmuration, a sort of "elastic band," if you will, that bonded these aves closely together in the air and was quite difficult to break. Helena especially felt a high regard for her personal flock as they tossed and turned in the air, experiencing the same spikes of adrenaline as they defied gravity. Together, they relished the extraordinary experience of flying in a Murmuration.

The mass flock rippled! It rolled! It barreled! It lolled! Indeed, the Avian Murmuration was a form of art—a living mosaic that continuously phased, condensing one second and expanding the next, building itself up and then collapsing again. All this unraveled at daybreak, and families gathered at the distant shores to watch, enamored by this natural wonder which hailed the coming of spring. How could a flock of thousands of people truly coordinate such a massive maneuver while ensuring that nobody crashed into one another? That was the true mystery of the Murmuration: how a flock of such magnitude, despite its own inclination towards disorder, inevitably maintained its strong, cohesive character instead of collapsing in on itself.

As all good things must sometime reach their end, the flock dispersed. Drunk with exhilaration, the aves knew one last thing remained before they sealed this special memory away for good: it was time for the dive. One by one, their wings ceased to thrust, and their bodies succumbed to gravity. Like raining missiles, they shot deep into the waters below.

High in the air, Helena steadied herself as a shriek drew her attention down below. Recalling Jamie Moore and Mikey's conversation from earlier that morning, she half expected to see a purplish body with a face as swollen as a pufferfish. What Helena actually saw was not far removed from what she had imagined—only this person had lost their life just moments ago. A body bobbed lifelessly among the waves, its wings mangled and neck cracked at an unnatural angle—the young ave had not pulled off their dive successfully.

"Lena," a voice called as Helena's stomach filled with debilitating dread. She turned to meet a set of familiar amber eyes.

"I'm not sure if I can do this," she confessed to Yulix, all while fear threatened to consume her.

Yulix outstretched his hand to her. "You won't do it alone."

Hand in hand, they nosedived towards the lake. Together, they narrowed their wings and cut through the air like two flying daggers. As the waters below rushed closer and closer towards them, and the wind trilled past their ears, Yulix eventually let go of Helena's hand. Despite her fear and instinctual desire to bail out at the last minute, Helena kept on going and bided her time, waiting for the golden window of opportunity to appear. *The penultimate moment,* she thought. *The sweet spot. Wait for it. Not yet...NOW!* She sucked in a breath and submitted to her instincts before impact...

Helena could've sworn she saw her life flash before her eyes as she pierced the water's surface. It wasn't exactly a pleasurable experience—she may as well have gone head-to-head with a solid block of ice—but thanks to momentum and adrenaline, Helena resurfaced before she could think twice about it. As she floundered for air, mouth drawn wide open in a gasp, an incredible realization struck her: she had done it!

At fifteen years old, Helena had completed her first Murmuration.

Yulix resurfaced just feet away from where Helena treaded water. Strands of wet, dark hair clung to his temples and cheeks as he, too, gasped for sweet oxygen. His nose bloomed pink from the water's chill temperature. He spotted Helena, who shivered from the cold and lingering adrenaline. They looked at one another with pure admiration before succumbing to joyous laughter.

Upon reaching the nearest shore, Yulix pulled Helena in for a tight embrace.

"May this day mark the beginning of a new and prosperous life for you, dearest Lena," he said softly. Helena's heart squeezed with affection. "I'm sure your mother would have been proud to see the fine young woman you've blossomed into."

Feeling her throat swell with emotion, Helena only held him tighter and said nothing. They spent a considerable amount of time in this embrace, swaying in the shallow waters in a gentle waltz as their wings curled over one another, shielding them from the rest of the world. Helena did not want to let go. Part of her was afraid that the moment she did, everything would change.

When they did part, and the world did not end, Helena could only distantly observe the crowds of celebrating aves gathering along the shores. She knew she should have mirrored them and felt their exact joy, so why was it she could not shake off this peculiar feeling? Could it have been loneliness, despite the entire ceremony being centered upon the notion that she would *never* be alone? Or was it the premonition of a darker time looming ahead?

Helena watched as they dragged the body of the lifeless ave ashore. She couldn't know for sure.

The toll of pulling a roost, a Murmuration, *and* an after-party in only twenty-four hours left Helena practically bedridden the next day. She was only fifteen, after all, and she relished her warm bed until late afternoon, when she decided she would head over to Blade's Peak for a flying session. First, however, she decided to pay a visit to her father.

Raphael Nightingale chopped a bundle of carrots for their evening stew at the kitchen counter, his wingless back facing her as he did. He was, in essence, a man of the earth; his skin was the color of rich soil, and he was short and stout, like the trunk of a stunted tree. The two of them often received odd looks, for Helena was paler in complexion and towered over her father a solid foot and a half. When questioned if she was his trueborn daughter, he would laugh and say, "That's what they told me! I sure as Hades hope so!"

Jokes aside, Raphael never doubted that Helena was of his blood, for she possessed the same striking green eyes that were said to run in the Nightingale family. Everything else, according to Raphael, she inherited from her late mother, Efevra Wilfur Nightingale—including her stature, her beauty, and her proclivity for flight. Raphael never failed to mention the time he first set his eyes on Helena's mother:

"She flew with as much grace as a dove flocking over a funeral," he would reflect, his eyes often blurring with tears of nostalgia. "Your mother was a quiet and decent woman, reticent in her thoughts and whereabouts, though in the air she was a force to be reckoned with."

Helena only knew her mother a short time in early childhood before she passed unexpectedly from illness, leaving Raphael to look after his only child. He never remarried.

Raphael was, as it turned out, a *wigeon*. The word was used to describe any avian—typically an adult—who could not fly. There were many kinds of wigeons; some had wings, yet simply never learned to fly—though such cases were rare. Most wigeons, however, were aves who had failed to earn their wings as children, for reasons never quite understood. The Magical Law of Attainment was simple: *all avians must earn their wings.* This was usually accomplished by performing an act of service worthy enough to earn them: a simple act of kindness, perhaps, or of self-sacrifice. No ave knew for certain when they would earn their wings—if they ever would at all—but it typically occurred in early childhood, when intentions were truest.

Because wigeons were unable to earn their wings, this often gave others the impression that they were inherently bad people…but this couldn't possibly be true, because Helena knew her father, and Raphael was not a bad person. A tad misunderstood, yes, and a bit of a loose cannon—but never *bad,* or evil, like most prejudiced aves often assumed.

"The Avocets dropped by earlier," Raphael said as Helena entered the kitchen. Using his knife, he scraped a handful of chopped carrots into a pot of boiling water, then jerked when the scalding water splashed on him. "They brought us a gift!"

He angled the knife carelessly towards the countertop.

"Watch where you're pointing that," Helena muttered before heading over towards the red box on the counter; it was no bigger than the palm of her hand and wrapped in a single, golden ribbon. When she opened it, she saw half a dozen candied grapes inside, each coated in a shiny, golden layer of nectar.

"Nectar bombs!" she cried in delight. She took one grape and popped it in her mouth. Her face puckered, for nectar always had that initial twang before it fell serendipitously into its sweet and floral profile. Raphael took two for himself, tossing both into his mouth and humming in approval.

"Our neighbor, Madam Maria—may the winds uplift her soul—used to hand these to me and my brother every Friday on our way back from school. One each—never more, the stingy old callus…" He suckled the tasty treat in nostalgic gratitude before sending a curious look her way. "The Avocets have a daughter, you know…what's her name? Mandy! She'd make for a good companion, you know!"

"Her name's Macee," Helena said, rolling her eyes. "All the same, I don't care to be friends with her. She's odd."

"Odd! How so?"

"She has this weird habit where she takes the communal stairwell."

Raphael turned back to his brewing pot, stirring its contents with a wooden ladle. "And?"

"She has wings!"

"I fail to see the crime, my dear!"

She huffed. "I just don't see the point in taking the stairs to get to your treehouse when flying would take just a fraction of that time! And it's not like she doesn't know how to fly—I've *seen* her do it before. It's loony, and I think it's rather pretentious on her part...there are plenty of people who would do *anything* to have a pair of wings like mine or hers!"

Helena was obviously referring to him, but Raphael didn't seem to mind. He swallowed the candy in his mouth and added a finishing touch of salt to his soup before responding.

"Perhaps instead of focusing on how people wish to be like you, you should consider taking the time to be like them."

"Now, what does that mean?"

"I'm saying you need to ground yourself, Lena."

Helena rolled her eyes and looked away.

"I only say this because you spend too much time twirling cotton in the skies," Raphael continued, setting down his ladle. "I worry about you. Even the bird must come down eventually, and too much time in the air detaches oneself from reality. You are in dire need of a grounding force in your life...that's why I think it's important you have friends. Friends are a good thing to have when one is not blessed with siblings. When you have neither, it's a recipe for a lonely life."

"I have friends!" she retorted.

"Or rather one."

"Yulix is all I need."

"*Chh!!* That boy is busier than ever with the duties of knighthood, and unless he plans on renouncing it all for the sake of your hand, I wouldn't rely entirely on one man's company!"

"Father!" she cried, mortified.

"It is the truth! Now, I have much admiration for the boy, for he has seen over you the last few years when I couldn't, but I find it a great slight that after filling our heads with thoughts of betrothal, he suddenly petitions to become a member of the King's Guard!"

Yulix had already been dubbed a knight, but joining the King's Guard was another matter entirely. In doing so, he would become a sworn protector of King Haeron IV, and one day command armies and wield a powerful and magical sword...it also meant that he would swear an oath of chastity, renouncing any and all chance of matrimony.

"He owes us nothing," she said, her gaze falling. "I could never expect him to give up his duties for me..."

"When a man truly loves a woman, Lena, no sacrifice is too big nor too small. Remember that."

Helena suddenly found herself to be in a very irritable mood.

"It doesn't matter," she snapped. "I'm perfectly fine with or without friends, thank you very much! Perhaps worry more about yourself, given all the rumors going around!"

"I'd become a senile old sack if I paid much attention to fool's gossip!"

"Well, you'd best listen this time! There's talk of people disappearing—many of whom are unaccounted for."

"A shame," he admitted, "but what does that have to do with me? I very much doubt they would gain anything in kidnapping an old mule like me!"

"That's not the point, father," Helena said, visibly annoyed. "Once people start panicking, they'll be eager to pin the blame on someone else—and it won't be long until they start saying that wigeons are behind these disappearances!"

Raphael's eyes flashed. "What good is it to listen to the mewing of a fool? Give ear to one fool, now two walk among us! Forget such garbage, Lena, and never bring it up again!"

"Oh!" Helena huffed. "You never take anything seriously..."

"Where are you going?" he demanded as she marched out of the kitchen.

"To the lake," she replied stiffly, making her way towards the front door.

"To twirl cotton until your head is full of air, no doubt! It seems you command yourself, nowadays! Don't think I've forgotten your little excursion to the roost last night—you've yet to fully answer for your sneakiness!"

"You're just mad that I can afford to fly out and not be stuck inside this house all day—like you!"

*"Insolent little girl, just like your mother—"*

Helena slammed the door shut. Before Raphael could follow her outside, she leapt off Heartwood Understory and headed out to Blade's Peak to clear her head.

She glided just above the waters of the great lake, dipping her hand and feeling the water spray across her skin. Helena spent the next several hours practicing the most basic aero maneuvers: barrel rolls, splits, and reverse splits. She did this and more with imaginary enemies at her tail, evading their arrows and swords by tossing and turning in midair, making steep vertical dives and climbs, twirling in the air until the howling winds in her ears carried away her anxieties...including the guilt she felt over the outburst she had committed against her father.

Before she knew it, most of the shores had emptied and the sun was nearly setting. Concluding a successful flying session, Helena made a landing run along the grainy shore, her long legs carrying her momentum forwards until she came to a gradual stop. *Even the bird must come down eventually,* Raphael's voice came to mind, and Helena's heart weighed heavily at the thought of her father. *I should go back and apologize,* she thought to herself. But before she could kick off the ground again and go home, a blood-curdling scream caused Helena to stop and look towards the farthest end of the shore.

*At night, avoid that lake like the plague,* Jamie Moore's words echoed. The feathers on Helena's wings prickled with goosebumps. She lingered on the balls of her feet, considered taking off and pretending she never heard it, then wiped her sweaty palms dry and took to the air once more to investigate.

A girl, it was. No more than eleven years. She lay fallen on the ground clutching her ankle, her ashen wings matted and coated with wet sand. Helena rushed to her side, bewildered, and assured her that everything would be fine.

"I was flying," she told Helena in tears. "I landed by that stone over there, and my ankle went out from underneath me..."

"You must've hesitated on the landing," Helena explained, a trifle disconcerted. She crouched to take stock of the girl's condition, though she was having trouble identifying which ankle was the injured one. "When you make a landing run, you're supposed to carry your momentum *forwards*, otherwise you can slip and break an ankle. Don't worry—it's happened to me before. That's why you should never fly alone at your age."

The girl blinked her tears away and looked up at Helena.

"That makes two of us."

*"HEY!—"*

A foul-smelling sack fell over Helena's head as someone tackled her from behind. Her mouth gasped against thick cloth, fighting for air as several bodies wrestled her to the ground. Both Helena and her great wings flailed with all their might, but after much struggle, her assailants succeeded in pinning and tying a thick rope around her. Panting, she lay useless on the cold, moist sand.

"That was easy," the girl said, her voice now free of any distress. "Hmph! Telling *me* how to land, as if she were the greatest flier in the world..."

A second voice answered her. "*Easy?* Wes and I did all the hard work! No wonder we only ever snatch wigeons—flockers like these aren't worth the trouble of tying up!"

"Shut up, the two of you," a third person sounded. "Ribeye, hurry and help me lug her on the boat. Sofie, you get the anchor..."

There was a united groan as they lifted Helena from the ground. They certainly had a hard time with her—Helena was on the heavier side, given both her wings and stature. Nevertheless, they hauled her onto a creaking canoe and tossed her onto its paneled floors, where she landed with an *umph!* Before long, a round object pounded the wooden floor by her head, rolling and crawling across the hard floor of the canoe.

"*Help me!*" Helena cried, despite the sack being fastened around her head.

"Shut her up! Last thing we need is another flocker to come sniffin' around..."

Someone ripped the sack off Helena's head, and crisp, cool air greeted her face. Two hollowed faces stared down at her: one was the avian girl who had baited her, Sofie, the other a wigeon boy with a pink birthmark covering the left side of his face. Helena guessed that one was likely to be Ribeye.

He forced a filthy rag into Helena's mouth before she could scream. Behind them, another wigeon boy kneeled watchfully as his collaborators rowed further into the lake. To Helena's side, a thick ball of granite rolled with the motion of the waves.

"You sure this is the one, Wesley?" Sofie asked, hesitant.

"Sure as ever," he replied. "Wings as dark as thunder clouds, they said."

Ribeye uttered a sound of approval. "An' she's worth a lot more because she's a flocker, I expect!"

"What good is that if we haven't even gotten paid? We've delivered nearly two dozen people to those Krows—*where's our coin?*" Sofie demanded.

"Are you doubting him, Sofie?" Wesley said sharply, a mad look in his eye. She shrunk. "The Stork is true to his word and will reward us if and only if we do as he says!"

*Who is the Stork?* Helena could hardly think straight through the blood pounding in her ears.

"That's *if* she even makes it to the other side," Sofie said quietly. "What if none of this works and we've just been drowning folks at the bottom of the lake?"

"Even if it doesn't, I heard the water pressure makes your head explode!" said Ribeye.

Helena's muffled screams began anew.

"It works," snapped Wesley. "So long as we're right above the portal, we just drop her in and send her to the other side. She should be down in Nadiir in no time."

Blazing alarms sounded within Helena's head as Ribeye chained the anchor to her ankle. *Nadiir.* The place where they sent avians into exile? Did these lunatics really mean to send her down there with an anchor attached to her foot? *Impossible*, she thought—only the king had the power and authority to send people into the netherworld...

"You hear that, flocker?" Ribeye called Helena with a snicker. "We're sending you right down to the big man—you'd best hope you're good at holding your breath!"

How long would she have to do such a thing? Would she even make it alive to Nadiir? What, or better yet, *who* awaited her on the other side?

After an hour of endless rowing, the canoe finally slowed to a gradual stop.

"Ribeye, the anchor." Wesley commanded before he began to utter bizarre commands to his clueless peers:

"Just a bit forward…no, not that much! We're off a few degrees…not that way, dipshits! We have to be accurate, or else she won't make it—there! That should be it. Get ready, and—*shit!!!*"

*Whoosh, whoosh, whoosh.* A steady, powerful cadence of wings approached. Ribeye dropped to the floor beside Helena, the two of them invisible in the poor lighting of the lake. As Helena lay face-to-face with her captor, he placed a finger to his lips. *Don't make a sound,* he seemed to say, as the point of his knife met the soft chub of Helena's throat. *Or I'll kill you.*

"You there!" a familiar voice called. "Hold it!"

It was not at all like Helena to be out this late, and Yulix knew this well. He also knew her well enough to know that Blade's Peak should be the first place he searched in case she ever disappeared. It was Helena's affinity for flight that led to Yulix miraculously finding her that night. Could it perhaps also be the reason why these bandits set their sights on Helena in the first place?

"You stand before Ser Ulyxes Cazador, Knight under the silver banner of Avalon! Explain yourselves!"

Wesley's voice jumped up an entire octave. "Sir, my friends and I were just going out for a nightly row. Please don't tell our parents…"

There came a ponderous silence from Yulix—Helena knew he was likely scrutinizing the scene with eagle-like vision. She listened with her heart pounding against her chest and adrenaline pooling in her veins. She knew she had to act quickly, within the next few seconds, to catch his attention. Or else he would leave  she had been right under his nose…

"It's dangerous for you kids to be out here at night. Especially considering the rumors going around."

"What rumors, sir?" sounded Wesley's innocent voice.

"Is something going on in the villages?" asked Sofie.

"People are going missing," Yulix replied.

"Oh, no!" they cried in unison.

Helena nearly rolled her eyes at their hypocrisy.

"I think it'd be best if you two headed home now. It's late."

"That won't be a problem, sir! We'll just be on our way…"

Helena's heart sunk as the thrust of his wings quickly grew distant.

Ribeye twisted his head towards his friends, whispering, "Is he gone, yet?"

In a split second, Helena seized an opportunity to lean over and head-butt him so hard that he was momentarily blindsided. Then, she spat out the gag in her mouth and screamed with all her might.

Wesley bellowed, "WHAT ARE YOU WAITING FOR? TOSS HER OVERBOARD!"

A moment later, Helena was thrown into the petrifyingly cold water with an unconquerable weight at her feet. No matter how hard she kicked and flailed, her efforts did little to slow her rapid descent into the dark depths of the lake. In a strange way, the experience seemed to be everything that was the *opposite* of flying—a terrifying reversal to the control she exhibited in the skies. Helena was sinking—and she was sinking fast!

There was a disturbance up above as a distant object pierced the water's surface, leaving a long trail of frothing bubbles as it hurtled its way towards her. Helena recognized this familiar figure—Yulix! He had dove in to save her! But was there any point? She was sinking faster than he could swim. Freezing water choked away the oxygen in her lungs, and the canoe that brought her here was now a small speck in the distance. Down below, she spotted a mysterious vat of space, swirling with water and darkness. *It's over,* she thought. *I'll soon be swallowed and drowned…*

Then something unusual happened. Soon after the swirling maelstrom engulfed her, Helena found herself no longer bound to stone, nor sinking in water—*she was falling!* She could finally breathe again, and she screamed as she fell into a space where darkness reigned true. Here, there was no top, nor bottom—only an endless abyss in which she fell further and further down…and then, in the blink of an eye, she fell into another portal, bigger and brighter, and was flung headfirst into a sky of raging clouds. The winds were bitter and cold, and Helena, wrought with fear and confusion, could not propel herself as gravity pulled her further down.

Just as all hope was lost, a hand caught hers—Yulix! He had also made it through the mysterious passageway and now bore both their weights.

"Yulix—it's s-s-so cold…" The icy wind chilled Helena's soaked body to the bone. Suspended in midair, Helena caught a dim glimpse of her surroundings: they were high in the sky, stormy clouds racing all around them, despite having been submerged at the bottom of a lake just moments ago…

"Lena, listen closely to everything I'm about to tell you. Once I'm finished, neither you nor I will say so much as a word anymore—not a word, Helena! This is imperative. We've fallen into Nadiir. If by some measure we end up separated, find shelter and stay indoors until sunrise. Do not trust anyone. *Anyone*, Lena, not even me! Now, we will move silently and resort to hand signals. Start moving your wings to get your blood pumping, and follow my lead. The sooner we get out of here, the better our chances at avoiding a fight."

Bits of information sifted clearly through her mind, though others clumped together like wet sand. She was in Nadiir—the lands of the fallen! But, wait—avoiding a fight with *whom?* What did Yulix mean she shouldn't trust him? It was impossible to think with upscale winds rushing at her like a blizzard, in temperatures that made her wings feel like they'd aged fifty years in a matter of moments. Nevertheless, she pumped her wings until she regained the strength to propel herself in the air, after which she and Yulix navigated through the clouded masses in tense silence.

Something moved in the shadows. It was too dark to know who—or what—it might be. Back-to-back, the two friends braced themselves for a fight. Then, multiple things happened nearly at once: a series of metal objects zipped through towards Yulix, but he was quick enough to spin in midair and deflect each thrown dagger with his wings. At the same time, Helena thought she heard Yulix call her name from her far right. When she turned and saw nothing, something hurled itself from the opposite direction and smashed against one of her wings, effectively disabling her.

No longer able to sustain herself, Helena fell headfirst into the clouds, swallowed by eternal darkness.

# Chapter Three

The night clouds of Nadiir were thick and frothy. Helena would have dived into them if she could. She lay upon a bed of dry yellow grass and could not move for many minutes, for her entire body felt as if it had been battered by a tremendous force. She could not recall the moment she made impact with the earth, though her shaky memory did remember that when she fell towards Nadiir, wounded and helpless, some intersecting force had slammed into her from the side—as if catching her and saving her from her fall. The next thing Helena knew, she lay face up on the floor of Nadiir, unmoving, forced to listen to the moaning of the wind and the faint stirring of the ominous forest around her. Then, a terrible metallic scent reached her nostrils.

*"Oh!"* Clenching her jaw, Helena sat up and pulled her left wing over her shoulder to examine it, then stifled a sob; her feathers and bones had been reduced to scarlet-red splinters! Shock numbed most of the pain. Helena faced a daunting reality. She would have no choice but to travel on foot through this forest, leaving her far too vulnerable against whatever perils it may present. If the scent of her own blood smelled strong to Helena, she could only imagine how it must smell to the creatures of the night out roaming for a midnight meal…and with a broken wing, how could she escape?

With the remaining strength in her limbs, Helena ventured through the eerily quiet forest, remaining vigilant for whatever dangers that might present themselves in the unfamiliar realm of Nadiir. The bark on the trees was deathly, with deformed limbs sprouting purple leaves that looked almost black in the dark of night. Even the air seemed to weigh more and proved difficult to breathe. Helena felt out of place, as if walking through a dream—*No!* She thought suddenly. *Avalon* was the dream. And this...this was the start of a never-ending nightmare.

Up ahead, in the dull haze of the night, loomed the silhouette of a gloomy and foreboding mountain, its summit mostly concealed by murky grey clouds. As Helena approached it, the landmass towered over her, its huge spurs thrusting greedily from either side like a pair of enormous arms ramming into the land itself.

How far and how long Helena traveled, she could not say. It could've been miles; it could've been all night long. One thing was for certain, however: the shock of her injury had receded almost entirely, leaving in its wake an unbearable pain that radiated from her left wing down her shoulder blades and to her lower back.

Helena stumbled to a halt, feeling faint. Something had come out from the trees. It was but a breath of the wind, but she could not deny it—a familiar voice had called out to her in the dead of night.

"Lena..."

In an instant, the voice had pulled her from her daze—it was Yulix!

Again, his voice called out to her, and Helena followed steadily after it like a lost pup, searching for her dear friend. He'd escaped whatever had attacked them in the Nadiirian skies! Helena clung to this hope like a light in the darkness. Yet still, as dead leaves crunched beneath her every step, it did not tame the uneasiness swirling through her stomach nor the goosebumps prickling across her arms. Why would Yulix not reveal himself? It felt like she had traveled across the entire forest by the time the bodiless voice led her into a large and empty clearing.

*Something was off.* The hum of insects had ceased, and the hooting owls had fallen to a still hush. Helena turned to hurry away when suddenly—

*No!* Something lunged at her from behind. Helena's hands instinctively flew to the nape of her neck to protect herself against the snarling creature whose weight crushed her against the ground. Only one thought ran through her head, the thought that one of her worst fears was coming to life: *her wings were about to be ripped to shreds!*

There was a sharp, mangled cry, and Helena could breathe again at last! A wolf fell dead to the floor beside her with an arrow lodged firmly into its furry neck. For several moments, Helena was too afraid to even move, but eventually she garnered the courage to look up at the man standing just feet away from her. His silky wings were obsidian, glassy like the night sea, and they tapered to a sharp, narrow edge. He wore a fine vest of silver brocade with sleeves of black silk, and dark pants tucked into leather boots. His feathers puffed as he tossed aside the bow he'd used to slay the wolf, which now lay stiffly at Helena's side.

"Little bird, what have they done to you?" he said. His face held a faint look of horror as he approached the awestruck Helena, who could not find it in herself to move away. The stranger was lean and handsome, with rich brown skin and the kind of face that robbed the air from out one's lungs. His black beard was trimmed to perfection, and his dark hair was slicked back.

Ever so cautiously, he crouched and examined her maimed wing with the lightest caress.

"What is your name, and how did a lovely creature such as yourself end up in this state?"

Helena felt her cheeks flush with warmth. She shifted into a sitting position and gaped up at this captivating man. This close, she could see the crow's feet lining the corners of his keen and hypnotizing eyes...

She could not help but answer feebly, "My name is Helena Nightingale, and I fell. I can't fly, and I don't know my way back home..."

"You're Avalonian."

"How did you know?"

His lips curled into a disarming smile. "Why, anyone could recognize the signature sterling silver feathers of an Avalonian—you're the stormier of the litter, certainly! You come together in crowds and do that thing...what's it called? Mumbling? Marmalade?"

"Murmurate," she said, a little too eagerly. "But you're not from Avalon, are you? Your wings are unlike anything I've ever seen..."

"I'm afraid not, little bird—though what matters right now is that we tend to that broken wing of yours. Come, we must take you to get it fixed."

"I can't go," she said. "My friend needs my help...I heard him call for me—*ah!*" Helena cried out as a sharp pain shot up her injured wing.

"Nonsense, look at the state you're in! You require immediate medical attention. From the looks of it, we have little time before infection settles in—and if it manages to spread into the stem, you could lose your entire wing. *Permanently.*"

No other words could ever evoke as much fear as those, and Helena's face twisted in anguish. Rising to his full height, the man cast an enrapturing gaze upon the wounded girl and offered his hand. The thought of losing her wings was so frightening that she considered reaching for it at once.

"I need you to trust me, Lena. I can get you the help you so desperately need."

Heart fluttering, she took his hand, blinking several times before the trance broke.

"...What did you just call me?"

His black feathers puffed inquisitively.

"Only two people have ever called me by that name."

At once, the image of benign salvation this man had created shattered; his eyes filled with darkness, and he spoke to her in a voice that was not his own:

"Lena, listen closely to everything I'm about to tell you."

Helena knew that voice well. It belonged to Yulix; it was unquestionably identical, yet so *perverse*. Helena fell backwards with a gasp. What horror to behold this stranger with the voice of an angel but the likeness of a devil! Whoever this imposter was, he'd stolen Yulix's voice, and now the fate of her friend remained unknown.

*"You're a demon!"* she cried, scrambling away from him. But the man had already predicted her next move; he lunged forwards and stomped on her maimed wing to keep her from moving further away. Helena yowled in agony.

*"Let me go! Please! I've done nothing wrong!"*

His dark eyes drank in her fear. He seemed entirely satisfied with her reaction, and when his face returned to its more appealing nature, he said, in his *true* voice:

"Always so blameless, you Avalonians. Incapable of doing wrong...has it ever occurred to you that you might not be as innocent as you think you are? While you go about enjoying the splendors of your world, indulging in the finest nectar and twirling the air like fairies, the victims you've cast down into exile toil in their own misery and can only dream of such pleasures."

There was an edge of bitter jealousy to his voice, and Helena knew exactly who she was dealing with as soon as he said the word *exile*.

"You're fallen."

"Quite an assumption, indeed! But let us first clarify a few things before we come to such hasty conclusions, shall we? What is a fallen avian, exactly? The term originated within the Upper Realm, over two hundred years ago—around the start of the Avalonian Empire. Avalonian society was a superstitious cesspool then, prone to mass hysteria and paranoia. Countless avians were accused of dark witchcraft, many of whom were undoubtedly innocent. If they were not exterminated, then these avians were banished and cast down to Nadiir, a desolate nether region inhabited predominantly by savage wigeon tribes and kingdoms. Such a place was only suitable for the lowliest of avian kind! Their wings were clipped, their wrists bound in shackles, and they were cast down into the Nadiirian abyss via portals, earning them the infamous name of *fallen avians*.

"Today, such exile is no longer a daily occurrence, as it was back then, but rather one of the highest forms of punishment in Avalon. Nowadays, an Avalonian must commit a heinous crime to be banished into Nadiir. So, to answer your question, Helena, no! I am *not* fallen, because one would have to be born in Avalon and subsequently exiled to Nadiir to qualify as such—you fit the term far better than I do, I'm afraid!"

"I'm only here against my will!" she cried hotly. "I am *not* fallen."

"It matters not how you got here, only that you *are* here."

She scowled. "If you don't consider yourself fallen, what are you, then?"

"Merely a descendant of those who fell."

"I...I don't understand..."

"I, like my other black-winged brothers and sisters, was born in Nadiir. We are descendants of the avians whom Avalon banished long ago. The proper term for us is *Nevarians,* and there are a few notable traits that distinguish the Nevarian from lesser aves: we typically have dark wings that range in shade from abyssal black to charcoal grey; if I didn't know any better, I would've taken you for Nevarian, seeing how dark your wings are, my dear! We also happen to be natural *mimickers*. That means I store every sound I hear deep within the catacombs of my mind and can vocalize them at will! Some sounds I've witnessed myself; others are only broken bits of phrases I've borrowed from other Nevarians."

At last Helena understood why Yulix advised her to keep her words to a minimum. This man was a vocal thief; every word out of his mouth, however familiar, was designed to trick and lure his prey for the kill...and Helena had taken the bait.

He chuckled at Helena's stupefied silence. "I know, I know, it's too much information for a light-headed Avalonian to process. But as much as I'd enjoy giving you more history lessons, it's time we tend to that injured wing of yours. I fear infection may have already settled in..."

"Get your hands off me!" Helena protested as he gripped her harshly by the wrists and pulled her up to his level. He secured her in his arms, holding her tight against his body. But as much as she thrashed, feathers flying everywhere, she could not escape his iron embrace.

"In many cases, the best way to reduce the spread of infection is to remove the problem altogether! Hold still, dear Lena..."

"What are you doing? *Let me go...no!*"

What took place in the next few moments happened quickly. The man pulled out a dagger unlike any other Helena had seen before. It had a golden grip with a rubied end, and its jagged blade was made of a strange, emerald-like material. As it was raised up into the moonlight, it gave one last, deadly glimmer before plunging into Helena's chest.

There was an explosion of light, and Helena lost all sense of sight and hearing, but the pain was ever so present where the dagger pierced her skin. *This*, Helena thought vividly, *is what it feels like to be branded with a hot iron rod pressed against your flesh.* An acrid scent invaded her nostrils. Worse yet, the blade moved up and down, diagonally, side to side, and across her chest, as if she was being carved up like a piece of meat. Each stroke was as excruciating as the last. Though it felt like an eternity, it was over in the blink of an eye, and the effects were devastating. Helena lay seizing for the next minute, hands clutched at her chest, with a painful ringing in her ears.

What little strength remained in Helena allowed her to lift her head and behold a faint spark of light buzzing lazily around the palm of the man's hand. It could have been mistaken for a firefly, given how small and fragile it looked. He put away the dagger before she could take a better look at it, and as it disappeared, so did the mysterious speck of light. Helena paid this no heed, instead looking down at herself to see the carnage wrought upon her chest...but there was not a drop of blood nor a single laceration to be seen! In fact, there was nothing indicating a blade had punctured her skin at all! Nevertheless, a burning sensation lingered in her chest that radiated a sickly warmth across the rest of her body, and she was overcome by a terrible weakness.

*"What did you just do to me..."*

"I took your wings away. You remain, for the time being, a wigeon—and if you ever hope to see them again, you will have to do exactly as I say, when I say it."

"Took them away? I don't...I don't understand...that's impossiblc..."

"Look over your own shoulders and tell me I haven't done just that."

Helena didn't need to look. She could feel how her center of gravity had already shifted. Her body felt as light as air, and the unbearable pain in her left wing had ceased to exist. They were gone.

That was when a wail escaped Helena's mouth, and she tried to crawl away, blubbering like an infant.

*"Oh, this all must be a nightmare...it can't be happening...father! Help me, father!"*

As Helena cried out for Raphael, the Nevarian chuckled pleasantly.

"He is no longer your father, child—I am. Don't you see? This is what I do. I take the despondent and the downtrodden under my wing so that I may father them, guide them, and teach them the truths of this world, however painful they may be. I deliver them into a new life of freedom and understanding! That is why they call me The Stork!"

It was him. *The Stork is true to his word,* she recalled Wesley telling his co-conspirators, *if and only if we do as he says.* Those bandits had succeeded in bringing Helena to the one person who had devised this entire scheme.

"My people have toiled for centuries on this forsaken continent," the Stork continued, "gnashing our teeth and cursing the Kingdom of Avalon for banishing our ancestors and confining us to the Lower Realm...but there is no use drowning in contempt for the people who spurned you if you don't use that very hatred to get back up and exert your revenge. It's the only thing that can happen after falling, isn't it? The Fallen can only rise!"

"I didn't do anything to deserve this!"

"No," he agreed, his voice a low hum, "you didn't. But it is the present that must answer for the works of the past. Come now, Nightingale. Follow me."

*"I'm not going anywhere with you!"*

"I will not ask twice."

Just as the Stork moved to seize Helena, a rock the size of a fist flew in and hit him in the side of the head, causing him to bend over and emit a harsh groan. The Stork raised his fingers to his temple, and they returned to him stained a dark crimson. It was the work of a courageous young man, a wigeon who stood a good distance away with another rock in hand. The Stork whirled to face him, his wings flaring to reveal a menacing wingspan, and a beastly groan emanated from his throat that nearly made the wigeon stumble back in fear.

"Does my true nature scare you, runt?" the Stork said viciously to him. "At the very least my wings must appeal to you—I preen and wax them myself! Spare yourself the trouble and *leave* before I have you gutted like an animal. Feathers can be sharp, when given the chance..."

But the wigeon held his ground.

Without warning, the Stork leapt at him, pirouetting in the air and spinning so fast that his razor-sharp feathers scored the wigeon's cheek. The boy fell back with a yell, clapping a hand to his face as the Stork closed in on him. These images spun round and round Helena like kaleidoscopic colors, and it felt like every sound, every breath, and every cry had been amplified a dozen times in her eardrums...and then everything stopped.

The Stork looked to the horizon, then to Helena, and back to the horizon once more, his face exhibiting a troubled disposition that suggested the approach of an enemy much greater than himself. Helena looked to the east, expecting to see a beast of sorts, but saw nothing but the paling sky in the face of dawn. What was he so afraid of?

"This isn't over," he said. Without another word, the Nevarian spread his wings and took off, disappearing into the tree line and leaving a half-dead Helena behind alongside her savior.

After some time, the wigeon boy slowly regained his composure, taking shaky, profound breaths to steady himself. A nasty crimson gash ran across his left cheekbone, and blood flowed freely down that one half of his face. Yet somehow, he still got to his feet, knees wobbling, and ran to Helena's side.

*"Stay with me!"* he said, his voice fading in and out of Helena's consciousness.

Helena's chest felt like it had been ripped wide open. The world around her felt washed in static, and a kind of terrible shame filled her as the wigeon boy's deep brown eyes took in her feeble appearance. She felt, for lack of a better word, *naked*. Discarded. She wanted so desperately to hide, but there was nothing to shield her vulnerable body from his piercing gaze. Her wings—her beautiful wings—were gone.

Unable to bear the weight of her eyelids any longer, Helena went out like a light.

# Chapter Four

In the days that Helena spent unconscious, the image of a quaint white bird pervaded her dreams, pale and glowing like the rising sun against a set of misty hills. She felt a profound longing for this creature—why, she could not say. Often, she dreamt that she was running through a grim and unfamiliar forest, wingless, and throwing fearful glances over her shoulder as an impending darkness drew ever nearer—all before she would stumble across the same dove lying center of her path. The bird would flutter out of Helena's reach before she could touch it. *Stay with me,* she would cry, her hand outstretched, before the shadowy tendrils of darkness snagged her and swallowed her whole. As persistent as these dreams were, however, even these images grew as wispy as vapor and dissolved into nothing as Helena's consciousness became steadily anchored into the real world.

A few things registered immediately upon her waking, such as the profound ache in her chest that felt as if it had been torn in half. There was a second prevailing sensation, however, whose nature Helena could scarcely forge into words; but for lack of a better phrasing, it sufficed to say she was *hungry.* This hunger, she soon realized, had little to do with any need for food, but with a vacancy occupying the inner workings of her spirit. Something was missing—no, something had been *taken* from her. Something that she so desperately missed but could not find. There was nothing more she could do other than to delve into this defeat. It was a terrible feeling, not unlike rock bottom...but it came with the definitive assurance that the only direction left to go was *up.*

Helena rose, heaving herself out of bed and breathing raggedly as she clutched tightly to the bedpost to keep herself from falling. She staggered towards the closest window, not caring what chair or vase she toppled over in her path, and pulled open the shutters. A cool, pleasant breeze greeted her face as she beheld the pale moon, which shone over a dark and dreary landscape of forests and hidden secrets, much like the terrible place in her dreams. *Nadiir,* she thought.

Helena's first instinct was to escape. She placed two hands over the windowsill and was about to haul herself over its ledge when a voice startled her:

"Yer as good as dead if you do that."

With a gasp, Helena whirled around to spot a figure stirring in the far corner of the room. They had been sitting in the shadows the whole time, and though it was too dark to make out much of their appearance, the bright, beaming moonlight shone past the window's shutters and cast itself upon the ashen, hairy face of the young man she had seen that night with the Stork. *Stay with me,* she vaguely recalled him saying to her. A long, slender scar curved along his cheekbone, just beneath his eye.

"The Krows come to play at this hour," he cautioned ominously. "Best wait till morning if yer to flee, unless you want an encore of the scene we played a few nights past."

Memories of the night descended upon her like a waterfall, and Helena dizzily pressed her hand to her forehead, swaying on her feet.

"No," she moaned, backing up against the windowsill. "It can't be...surely, it was all just a dream!"

That was when the glint of a nearby mirror snagged her attention. Helena crept closer to it, floorboards creaking underneath each of her steps as she studied the eerie image before her. With such poor lighting, the green-eyed girl in the mirror looked rather sickly; her face was deathly pale, and scratches marred her collarbone, neck, and arms. Her utilitarian suit was gone, and replaced by a loose tunic and trousers. Wigeon garments. But all this paled in comparison to what truly horrified her the most: her wings were gone.

Recalling the cursed name of the *Stork*, Helena gave one last shudder before her knees gave way beneath her, and all else was forgotten.

Part of Helena wished she never woke up the next morning. Though she did, and shortly after rising out of bed, she found herself maneuvering through a jarring and disorienting reality. She made her way out of the bedroom and through the looming corridors of the dead-silent house, the world suddenly much too big, and Helena much too small without her wings. She felt lighter, but it was not a pleasant feeling; there was a disequilibrium present in her steps, where she occasionally swayed too much to one side or nearly tripped over her own feet. There were times when, out of habit, she half expected to bump a wing or two against a shelf or doorframe, only to glide effortlessly past them; she felt that nothing could have been more devastating.

Helena wandered like a ghost around the empty house, finding only a homely looking parlor with a hearth, a few spare bedrooms, and a kitchen with a window overlooking a vast stretch of green hills and pasture in the east. As the pale, diaphanous rays of the morning light shone through the windowpane, Helena spotted two large figures approaching the house from the main road.

A series of high, lyrical neighs beckoned Helena outside and onto the front porch, where she met two wigeon riders and their horses, which were laden with parcels of food and other goods. The first rider to dismount his horse was a brawny, earth-toned wigeon, tall and proud, though there was a coltish movement about his arms and legs as he approached her. Helena instinctively backed away from him, and the man stopped and raised his arms in surrender.

"I come in peace," he declared, and ever so slowly removed his hat as a sign of respect. The tenor of adolescence was amply visible in his friendly brown face—he was not a man, but a boy around Helena's age, though perhaps slightly older...He struck Helena as almost harmless...still, after everything that had happened to her, she could not let her guard down. She stood poised, her muscles tensed in anticipation of the slightest chance that she would need to make a quick getaway.

"I understand you're scared," the young wigeon said. His voice was kind. Gentle. "But you're safe here, and you can trust us. My name is Jared Pathfoot. Who might you be?"

Her voice was hoarse when she answered: "Helena Nightingale."

"Well, Helena Nightingale, you've been out cold for the last couple of days! I had begun to worry, but I had faith you would wake eventually, and I'm pleased to see I was right. My friend Noa here was the one who found you and brought you in that fateful night."

Helena's eyes flickered to the other wigeon, who remained mounted on his horse. She recognized his olive-toned cheeks and scruffy black beard. And of course, she couldn't fail to miss the long, pink scar across his cheekbone—a grim reminder of his encounter with the Stork. The mistrustful look painted on his face dissuaded Helena from showing any form of gratitude towards him.

"Where am I?" she demanded.

"You're in Nadiir," Jared answered at once, "on a small farm located along Krow's Foot."

*What a silly name,* she thought, disconcerted.

"It mostly takes the name because these lands are infested with *Krows,*" he clarified, after noticing her expression. "Those are the bad avians. They call themselves Nevarians, but down here, most people refer to them as Krows."

"They have wings like death," Noa finally spoke. His voice bore a familiar accent that Helena could not quite pinpoint, which admittedly nettled her.

"I would label those mimicking demons as anything but aves," Helena said with an air of disgust.

"I agree," said Jared with a smile. "I find the term *nave* suits them much better."

Helena could not care less what they called them—her mind was too busy stirring nervously at the thought of them lurking in the shadows of the forests that surrounded them.

"I'm grateful for your help," she said, "but I'm afraid I can't stay much longer. Can either of you tell me how I can get back home?"

The two wigeon boys looked at one another, chuckling, as if this perfectly reasonable question was amusing. Helena, clueless as to why her question was so funny, felt her cheeks grow warm.

"To Avalon, you mean?" said Noa amidst chuckles. "If that's the case, I'm afraid there is no way home."

This news struck Helena like a mallet to the gut, but Jared's lighthearted laughter softened the blow.

"Oh, you of little faith," he said. "There's no direct way to Avalon that we know of *yet*."

Helena looked from one to the other in sheer puzzlement.

"You see, Helena…you and Noa share a common fate: both of you were sent down here to Nadiir by the man who calls himself the Stork. I found Noa not long after he fell, just as he found you. I was born here, you see. We've been searching for a way to get to Avalon together ever since."

*A Nadiirian*, Helena thought, wondering how someone could bear to live in a place like this…

"How long has it been since they abducted you?" she said sharply to Noa. He seemed reluctant to answer.

"It's been close to five years since I've touched Avalonian soil."

*"Years?"* she cried, horrified. "You mean all this time you haven't made the effort to get back home?"

"Take a look around you," he snapped. "We've hit the rock bottom of the universe, and it's not like we can just fly back home, can we? We don't have wings!"

"Not yet, at least!" interposed Jared.

Something about this response rubbed Noa the wrong way, as if it were a sore topic of conversation that he was tired of hearing brought up again. He rolled his eyes and muttered, "Chasing fairytales again, I see!"

Jared frowned. "Can't a man hope for the best?"

Noa uttered a huff of disapproval. "Sure he can—but on more sensible things! Now, I've told you once before and I won't shy away from telling you again—if you haven't earned yer wings by now, *you never will.* The sooner you come to terms with it, the better."

Without another word, Noa spurred his horse onwards and trotted off to stable it, leaving Helena and Jared to dwell in stunned silence. Noa's brutality evoked within Helena feelings of sympathy for Jared, who was clearly wounded by these words. It also sowed the seeds of Helena's dislike for Noa, whom she had not known for even a day, yet had already given her the impression of being an impertinent young man with a callous disregard for others. Nevertheless, it was in that moment that Helena understood that Jared, despite teetering on the cusp of adulthood, had not yet abandoned his hopes of earning his wings. Given recent events, Helena was unsure how to feel about this.

They gathered later in the kitchen for breakfast, and Helena was stunned to see that even the poorest of meals in Avalon were of higher quality than what Nadiir had to offer. Jared served Helena a meek plate of three, sunny-side-up eggs, a slice of tough rye bread, and a side of withered greens—if you could even *call* the limp pile of purple and black weeds that! One egg's yolk had already burst and trickled through Helena's dismal plate like a river of gold.

Even then, this was far more food than Helena was used to. *I hate flying on a full stomach* was the excuse she always used. But in efforts to be polite, Helena ate her food diligently, chewing slowly whilst Noa ate with haste and without shame. He grabbed his portion of bread and tore it into pieces, dipping each piece into the creamy yolk of the eggs with his greasy fingers before tossing them high in the air and catching them in his mouth, then sucking his fingers clean afterwards. When finished, he bent over and licked the runny egg yolk residue from the plate, chugged a glass of milk within seconds, and gave a nauseating, gaseous *burp*. Helena sat across the table from him, gawking.

"Your accent is familiar," she said to him, doing little to conceal the disgust on her face. "You're from Wigeon's Walk, aren't you?" The oceanic tilt to his voice could only come from Avalon's southern harbors.

"Aye," he said, wiping his hairy mouth with the back of his hand. "Wigewalk, born and raised."

"Oh," she said stiffly. "I've visited a few times, though only to see its beaches."

"Aren't you a lucky wigeon? I, on the other hand, spent my entire life toiling by the harbors, loading ships and trading goods—you know, the work them *flockers* don't want to do."

Helena didn't care much for that word—it was riddled with contempt, at least it was the way he said it. She didn't press him on the subject anymore after that. What Noa said, however, checked out with what Helena knew of

Wigeon's Walk, or *Wigewalk* as he liked to call it. Its harbors were hotspots for working wigeons who dealt with the laborious tasks involved in handling precious cargo and trading goods, and who often manned ships to set sail across the seas. It was the rich and powerful avian families who commissioned these dangerous expeditions.

Jared, who sat nearby, set down his utensils and cleared his throat. "It would be wise to discuss what happened a few nights ago."

"That it would," Helena agreed sullenly, pushing her plate away. "But for what it's worth, I hardly understand what happened, either."

Helena recalled the events of that night in fragments, describing them as if they were a dream. She felt almost as if she were talking herself through them, rather than telling a story of her own experiences. She began with the events at Blade's Peak and was in the middle of explaining how she had just finished practicing aero maneuvers when Noa's impatient voice cut her off:

"Practicing *aero maneuvers?*"

Helena faltered, momentarily displaced, and felt a surge of annoyance at Noa's scrutinizing gaze. What part of that was so hard to believe?

*Oh.* Helena realized that her story didn't make sense to them because they weren't yet aware of what happened to her. Neither of them—not even Noa, who had saved her that night—had been present the moment the Stork stole her wings. As far as they knew, Helena had always been a wigeon.

"Hold your tongue until she's finished," Jared commanded, though he appeared just as bewildered by Helena's apparent contradiction as Noa was. "She has a right to tell her story...however bizarre it might be."

Only with great reluctance did Noa lean back in his chair and cross his arms over his chest; Helena imagined that he was likely biting his tongue. But they had no other choice but to listen to Helena's story, which she felt obligated to start over again from the beginning. And for the most part, they remained faithful listeners, their eyes occasionally widening as Helena described the more engaging parts of her story. They seemed especially skeptical when Helena recounted how she had suffered a hit to the wing and fell through the portal into Nadiir, but held their tongues and leaned forwards in anticipation.

"And then what happened," Jared pressed, "after you fell?"

"I lost my wings."

Even Helena realized how insane that sounded. A hairbrush, an earring, a pet...these were all things one could conceivably misplace—but *wings?* If Helena had lost anything, it would be her marbles! Or so it seemed.

Jared was at a loss as to how to react to this. "You...*lost* them?"

"They were *taken* from me," Helena clarified, just before Noa's howling laughter carried across the room.

"I've met delusional wigeons who think they'll earn their wings, but I can't say I've ever met one who claims they've lost them! She must've hit her head hard on the way down here!"

Helena's cheeks burned with anger. "I'm telling the truth!"

Jared shook his head. "I'm having a hard time understanding what you mean by *taken.* Perhaps you mean to say they were cut off? But that can't be! You would have stubs to account for it, if that were the case. But you don't."

"They're gone," she answered gruffly, "without a trace. It's as if I never earned them."

Noa gave a loud snort. "Likely you didn't."

Helena's jaw clenched. *"I earned my wings."*

"How'd you earn them, then?"

"That's none of your business," she snapped. How an ave earned their wings was a subject you wouldn't reveal to just anybody, and it was impolite for one ave to ask another. Even if Helena *did* choose to disclose how she earned her wings, it wouldn't be to this, this...insolent wigeon who vexed her so profoundly!

"Why, didn't mean to ruffle yer imaginary feathers!" Noa said, chuckling.

Helena had enough. She pushed herself up from her chair and made to exit the room, but Jared raised his hand to stop her.

"Don't go," he implored. "Forgive us! We're just trying to make sense of what you're saying! It's not every day that someone loses their wings...grant us a bit of grace in trying to understand your situation, and maybe then we can help you. Please, Helena. Stay."

He looked up at her pleadingly. Mustering a deep breath, Helena slowly sat back down, crossed one leg over the other, and cast annoyed glances at the sailor boy.

Jared sighed and began again. "Look, Helena...when an avian earns their wings, they earn them for life. This is the first I've ever heard of an avian *losing* their wings. Tell us—how did such a terrible thing happen?"

"That night, a strange man used dark sorcery to take them away," she said, recalling the traumatic event. "He had an enchanted dagger unlike any other I've seen. Its blade was green and crystal-like...When he stabbed me, it felt like I was being carved up and burned alive. Next thing I knew, my wings were gone, and I've been a wigeon ever since."

Jared leaned forwards to rest his elbows on his knees, his deep brown eyes conflicted with everything he had just heard.

"Do you know the name of the man who did this to you?" he asked intently.

Helena hesitated, for the name itself caused her to tremble. "He calls himself the Stork."

At once, Jared and Noa shared a knowing look.

"So, you two *have* heard of him," she observed.

Jared nodded grimly. "He's the leader of the Nevarians. They've terrorized our towns and villages for years, snatching people in the dead of night—usually young victims, like you and me. Nowadays, stepping foot outside your door past sundown means a death sentence. Not only that, but it appears that in recent months the Nevarians have secured a connection to the Upper Realm. They've started using it for all sorts of nefarious purposes—including abducting Avalonians."

Helena gave a dismal frown. "It's the first time I've ever heard of these so-called Nevarians."

"They are a budding population, with fresh wounds and a potent thirst for revenge against Avalon for what it did to their ancestors. They even have a strange phrase they like to quip to each other, over and over again. '*The Fallen will rise.*'"

"And always in the same voice," muttered Noa. "I got no doubt those Krows are demon-spawn. It's skin-tingling, the way they copy you like parrots..."

Helena shivered at the thought.

Jared's face turned grave. "I didn't think things could get any worse...but now, with what you're telling me...I fear for what's to come. Taking your wings away would be as if the Stork *undid* the very act of how you earned them, Helena—which sounds impossible. You're certain it was *him* who did this to you?"

"I wasn't the only one who saw him that night," she said, shooting daggers at Noa. "Unless *he's* so stubborn as to say he didn't see anything..."

Noa seemed disinclined to grant Helena any sort of vindication.

"Look, it may have been him; it may not have been. The Krow didn't stick around long enough for me and him to swap names—but even if that *was* him I saw, I wasn't there to see the Stork steal her wings, as she claims, so who knows if what she speaks is truth?"

The sheer audacity of this wigeon to insinuate that she was a liar! Helena opened her mouth to speak, ready to command him to believe her, but her anger fell away and she closed her mouth instead. It was no use. There was no way to prove what had happened to her that night.

Helena felt almost as if Jared's noble brown eyes were seeing through her own. She was broken, there was no doubt about that, and something had been taken from her. Something, he seemed to discern, that went beyond the mundane eye.

"I believe you, Helena Nightingale."

Helena fought the desire to break down in tears, though she could not explain why she felt the need to cry. Perhaps it had to do with the simple fact that Jared had not known Helena even for a day, yet still took her at her word on something that even she wasn't sure had really happened. She just knew that it was a beautiful feeling when someone believed you.

"Thank you," was all she said. Noa, however, seemed unsatisfied with this exchange and slumped back against his chair with a scowl.

Jared suddenly sucked in a sharp breath, his brows scrunching together, as if something didn't make sense to him. "If the Stork wanted you dead, he would have killed you without a second thought. But he left you alive—why?"

"Perhaps we'll find out soon enough," she said, her eyes flickering fearfully up to Jared's. "It won't be long until he finds me again..."

She recalled something the Stork had uttered after he took her wings away: *If you ever hope to fly again, you will do as I say, when I say it.* For reasons even she wasn't sure of, Helena kept this to herself. These thoughts sparked fear in her and made her chest ache. *No, she thought...I couldn't bear to see that monster again...not after what he did to me...*

Jared reassured her. "He won't be able to find you. We're located further along the upper leg of Krow's Foot, and their numbers tend to dwindle up north, so you're less likely to run into one of them around here. As long as you don't stray from the house at night, you're safe."

"*Safe,*" Helena repeated disbelievingly. "How can you be certain of that?

"Because Krows only ever come out at night," Noa muttered.

"You're saying that Nevarians are nocturnal?"

Jared nodded grimly. "They burst into flames if they step into the sun. That's why they'll never stick around long enough to see dawn. Because of that, we have the advantage of a *daylight buffer zone*—the sun is our best defense against them. That is how us Nadiirians evade falling into the hands of those wicked Krows—we only make errands during the day and are always back before nightfall."

"And if night falls and you're still not home?"

"That's exactly what happened to Noa the night he found you. Isn't that right, Noa?"

They looked expectantly at the wigeon boy, who sat sulking in his seat. When he realized they were waiting for some kind of response, he rolled his eyes and muttered under his breath, like a child being forced to confess to some misdeed they had committed.

"Time got away from me that day. I knew going back during the night harbored the risk of being tailed by a Krow, so I decided to camp out in the forest until dawn—that was right around the time I heard yer cries for help. When I saw the bloody Krow had his hands on you, I went and found a rock fat enough to sling at his ugly face...the coward fled as soon as he caught sight of the light."

"I never thanked you," Helena said, meeting his brown eyes. She didn't really enjoy the thought of this spiteful boy finding her in such a vulnerable state, as he did a few nights ago. Nevertheless, she felt indebted to him. "So...thank you."

Noa did not reply, but acknowledged her gratitude with a stiff nod of the head before looking away elsewhere.

Jared seemed pleased with this interaction. "The moral of the story is, if the sun ever beats you home, find cover from the sky and stay where you are until sunrise—*never* travel at night, unless absolutely necessary. It was past sunrise when Noa brought you here, so the Stork couldn't have followed you. You're safe."

*Safe.* It was hard to believe it could actually be true...but with an uncertain future lying ahead of her, Helena clutched to her newfound hope like a warm blanket.

"How, then, do we find a way back to Avalon?"

Jared leaned on his knees and sighed. "There's no conceivable way to travel from the Lower Realm to the Upper Realm without the use of magic. From the looks of it, we have only two options. The first would be to locate the same portal we fell through and use that to travel back to the Upper Realm."

"Which is impossible," Noa muttered. "That portal is thousands of feet in the sky, and there's no way for us to reach it, being stuck down here."

*It's not fair,* Helena thought bitterly. If she still had her wings, there would be nothing stopping her from flying through that portal and returning to Avalon...

"What's our second option?" she asked Jared hastily.

"There's only one person that we know of who has the power to open a gate between both Realms."

She knew the answer at once. "The King of Avalon."

He nodded. "If, by some turn of events, the King was informed of your fate, there's a chance he might open a portal and grant us entry into Avalon. For that to happen, however, we would need a messenger. That person would have to fly through the portal to deliver the news that you and Noa are stranded in Nadiir."

"Again," Noa began, "that's out of the question since none of us can fly, and we don't know a single flocker around these parts willing to risk their lives just to get through that portal..."

"If one of us earns our wings, we might be able to pull off such a mission," Jared said hopefully.

"There you go again, Red, beating the dead horse to a bloody pulp!" Noa cried out in exasperation. "Must I waste *any* more precious air on you?"

"Why are you so eager to snuff out his hopes?" Helena couldn't help but interject. "At the very least, he's *trying* to conjure up a solution, instead of dismissing every idea without a second thought!"

Noa's eyes narrowed into slits, and he angled his entire body towards her. "I'm doing him a *favor*."

"By shooting him down every chance you get?"

He chuckled, shaking his head. "Tell me, bird...at what age did you earn yer wings? *If* you ever did, that is."

"Six," she said through gritted teeth, never lowering her gaze.

A snort escaped his lips. "Alright! Let's just assume you did earn yer wings that young—"

"—I did!"

"—Then you just proved my point. Most flockers earn their wings when they're kids, usually by the time they're ten years old—Red's two away from twenty! If he hasn't earned them by now, he never will."

"There's no set age you have to earn them by!" said Jared stubbornly. "Most aves earn them early in life, that's true, but I've heard stories of aves earning their wings at fifteen, even twenty years old..."

"Hah! You'll be earning them at eighty, by the looks of it! By which time I reckon you'll be too old to use them. Open yer eyes and smell the salty sea air, mate—they're *not* coming. Don't you know that any ship that runs on false hope is doomed?"

"Spare me your wisdom, sailor," Jared snapped bitterly. "My time will come—just you wait!"

"If we spend our hopes on things that will never happen, we might as well resign ourselves to living the rest of our miserable lives on this wretched continent!"

They fell into another cold, rigid silence. Luckily for them, a startling realization struck Helena...

"I know how we can get back home!"

The two wigeon boys looked at her.

"My friend Yulix was with me the night of my fall. He's out there somewhere, I know it! If we find him, I'm certain he could fly back to Avalon and convince the King to help us get back home!"

This possibility seemed to stir some hope within Jared, although Noa still wasn't convinced. After much consideration, it was Jared who took the initiative to speak up:

"Finding your friend may be our best bet. If he fell at the same time as you, then he couldn't have gotten far. Of course, this all depends on the hope that he isn't already dead."

Helena winced at this.

"It's time we go home," Jared said to Noa, who did not seem too enthusiastic at the idea. Nevertheless, he did not object.

Helena was more than eager to return home, but something was holding her back. *I took your wings away. If you ever hope to see them again, you will have to do exactly as I say, when I say it.*

She would never admit it, but Helena suspected she would not be returning home for a very, very long time.

# CHAPTER FIVE

Having already suffered the devastating loss of her wings, Helena was surprised to discover that enduring the aftermath was a fate far worse than death. She could have been jabbed a thousand times in the chest, or torn apart and ripped to shreds by savage wolves; she could have been strangled to death and brought back to life, only to be killed once more—and none of those deaths would have wrought the anguish she felt staring at her tragic, puny frame in the mirror every day. As much as it pained her, she couldn't help wringing herself like a wet towel to get a full view of her bare back.

In the past, Helena had either dressed herself in her utilitarian suit or some variation of a backless top to accommodate her wings. Now, after losing them, she could not bring herself to use her U-ball, for the nostalgia that it carried with it was too painful. So, she settled with a plain tunic made of linen and a pair of trousers—*what any wigeon would wear in their day-to-day life*, she thought bitterly. Slipping on this clothing felt like putting on someone else's skin, and it fit her far too generously with the empty space where her wings should have been. As if this wasn't bad enough already, a scar had materialized upon her chest where the magical dagger had impaled her. It was long, hideous, and purple, and Helena knew it would forever serve as a grim reminder of the day she lost what was most precious to her.

It was precisely this internal struggle that put Helena and Noa at odds with one another right off the bat. It was hardly a secret that the wigeon boy disliked her—and the feeling was quite mutual! He was a proud spirit who mistook Helena's grief as a slight towards his wigeon nature. At night, when Helena's sorrows were most potent, her muffled cries carried through the thin walls of the farmhouse...and the next morning, an unspoken resentment lingered in the wigeon boy's eyes whenever she passed. For he knew far too well that Helena's tragedy was a simple face of his everyday existence, and from that tension sprouted the seed of their animosity.

Jared was kinder and more courteous to Helena than his sailor counterpart, often going out of his way to do things such as opening the door or pulling out her chair for her. But Helena saw right through him. *He's not really a good person*, she thought bitterly. *It's all a vain attempt to earn his wings!* And at the height of her grief, Helena secretly hoped that day would never come. She felt indescribably bitter at the prospect of Jared earning his wings and getting to fly when she couldn't. If Helena couldn't enjoy the wonders of flight, she didn't want anybody else to.

Helena often mulled over how Yulix and her father would react to the news of her loss. Yulix had always admired the pleasant, dark shade of her wings, which he often compared to storm clouds. Surely, he would want nothing to do with her now. Raphael would be ashamed to have another wigeon in the family, no doubt. *Or maybe*, she thought darkly, *it would bring him some sort of satisfaction to see me stuck inside the house all day, just like him. To keep the bird locked in a cage.* Helena loathed herself for these poisonous thoughts, but they could not be helped.

Late at night, when she had nearly exhausted herself in self-pity, Helena almost always thought of her mother. The years had fogged Helena's memory, but she could still recall clearly her mother's keen, dark eyes and wispy, black hair. *You were as good a flier as your mother*, Raphael often told Helena. *She, too, took to the sky to escape her woes.* Now, Helena no longer had the means to escape.

Missing her mother, Helena rolled over in bed and wept.

Jared found her one morning sitting on the edge of her bed, staring with red-rimmed eyes at the little black mass in her hands. When Jared tossed a pair of brown leather boots to her side, Helena quickly stored away her U-ball and looked at him.

"Ride with me," he said. "It's time you get some air."

*Air*, she thought, *yes*. "Where will we be going?"

"A few miles north, a little way from Wick Town. I was hoping it would take your mind off things."

Eager to catch a breeze, Helena rose out of bed and pulled on the old pair of boots. Though they fit her feet a little too snugly, she followed Jared outside so she could learn to ride a horse for the first time.

The gleaming, rusty brown stallion towered over Helena. Beneath its mighty chest she could just see the outline of its heart pumping in large bursts of energy. A long white patch laid across its chest and the front of its stomach, earning it the noble name of Underbelly.

"This may be a little higher than you're used to," Jared said after helping Helena mount her horse. She clutched the reins tightly as the red stallion gave an antsy jerk.

"This is nothing compared to the heights I've soared," Helena said proudly, and Underbelly responded with a squeal. Even the horse could tell her words were filled with doubt.

She soon regretted saying anything at all. Jared demonstrated the basic commands and gestures to maneuver a horse, but it was an experience completely alien to Helena. Her stomach lurched as the horse suddenly broke into a trot, and she soon lost control. Helena's pelvis pounded painfully against the saddle. Her left foot slipped out of the stirrup, and she felt herself slipping off the saddle...

"Pull the reins!" Jared shouted behind her.

*"I'm falling, I'm falling!"* she cried.

Jared yowled, prompting his steed to rush to her side, and pulled Helena's reins hard until both horses came to a jolting stop. Frazzled, Helena leaned forwards to catch her breath, pressing a hand to her pounding chest and aching scar. Underbelly gave a shrilly whine and shook its head almost indignantly at the fiasco that had just taken place.

"You have to be assertive," Jared told her sternly. "Horses can sense fear! Watch and observe."

He spurred his horse forwards, his steed's ears pointing back at the sound of Jared's commanding voice. They accelerated into a healthy trot, both rider and noble beast holding their heads high, before circling back in a slow walk. Jared's hips shifted comfortably with every step of his horse.

"Riding requires confidence, balance, and great concentration in the lower body—an area I assume you're unfamiliar with. Sit up tall. Allow yourself to sink into the groove of the ride. Rock your hips, if you need to. It's all in the legs."

*It's all in the legs,* Helena mused, not quite grasping the concept at first. Still shaken from her previous mishap, Helena could only swallow her pride and shabbily mimic Jared's profile. It took some getting used to, and her groin ached terribly, but Helena eventually relaxed and gained better control of her horse. When she finally felt ready, the pair embarked on a simple, slow walk down a path that ran alongside a trickling creek. This time, Helena felt a lot more at ease, and her tight grip on the reins finally loosened.

"You're not so bad," she told Underbelly, who responded with a rather haughty snort.

"I never thought I'd be in this position," she admitted afterwards, "down here, riding a horse. It's usually meant for...well, aves don't really make use of horses, do they? Why ride a horse when you can get where you want to go twice as fast through the air?"

"I can tell you're practical," Jared said with a smile, "but here in Nadiir, it's the fastest way to get around. Second to having wings, that is. I suggest you get used to it."

Helena's good mood turned sour. "How can I? It wasn't always like this..."

"Keep thinking like that, and the world will move on without you. The best thing to do is to make the most of your current situation. It's the only thing a wigeon can do."

Helena turned her head away and scowled. How could he expect her to accept such a reality so soon, and unconditionally? She was aware that Jared's advice came in good faith—perhaps, being the wigeon that he was, he saw something of himself in her suffering. Helena was adamant, however, that their battles were not the same. In her eyes, it was a lot worse to live your entire life with something and then one day *lose it,* as if being woken from a beautiful dream. Jared would most likely never know such a loss and would never have to navigate the murky field of grief that Helena had found herself stuck in...

"I just can't fathom being stuck in a place like *this,*" she said, gesticulating around them, "let alone for years! I'd have tossed myself off a cliff already!"

"Try living your entire life down here."

"I'm sorry," Helena said, frowning. "I didn't mean—"

"I know what you meant," he said with a stale smile. "Nadiir is my native home, but it is as flawed and wild as it is beautiful."

"How has *he* gotten along the last five years?" Helena asked, nodding back towards the farmhouse. She found herself somewhat reluctant to say Noa's name out loud.

"Contrary to what you would expect, he's fared well. Noa has a keen sense of adventure, and that makes him adaptable to almost any environment...of course, he also has a temper as turbulent and volatile as the wayward tide. But his loyalty never wavers."

"Yes, he's quite the character," she muttered. "How did the two of you come to meet?"

"It's...complicated. I'm not sure if I'm even at liberty to say—Noa hates when I bring it up."

"Oh, please. How complicated could it be?"

He hesitated, debating whether he should continue. "Noa spent most of his life toiling at the harbors for money—I suppose that made it easier for him to develop something of a fondness for mischief. He was only twelve when he joined a gang called the Blood Feathers. Noa didn't know it then—or so he tells me—but the Stork had been working in collusion with them, promising bounties for Avalonians like you."

Helena recalled the faces of the three adolescents who had abducted her at Blade's Peak. Wesley, Ribeye, and Sofie were their names.

"He and a group of Blood Feathers ambushed a few working wigeons in the countryside and took them to Blade's Peak to be dropped into Nadiir. Some of the higher ranking Blood Feathers, however, had the sudden inspiration to torture the victims. Then, when they ordered Noa to finish one off, as in silencing them *permanently*, he refused...but the Blood Feathers have a no-backing-out policy, you see. And when he resisted, they tossed him in the lake alongside the rest."

"I don't believe this...he's worked for the Stork, and you *trust* him?"

"I do. He was just a boy, after all, and people often underestimate what a person is willing to do when they're starving. Besides, you wouldn't want a mistake you committed years ago held over your head, would you?"

Helena looked away and scowled.

"I found him one fateful day on my way back home. He was chained inside a cave, and I helped him escape. After that, we could never stay in one place for more than a day, and we always slept with one eye open. We were all we had—my folks had passed a few weeks prior to us meeting, after catching a lethal cold. Still, as an orphaned boy of only thirteen, I had lived long enough on Nadiir to know how to evade trouble, and Noa caught on quickly: mind your business, stay indoors at night, and never, *ever*, admit you're from Avalon."

"Why not?"

"It attracts a lot of negative attention. There's a prevailing myth that those from the Upper Realm have magic in their blood—and many Nadiirians would kill to be *'up in Paradise,'* as they say."

Helena shot him a side-eye. "Even you?"

"I'm not so desperate as some, but I understand the sentiment. Lush, fertile lands, endless possibilities. Being able to raise a family and not having to worry about your children being snatched by a Krow at night...it's enough for any man to risk his life just to cross over. Living in Nadiir can be quite dangerous."

"And what dangers would you say pose a threat to a person like me down here?"

"Wigeon poachers run amuck in these lands hunting avians for their feathers, which make a useful ingredient in medical salves. It's either that, or they sell them off as slaves. If they find out you're from the Upper Realm, though, you become twice as valuable as any Nadiirian, whether you have wings or not."

"That's horrible!" Helena exclaimed, frightened. "But I find it hard to believe that *avians* actually live around here—I haven't seen a single one since I've gotten here! Only wigeons and naves..."

"You won't find many around these parts because of the reasons I've just told you. The people who do earn their wings...most of them leave and never come back. They tend to migrate north and settle at higher elevations, like mountains, valleys, or cliff sides—where it's safer for them. I've never visited the North, but when I earn my wings, it'll be the first place I go—you know, once I can soar miles on end without getting tired!"

Helena felt a pang of jealousy at this.

"Flying is more tiresome than you think!" she couldn't help but interject.

He tilted his head curiously. "How so?"

"Well, you couldn't possibly soar across the continent in a day...you'd have to account for climate and shifting weather patterns. Moreover, an ave can only fly as far as their endurance will allow...as my father says, even the bird must come down eventually."

The memory of her father flashed before her eyes, and Helena's heart squeezed with sadness.

Jared laughed, easing Helena's sorrow. "And here I thought flying was as simple as slicing through butter! There's still much I have to learn, it seems."

She eyed him and sighed. "Tell me how you do it."

Jared looked at her with gentle surprise.

"You've spent your entire life wishing for a pair of wings, and even after a decade has passed and you still haven't earned them, even when your own friend says you will never earn them, you still cling to the absurd hope that you'll earn them one day. How have you managed to remain so, so...*optimistic* after all these years?"

"If I don't believe in myself, nobody else will," he said with a light smile. "It's almost silly, I know, but sometimes I can't help but feel that the universe wants me to prove myself somehow. I *will* earn my wings, one way or another. How? Well...I suppose only time will tell."

"Only time will tell," Helena said in agreement, and the conversation ended there. Before long, the two of them turned their horses around and made their way back to the farm. Helena pondered over their conversation the whole ride back. Who knew if by the end of this journey—*if* it ever ended—both of them, one of them, or neither of them would have their wings? Helena, however, wouldn't resign herself to a life of wigeonhood just yet—she held on firmly to the belief that all of this was just temporary. She would get her wings back one day. She didn't care how long it would take.

Perhaps, in that way, she and Jared were very much alike.

Helena ended the day with sore legs and a sore backside—a feeling she never expected she would ever experience—and fell asleep like a child after a long day of play.

Helena, Jared, and Noa spent days riding southwards along the length of Krow's Foot in search of Yulix, keeping a keen eye for any silver feathers, tracks, or breakage in trees that they might come across. One day, the group split up to cover as much ground as possible, and Helena was left on her own. *Be back by nightfall*—that was the golden rule. By this point, Helena had ridden Underbelly plenty of times, but something about this mission made her stomach churn with unease. Anything could go wrong—falling and breaking an ankle, encountering a wild beast, crossing paths with poachers...*anything!* What's more, from the top of a hill overlooking the southern countryside, Helena could see the faint blue-grey outline of a familiar mountain on the horizon. A darkness gathered behind it, suggesting an ugly storm was on its way. Ignoring the uneasiness that the mountain made her feel, Helena sucked in a deep breath and spurred Underbelly onwards.

They ventured across the countryside, following dirt paths and roads, overcoming hills both big and small, and worming their way through the narrowest of valleys. Then, after many hours of constant riding, Helena called Underbelly to a sudden stop.

She had spotted something shiny entwined amidst the fronds of a tall, shady tree. Helena prompted Underbelly to move underneath the tree's branches, then extended her arm out and plucked the feather from the leaves. The silver feather glimmered like a long, polished blade beneath the bright light of the sun overhead. It was as long as Helena's forearm. She knew Yulix well enough to recognize the distinct silvery-white pattern of his feathers, which tapered to a soft grey at their base. Its tip was stained unmistakably with droplets of dried blood. *Please be alive,* she thought, looking anxiously to the skies. The sun was well past its apex, and Helena decided that she would venture a bit further before returning and sharing her critical discovery with Jared and Noa.

It was late, and Helena knew that. She would hurry home soon. *Just a little bit further,* she thought stubbornly—after all, Yulix could've been nearby in desperate need of help! The grim mountain's outline doubled in size as Helena headed further south. Then, as she and Underbelly trotted past a stream, a snake unexpectedly burst from beneath the water and skidded across its surface. The sudden movement spooked the unsuspecting horse. With a shrieking neigh, he jerked to a stop and reared back. Helena lost grip of her reins and fell backwards, landing harshly on the rubbly gravel. The impact of the fall knocked the wind out of her lungs, and Helena felt a bit of déjà vu as she stared up at the orange sky, breathless.

Helena swore as she watched Underbelly shoot off into the distance, disappearing into a thicket of bushes and trees. She looked to the western sky and saw it was already beginning to darken—time had slipped from her fingers! By now, Noa and Jared were probably at the farm wondering where she was...

*Never travel at night.* Jared's words rang in her head. Helena knew better than to try to go home. She decided she would camp out for the night. Because it was sure to get chilly with the oncoming storm, Helena took her U-ball from her pocket and squeezed it, causing it to unravel underneath her wigeon clothes and provide an extra layer of warmth. Helena decided she would look for Underbelly before setting up camp, as the antsy horse could not have strayed far. It took a good while before Helena perceived any sign of him; she could hardly see a thing when the stallion's familiar nickers sounded nearby.

*BRRGGHHH...*

"Underbelly?" Helena said, rubbing her eyes. She could've sworn she heard the blow of her horse's lips...

*NEIGHHH...*

Yes, Helena was almost certain it was her horse hidden behind that thick congregation of bushes and branches. She heard his heavy, burdened breath, which she had grown to recognize as easily as her own. Helena approached slowly, clicking her tongue and being careful not to frighten him and set him off. Yet as she neared, the hairs along Helena's arms prickled, and apprehension bubbled in the pit of her stomach. Something was not quite right...

*WHAM!* A shadow lunged at Helena from the bushes and tackled her to the ground. The Nevarian's sharp black wings tore every nearby branch and leaf to shreds as she wrestled with Helena, who struggled with all her might to gain the upper hand. Black feathers and debris rained down around them, and in less than a minute, the Nevarian had Helena pinned to the floor.

*"Shut up!"* the nave hissed, clamping her hand over Helena's mouth. "I've come to deliver a message from the Stork. Listen closely. I shall only recite it once..."

Heart hammering against her chest, Helena could only gaze wide-eyed as the Nevarian delivered the message:

"Helena Nightingale," the ave intoned, in a voice that was not her own. Helena could not forget the Stork's voice, even if she wanted to.

"After having successfully evaded my men and fled north, it appears your Avalonian friend has returned with a group of seven other scouts to attempt a search and rescue mission for you! Heed my words, Nightingale! The time has come for you to make your choice. You can choose to reunite with your beloved friend and attempt to return to Avalon, where you would live out your days forever wingless. Or, if you ever hope to fly again, you can meet me at the summit of Mount Sulfur tonight. I have a surprise that I'm quite certain will be of interest to you...if you have any intention of finding out what it is, make haste and come alone. Until then, Nightingale..."

*Yulix was alive.* The brave knight must've gone incredible lengths to return with a rescue team for her...but at the very least, she was relieved he was still breathing. Still, Helena found herself at a crossroads: she could choose to reunite with Yulix, and together they would find a way to return to Avalon...but that would reduce the chances of getting her wings to zero. If Helena ever hoped to fly again, she would have to accept the Stork's request and meet with him at the top of Mount Sulfur.

With a hiss, the Nevarian woman let go of Helena and leapt up into the night sky, winging off towards the distant mountain to the south. She had completed her mission by delivering the Stork's message to Helena and looked unlikely to return. As for Helena, she rubbed her sore neck and pondered her next course of action. After much deliberation, she rose to her feet and began looking for Underbelly.

After all, Helena would have need of a good horse if she wanted to get to the top of that mountain as quickly as possible.

# Chapter Six

Mount Sulfur drew ever nearer as Helena approached its northernmost spur on horseback. Storm clouds shrouded the skies in a dark and nebulous mass which engulfed the entire upper half of the mountain. Sharp rain stung Helena's eyes, and loose strands of hair clung to her wet face as she and Underbelly hurried blindly through the pitch-black landscape, which was illuminated only by startling flashes of lightning.

As the paths up the mountain became steeper and slipperier, Helena had no choice but to tether Underbelly to a nearby tree and proceed on foot. Ankle-deep in mud, she treaded carefully up the narrow, rising ridges of the mountain—a journey far more strenuous and humiliating than anything else she had experienced. A painful stitch lingered in her side, and her thighs cramped terribly...having a pair of *functional* wings would've been extremely helpful, given that aves seldom used their feet to travel any distance more than ten feet! It was growing all the more difficult to breathe at this altitude, and Helena's chest ached...

She knew she had encroached upon enemy territory when she spotted a feather entangled within a thorny bush. Holding it up to her eye level, she observed droplets of rainwater rolling off its waxy black coating. Nevarian. Helena spotted another feather not far over, half buried in mud. And another, and another. These feathers led her to a great tunnel entrance. As it was difficult to discern the scene with rainwater flooding her eyes, Helena slid behind a large bush to get a closer look.

Helena counted five tents gathered around a large tunnel entrance leading into Mount Sulfur. Black-winged Nevarians filtered in and out of this tunnel like ants, carrying crates of meat that appeared to consist of slain warthogs, goats, and lambs. They also moved to and fro ferrying munitions of gleaming iron weapons: swords, knives, spearheads, and morningstars. Their armor was lightweight, yet durable. They wore iron chest plates which opened wide in the back—a typical avian feature designed to accommodate the wings, but admittedly always left the ave's back vulnerable to arrows or spears—with the sigil of what looked like a crow engraved upon their chests.

While eavesdropping, Helena noticed another skin-crawling detail: every Nevarian demonstrated the innate ability to mimic speech. They quipped to one another like parrots, tossing sounds and words back and forth like a ball—and always in the exact manner in which they heard it! A few select phrases dominated the grounds: "THE FALLEN WILL RISE," and "LONG LIVE NEVAR." They parroted these phrases from a source Helena did not recognize. In a hurry, and with chills running down her spine, Helena quickly turned her back and continued her journey up Mount Sulfur.

After what seemed like hours of physical toil, Helena at last came to a stop. She beheld a masterful portrait of sky, and only sky, where a thick blanket of clouds settled below and concealed the lands beneath, which were plagued by harrowing rain and thunder. These were the great heights at which she once soared, as easily as one would stroll through a garden, but now she could only attain them as any ordinary wigeon could: by using her own two feet and trekking up the mountain. Helena marveled at the endless field of clouds, made silver by the pale rays of the moon. It was, in essence, a paradise untouched by conflict.

She had arrived at the summit of Mount Sulfur.

Almost hypnotized, Helena admired a set of six birds gliding over the clouds in a delicate 'V' formation. She hadn't yet realized that someone else had joined her in marveling at the breathtaking scenery.

"Birds are wonderful, tireless things," the Stork said, almost dreamily. "They can fly for hours on end, if they so desire. The Albatross, for instance, hosts migrations that can last months, even years without rest...can you imagine such freedom, Nightingale?"

Helena gave a doleful sigh as she watched the birds soar effortlessly across the sky. The Stork continued.

"We avians are not birds, however. We *weigh*—some more than others—and it is only a matter of time before we must come down eventually. How unjust it is, having something as splendid as flight at the tips of our fingers, and yet always having to land, like waking from a dream! Oh, but you were once as swift as a bird, flying circles over Blade's Peak as if your life depended on it! You would've spent your whole life flying if you could've, isn't that right?"

A single tear trailed down Helena's cheek as her eyes lingered on those geese. "How long have you been watching me?"

"A little over a year, now. My eyes and ears up in Avalon always wrote to me of the girl who lived at Blade's Peak—the one who dwelled from sunrise to sunset. The Nightingale, they called her. Daughter of an irritable old wigeon who goes by the name Raphael Nightingale."

The fact that he knew her father's name alarmed Helena greatly.

"After spending much time observing you, I began to wonder...how relentless is this ave's ambition to fly, and to what lengths would she go to retrieve it lest it be taken away from her?"

Realization struck Helena, and she clenched her hands into fists. "You took my wings away out of some dark whim?"

"If you think me so imprudent, Nightingale, as to take away your wings out of mere impulse, I would advise you to reconsider such a notion. Everything I do, I do for a reason. In truth, I took them away in the hopes that you and I could broker an agreement between us...a transaction, if you will. You give me something I want, and in exchange I shall grant you your wings back. How? Let me explain..."

The Stork took several steps back and unveiled the very weapon he had used to steal Helena's livelihood; the dagger's crystal-like blade was the same as when she last saw it, long and sickly green. Surely, no ordinary object could've possibly invoked such a reaction from her! Helena jerked away from it as if brushing up against a flame. Oh, how she loathed the sight of it, and how her scar throbbed like a pounding heart...

"This dagger dates back thousands of years. Only recently did I acquire it after investing precious time and resources in tracking it down. It is said to have powers of great magnitude, including the ability to examine and manipulate the soul. With it, I was able to penetrate the confines of your soul and examine it..."

As if wielding a wand, the Stork conjured a blinding, glimmering orb of light from the blade with an effortless jerk of his wrist. The orb lurched outwards as if trying to escape, but something tethered it to the cursed weapon, and it fluttered frantically around the Stork's head. Helena saw its familiar white wings and realized that this bird was the same one that frequently visited her in her dreams!

"Do you know what this is, Nightingale?"

"It can't be..." Stupefied by the captivating light, Helena couldn't find the words to answer his question. Helena felt as if she knew it all her life.

"This orb of light I have in my hands is your *mirage.* You have seen it once before—the day you earned your wings."

Of course! How could she have forgotten? There was a good reason why this little bird filled Helena's dreams, and why a longing ache radiated from within her chest as the dove floated in front of her. It had been so long ago...but she could still recall the day she earned her wings, and when a bright, shining light formed out of nothingness. It fluttered joyously in midair, as if celebrating Helena's milestone with her, before diving into and nestling inside her six-year-old chest. And from there sprouted her wings...

*"All avians must earn their wings,"* the Stork began. "That is the fundamental principle that governs our universe. The mirage is the mechanism through which the avian's wings are bestowed upon them. Its name derives from the belief that it reflects the image of your soul—and yours happens to take the form of a dove! The night of your fall, I took your wings from you by taking away your mirage."

Oh, the sheer humiliation of knowing this man had seen every inch of her mirage was almost too much for Helena to bear! It felt like an equivalent to his seeing her naked, and it sparked an inner outrage.

Her eyes burned. "You've stolen my mirage, and you've—you've perverted it with your eyes!"

"Oh, I'll never understand the taboo against sharing how you earned your wings. If you were such a dutiful child in earning it, why don't you show it off with pride?"

Helena found herself repeating a phrase her father would often say to her: *"Honor myself, and my honor means nothing!"*

At these words, his face darkened. "Such noble words, and yet here you are, Nightingale! Why did you agree to meet with me? The answer is ever so clear, for you know as well as I do that you'd be willing to do anything to get your wings back...even if it meant getting your hands dirty. Isn't that right?"

At that moment, Helena resisted the urge to claw her way through the Stork and claim what was rightfully hers. It was excruciating to stand so close to it, as if she had crossed an entire desert without water, and now a bountiful oasis presented itself before her. She would do anything if it meant flying once more...

"Enough of this," she said, defeated. "Just tell me what you want."

His fine lips curled into a greedy smile. "Listen closely, for I will only tell you this once. There is an object of considerable value that I want you to retrieve for me—an artifact, to be exact, hidden within a network of caverns which are said to be nearly impossible to locate."

"And you expect *me* to find it?"

"I don't. There are two individuals roaming Nadiir, however, who can: two avians from the Upper Realm who go by the names of Olip and Penelope Duskmuth. They are, in fact, siblings, and the two of them smuggled themselves into Nadiir to find this artifact. They are excellent navigators and are the only ones who possess the knowledge necessary to locate it."

"So why don't you have *them* find it, instead?"

"Do you think me so foolish as to not have considered the possibility? I made my offer to the twins, but they refused. Now, I find myself in need of someone less...conspicuous to find them and uncover the true location of the artifact."

"You haven't even told me what it is that you want me to retrieve for you."

"That," he said sharply, nettled by her comments, "you will find out in due time. You will seek these two individuals and gain their trust. It might be of interest to you to know that they are Nocturnal avians, so they may be a bit wary of you at the start. Do whatever it takes to coexist with them, for they are the key to achieving your objective. They mustn't die—not until you find the artifact—after which you will bring it directly to me. Do this, and only this, and I will return your mirage."

He snatched the flying bird from the air. It squirmed, and as it did, so did Helena. "Naturally, you have the freedom to turn down my request or change your mind at any time. But know that in doing so, I will not hesitate to destroy your mirage, and you will never know flight again."

Nothing frightened Helena more than those words. Taking her under his wing, the Stork turned so that they faced the startling expanse of the sky before whispering in her ear.

"There is a reason why wigeons envy us avians so arduously in their thoughts and dreams. Countless of their number have died trying to replicate what we have achieved naturally. What are we, if not the wigeon's wildest dream? Is that what you want, Helena? To spend the rest of your miserable life pining for an impossible dream? To give up that which is the only thing keeping you from utter mediocrity?"

If this man meant to reach into and scratch the deepest surface of Helena's fears, he had succeeded.

"I'll do it..." she said at last.

"How delighted I am to know we will spend the next several weeks in collaboration, Nightingale!"

"...on one other condition."

The Stork's feathers puffed. He took no pleasure at the thought of Helena adding her own clause to their bargain. Nevertheless, he listened to what she had to say.

"There are two boys with me—a native Nadiirian and an ex-Avalonian Blood Feather. When all this is over, and I have done as you've asked, not only will you return my wings, but you will pardon any grievances you may have against them and allow us to return home, no questions asked."

Though the Stork's face remained still, his eyes flashed with what appeared to be ire. "You ask me to pardon a defector from my cause? Such a case allows for little mercy."

"He was only a child, then, and my conditions are final," she said firmly.

"Very well," he said at last, his dark eyes glittering with mischief. "I am not unreasonable. With this deal, you will buy your friends' freedom, and no harm shall come to them—so long as you uphold your end of the bargain."

"Just to be clear, they are not my friends. They're just some people I met the other night, is all."

*I'm only returning the favor for their help,* she thought. *This way, we'll be even.*

"No doubt it would hurt them to know you regard them so little."

Jared's honest eyes flashed before Helena's, and she stifled the feeling of guilt bubbling at the base of her stomach. The Stork clasped his hands together with a satisfied, victorious grin.

"Then we have ourselves a deal! I'm afraid that concludes our time together. And so begins your long and arduous journey! The next time you hear from me shall be through a little bird. Farewell, Nightingale, and remember that nothing good ever happens after dark..."

The Stork receded back into the darkness, taking Helena's mirage with him and leaving her feeling colder than she ever had before.

Helena waited out the remainder of that stormy night on the peak of Mount Sulfur. The kiss of dawn fell upon her cheek and stirred her from a restless sleep. The sky was a clear, pale blue, and a wonderland of frothy white clouds blanketed the world like sheep's wool. As Helena gazed longingly at the sight, relishing the cool, whistling breeze, something stirred in the distance. A small V-shape emerged from beneath the clouds, bursting into the clear blue skies. Anyone else would've taken it for a flock of birds, but Helena knew better. She jumped to her feet and moved to get a better look. Seven aves with brown wings soared higher and higher above the clouds, heading away from the mountain. Their shining armor glimmered in the crisp light of the morning, almost as brilliantly as the silver wings of the headbird of the flock: Yulix.

Forgetting everything that had happened to her in the last twenty-four hours, Helena waved her arms and yelled with all her might.

*"COME BACK! TURN AROUND!"*

The remaining avian instinct in Helena caused her to sprint and launch herself off a log, expecting the wind to carry underneath her wings and propel her body upwards. But now, in a devastating reminder of her present condition, she found herself falling and crashing to the ground instead. Her wings were gone. They no longer existed. All that remained was a girl whose knees now bled against the earth. Stranded. So painfully pedestrian. That day, as Helena watched her kind disappear into the clouds, she was reminded so cruelly of what had been taken from her...and what she had to do to get it back.

*"Even if it takes weeks, or months, or years,"* she said amidst tears, *"even if it costs me my life—I'll take back what's rightfully mine."*

# CHAPTER SEVEN

I t was late afternoon when Helena arrived back at the farm. She was riding Underbelly up the main road when Jared and Noa rode out on horseback and met her halfway. Their disbelieving eyes alighted upon the tall, slender girl whose normally tight braids had come loose and exploded into a dark, unkempt mess. When the three of them dismounted their horses, Helena came face-to-face with Jared, who looked relieved and somewhat vindicated by her presence, and Noa, who looked rather bitter Helena had returned after all.

"What did I tell you? Relentless as the wind, she is, always carrying through!" said Jared, grinning. Noa only rolled his eyes and scowled.

"For the record, I never doubted you were alive, Helena!" Jared said. "But I will admit I was concerned the Krows had gotten to you."

*You weren't wrong,* she thought wryly.

"We agreed to rendezvous at the farm by sundown, did we not?" snapped Noa, a suspicious gleam in his eye. "Why didn't you?"

"I lost track of time," she explained. "I found traces of Yulix scattered amidst the forests of Nadiir and time slipped away from me while I was trying to find more. I would've stayed put, like you instructed me, Jared…only I was ambushed."

"Ambushed," cried Jared sharply. "By Nevarians?"

Helena knew it would be tricky to explain the events that had ensued last night after sundown. Based on the glowering, accusatory look plastered upon Noa's hairy face, she anticipated that the conversation ahead of them would be unpleasant to navigate.

"Just one. They had no intention of capturing or killing me—they were simply delivering a message from the Stork."

The two wigeon boys exchanged alarmed looks.

"What sort of message?" demanded Noa, his heavy brows sinking further with mistrust.

"Well?" said Jared expectantly. Helena was reluctant to answer. Her eyes flickered nervously between Jared's look of disapproval and Noa's withering glare. She sighed. There was little point in hiding the truth, though she dreaded the reaction to come.

"He asked to meet with me in private."

Something in Noa's eyes ignited; there was a smug look on his face, as if all of his suspicions about Helena had rung true. He pressed his lips together tightly, as if withholding a profound reaction and waiting for the signal to unleash it...

"And you accepted this invitation?" Jared asked, frowning. It seemed he already knew the answer.

"Yes."

"*YER A RAT!*" Noa had even startled his own horse, for it let loose a piercing neigh and tossed its head up and down in response to Noa's outburst. "*I told Red you were rotten, and he didn't want to believe me! This entire time you've been waiting for the perfect opportunity to sell us out, haven't you? How was it, then? Did you chat him up nicely and bid him Fairwinds before tossing us overboard? Did he promise you silver and gold? A hundred taluns a wigeon?*"

"Why, I might ask you the same thing, *Blood Feather!*"

Helena knew she had struck him where he least expected it.

Noa reeled from Helena's retort, then shot Jared an accusatory glare. "*You swore you would never speak of that again!*"

Jared squared his shoulders and said, "There's no use in hiding the truth, Noa—"

"I was twelve, Red! *Twelve!* I reckon I'll be on my deathbed, and you'll *still* be finding ways to hold that over my head and make me feel terrible—"

"You know that's not my intention. You'll run a never-ending race if you keep trying to outrun your past—"

"Oh, I don't need to hear another one of yer bloody sermons! Until either of you knows true hunger like I have, you got no right to criticize the mistakes I made as a mere boy!"

"Then what right do you have to call me a sellout?" Helena demanded hotly. "And for the record, I never sold anyone out—I met with the Stork because I didn't have a choice in the matter. He has my mirage!"

At once, they fell silent.

"Impossible!" whispered Jared.

Noa's tirade fizzled, and he looked warily at Jared. "What's she going on about?"

"How did he get his hands on it?" Jared pressed, ignoring Noa.

"He used the enchanted dagger to remove my mirage," she answered at once.

"Yes…" he mused. "Of course! How could I have not considered it before?"

"Oh, don't mind me!" Noa said, snorting. "I'll just stand over here, clueless as to what the pair of you are talking about!"

Noa had never earned his wings—Helena knew that well enough, so she was not surprised to hear that he was unfamiliar with the term. Jared, on the other hand, seemed well versed on the subject—which made sense, given how he longed for a pair of his own. He was more than eager to explain what a mirage was—though, for whatever reason, Noa didn't seem too enthusiastic about the topic.

"When an avian performs an act worthy enough to earn their wings, the purest light imaginable spawns in midair, almost too bright to behold, before planting itself inside them like a seed and sprouting into a set of pure white wings. Every avian's mirage is different, you see—often taking the form of whatever you did to earn it. My father once told me that an ave only ever witnesses their mirage twice in their life: the first time is when they earn it, the second time is only in death…"

These words sent chills running down Helena's spine. If she had seen her mirage for the second time already, one could say she was already dead…she certainly felt like it, at times.

Noa tapped his foot in annoyance. "Okay. So, what does any of that have to do with *her?*"

"It explains exactly how the Stork took Helena's wings, Noa. The Stork severed the bond between Helena and her mirage, leaving her as if she had never earned them...unbelievable! By confiscating her wings, the Stork has managed to defy the very Law of Attainment!"

This last sentence was enough to send a wave of shivers down Helena's spine.

Noa, evidently annoyed that even Jared knew more about mirages than he did, said, "Well, I couldn't care less about how a flocker earns or loses their wings. Where I come from, we don't spend our time talking about *magical fairy auras.*"

"Neither do we," Helena answered brusquely. "In fact, it's frowned upon to boast about how you earned your wings because mirages highlight the good in us—if you spend all of your time bragging about your good deeds, does that truly make you a good person?"

"Riddle me this, then, bird—I don't have a mirage. Does that make me a terrible person?"

"You're a delight to be around..." she muttered.

He snorted. "Well, I don't need some *mirage* to know whether I'm a decent person or not!"

*Neither do I,* she thought savagely. *I can tell just by looking at you.*

"Let's focus on what's at hand," Jared said, reining in the conversation. "Helena, what happened last night when you went to meet with the Stork?"

"He sought a deal with me," she explained, although something about Jared's earnest disposition made her feel almost unworthy. "He told me if I helped retrieve something for him, he'd return my mirage."

Noa scoffed at Helena. "And you believed him?"

Noa clearly thought that her silence was telling, as he could not contain the burst of laughter that erupted out of him.

"Goodness, bird!" he said, wiping the tears from his eyes. "It seems you really were born just yesterday! Even I know darn well that the Krow has no intention of returning yer stinking feathers, but I'll wager you accepted wholeheartedly!"

While Jared had fallen into a strange, contemplative silence, blood rushed to Helena's head at the sound of Noa's jeering laughter.

"Either of you would have done the same, had you been in my position! Or are you so proud as to say you would reject a pair of wings, if given the chance?"

"The difference between you and me, bird, is that I don't need feathers to feel good about myself—I'm content the way I am, and you'd do well to take note! The sooner you come to terms with yer reality, the better off yer going to be for it!"

"I'm not coming to terms with anything," she snapped. "I'm going to take back my wings, and to do that, I'm going to find whatever the Stork wants and bring it right back to him."

Jared spoke with sharp interest. "What does he want you to find?"

Helena faltered slightly at his intensity. "He's looking for an artifact hidden somewhere in Nadiir. He never specified what it was and didn't give me much detail on how to find it...but he did mention two avians in Nadiir who happen to be searching for it, as well. They go by the names of Olip and Penelope Duskmuth. As far as I know, they're our ticket to finding the artifact."

Noa scoffed at the idea. "Let me get this straight...in order to find this thing, the Stork is having you find someone *else* who will do the job for you? Not only that, but two people you've never met in yer life, and who could be anywhere on this cursed continent? It seems to me, bird, yer at a complete disadvantage!"

*He's right,* Helena thought, though she would never admit it to his stupid face. What little Helena knew about Nocturnal avians amounted to the simple fact that they were a wandering species who never lingered in one place longer than they cared to be. It would be nearly impossible for Helena to find them down here; she wouldn't even know where to start.

"That's why I was hoping you two would come along on this journey with me and help me find them."

"Forget it," Noa said sharply.

Helena then turned to Jared, who looked torn. "I can't find this artifact alone. If we give the Stork what he wants, there's a chance he'll let us all go home."

He frowned. "What about your Avalonian friend? I thought our plan was to have him get us back to Avalon, not the Stork."

Helena's mind flashed back to early morning, recalling the way Yulix's silver wings gleamed under the bright sun, and her chest ached with longing.

"Yulix is alive," she said at last, "and I have faith that we'll meet again soon...but I'm not leaving Nadiir until I get my wings back."

Something about Helena's resolve must have resonated with Jared, for he looked at Helena with an air of admiration. Before long, he knelt on one knee before her.

"What in the mighty seas has gotten into you?" Noa exclaimed wildly, looking down at his friend in utter indignation.

"Helena Nightingale," Jared began, taking Helena's hands in his, "I want to join you on your quest for this artifact. If you accept me, I vow to be your sworn protector and to guide you along your journey. And if the world is just, and I succeed in helping you get your wings back, perhaps then I will be worthy enough to earn my own! What do you say? Will you accept my help?"

Helena blushed bright red at the dramatic gesture, which seemed nothing short of a marriage proposal!

"Yes!" she said at last, and Jared returned a beaming smile.

"You hopeful fool!" Noa cried out in outrage. "You'd pledge yer life to a girl you just met in the silly hopes of earning yerself a miserable set of feathers? Fine! Let's say you help the poor girl turn over every stone and boulder in Nadiir looking for that artifact, and you still don't earn yer wings—do you fancy the idea of *her* getting wings and not you?"

"I *will* prove myself worthy on this journey. Of that, I've no doubt...and if you come along, you may yet prove yourself worthy enough to earn yours! Join us!"

Noa crossed his arms and rolled his eyes, tapping his foot impatiently.

"If I'm to join this miserable quest, it won't be for the sake of becoming one of them flockers!" he said, shooting a dirty look at Helena before turning to Jared. "I'll follow you because yer my captain, and a ship without a dedicated crew is mighty well damned! You should know better than to try to leave port without me!"

Jared's face broke into a grin. "Even you could not pass up the opportunity for an adventure like this! Welcome aboard, brother."

Helena was glad Jared was choosing to join the cause. Not so much for Noa, but...she knew if there was any hope of her getting to fly again, her luck would be greater in numbers. Thus, it was settled! The three wigeons would embark on a long journey to find the Stork's artifact, get back Helena's wings, and eventually return home to Avalon...but, for that to happen, they had to first locate the Duskmuth siblings. And they could be anywhere within the giant continent of Nadiir...

"We should start moving now and gain some distance before sundown," Jared said as he mounted his horse. "We'll head north towards Wick's Town and ask around for any strange sightings—Noa! Take the lead and keep an eye out for any dangers lurking about."

"Aye!" Noa mounted his horse and, with a spirited whoop, raced north towards Wick's Town.

"You've a loyal friend," Helena observed after mounting Underbelly. She watched the figure of Noa and his horse become smaller and smaller.

Jared smiled. "That's the thing about wigeonhood, Helena, that you've yet to understand. Us wigeons have to stick together because we're all we have."

Helena chewed her bottom lip. She thought it best to keep her thoughts to herself. Jared's notion of wigeonhood might have been touching, but it was something that she fervently hoped she'd *never* understand.

# Chapter Eight

The group covered a good distance north over the remaining course of the day, bypassing a few wigeon cottages along the way and stopping at a place called Wick's Town. It was nearly sunset, and though there was less chance of running into a Nevarian this far up Krow's Foot, they did not want to take any chances by traveling at night. So, they found repose at a homely inn and tavern called *The Night Owl's Nest*. Here, they stabled their horses and ate a meek supper of mutton stew with a slice of toasted rye bread on the side. Afterwards, the boys helped themselves to a few cold pints of ale. Helena had little affinity for drinking, so she retired upstairs to their quarters, where she pondered tirelessly over what might happen in the days ahead before falling into a troubled sleep.

The next morning, the group gathered around a table in the tavern, sipping on bowls of warm porridge as they looked over their map of Nadiir and pondered their next course of action. The map they used was not very helpful, for Jared had acquired it from a wigeon cartographer; much of the northern lands beyond the Great Isthmus of Nadiir were marked as unknown, with *HERE LIES THE WINGED MAN* written in giant, bold letters across the region. They would have done anything to get their hands on a map crafted by an avian cartographer, whose maps were often much more detailed and offered a handy bird's-eye view of the quickest routes, differences in elevation, and even the river systems that ran across Nadiir. Since the group did not have one of these precious maps on hand, however, they had to make do with what little information they had.

An old wigeon woman interrupted their musings after barging in through the inn's front door. Her knotted and silver hair reached down to her ankles, and she ran amuck throughout the tavern, flapping her arms about like a bird. *"Caw, caw!"* she went. It was hard to discern her words amidst her panicked squabbling, but Helena managed to catch a few of them:

*"White-winged demons,"* she cried. *"They have faces like death—two holes for eyes!"*

Helena's group heard this and looked at one another in grim realization. The old woman's description matched the profile of a Nocturnal. When they called the woman over to ask her where she had seen such a horrifying sight, she came barreling at them, her hands flailing all about as she explained where she saw the white-winged demons.

"West of here, following up the main river," she said. "Spotted the demon last night on the riverbank, I did, feasting over a dead corpse! Don't look it in the eyes, or turn to stone, you will!"

It wasn't much, but enough to point them in the right direction, at least. The group set off westwards along the main river, which stretched on for miles and miles on end. Helena rode Underbelly, whom she had found to be a faithful and reliable companion. By late afternoon, they were making their way down a long road, bypassing endless columns of shady trees to their left; to their right flowed a large and winding river, which sparkled and rippled against the hot afternoon sun. Noa, who had been leading the way far up ahead, came bounding back on his horse, which seemed agitated.

"You've got to see this, Cap'n," he said before spurring his horse around and trotting hastily in the other direction. He stopped by a ledge overlooking a steep ditch. His horse shuffled anxiously and swished its tail in aggravation—it seemed to have caught a strange scent.

"There," Noa told them once they caught up, "down yonder." He gestured towards the grassy bottom of the ditch, and they clambered down on foot to investigate further.

If it hadn't been for Noa's keen eye, they would've overlooked the well-disguised den, which was cleverly hidden by an awning of dead boughs and green fronds. The den was large enough to fit two, maybe three people. But most interesting of all was the collection of stones and foliage gathered around the entrance, as if whoever resided there had used these materials to barricade themselves inside. Jared crouched and picked up a stone, turning it over in his hands before balancing it carefully on top of another tower of stones.

"I doubt any wild animal could've built this," he murmured, knitting his brows in deep thought. Jared then leaned forwards and ducked his head under the low, grassy entrance as he examined the interior of the den. He returned with a handful of white fluff—feathers as white as snow.

"*Oh!*" Helena cried. "It has to be them! They likely use these dens to hibernate during the day."

Jared nodded. "It appears they use stones and other debris to seal their dens shut and make them sun-proof—look!" He pulled out the half-eaten carcass of a cooked rat.

Helena uttered a moan of disgust at the sight. She knew that rats and lemmings were a staple in the Nocturnal diet.

Noa took the rodent by the tail and lifted it eagerly to his face, breaking into a wide grin. "Why, it's harmless!"

"The two of you seem well acquainted," Helena commented, appalled by the way he swung the rat's body with careless abandon. "I take it there's not much else to eat on a ship other than rats?"

The sailor boy gave her something of a rueful smile before tossing the dead rat aside and dusting his hands off.

"It's not unheard of. I haven't had that sort of luck...yet."

Helena shuddered at the thought and turned to Jared, who was still crouching and sticking his head inside the den.

"This must mean they're nearby," she said, with a touch of hope in her voice.

Jared balanced on the balls of his feet and let loose a sigh. "We've no idea how much time's elapsed since they were here. They could be halfway across the continent for all we know..."

"Or right around the corner!" Noa interposed. "I imagine Nocturnals can only cover so much ground at night before the sun rises—can't get very far if yer too busy hiding from the sun!"

"A hopeful argument—if we were talking about wigeons. But an ave can cover twice the distance a wigeon can." Jared rose to his full height and dusted off the stray white plumage that had stuck to his shirt. "Still, I can't help but think we're headed in the right direction. Let's keep moving and stick to the river."

"Aye, Cap'n," Noa said with a two-fingered salute, then bounded back up the ditch.

The group carried on for several more miles until the river curved north and branched in two. They had a choice to make: if they continued northwest along the river, that path would lead them towards the rural countryside, where there would be no nearby towns or villages in the vicinity. If, on the other hand, they followed the river branch that strayed eastwards, they would run into the Forest of Emery, which, according to their map, stretched on for miles. They were unsure which path to take.

"The sun is going to set soon," Helena said suddenly, frowning as she angled her head up towards the bright orange sky. The glaring afternoon heat had diminished into a cool evening wind, which fanned the stray, loose ends of Helena's braided hair, as well as Underbelly's silky mane.

Noa snorted and replied indirectly, "Would the bird like us to put a stop to the sun?"

"I have a name, if you would kindly stop calling me that."

"Yer the one who says she's got wings," he said, laughing and flapping his arms like a crazed goose.

Helena jutted her chin out, affronted. "Hmph! Well, I was merely pointing out the obvious! The sun is bound to set soon, and the closest town is eons away. We'll soon be stranded out here in the open—and *nothing* good ever happens after dark."

"Helena's right," Jared said. Noa rolled his eyes. "We're too vulnerable out here. We should head east towards Emery and set up camp there. That way, we'll have some coverage from the night sky."

"A shame. I think we're overdue for a nice encounter with a Krow around these parts," Noa said with a diabolical smile, as if the wigeon boy *wanted* another scar to complement the one on his face.

"Krows aren't the only thing we have to worry about down here," Jared said darkly before spurring his horse into a quicker gait, leaving Helena and Noa with no choice but to follow him.

The Forest of Emery was an eerie accumulation of trees where little light shined through its canopies. With the sun nearly set, they ventured headfirst into a dim and ominous realm of dead leaves, rotting logs, and glistening spiderwebs. Jared led the way with a torch in his hand. After much riding, they settled into a dense, hidden thicket. Here, they tethered their horses and left them to graze the nearby grass while they worked to set up camp. They were careful to make a campfire small enough to give them warmth while avoiding unwanted attention from the skies above. Using their bags as makeshift pillows, they wrapped themselves in their thin quilts and hoped it would be enough to fend off the impending nighttime chill.

The forest was infinitely more terrifying at night. Every tree, bush, and log untouched by the light of the campfire fell into pitch-black darkness. *Hoo,* the owls went—that is, if they were *truly* owls. Were those genuine crickets rubbing their legs together out in the forest? Helena imagined Nevarians, with their obsidian eyes and devilish grins, hiding behind the trees and bushes and imitating forest sounds to taunt their prey before lunging in for the kill. She slept with one eye open in case a winged demon descended upon them to swoop them up into darkness...

The fire had reduced itself to a heap of embers by the time Helena stirred from her uneasy sleep and sat up. Her eyes had acclimated to the darkness, helping to drive away her childish fears of the dark. She could just make out the crescent moon through a break in the tall canopies of the trees; it seemed to peer down at them warily. Jared lay face up in a deep sleep with his arms on either side of his head, breathing steadily.

The wrinkled quilt lying a short distance away from the fire didn't concern Helena...at first. She assumed Noa had gone off to relieve himself...only a sane and healthy person seldom needed half an hour to do so. Rising carefully so as not to rouse Jared from his slumber, Helena set off to investigate the footprints leading deeper into the heart of the forest...

Helena kept her eyes trained on the trail of footprints leading her past rows and rows of dark oakwood trees and bushes. *Hoo-hoo, hoo-hoo.* A stark white owl perched upon an overhanging branch, training its sallow face and haunting black eyes upon her before taking off soundlessly into the night sky.

Helena reckoned she was a good distance from camp when she spotted a glow off in the distance. It beckoned her further into the forest, where she caught the strong, attractive scent of a woodfire. Both signs seemed to align with the straightforward nature of Noa's footprints. Helena came to a stop before a huge, brightly lit clearing, where she counted five horse-drawn wagons whose horses grazed upon the bountiful vegetation beneath them. A bright and central fire, its flames chasing each other upwards into the black sky above, governed the scene. Shadows danced across the faces of the wigeon men that gathered around it: they howled in laughter as they drank themselves to filth.

Helena used the darkness to her advantage, her heart thumping as she slunk her way around the perimeter of the camp, hiding behind trees and bushes. She was bypassing one wagon when a nauseating scent hit her like a punch to the face. *Ugh,* she thought, resisting the urge to gag. The stench was oddly familiar, reminding Helena of the times when she had forgotten to preen her wings—which hadn't happened often, as Helena always strove to maintain her wings in pristine condition! But alas, nobody was perfect. Regardless, the result had been a nasty accumulation of dead skin cells, dust, and oily residue: *feather musk.*

The hair along her arms rose. Helena took a step forwards, swallowing her fears as she pushed aside the flap of canvas covering the wagon, then sucked in a sharp gasp. One—no, *several* pairs of wings resided inside the wagon, mottled brown feathers stacked on top of one another in nauseating piles, with no owner in sight. Remnants of fresh, blood-stained tissue still lingered on the bones as if they had been sawed off only hours ago. Helena resisted the urge to bend over and hurl any remaining food in her system. Somewhere out there within the abysmal wasteland that was Nadiir, another poor soul was enduring a fate worse than Helena's. Though Helena had her wings stolen as well, the least she could say was that she bore no stubs on her back to account for it...that, she was certain, was a fate too grotesque to even contemplate...

*Poachers,* Helena concluded at once. These were the people Jared had warned her about: evil wigeon men who spent their time hunting aves and exploiting them for profit. *Flee,* Helena's instincts told her. But it was too late—somebody grasped her roughly by the shoulders and turned her around.

The wigeon man towered over Helena—or perhaps she had shrunk so low that it only seemed that way. His fat, crooked nose scrunched up in anger at the sight of her. *"Gotcha, ya little rat!"*

Just seconds later, Helena found herself shoved at the feet of the countless men who gathered around the fire. Whistles sounded at her arrival, and the chattering ceased.

"Found this one here sniffin' 'round the goods," the ugly man said.

"Well, now," said a coarse voice. A pair of brown leather boots stepped in front of Helena, and her gaze traveled upwards to meet a pair of radioactive yellow eyes. This man—their leader, it seemed—had skin the color of a sausage, red and greasy, and she could smell the liquor on his breath from where she lay. "Snoopin' an' stealin' don't pay, now, darlin'..."

Helena's heart drummed as quick as a hummingbird's as it dawned on her that she was surrounded. Her panicked eyes searched for a break in the campfire circle, anywhere where she could make a run for it, when suddenly—

"The bird's with me," a familiar accent sounded from just across the campfire. Never in her life did Helena think she would ever be glad to see Noa, of all people, sitting on a log beside these strange men. The flames danced in his eyes as they met hers. *What are YOU doing here,* both their faces seemed to be saying to each other.

The face of the yellow-eyed man fell at this news. Helena's captor half-shoved her over to Noa who, after catching her, seemed equally repulsed by her and also shoved her away from him. Helena wondered if he felt the depth of her sharp, reproving gaze before planting herself at his side.

"Noa," she whispered tensely. "We have to leave!"

He did not argue. Without looking at her, he replied quietly, "Just let me do all the talking."

"I ferget what I was sayin', right before we was so divinely interrupted!" the yellow-eyed man said. His eyes lingered on Helena, who averted her eyes from his unsettling gaze and stifled her heightened breaths. The man slapped his knee. "Oh, right! I was sayin' how I didn't expect to find a young wigun like yerself all alone in the middle of nun!"

"The call of the wild beckons all!" Noa said with a devilish grin.

"Cheers to that!" the man replied with a bellowing laugh. He raised his glass, and his men lifted their glasses in murmuring agreement. It seemed that fitting in around a herd of drinking men was a forte for the young sailor.

"You got a strange accent on ya, boy. Where you from?"

"I teetered a few years between the Finger and Kricket Pence, out east a ways," he replied cooly. "Worked mainly at the docks before I came down here."

"Pence, eh? What brings you this far inland near the border of Krow's Foot?"

Helena stiffened, but Noa leaned forwards in anticipation as his dark, keen eyes met the leader's.

"We're looking for someone," he said with a mischievous gleam in his eye. "We heard rumors of a white-winged demon roaming these parts. Caught any scent of that sort?"

"Only skinwalkers 'round these parts," the wigeon man answered brusquely before taking another swallow of his drink. He shook off the sting of the drink and sucked on his teeth.

"Skinwalkers?"

"Black-winged demons who hunt men at night an' steal their tongues."

*Stealing their tongues must be a reference to Nevarians*, Helena thought.

"That's one of theirs, ain't it?" Noa asked. He shot a nod to the wigeon man's right where—sure enough—a black feather hung from a string nailed to the wooden frame of the wagon. Helena felt the hair rise on her arms at the sight of it.

"Sure is. Them skinwalkers is slippery as eels, they is. But when we do finally trap one o' them devils, their feathers make nice to keep the rest of 'em at bay—ward off evil with evil, as it were. Put one at your front door, and they'll never come knocking at night. The folks down the main river pay a pretty coin for a handful of 'em."

The wigeon poachers sipped at their glasses of liquor, blissfully unaware that Helena and Noa were Avalonian—they must have brushed them off as ordinary Nadiirians. Helena trembled at the idea of these men finding out who they were. They must've seen her face turn white, for the man with the yellow eyes took one look at her and laughed.

"Yer girl hasn't said a word since she got here! Skinwalkers got her tongue?"

The rest of his circle snickered.

"She ain't mine," Noa said through gritted teeth.

"A darn shame! I'd've claimed that one already, if I were a young'un like yerself...you don't see many beauties like that 'round these parts, no sirree. I'd say she's out of this world."

Helena felt nauseous as the men erupted in a wave of approval at his words.

"You know what else I been hearin' these days," he began again, having to tear his eyes from Helena to return to their conversation. "There's been some funny talk 'bout 'em skinwalkers gettin' up to some heinous schemes down south. The locals 'round here say they even secured a connection to Paradise."

Noa tensed next to her. But when he spoke, he kept his tone casual. "Is that so?"

Another man spoke up. "Yessir, I know folks out by Krow's Foot who say they been usin' it to smuggle in goods from up above...jewels, nectar, spices. You know, the sort you won't find down here."

"Woo!" sounded another. "What I wouldn't do fer just a pint of liquid gold..."

Dreamy murmurs of agreement sounded at the thought of a glass of nectar.

"Some folk say they been bringin' in more than just goods," the wigeon man said, a greedy gleam in his eye. "There's talk that they've been bringing in Paradisers."

"You mean exiles?" one asked.

"Nah, I'm talking about ordinary regulars from Paradise. The winged ones make a fine harvest if you're looking to sell their feathers, and the wingless ones are plenty useful as minions. I'm tellin' y'all...if they keep this up, it won't be long till they start puttin' a dent in our profits..."

Noa rose to his feet, and Helena followed suit at once. "Well, we best be gettin' a move on. If you haven't seen anything out there..."

"Nonsense, stay a spell longer! It's dangerous being out this late, y'know!"

"We'll be on our way," Noa said, politely yet firmly. He and Helena began making their way out past the campfire and back the way they came from.

"Hold on a sec," the yellow-eyed man said, and they froze. "What's that popping out from underneath her sleeve, there?" The man jerked his head towards Helena, who had entirely forgotten that she was still wearing her utilitarian suit beneath her wigeon clothes. "I know a Paradiser's suit when I see one. You get that from Pence, too?"

Helena's heart skipped a beat, but she was quick to respond. "I got it from a trader who told me it once belonged to an Avalonian exile. He swore it'd make me fly like one of those flockers—and I believed him."

A weird sensation passed over Helena upon saying the word *flockers*—even Noa glanced over at her in slight surprise.

"So! The girl ain't a mute after all," the man said. His thin lips dropped so severely that he was practically glowering at the pair. When those yellow-rimmed eyes fell upon Helena, she felt that familiar premonition of disaster in her stomach. There was a wicked gleam in his eyes as he said, "Well, then. You two best hurry off now, back to wherever you came from."

"He knows," Helena whispered harshly to Noa as they quickly made their way out of the clearing. Perhaps the man had known she was Avalonian the moment he laid eyes on her...

"Just shut up and run!" he hissed, and they burst into a sprint as soon as they reached the tree line.

They bounded back to their camp and roused Jared from his deep sleep.

"What's happened?" he asked, bewildered.

"Poachers," Noa said, bolting for the horses and untying them from their tethers. "They know we're from the Upper Realm—or at the least, they strongly suspect it by now. It won't be long till they're snapping at our heels. We need to leave—now!"

Jared decided it was best to flee now and ask questions later. They gathered their belongings and mounted their horses, hastening to leave the campsite at full gallop. The moon shone overhead, looming down on them like an elusive phantom trailing their every move. They rode blindly through the forest until they saw no sign of the poachers on their tails, after which they came to a brief stop to catch their breaths.

"What's gotten into you?" Helena said to Noa. "Cozying up with poachers? Do you *want* us to get killed?"

Scoffing at her, Noa crossed his arms and looked away. "I don't have to explain anything to the likes of you!"

"Then you'd better answer to me," Jared said, visibly furious as he spurred his horse around to face him. "What happened back there?"

"I didn't think much when I first saw them," Noa said, suddenly more abashed after Jared's reprimand. "I would have left as soon as I came upon them, but I realized they were poachers, and I figured if anyone would've known where we could find a Nocturnal, it'd be them. Everything was swell until *she* showed up and blew our cover!"

Noa's accusing finger fired Helena up from the inside.

"I wasn't the one who wandered headfirst into a death trap! Really, I didn't take you for such a reckless fool when I met you..."

"Strange, yer kind tends to assume a lot about wigeons like me!"

Jared looked to the sky and muttered, "Here we go..."

Helena's eyes narrowed. *"My kind?"*

"Haughty, arrogant flockers who think themselves better just 'cause they got feathers!"

"Oh, so I'm a flocker, now? Weren't you the one who didn't believe me when I said I lost my wings?"

"Now that I look at it, it makes rightful sense to me..."

"What's that supposed to mean?"

"Well, there's a saying that you flockers spend so much time in the air that there's little oxygen left in yer brains by the time you come down! Yer kind is featherbrained, empty-headed, and nothing of what you say is of any value—which, dare I say, fits your description quite nicely! Yer as lightheaded as they come!"

Helena's laughter was dry and mirthless. "If I didn't know any better, I'd say you were *jealous*."

The way his eyes nearly bulged out of his head, she might as well have slapped the boy in the face, which contorted into a dark, nebulous cloud of thundering fury. *"What the devil did you just say?"*

"Now's not the time!" Jared shouted. But Helena could not hold her tongue back any longer...

"You heard me! Ever since you met me, you've done nothing but bully me and call me a liar. You've never flown in your life—and likely never will—and it probably kills you inside to know that while there's still some slim chance of me getting my wings back, you'll stay *stuck like this forever!*"

In the heat of the moment, it never occurred to Helena that Jared might have been caught in the crossfire. She was too busy looking to strike the sorest nerve she could find on the wigeon boy...and it worked.

*"HAHAHAHA!"* Noa threw his head back in an obnoxious peal of laughter. "Me, jealous of you? A delusional wigeon with the absurd hope of getting her wings back? As if I would ever feel a drop of envy for the likes of you! I don't spend my time making a victim of myself, moping every night about not being able to fly. Don't think we haven't heard you—yer like clockwork. As soon as the lights go out, you start up with yer moaning and groaning. *'Boo-hoo, they stole my wings!'* I, at the very least, know my worth as a wigeon man. It's you who thinks a person carries their worth in an assemblage of feathers. Tell me, bird—take those feathers away, and what are you?"

Every word cut cleanly to the bone, and the two wigeons remained in a deadlock for many tense moments. Then, a slight tremor rumbled beneath them, and Underbelly nickered uneasily. *Thrum, thrum, thrum!* Those were the distant sounds of hooves pounding against the earth...and they grew stronger every second.

Jared's quiet voice spoke up:

"We have to get a move on—they'll be on us any moment, now."

Without question, Noa took off with a sharp, *"Yah!"*

"Jared—" Helena started, ashamed of what she had said. But he and his horse started off before she could apologize, leaving her no choice but to follow.

With pursuers on their tail, their quarrel was soon forgotten. They fled as fast as they could, the trees flying past them in a blur. The light behind them steadily grew as several riders gained on the fleeing Avalonians. Helena heard their howling cries in the distance:

*"Yeeeah, we got 'em'!"*

They were forced to pull up before a steep chasm in the ground—too risky, too dangerous for any horse to climb down safely. With a heavy heart, Helena bid her goodbyes to faithful Underbelly as the three wigeons dismounted and descended the sharp slope on foot. Together, they clambered down, moving as quickly as one could go without stumbling and falling. Just as they reached level ground, a *wizzp* came from up above them, and an arrow thunked into a nearby tree, narrowly missing Helena's shoulder. They trampled blindly over the mulchy, unsteady terrain as the voices of their pursuers grew steadily louder behind them. Helena could hear the shrilly cries of their horses, who fled at the sight of the wigeon poachers.

Jared fell slightly behind, ushering his friends to keep going until his foot got caught amidst a tangle of roots; he was sent barreling over, hitting his head square against the blunt edge of a nearby fallen log. He let slip a heavy *umph* before his body fell limp. Noa darted to his side to help pick his friend up, but Jared's weight was twice his own.

*"Help me move him, bird!"*

Helena turned without hesitation and rushed to Noa's side. Their combined efforts only moved Jared's body a measly four feet before someone snatched ahold of Helena's braids and yanked her backwards.

*"Let go of me—"* she snarled, but she was quickly forced to her knees. One man pinned Noa against a tree, nearly crushing his throat with his forearm. A familiar, yellow-eyed man appeared before Helena, stepping so close that his rotten breath fanned her face like broken wind.

"There she is," he said with a crooked grin. "Can't ferget a face done like hers, no doubt about it."

Another poacher, this one with a weasel-like face, threw a hard kick to Jared's side. "Billy, I think this one here's dead!"

*"You'll pay for that!"* Noa snarled. For his trouble, he received a solid blow to the jaw which nearly rendered him unconscious. Helena screamed.

"Shut up!" the yellow-eyed man hollered at her. He turned to his peer. "He's not dead, slick. Boy's asleep, is all. But he's got a nice surprise waitin' for him when he wakes up…"

Helena's thighs cramped as she kneeled, and her eyes wandered off to the side, where darkness clung to the trees and bushes. The clouds shifted, and a stream of light shone upon a lone bush, briefly illuminating something cold and shiny. A pair of wide, grey eyes stared back at her from behind the bushes.

*"Help,"* Helena choked out before they disappeared.

The yellow-eyed man gave an atrocious laugh. "Who's gonna help you out here, poppet? Ain't nobody around for miles! Only creatures and skin-walkers roam hereabouts…" He raised Helena's chin gently with a finger, running his tongue over his rotten teeth. "Kricket Pence—that was all a fib, wadn't it? Yea, even if y'all don't got wings, I can tell clear as day you lot ain't from 'round these parts. Yer from Paradise."

By that point, Helena's pounding heart threatened to explode.

"You kids know how much folks down here would be willing to pay for a couple Paradisers? Not as much as a Paradiser with wings, mind you—but a lot more change than what you got janglin' around in yer pockets! Yessir-ree…they don't make 'em down here like they do in Paradise…" A dark, lustful shadow fell over his radioactive eyes as his hand began tracing patterns along the curve of Helena's cheek. "Yer as fine as they come. Pretty as a dove, skin as soft as a petal…I know a lot of powerful men who'd pay a pretty dime to have you in their midst…but I think it'd be better if I kept you fer myself."

Helena did not know the horrors that awaited her. She looked down at Jared and wondered if it would be better if he never woke up. How pitiful! Falling prey to Nevarians, *that* was believable…but never did it occur to Helena that wigeon drunkards would ever pose a threat to her existence!

Panicking, Helena did what she did best—she yelled, yelled until her throat seemed to crack. Then, someone struck her head from behind, and time became sluggish. Helena's world spun around her.

Next thing she knew, she was on the ground. Noa hovered right over her, shouting at her, but she could not register his words. His eyes were wide and panicked. He repeatedly ducked his head, for there appeared to be some unknown presence in the night sky. Jared lay next to them, still unconscious, but at the very least Helena was glad to see he was still breathing. As for the poachers, they had vanished, all except for the yellow-eyed man who stumbled away in fear. His voice cried out into the night:

*"Roy! Munswick! Jeb! Oh, Lord, I'm sorry! I'm sorry for what I done! Save me from these demons! Don't let 'em kill me—"*

Then, he was snatched up in midair like a mouse in the dead of night. What had taken him, Helena could not say. The man's agonizing screams echoed in the distance before they ceased. Permanently.

Helena tried to stand, but Noa pulled her back down.

"Keep yer head low," he hissed, "and don't move a muscle!"

An eerie silence remained. They huddled together, scared to take so much as a breath. Those men had been whisked away and killed...and they were probably next!

Several heartbeats later, out beyond the trees, two pairs of ominous orbs materialized in the darkness. They locked onto them, unblinking. These were predatory eyes. Night vision eyes, designed to detect the slightest movement in the swallowing darkness.

Eyes perfect for a nocturnal hunter.

# Chapter Nine

The two pairs of glowing eyes off in the darkness fixed themselves upon the three helpless wigeons. Noa pressed closely against Helena as Jared began stirring back into consciousness. None of them were sure whether these two figures in the darkness were their enemies or their allies. They had taken the yellow-eyed man and seemingly killed him—but who knew if they were next in line on their kill list? On a hunch, Helena slowly approached the furtive figures lurking in the shadows.

"Bird, get back here!" Noa hissed.

She paid him no mind. Instead, she swallowed her fears and spoke aloud to the darkness:

*"In numbers, we prevail."*

A cold, raspy voice replied, *"And in darkness, we serve the light."*

From Helena's lips came a breath of relief. She had heard this phrase many times before; it was the motto honoring the alliance between Nocturnia and the Kingdom of Avalon. The two individuals before her were *Nocturnal avians,* and there was a good chance they were the same ones Helena had been instructed to locate. It was too late to confirm that, however—with a combined hiss, the two avians launched themselves up into the skies and fled the scene.

"No!" Helena cried, chasing after the distant figures as they flew away. "Come back!"

But they vanished as mysteriously as they had appeared.

Helena ran back to her friends to reveal her discovery. "It's them! We have to go after them, before it's too late—"

She stopped when she noticed Noa holding Jared's lolling head in his lap. A dark trail of blood trickled steadily down the side of his head from the heinous gash along his temple. With a stir, Jared groaned.

"He's out of it," Noa mumbled bitterly. "Must've hit his head hard on the fall…"

"No, no, no!" Helena paced back and forth, biting her nails as she struggled to come up with their next course of action. "We can't lose those avians…help me get Jared back on his feet so we can start making our way down that trail—"

Noa sent her a dirty look. "Does he look like he's in any condition to walk?"

"This might be our only chance at finding that artifact, Noa!"

"What makes you so sure it's even them? They could be Krows for all we know!"

"The longer we sit here and debate about it, the higher our chances are of running into *actual* Krows," she told him. "Besides, look at the state you two are in! Your face is swelling up like a chipmunk's, Jared might have a concussion—not to mention, we're starving! These people might be our only chance at food and shelter!"

Noa weighed his options. At last, holding Jared up between them, Helena and Noa began stumbling off in the direction the Nocturnals had fled. They clambered their way through the darkness, swaying this way and that as they struggled to keep Jared upright. Then, Helena's quiet voice sounded:

"I'm sorry for what I said earlier," she confessed, her face riddled with shame. "I was on edge and angry. I didn't mean to offend you—either of you."

Noa did not respond at first, though it was clear as day that he was eager to put the ordeal behind them.

"There's a chance I might've been a little harsh on you, too, bird," he said after a while, keeping his sight focused straight ahead. "In that case, we'll forget we ever said anything."

Perhaps the haggard frame of Jared in between them was what softened their hearts, or their perilous brush with death just moments ago. Or maybe, after much travel, they had realized they were all in desperate need of a good night's rest.

They arrived eventually at a lone campsite pitched before a small, unlit cave. Helena knew at once they were not alone—the fire which lay at the center of the campsite burned brightly, and around it lay the remains of several rodents—mice, rats, and lemmings—which had all been picked cleanly to the bone. Clearly, they had reached Nocturnal territory.

*"Company!"* a foreign voice rasped from somewhere within the dark cave. Helena's palms were clammy as she took one step towards the cave, then stumbled back as a blood-chilling hiss echoed from the shadows. *"WE HAVE NOT YET GRANTED YOU PERMISSION TO ENTER!"*

Helena's voice cracked as she pleaded with the unknown avians. "Please, we seek shelter! What can we do for you to take us in? We have no money—"

"We do not take worldly offers as payment. If it is truly shelter that you seek, you must answer our riddle. If you fail to provide the correct answer within three attempts, we will expel you from these grounds—by any means necessary."

*Any means necessary.* Helena dwelled on those last few words, which were as chilling and foreboding as the wind that howled that night. Helena looked back at her wigeon companions. Jared leaned on Noa with a dreary look on his face, and she knew they would not last the night out in the wild alone. Knowing she could not give up this one and only opportunity to locate the artifact, Helena agreed to their challenge.

And so the riddle went:

> *I can fly in all directions,*
> *Yet two I so prefer.*
> *With every push, I shove,*
> *And as I depart, I return.*
> *I can fly in all directions,*
> *Yet fixed in place I remain.*
> *To and fro I go,*
> *My presence remains the same.*
> *What am I?*

*I fly in all directions.* Well, that couldn't be anything other than a bird! But birds could fly in every direction *except* backwards, so Helena ruled that out...

"A bird!" Noa yelled, to Helena's horror.

"You have two attempts remaining."

"At least tell me what you're going to say before babbling like a fool," she snapped at him. Noa scowled right back at her as Jared settled on a nearby log, holding his head in his hands. Judging by his pained expression, he would not be able to offer much aid in solving the riddle.

Helena paced back and forth, tree to tree, chewing her bottom lip until tender. *With every push, I shove, and as I depart, I return.* And then it struck her like a mallet—it had to be something with an ebb and flow! Back and forth...*To and fro!*

"A wave," she told the Nocturnals.

"You have one remaining attempt. Choose wisely."

The stakes were now set. Noa was the first to propose abandoning the game altogether, but the Nocturnals made it quite clear they could not opt out of this riddle without dire consequences. It was difficult to imagine what these consequences entailed, though death certainly seemed a strong possibility. They spent ten minutes pitching ideas back and forth, coming up with a circle, a ball, a door, a zipper—even a toothbrush! But none of those seemed solid enough to wager their lives on.

"Spare us a clue, would you?" Noa begged.

After thorough consideration, the Nocturnals gave them their one and only clue:

"I am often bound by time."

All the warmth in Helena's body seemed to flush straight down towards her feet. The likelihood of her nailing the answer to this impossible riddle was slim to none, and the three of them would most likely die. *Time?* What could possibly be bound by time that they could guess in one try? Helena lifted her hand to her chin, mulling over this information for several minutes. Droplets of sweat gathered on her forehead. They had only one more shot at guessing the correct answer, and the clock was ticking...yes, ticking...*tick, tock, tick, tock...back, forth, back, forth...*

In a burst of inspiration, Helena asked Noa, "What's the surest way to tell time?"

He merely shrugged at her. "A clock?"

"Yes! We're onto something!"

"Pardon me, bird, but what the devil does a clock have to do with any of what we just heard?"

"Clocks have a cadence. Tell me, what kinds of clocks do you know?"

He blew out a heavy sigh. "I've seen all sorts on ships bringing back goods for trade. I've seen gadgets as small as apples that ring next to your bed. I've seen those cuckoo ones with the little bird that pops out every hour...oh, and I've also seen those big, fancy ones that only the rich old lady flockers buy, all heavy and lacquered and obnoxious..."

*"That's it!"* she cried, startling Noa. "Grandfather clocks!"

He looked at her askance. "Those can't fly, you know!"

"Stay with me, Noa! Grandfather clocks are obnoxious, but why? Open the glass door and look inside, and what do you find? What swings back and forth inside the glass cage?"

"I am often bound by time..." Noa whispered, before his eyes nearly shot out of his head. *"Yer right!"*

Helena laughed, her eyes glistening. "With every push—"

"—I shove!"

"And as I depart—"

"—I return! THAT'S IT! IT'S AT THE TIP OF MY TONGUE—"

*"Pendulum!"* Helena shouted finally.

Two slender bodies stepped out from within the cave. The first belonged to a young avian woman with long, night-black hair framing her heart-shaped face. Beside her stood a man whose hair was just as dark, and whose entire right arm was missing up to the shoulder. The soft pearlescence of their white wings was easy on the eyes compared to their more ghoulish features: skin of plain alabaster, beady black eyes, and paper-thin lips so similar, the two aves had to be related somehow. The woman fixed her unblinking gaze on Helena.

"Congratulations. You solved our riddle." It had been a glorious, hairsbreadth victory for the two wigeons, but the Nocturnal said this in a manner most unimpressed. "Although, it's worth noting we've solved riddles on a far more difficult scale. My brother Olip here solved this one on his own..."

Helena opened her mouth to respond, but the Nocturnal paid her no mind.

"...on his first try..."

"That's—"

"...on his first birthday."

"Should we bow?" Noa muttered sarcastically. Helena nudged him hard in the ribs to shut him up.

Jared eventually gathered enough strength to rise to his feet. He stumbled over with a pained expression, pressing his hand tightly against his forehead as he cast disconcerted glances at the peculiar avians before them—this was likely the first time the Nadiirian boy had ever laid eyes on a Nocturnal. It was unclear to Helena whether that was the case for Noa. Still, he seemed deeply perturbed by how their heads moved though their eyes did not, and how their wings were so thin and frail they almost seemed translucent.

Olip, the male Nocturnal who was missing an arm, hovered over his sister's shoulder; his entire head swiveled from one person to the next, his round, button-black eyes regarding the Diurnal strangers with silent wariness. He flinched when Helena offered her hand to the female Nocturnal, who was clearly in firm control of the entire situation.

"The name is Helena Nightingale."

Their handshake was exceptionally loose on both ends. "Olip and Penelope Duskmuth," she said.

*We found them,* Helena thought.

After everyone had introduced themselves, Jared said, "We owe you our lives. Those poachers would've killed us—or worse."

"They will no longer pose a threat to you or your friends."

"You mean they're...?"

"Taken care of."

Helena felt a strange urge to cover her neck.

Penelope gave a lengthy sigh. "You can direct your thanks towards Phellicarus. She was nearby when she heard your call for help and hastened back to camp to inform us."

As if on cue, a shadow in the tree branches flashed down from above, and a wigeoned figure landed before them on two lean, graceful legs. Helena and the others staggered back as they took in the wild caricature that was this wigeon girl, who looked like she could be no older than Helena! Her eyes were a striking silver, her blonde hair was cut short like a boy's, and her bare feet were wide and misshapen by bunions and hard callouses! Most curious of all, though, was how when Phellis occasionally oriented her body to the left or right, showcasing her wingless back, Helena could make out a pair of solid, stubby white bones protruding from two slits cut into the fabric of her shirt. Wing stubs.

"Howdy!" the wigeon girl said. "My name is Phellicarus Faye, but only a true friend calls me Phellis!"

"You saved us!" Jared exclaimed.

"Yea," Phellis chirruped, "I saw what them poachers was about to do, so I ran back to fetch my pals here to help!"

Helena, frozen, found herself unable to come up with a proper response. She didn't mean to stare, but...those stubs...

Jared gave a lighthearted chuckle. "Were it not for you, we'd all be dead by now. Thank you!"

Phellis beamed. "No need to thank me! Wigeons help wigeons—ain't that the law of the land?"

"Darn right it is," Noa quipped. He flashed a rascally grin at the young girl, and they shared a mutual fist bump. Something in Phellis' eyes glittered as she gazed up at the scruffy wigeon boy.

Helena tried her best not to roll her eyes as they fawned over their gang's newest wigeon member. And yet, seeing the three of them getting along so easily made her feel a bit lonely. Even though she was a wigeon, like them, she did not *feel* like one. She felt even worse when looking over at the two Nocturnals with their snow-white wings and cold, beady eyes...Helena had never felt quite so out of place.

With the six of them facing each other—four Diurnal wigeons and two Nocturnal avians—Jared stepped up and said, "The three of us are trying to find a way to Avalon."

Helena felt a pang of panic at Jared's honesty—she was unsure what information he was willing to disclose to these strangers. They knew nothing about these Nocturnals or their motives...a single mention of the artifact or the Stork, and the pair would likely flee. They had to choose their words carefully.

"Ditto!" Phellis sounded. "Did they throw you down a lake like some dark secret, too?"

"Yes!" Helena exclaimed. "How long has it been since you fell?"

"Reckon it's been a few months since then. After I fell, them night-crawlers kept nipping at my heels, but I'm fast for my age, see. I crossed all sorts of rivers an' forests an' towns to evade them. I'm good at that stuff...running, I mean. I shake them nightcrawlers off like dust," she said with a proud smirk.

"Nightcrawlers, huh?" Noa mused. "We call them Krows."

"Don't matter what you call them—they kill you all the same! Anyways, it wasn't long before I found my good pals Olip an' Penny here—"

"—*What* did we say about nicknames, *Phellicarus?*"

"Woops," Phellis said, giggling. "Olip an' *Penelope!*"

Helena tried her best to act normal as Olip's star-speckled eyes lingered on her like an owl's. He still hadn't said a word since they met, but a great depth lay behind his gaze, and Helena got the feeling she was being read from the inside out.

"I still fail to understand," Helena started afterwards, "how I was in Avalon one moment, and then in Nadiir the next..."

Phellis murmured in agreement, and Penelope hastened to quell their confusion.

"The Upper and Lower Realms are separated by a dimensional plane called the *Nadiirian Plate.* Natural gap-junctions exist between both realms as portals, which bridge the distance between them. They are rare, and often spontaneous, but a semipermanent portal seems to have materialized at the bottom of the lake at Blade's Peak, and just over Krow's Foot. It is formally known as the *Eye of Nadiir.* Nevarians and their conspirators have been capitalizing upon this junction to smuggle goods and victims to Nadiir."

The group exchanged helpless glances during this long-winded explanation. Phellis looked at them apologetically and shrugged as if to say, *I get it, she can be a bit much.*

Noa glowered at the twins and their impressive plumage. "Alright then. So what's stopping you two from flying yerselves up that portal and back to Avalon?"

Penelope gave a little scoff. "It's not quite as simple as just *flying back home*—Krow's Foot is infested with Nevarians, who guard the Eye of Nadiir jealously. It would take a well-coordinated effort to navigate that maze of naves and escape unharmed...but aside from all that, my brother and I have no intention of returning to Avalon just yet. Unlike the four of you, we were not victims of an orchestrated kidnapping. We traveled through the portal and came down to Nadiir willingly."

Helena braced herself for the information that was to come.

"Who'd *want* to come down to this shithole?" Noa sputtered in disbelief. His brash comment sparked a flurry of giggles around the group, the loudest coming from Phellis. Helena certainly wished she had been given the choice whether to come down here or not...

Noa's sailor's tongue did not amuse Penelope, who regarded him disdainfully.

"My brother and I are students at the Northern Borealis Institute of Research, one of the most prestigious academic institutions within Nocturnia. We dabble in the fields of archeology and anthropology, respectively. We came down this...*shithole*, as you say, on an expedition to find and collect evidence needed for our studies regarding the origins of avian kind."

Helena was glad she did not have a pair of wings, for they would've puffed up with intrigue and given her away in an instant.

"Evidence like what?" Jared asked curiously.

Penelope's lips pressed into a thin line. "That is none of your concern. We've done our part in helping you, and we will allow the three of you time to get whatever rest you need. Afterwards, it would be best we go our separate ways."

Phellis' ears seemed to perk up at Penelope's words, and she looked at the wigeon group with great disappointment. "Separate ways?"

Penelope responded with a stiff-headed nod.

"Oh, but we've only just met them!" Phellis cried, giving the Nocturnal a pleading look. "Please, please, *please*, Penelope! Don't send them away!"

"If it upsets you so, feel free to stay behind," Penelope snapped at her coldly.

Phellis was taken aback by Penelope's frankness. "But I thought we were friends! Don't it tickle your heart to see me go?"

"You kept a serviceable watch during the day—nothing more. But I can only imagine how...great it must feel to finally be amidst other people of your...caliber. It would be a shame to take that away from you, dearest Phellis." Penelope's words weren't earnest in the slightest; it was amply visible to Helena how eager she was to dispose of Phellis.

Helena braced herself before saying, "Take us with you!"

Penelope's heart-shaped head swiveled a full ninety degrees towards Helena.

*Don't blow this,* Helena thought. "Please reconsider! This is a foreign land with dangers lurking in every corner. What happens if a group of hunters finds your den while you're hibernating? Without us, you'll be vulnerable! You'll need a Diurnal to keep watch during the day—the more, the merrier. Think about it—you provide us with protection during the night, and we'll return the favor during the day. We can help you find whatever it is you're looking for, just please take us with you! We won't last a night out here alone—you saw what happened with those poachers."

Penelope's solemn, black eyes seemed to be analyzing Helena from within. Helena sensed that there had to be a reason why her argument had resonated with Penelope's calculating nature. What that reason might be, she hadn't a clue—but there had to be one! At last, Penelope responded with:

"My brother and I will discuss this privately."

With a sharp turn of her heel, Penelope vanished back into her cave. Olip sent the group one more wary glance before scuttling after her.

"Got any food around here?" Noa said, breaking the tense silence that followed. "I'm starving."

"Reckon you're not gonna want what they're having," Phellis said under her breath, sending a nasty glance towards the dead rodents. "I got some leftover bread an' goat's milk, if you're into them kind o' vittles."

Jared touched the tender wound on his head and grimaced. "I don't suppose you'd have anything that might alleviate this massive headache, would you?"

"Sure do! Let's get to healing that noggin' of yours an' then gather 'round the fire to eat. I'm a great storyteller, if you can believe that!"

Penelope's quiet humming sweetened the air as she hovered over her brother's wings, running her nimble fingers through his white feathers and sifting out any dust or bugs. She was preening his wings—a standard hygiene practice, but one which was considered a form of endearment, like braiding someone's hair. Olip gazed quietly up at the stars while Penelope handled his wings with the tenderness of a mother. Helena found her eyes jealously gravitating towards the pair, who sat apart from the rest.

The lumpy slice of bread in Helena's hand was as hard as a rock, but she softened it with warm goat's milk. Helena was so hungry, she devoured her food and drink in less than a minute—not nearly enough time to match the lengthy expanse of Phellis' energetic campfire performance.

"Long, long ago," she began as the fire's shadows danced across her face, "there was a wicked, wicked man who lived in ancient Avalon an' did terrible, terrible things! They say he had the eyes an' tongue of a lizard, to go along with an ugly pair of wings as tough as old shoe leather. Legend has it, he was the first ave ever exiled from Avalon into Nadiir. That's the gist of it, anyhow. Up in Avalon, he's best known as the *Fallen Avian...*"

Helena's head perked up at that familiar name. Jamie Moore had mentioned it on Murmuration's Eve, after discussing the late-night disappearances. *My dad thinks the people behind the nappings are sacrificing them in the name of the Fallen Avian...*

Phellis continued. "They got a funny name for him down here, though—*Nevar.*"

"As in *Nevarians,*" Helena said, swallowing the last soggy lump of her bread.

"Tit for tat. Turns out, those nightcrawlers are direct descendants of his..." She leaned in with an ominous gleam in her eye. "Would you believe me if I told you some of them words you hear them spit are the exact same words *he* muttered way back when he was alive?"

There wasn't a person sitting around the campfire that night who was a stranger to the Nevarians' haunting gift for vocal mimicry, and the tension became as thick as butter. *The Fallen Rise.* Helena recalled that strange, cold voice in her memory. Back home she had paid little regard to scary stories, but this time she could not help but look over her shoulder a few times...

"She's toying with us," Noa said dismissively. He sat across the fire from Helena, next to Jared, who had a clean bandage wrapped around his head. Penelope had been the one to tend to his wound, applying a mysterious, shimmery white salve which Jared claimed had cured his headache in an instant.

Phellis cried, "I'm serious! Penny here calls them—"

*"Phellicarus!"*

"Oh, fine!" she said, sticking her tongue out at Penelope when she wasn't looking. "That *woman* over there calls them a *parroting species.* Tricksters who repeat anything they hear. But that's the rub, ain't it—they gotta *hear* something first to mimic it. If they don't hear it, they can't say spit!"

Helena snorted. "And you believe the voice they mimic is the Fallen Avian himself?"

"Well, that voice has gotta come from somewhere, don't it? I bet my buttons it's his."

Helena fell into a sullen silence.

"Fallen avians are not unheard of in Nadiir," Jared mused, "but I must admit it's the first time I've heard of *The* Fallen Avian...it sounds almost like a bedtime story you'd tell a child so they don't misbehave."

Noa feigned a shrill old woman's voice. *"You'd best not steal another cookie, Red, or the Fallen Avie's gonna pull at yer toes!"*

The two boys burst out in laughter, and the tension broke. Phellis huffed and crossed her arms.

"Laugh all you want now," she warned, "but the Fallen Avian is real, and some folk even say he's coming back to punish us Avalonians for what we did to his people!"

"Well, I didn't banish the fool!" Noa said defensively. "Am I to carry the weight of my ancestors' doings forever?"

"It don't matter what you done or haven't done! Fact is, them nightcrawlers are stuck down here, an' we're the ones who put 'em there. Nadiir is no paradise, if you ask me. But don't tell me you wouldn't be colored green at the thought of someone else living up there, way better than you, while you're stuck down here, *and* you're allergic to the *sun!*"

"So, it's true?" Helena asked, breaking her silence. "Nevarians can't step foot outside during daylight hours?"

"Reckon they'll char like a hardy steak on a grill if they do!"

"It's why they flee from the sun like their life depends on it," Jared commented. "Because it very well does!"

"Yessir! You'll find heaps of them nightcrawlers in underground tunnels—usually inside mountains...all this and more is why they hate us Avalonians so much. It's like they're cursed, living at the bottom of the barrel with no way out!"

"You seem to know a lot about these people, Phellis," Jared observed keenly. "More than I do, it seems, and I've lived here all my life."

Phellis appeared somewhat embarrassed. "I've had my fair share of encounters with them nightcrawlers. Most of them will try an' kill you on the spot...but a few of 'em—very, very few—are decent until you cross 'em. Learnt that the hard way."

The group exchanged alarmed looks.

"What do you mean?" Jared pressed.

Phellis gulped. "Well, you see...I spent a good deal o' time travelin' Krow's Foot with nothing more than a few coins in my pocket. I was starvin' an' scared, an' some nightcrawlers'd give me a hunk of bread if I did them a favor or two—delivering money, or eavesdropping, that kind of stuff. One day, though, I ran off with a bundle of jewels they wanted delivered, an' they caught on. I found myself backed against the wall with three nightcrawlers at my neck. They would've done away with me if it weren't for Olip an'

Penn—*ahem*...that is to say, Olip an' *Penelope*. They saved me, just like they did you guys."

Phellis saw the wary looks on their faces and cried, "Look, I know what y'all are thinking, but I'm no rotten apple—I promise! Now, I'm not proud of what I done, but I had no choice—"

"No one's judging you, Phellis," Jared said, casting a quick glance at Noa. "You did what you had to do to survive."

Noa kept his sight fixed on the fire as he murmured, "That's all a wigeon can do."

For some reason, both Noa and Jared seemed wholeheartedly accepting of Phellis, despite her having just admitted to working with Nevarians in the past. Helena, on the other hand, still remained dubious of this eccentric little girl and resolved to pay close attention to her mannerisms in case she was hiding any tricks up her sleeve...

Jared leaned forwards and sighed. "So, the Nevarians want revenge for their ancestors. The question is, what are they doing—or planning to do—to achieve it?"

"They already found a gateway into Avalon," Noa said darkly. "Perhaps the Krows plan to invade."

"But the Eye of Nadiir seems much too small for any real host to pass through, don't you think? With no direct entrance into the Upper Realm, an invasion feels unlikely, if not altogether impossible."

"Send a Krow or two up that portal every day for five years, and you already got a legion of Krows eager to spill Avalonian blood."

"I think the Crown would realize that there was an army filtering through Blade's Peak soon enough," Helena said. "They would put a stop to it at once."

Jared nodded. "That's why they've been acting discreetly over the years, only smuggling goods and people by the handful, otherwise their operations would be shut down instantly. Though, I wouldn't doubt there's already an established Nevarian presence in Avalon. How else are they getting Avalonian gangs like the Blood Feathers to do their dirty work?"

"With the tantalizing promise of wealth," Noa answered shamefully. Everyone stared at him.

"You never heard anything in your time as a Blood Feather?" Helena asked him.

Noa shook his head. "I was bottom tier, only used for delivering people or parcels from one place to another."

"Ditto!" Phellis chirruped. She seemed to revere the wigeon boy from afar on account of yet another thing they had in common.

Jared shook his head. "Whatever they're planning, it can't be anything good."

Noa yawned. "Why don't we ask the Stork? I'm sure he knows all about it!"

They fell into a tense silence. Even Penelope, who was still busy preening Olip's wings, had stopped humming at the mention of that name. For several minutes, all that could be heard was the crackle and hiss of the campfire.

"That man is sumthin' of a myth 'round these parts," Phellis started hesitantly. "Reckon I never got the chance to meet him...they say that he snatches kids an' that if you look directly into his eyes, he'll snatch your soul!"

*That's what happened to me,* Helena thought.

Noa rolled his eyes. "The Krow's not all that he's cracked up to be."

"How would *you* know?"

"I saw him with my own eyes!"

Phellis let slip a gasp. *"You've met the Stork?"*

"I clocked him in the head with a rock with my very own hands," he answered proudly. Helena could not help but roll her eyes as Phellis flocked to his side fawningly.

"What's he like? Ugly? Smelly? Fat? Oh, please tell us!"

*Far from ugly,* Helena thought to herself. She recalled his alluring dark eyes and handsome black wings, which were as polished and reflective as sea glass. He was older, yes, but possessed a charming, almost bewitching disposition that would've fooled Helena had it not been for his use of her nickname, *Lena.*

Helena was forced to endure Noa's heroic version of his encounter with the Stork, which began with a nail-biting exposition of being stranded in the middle of the woods at night, forced to rely on his wits and hard-won survival skills. Then, he came face to face with the Stork! Noa fearlessly flung a single stone that left a gash on the nave's face that spewed blood like a waterfall, before the Stork spun like a tornado and scarred Noa's face for life! Phellis examined his scar with amazement. Noa concluded by giving a rough imitation of the Stork fleeing the sun by prancing away and screaming like a little girl. This sent Phellis doubling over in laughter. Noa had been so engrossed in his own story that he failed to mention one crucial detail—

"What even brought you there in the first place?" Phellis wondered.

Noa's smile faded, and the air fell silent. Clearing his throat, he said quickly, "I was the one who found the bird after the Stork—"

Jared's voice snapped like a pine knot crackling in the fire. "Hush, Noa! That's not your story to tell."

His kind eyes flashed to Helena, as did everyone else's. A pair of wings would've sufficed to shield Helena from their wounding gazes. But she had to tell them the truth—as humiliating as it was. When she did, Phellis gasped, and two ghostly faces moved closer and loomed over the fire; Olip and Penelope's haunting stares were a lot more vivid under flickering firelight. For the first time, a small display of concern formed upon Penelope's icy face.

"What did you just say?" she asked Helena, her voice barely above a whisper.

"He stole my wings," Helena repeated, the second time hurting more than the first.

"You mean to say he cut them off," Phellis said, her brows furrowing.

"No. He took them away by removing my mirage. It's as if I never earned them."

There was a moment of silence before Phellis slapped her knee, hard, and cackled. "Well, isn't that the strangest thing I ever heard! You mean to say the Stork magically took your wings away?"

"It's no laughing matter," Helena said icily.

"Pardon me! I just never heard of a man magically turning an ave into wigeon...that's impossible!"

"Obviously not, if he did it!"

"How?" Penelope asked. Her black eyes filled with a deep interest, as if she believed there might be a kernel of truth in Helena's wild claims.

"He used an enchanted dagger to take them away," Helena answered hesitantly. She half expected Penelope to denounce her story altogether; instead, the Nocturnal fetched a small satchel from her den and rummaged through it until she found a fat, leather-bound notebook stuffed with protruding yellow notes. Its front cover was curled from frequent handling. Penelope flipped through several hundred pages until she stopped at one and practically shoved the booklet in Helena's face.

"Did it look anything like this?"

Helena took a step back so she could take a clearer look at the diagram presenting itself on the page before her. The image had been sketched roughly by hand, and it had smeared with time, but looked as if it had been traced directly from Helena's memory. There it sat before her: the intricate golden handle, the rubied end, and the very same crooked, green blade which had butchered Helena oh so many nights ago...

Helena found herself at a loss for words. "What are the odds..."

"The dagger you see here once belonged to Prince Elizar of Paptar," Penelope explained, reciting from some deep recess within her impressive memory. "Paptar was an ancient city in the Upper Realm that currently lies in ruins underwater. Its base cracked under the pressure of a giant earthquake, and it is speculated to have sunk entirely within the hour. There are many sources citing Prince Elizar's magical ability to turn ave into wigeon. Most historians assume this meant that he merely cut their wings off—but that is not the case. In reality, he possessed an enchanted dagger which allowed him to remove the wings of avians by severing the bond between them and their mirage."

"Exactly what the Stork did to Helena," Jared said grimly. "How does a weapon like that end up at the bottom of the universe?"

"Any object can travel far enough if enough men are willing to kill for it."

A chill fell upon them, and Helena rubbed her arms uneasily. Such a thing could only be cursed, not enchanted...

"What happened to this prince?" Noa asked, breaking the spell.

"He was said to have gone mad over time, executing hundreds of innocent people he had deemed guilty in his derangement. All before he slit his own wrists with that very same dagger."

It was hard to fathom how the same dagger that was used to take Helena's wings had once tasted the blood of a prince. Her scar throbbed just thinking about it.

Helena turned to Penelope. "If the Stork has that weapon, it means he has the power to steal the wings of other avians like me!"

"The Stork is much more practical than that," she replied. "He is only one man, after all, and I doubt he cares to spend his time de-winging other avians one at a time. While his possession of such a weapon is alarming, the Stork is after something far more dangerous."

"What might that be?" Helena asked intently.

Penelope's beady eyes were potent and penetrating. "An artifact."

It took a tremendous amount of willpower for Helena not to break eye contact with the Nocturnal, for she feared that the second she broke their gaze, it would give them away instantly.

"What kind of artifact?" Jared asked coolly.

"Its identity remains a mystery, but I have my suspicions. Treasure, elixirs, lost heirlooms...it could be anything. We won't know until we see it."

"I could fare with some booty," Noa murmured in approval, prompting Helena to roll her eyes.

"Where is this artifact?" Helena asked.

"It lies at the heart of a treasure-ridden vault somewhere within Northern Nadiir. My brother and I only recently acquired a treasure map leading to it, though we still have yet to decode the glyphs specifying its true location. Nevertheless...we are the only people in Nadiir with the means to find the vault and the artifact inside."

*That's why the Stork is after you,* Helena thought to herself.

"Whatever it is, the Stork must not get his hands on it," Penelope said, "for if he does, there's no telling of the consequences."

"Then let us help you!" Helena burst out. "You can't do it alone—you need our protection, just as we need yours."

Penelope glanced at her brother, whose bulging black eyes stared back at her fretfully. "We've considered your offer and believe it would be mutually beneficial for us to travel together for the time being."

Helena wanted to cheer!

"We will warn you now," Penelope added forebodingly, "that if you are truly willing to help us, the journey will require you agree to a few...terms and conditions that best accommodate our needs."

Jared squared his broad shoulders. "Let's hear them, then."

"Over the course of our journey, we will each have designated sleeping and activity blocks. My brother and I will hibernate from dawn to sunset, during which time you will keep watch over our den and attend to your own responsibilities."

"Sounds simple enough," Helena said.

"At least one of you must always keep watch of the den during the day. You must not abandon your post at any point in time, under any circumstance—this, I'm afraid, is nonnegotiable."

"Consider it done," Jared answered honorably.

"At sunset, we will rise to hunt, and you will be granted a few hours to sleep before we move together as a group at night, covering as much distance as we can before settling again before the dawn."

"We'd be getting little rest, if any," Jared observed.

"We'd be spending most of our nights traveling," Helena added.

"We'd be stuck with the likes of you," Noa muttered under his breath.

"And thus is the art of compromise," Penelope said. She paused a moment, then said, "We could always head our separate ways and avoid the trouble altogether..."

Helena answered before anyone else could.

"It's not a problem!"

"Very well," Penelope said. "For tonight, the three of you may settle in and make your sleeping arrangements so that you may rest. Meanwhile, my brother and I will hunt and monitor the skies for the next several hours. You will stay safe so long as you stay with Phellicarus and don't wander too far."

Helena gave a firm nod. "It's settled, then."

"We move at midnight." Without another word, Penelope and her brother took off silently into the night.

As soon as they were gone, Noa whirled around to Helena and exclaimed, "Thanks a lot for consulting us before tying the knot!"

Jared sent a wary glance at Phellis before whispering in Helena's ear, "You really think this is a good idea?"

"We need to stick together," she whispered back. "They're our only chance at finding the artifact and our best defense against the night! Besides...traveling with Nocturnals, how bad could it be?"

They looked over at Phellis, who sat slumped by the campfire. The flames illuminated her tired, worn face; she looked as if she hadn't gotten a good night's rest in weeks. She hadn't heard the conversation between Helena and Jared, but she stretched her long limbs as she gave a big, gaping yawn.

"You guys don't got a clue what yer in for," she said. "Hope y'all got as much sleep as you possibly could the last few days...'cause from here on out, you're not gettin' any."

# Chapter Ten

For the next several weeks, the group journeyed by night across Southern Nadiir in united efforts to locate the artifact. Olip and Penelope took high vantage points in the sky as they followed their faithful map—which guided them northwards—all while Helena and the others tagged along on horseback (It turns out that Underbelly and the other horses did not flee very far, after their encounter with the wigeon poachers!)The group almost always called a halt before dawn so that the twins could construct dens to hibernate within during the daytime hours. It could take the twins up to two hours to meticulously craft their dens—less if there was a cave or burrow available, more if they had to build them entirely from scratch so that not a thread of light penetrated their dwelling. They slept from dawn till dusk, rising punctually after sunset and leaving promptly to hunt. This granted Helena and her Diurnal peers a few precious hours of sleep before they would all resume their arduous journey at night as a collective, and the whole cycle would begin again. In a complete reversal of what her body was used to, Helena spent most nights moving instead of sleeping, as if she were slowly becoming Nocturnal herself...

Despite this rigorous itinerary, the Nocturnal twins offered them reliable protection against the perils of the night; twice they deterred a threat from disturbing the camp, the first being a rogue warthog, the second being a giant black bear. Although the hours in which the Diurnal group slept were few, they could do so with the assurance that Olip and Penelope would prevent any and all dangers from disturbing their sleep. They patrolled the cloudy night skies like phantoms in the air: undetectable and unforeseeable, courtesy of their signature flight style, the *silent glide*. Whilst the common avian had to actively *thrust* their wings to propel themselves through the air—which was often quite noisy—the Nocturnal avian possessed wings which gave them the striking ability to glide effortlessly, and silently, across the air.

The Diurnal group had agreed to keep watch over the twins' dwelling during the day in case anything—or anyone—sought to disturb them when they were at their most vulnerable. Penelope emphasized two simple, yet absolute rules. The first was that at least *one* person always stay awake and close by to keep watch over the den. Easy enough. The second was that nobody was permitted to disturb their sleep by making excessive noise or getting *too* close to their dens. Every night, Penelope reinforced this rule by using a stick to draw a great boundary between their den and the others.

"You are not to cross this line while we sleep," she would instruct them.

Noa, however, took this as a challenge. "If I feel the need to cross it, I *will*."

Helena shot him a glare. "At least try to *act* civil!"

"No one here tells me what or what not to do, bird!" He crossed his arms and sneered at Penelope, who merely returned his look with complete loathing. Lately, Noa's hostility had shifted unilaterally away from Helena and towards Penelope. The reason was blatantly obvious in Helena's eyes: Noa was a covetous fool who despised anyone who had feathers—especially someone as unusual as a Nocturnal.

"Forgive us," Jared said quickly to Penelope. "We are unfamiliar with your ways...truth be told, the precaution does seem somewhat unnecessary..."

Penelope sent a dirty look towards Noa. "This practice is customary in Nocturnia. Our people practice *purging,* a process in which *all* Diurnals are removed from the city and forbidden to cross its borders during daylight hours. This is to prevent the likelihood of Diurnals stumbling upon and disturbing our den while we sleep. Additionally, it decreases the likelihood of daylight raids, a method historically used to persecute our people when we are at our most vulnerable."

"There is no honor in such a thing," Jared said. "If that's the case, we will do our best to make sure nothing gets past these borders!"

"Yes, I'm sure you will," Penelope said. Her cold eyes lingered on Noa, then she left to finish her pre-dawn duties.

When she was gone, Noa snickered and said, "I wonder if they hold in their shit until sundown, too!"

"Keep your thoughts to yourself," Helena snapped, though she did have to stifle a giggle at the thought of Penelope clenching for the next twelve hours of daylight. Jared also looked away to conceal his smile.

"I only ask what the people are too afraid to ask! What's this talk of not crossing such-and-such line? They're so afraid of catching some sunlight when heaven knows they're in dire need of a tan...what's the worst that could happen if their fort collapses?"

"You'd best run away if it does," sounded the drowsy voice of Phellis. She had been lying on her side, sleeping with her cheek pressed against her arm. "If that wall comes tumbling down an' we see one o'em in broad daylight, we're cursed to a lifetime of bad luck..."

"Absurd!" said Noa.

"That can't possibly be true," Helena agreed skeptically.

Jared frowned. "What *would* happen if a Nocturnal exposed themselves to sunlight? Would they die, like Nevarians?"

"Beats me," said Phellis. "Whatever happens, it's something only one o'em could ever know. And I sure as Hades hope it stays that way!"

Even with her faithful friend Underbelly, whom she esteemed greatly, Helena had immense difficulty acclimating to the vast and ever-changing terrain of Nadiir. Phellis, being the athletic scout that she was, often trooped ahead of the group on foot to survey their prospective path. Olip and Penelope would be flying somewhere overhead in the clouds, while Helena and the others followed steadily on horseback. Underbelly bore most of the burden of the journey, being the hardy fellow that he was, but even he grew tired after hours of travel, and Helena knew no other option than to walk him by the reins. A hellish battle, that was! There was no way a living being could endure such torture—namely, *walking!* Helena had little clue how Phellis or the others managed so well, for her feet soon became laden with blisters that oozed pus, and her aching quads grew as heavy as lead. There were many times when Helena's legs nearly gave way underneath her. *Step, step, step,* she thought rhythmically, training her eyes on her sore feet. Nowadays, that's how she got through anything...by taking one painstaking step at a time.

If Helena wanted to bring about an end to this nightmare, which she most certainly did, she would have to get her hands on the artifact—but how, if she didn't even know what she was looking for? And in order for her to learn more about the artifact, she would have to get closer to the twins...but how was she supposed to do *that* if the twins spent all day either sleeping in their den or flying a hundred feet in the air? It all seemed impossible. It quickly came to Helena's attention, however, that someone else might be able to provide more insight on their Nocturnal brethren...

Phellicarus Faye was an eccentric girl who'd developed some valuable skills by the early age of fourteen; she was exceptionally clever when it came to tracking and baiting game, and had long, sinewy legs which granted her both the stride of a cheetah and the grace of a gazelle. Her exceptional endurance and stamina made her extraordinarily skilled at running long distances and scoping out the areas around them for any bandits, wigeons, or wild animals that could pose a threat to them and the hibernating twins.

One afternoon, Phellis brought in two lean hares from her daily hunt. The group had them skewered over the cooking pit, and grease fell readily onto the fire with a sizzle. Helena's stomach grumbled loudly upon inhaling the enticing aroma in the air; all this walking and traveling had made her hungrier—and more irritable—than usual. When the meal was ready, everyone gathered gleefully around the fire to tear into their crispy portions of roasted meat. They ate in awkward silence for many moments, which Noa found to be particularly dreadful. To break the dull silence, he cast one look at Phellis' shoulders and asked:

"So, how'd you earn those stubs?"

Helena nearly choked on her food upon hearing such a brash question!

Jared smacked him upside the head. "What's the matter with you?"

"Easy!" Noa said, scowling as he rubbed his head. "I was just wondering!"

Phellis had turned a deep shade of red, but shrugged it off with a nervous laugh.

"Oh, these? It's a long story, if you're up for it."

"Please! Anything to fill this dreadful silence..." he said. He shot a reproachful look at Jared and Helena, who only rolled their eyes and continued to eat as Phellis told her story...

Phellis, as it turned out, was not a *true* wigeon like Noa and Jared; she had, in fact, earned her wings at one point in her life, only she shared a similar fate with Helena in which she lost them tragically.

"I reckon I was no bigger than a calf at the time," said Phellis, sinking her teeth into a meaty leg and wiping the grease off her mouth with the back of her hand. "Even back then, Papa always had me up early to tend to the hens. A stickler, he was, in tending to 'em. Said if I was old enough to earn my wings then I was old enough to know what hard work meant on the farm. If I slept in even once, he'd whip out his belt an' he'd...well, I s'pose that don't matter much, anymore. He's dead as dust, now."

The group sent each other discreet looks of concern before shifting their attention back to Phellis, who looked suddenly ashamed.

"Coyotes had a habit of breaking in an' causing mayhem, y'see, but Papa always saw to shooting them dead with a bow an' arrow. One night, though, Papa was away from the farm..."

Phellis was now visibly distraught. She took a shuddering breath before resuming her story.

"I heard the cries an' commotions down by the coop, an' I went to see what all the hullabaloo was about...it wasn't no mere coyote this time. It was one of them big, lone wolfs, an' it was the color of soot an' coal."

"No," Jared couldn't help but say, his jaw falling open.

Noa inhaled sharply. "Don't tell me that—"

Phellis nodded. "My first instinct was to take off, but I reckon that was my mistake—I *ran,* I didn't fly. Before I knew it, I was on the ground, an' I felt something hot running down my back...I must've blacked out, 'cause next thing I knew, I was wakin' up at the doctor's with two stubs on my back. I cried for weeks."

Helena was speechless. Having your wings torn off and devoured or having an enchanted dagger cut into your soul—she could not decide which fate was worse! Perhaps it was not worth comparing; she and Phellis had both lost something so incredibly precious to them in ways that were incredibly traumatic. Helena could picture Phellis lying face down on a table, unconscious as the doctor, with his giant mechanical tools, sawed off her wings and filed down what remained. She could almost see the blood and bone dust flying everywhere...the thought itself was enough to make Helena queasy...

Jared could not seem to express his profound regret for the young girl. "I'm...I'm sorry for your loss."

"You were but a kid, too," Noa added, frowning.

"No more than ten, I reckon."

"I should have kept my mouth shut," he said, ashamed. "My apologies."

Phellis had a vacant look on her face, as if she were recalling a distant and painful time.

"I'm sorry." It was all Helena could bring herself to say. Phellis' somber eyes met hers, and they shared a moment of painful, mutual acknowledgment.

"It must have been tough, living without your wings," Jared said quietly. "How did you manage?"

Phellis shrugged. "It was hard at first, I'll admit...but then, after a couple months..."

Helena found herself answering, "It's like you never earned them."

The resignation in her own words caused Helena to feel disgusted with herself. What was she talking about? Helena *had* earned her wings, she *had* earned them honorably, and nothing in this world—not even time—could cause her to forget this precious truth!

"Phellis, what artifact are Olip and Penelope looking for?" she demanded suddenly, tired of beating around the bush.

Phellis froze, her wide eyes gleaming like two silver coins.

She stammered. "O-oh, well...I'm not sure if I should say—Penny told me to keep my mouth shut and pretend I don't hear anything they say..."

"They threatened her, no doubt," Noa muttered.

"You don't have to say anything you don't want to—" Jared began.

"You can trust us," Helena said sharply, and Phellis shrank. "You saw how willing Penelope was to send you away. They couldn't care less about you, a Diurnal wigeon! You said it yourself—wigeons help wigeons, right? Whose team are you on?"

Phellis gulped, her doe eyes flickering back and forth between her new companions and the shabby, ominous den behind them.

"I'm not too sure what they're looking for," she said. Her voice dropped to a whisper and the group huddled closer together. "They mostly keep to themselves, huddling in their caves plotting an' scheming...they talk an awful lot about ancient ruins and fossil records. Penny mentioned that once they get their hands on this artifact, they'll finally be free."

"Free from *what?*" Helena pressed.

"I—I don't know!"

It wasn't nearly enough to quell Helena's thirst for information about the artifact, and she found herself more frustrated than ever by the lack of clarity.

"You had to have heard something else," Helena insisted. "Come on, Phellis, you have to tell us!"

*"Enough,"* Jared's sharp voice sounded.

Helena realized she was now looming over Phellis with a crazed look in her eye as the wigeon girl shrunk back in fear. With a huff, Helena stalked off into the trees and walked to the nearest stream to splash some cold water onto her face. Her reflection in the water showed a dark halo permeating the skin underneath her eyes. Now, more than ever, she felt the weight of physical and mental exhaustion bearing down on her. She hadn't gotten a good night's sleep in what seemed like weeks—and by the looks of it, she wouldn't get another for a good, long while...

There yet remained a long journey ahead.

# Chapter Eleven

Krow's Foot was but a forgotten memory as the group approached the Great Isthmus of Nadiir; the narrow crossing was the only thing bridging the massive continental rift between Northern and Southern Nadiir. They spent hours treading carefully across its earthen bridge, which tapered more and more the further on they went. The crossing grew even worse as harrowing winds and rains threatened to send them all toppling over the edge. One slip or stumble, and they would fall hundreds of feet into the misty waters below! Olip and Penelope, for obvious reasons, suffered few obstacles in crossing the isthmus apart from a nettlesome wind, and completed the endeavor in a fraction of the time Helena and her peers did.

"We've officially crossed over into Northern Nadiir," Jared announced once they finally made it to the other side. "Look ahead!"

He pointed towards a budding, blueish outline in the distance: a beautiful sierra appeared to span the entire northwest. "The Mountains of Alazar! I expect a stronger avian presence here. There's a good chance we might spot a few voyagers in the sky around these parts..."

As she sat mounted on her horse, Helena gazed off into the northern distance longingly.

"Do you think Yulix is out there?" she said to Underbelly, who said nothing. "Hopefully, we'll reunite soon...*but not before I get my wings back,*" she added hastily.

The group soon found themselves in hot and arid shrublands with little grass, few trees, and frequent, tiresome hills. Here, the twins constructed their most impressive feat of architecture, yet: a dome built from raw adobe clay. It was hand-molded with nothing but a spade and a bucket of water, and baked to perfection by the hot, stinging rays of the sun. Penelope even had the sudden notion to decorate its walls with lovely, intricate swirling patterns of relief which reminded Helena oddly of Murmurations.

It was so hot one morning, in fact, that Helena felt obliged to remove her utilitarian suit from underneath her tunic and trousers. Meanwhile, Jared had left to hunt and Phellis was out on a scouting mission. Both would not be back for some time, leaving Helena, Noa, and the horses to watch over the Duskmuths' adobe dome. It was a task so dull that Noa felt he had no other option to alleviate his suffering than to converse with Helena, of all people.

"It's dead wind today," he said, thrusting his nose in the air and squinting up at the scorching sun.

Helena hadn't noticed it until he pointed it out, but the air was arid and still. There wasn't even the hint of a cool breeze on this hot, cloudless day. The shrubs and trees around them stood placid and unmoving, as if in a painting.

Helena fidgeted with her U-ball in one hand. "What about it?"

Noa shrugged. "Back at the harbor, dead wind meant no man sailed that day. It's bad luck. Wind breathes life into a ship, you see—it's what pushes her onwards. Without it, she's stuck in place."

Helena couldn't help but smile at this. "Back home, we have a saying: *nothing hampers the ave's spirit more than a cloudy, windless day.* There's nothing quite like the feeling of a full gust of wind propelling you from underneath and lifting you up into the sky..."

For the first time in all of their journeying together, Noa didn't have some bitter, spiteful comment to retort. Instead, he returned a firm nod of respect, his eyes seeming to say something along the lines of, *At least that's something we can agree on.*

They fell into another awkward silence. It was then that Helena, in a bid to cure their boredom, demonstrated to Noa the science behind her U-ball. At first, he regarded it skeptically but grew gradually more fascinated with both the magic and practicality of such a thing. He shivered as he squished it between his thumb and index finger, and the navy-blue substance raveled over his body and underneath his clothes.

"We don't have these fancy gadgets back at the Harbors...what else can it do?"

Helena walked behind him and pressed a small button at the nape of his neck. In a flash, his suit retracted back into a small ball, and she placed it into his hands.

"It's multipurpose," she explained. "If you squish it, it becomes a suit, which can come in handy on a chilly night. But if you stretch it between your fingers..."

*"Woah!"* He laughed incredulously as the ball shot out into the shape of a long, shimmering staff. With the way his eyes sparkled, Helena thought it was like watching a child discover a brand-new toy. "You flockers sure got some time on yer hands if yer sitting around crafting things like this!"

Helena felt a strange gratification in watching him fidget with the U-ball. If she didn't know better, she would think it was almost as if the two of them were getting along...but the moment ended, to her dismay, when Phellis came bounding back up a hill off in the distance. She bounced up and down as she beckoned them over.

*"You'll never guess what I found!"*

After walking many, many hills to meet her, Helena and Noah were vexed to find that Phellis had led them to a lonely sign next to an abandoned dirt road. It read:

Krotoa
Population: 109

Noa's face had turned a dark red from all the exertion. *"You made us come all this way...for a sign?"*

Phellis' face glistened with sweat. "Not just a sign, a *ghost town*. I scanned every inch of it from a distance and didn't spot a soul for miles. Wanna go check it out?" she said excitedly.

"Never heard a more senseless question," Noa said, a wicked gleam in his eye. "Of course I do!"

Helena looked anxiously over her shoulder towards camp. "We should probably head back. Penelope said at least one of us had to stay and keep watch at all times...we'll be in big trouble if anyone finds out we left the den unguarded."

"As long as neither of you go mouthing off to Red, we'll live. Let's go!" Noa said. He bustled down the path towards the remote town as Phellis tagged along behind him. Helena wavered once more. *You must never leave the den unguarded,* she recalled Penelope's ominous warning. But the prospect of discovering some form of civilization excited Helena—what was the worst thing that could happen? Penelope was fast asleep, and they would surely be back by nightfall—she never needed to find out that they'd been gone. Suppressing the feeling of foreboding in her stomach, Helena bounded down the dirt path after Noa and Phellis.

*It's dead wind today,* Noa's voice sounded in Helena's head as they arrived at Krotoa. The small town had a temple, a single learning hall that must have been a school, and several meek cottages scattered around, all of which were only occupied by an eerie silence. The group made their way through the central square; here, they found stands with all kinds of food and knickknacks, but there were no vendors in sight. Helena strolled by one stand, gaping at the headless mannequins dressed in coarse, asphyxiating wigeon gowns. Helena scurried away after she got the ill feeling that she was being watched.

"Population one hundred and *none,*" said Noa as they reconvened in the courtyard.

"What'd I tell y'all? Not a person in sight!" said Phellis.

"This can't be a ghost town," said Helena. "Look at the stands! Not even a trace of cobwebs...someone's been keeping the place up."

"I say we just loot it and boot it," said Noa. "Spotted a solid pair of boots two stands down..."

*"Greetings. "*

There was a chorus of screams and shouts from the group—a wigeon woman had taken them all by surprise after having appeared out of thin air behind them! Her long, coarse hair was wrapped in a faded pink bandana. Even though the woman was dressed from head to toe in rough-spun, homely garments, Helena reckoned her wide, tired eyes were the most unsettling thing of all...

"Welcome to Krotoa. Did you younglings need a place to stay for the night?"

"We were just passing by," Helena replied warily.

"Then perhaps a meal? Our local tavern offers a nightly special of pork and vegetable stew."

"We're not hungry," Helena said. "Where is everybody? You're the only person we've seen here."

The woman's red-rimmed eyes lingered on Helena before she answered. Something about her face seemed to scream, *Help me!*

"The residents of Krotoa are as lively as ever. If you find yourselves satisfied, then I bid you farewell and good luck on your journey. Although we do advise any wandering travelers to stay for the night, for traveling alone after dark can be especially dangerous..."

It was an odd encounter, indeed. As the group hurried their way back to camp, Helena felt perturbed at the thought of the woman and her strained, panicked eyes. Phellis put it best when she rubbed her hairy arms and said:

"*Eughhh!* That sure gave me the heebie-jeebies!"

Noa said, "One person managing an entire town...I don't buy it!"

"It begs the question," Helena said darkly, "where did the rest of the town go off to?"

The answer to that question came not long after sundown, after Penelope and Olip rose from their den to begin their nightly hunting session.

"We will return in a few hours," Penelope emphasized. She seemed to pay especially close attention to Helena as she added, "Remember what I said about not straying too far from camp."

Little did she know that a few hours ago they had, in fact, done just that to explore a nearby ghost town. Without another word, the twins took off into the night, granting the wigeon group the freedom to set up their sleeping quarters.

It wasn't long until Phellis, who had scurried off to hail the call of nature, returned to camp out of breath and wrought with excitement.

*"Guys, come quickly!"*

The group shot out of the adobe den and followed Phellis into the darkness and past several hills, which were illuminated by the starlit skies. Phellis led them to the top of a hill overlooking a great expanse of shrubland, where they all crouched behind a lone bush.

"What do you see, Phellis?" demanded Jared.

She pointed out into the distance and cried, "Down yonder!"

When they followed her finger they caught sight of a strong glow in the east. There was no other place it could be—it was the ghost town of Krotoa!

The sweet, melodic ringing of bells and music beckoned them closer towards the strange town, which glimmered in the bleak and dim setting of the shrublands. They lingered at its borders as they approached. Incredibly, the town was absolutely *crawling* with people; dozens and dozens of wigeons flooded the animated streets—all in beautiful gowns and suits, dancing to drums and violins underneath the starry skies.

"It must be a festival!" Phellis squealed.

"Impossible!" Helena cried.

"When the sun goes down, the celebrations begin, it seems!" Noa said, his eyes gleaming with excitement.

Jared looked at them askance. "Is there something I'm missing here? Why are you three acting so surprised?"

"We visited this place earlier in the day," Helena confessed guiltily.

Jared was furious. *"You did what?"*

Noa groaned. "Curse that insolent tongue o'yers, bird!"

"I'll say!" huffed Phellis.

"He has a right to know we left the den unguarded!" she said defensively.

"We swore to always keep watch over the den!" Jared said. He directed his anger towards Noa, who he knew had played a part in this brief excursion.

Noa rolled his eyes. "Nothing happened while we were gone—we may as well have never left!"

"If Penelope finds out we left them unguarded, she might be so furious as to *leave us*."

"She *won't* leave, because she doesn't need to know—unless *she's* so dense as to tell her, too!" Noa said. His look shot daggers at Helena, who rolled her eyes.

"I only brought it up because this town was abandoned earlier in the day! Don't any of you think this is strange? Where did all these people come from?"

Jared knew at once that something was off. "Ghost town? But that can't be—Noa! Phellis! Wait!"

The pair were already bounding off towards the town's bustling streets, leaving Jared and Helena to chase after them.

*"Travelers!"* cried a little girl with pink-ribbon pigtails. A slew of giggling children rushed at all four of them, picking and pulling at their clothing as if it were rare and valuable. They peppered them with the most innocent questions—Noa in particular, whom the little girls seemed to be most taken with.

"What's your name?"

"How did you get that scar?"

"You are very tan—are you from the beach?"

Helena grabbed his shoulder and said, "Noa, we need to leave—*now*."

One little girl replied, rather jealously, "Is she your *girlfriend?*"

Helena did not have time to gag at the question, as she was swept up and away by a current of dancers. Soon, even Jared was out of sight, and Helena had no choice but to kick her feet to the strumming beat of a banjo, mimicking the people around her. Their energy and drive were infectious! Even Helena found herself smiling as handsome gentlemen approached her and planted soft kisses upon her hand, while the daintiest ladies came up and complimented her braided hair. It was a night to be celebrated, they said, and Helena did just that! That is, until she heard:

"HELENA NIGHTINGALE."

There could be no mistaking the Stork's cool, calculating voice. Helena maneuvered her way through the crowds, scouring the rooftops and skies for any sign of black wings or feathers. The voice, however, sounded from all around her. It wasn't until Helena started to pay closer attention to the people around her that she realized they were all copying her every move: every time she ducked, they ducked. Every time she spun, they spun. Their eyes were dark pools of ink as they watched her dance...

In those chilling few moments, Helena considered that this town had been deserted the entire day, yet now, its streets were crawling with people at night. If Helena didn't know any better, she would have thought they exhibited signs of nocturnal behavior...

That's when it dawned on Helena: these people were not ordinary Nadiirian folk. They were *Nevarian wigeons.*

The commotion of the music drowned out Helena's cries for her friends. She saw Phellis kicking her feet and shuffling to the beat of the drums, oblivious to the enemy surrounding her. Helena moved towards her, but a great force met the back of her head, and in an instant all went black...

Helena woke with a terrible headache. Rubbing the back of her head, she looked around and found herself in a small clearing amidst shrubs and boulders. Two figures stood at the center; it was impossible to ignore one of them, a fearsome avian who made even the tallest boulders shrink in comparison. He towered nearly eight feet, his massive wingspan at least double his height, and he wore the familiar black sigil of a crow upon his chest. Despite his hands being so disfigured that they resembled two sets of pincers, he wielded a rugged sword with a tight grip. Next to him, a sickly Nevarian lingered by his side, parroting the incessant *"RUFF! RUFF!"* of an excited dog. Its pitch was needlelike and pierced Helena's ears. He shuffled around on all fours, his stout wings stretched out and flapping.

*"RUFF, RUFF!"* he yelped. *"Ptero, Ptero!* Majoravik has not—*RUFF, RUFF*—returned! He told Jimkins he would go piss, he said! Jimkins reckons it's been ten minutes..."

"Can't a man shit himself in peace?" a familiar, sarcastic voice said aloud.

"Noa?" Helena cried out. "Is that you?"

She shuffled around to see the sailor boy sitting on the ground alongside Jared. Both had their wrists bound behind them.

"Helena!" cried Jared. "You're okay!"

"How good of you to join us, bird!" said Noa. "I will say, every Krow-fest is incomplete when yer not around!"

"I'll remind you it wasn't *my* idea to come here," she replied crossly.

"All the same, yer a magnet for them Krows. They were looking for *you.*"

"Me?" she said nervously. "What for?"

"I guess we'll find out soon, won't we?"

It was then that Helena distinctly recalled the Stork's words: *the next time you hear from me will be through a little bird…*

"Nevarian wigeons," Jared muttered to himself, drawing Helena out of her thoughts. "I didn't see it coming…not this far out north…"

When Ptero wasn't looking, Helena scooched closer to Jared and whispered, "None of us did…not even Olip or Penelope. They must've taken it for any old town at night."

"What about Phellis?" he asked intently.

"She was still dancing, last I saw her."

"She's a clever girl, and will catch on quickly. It won't be long until she finds Olip and Penelope and tells them what's happened…"

"There's something off about this Krow," Noa said grimly. As he eyed the giant nave from head to toe, Helena and Jared followed his gaze. "He's not like the others. I just can't quite put my finger on it…"

Jared chuckled darkly. "Might you have overlooked the immense size of the beast?"

"No," Helena whispered, her voice grave. "Noa's right. Look at the color of his wings."

Though it was hard to tell at first given the dimness of the setting, his dirty feathers differed from the stark black feathers of the other Nevarians she had seen before. They had a familiar silver sheen to them which reminded Helena of her own. The Stork's voice sounded in Helena's head: *why, anyone could recognize the signature sterling silver feathers of an Avalonian!*

Noa's face went pale as he came to the same conclusion Helena had already reached. "Are you thinking what I'm thinking, bird?"

She nodded. *"He's fallen."*

The massive figure before them was not a Nevarian, but in fact, an Avalonian—more specifically, an *ex-Avalonian* who had been banished for committing treason against the Crown. Or perhaps he'd been exiled for some other crime—something so heinous that the Crown saw no other alternative than to send this colossal ave into Nadiir, where he could terrorize innocent Nadiirians instead of Avalonions. And Helena, Jared, and Noa were all at his mercy, tied up and huddled together like cattle awaiting slaughter.

Ptero seemed incapable of making anything other than large, slow movements—even his thought process seemed to take several seconds of delay. He made his lumbering way towards Helena, who whimpered and tried to scurry away. But Ptero caught hold of her by the ankle and raised her up so that she was left thrashing upside down in midair. Suddenly, Helena found herself face to face with Jimkins, who fanned her with his hot, rancid breath.

"Hair like a raven, eyes of green!" he whined greasily. *"The fairest woman Jimkins' ever done seen!"*

"Get away from me," Helena hissed. She smacked him after he tried sniffing one of her dangling braids, which seemed to bring him out of his lovestruck trance. He shook his entire body like a dog, blinking several times before saying:

"Jimkins shall now deliver the message!"

"Message for the Nightingale," Ptero growled. "From Master Stork."

Once again, Jimkins cautiously approached Helena on all fours. His eyes flooded with darkness, and all traces of emotion vanished from his face as he summoned the Stork's message from the depths of his memory:

"Helena Nightingale! By now, I expect you have already found the Duskmuth siblings and will soon locate the caverns in which the artifact resides. You will be put under immense pressure—its tunnels are said to be as impossible to endure as they are to find, and not all of you may make it out alive. You *must* be willing to do the unthinkable. As you hear this, your mirage is waiting patiently for the day of your return. I must admit, it's served me tremendously well in ex-

PLORING THE FIELD OF MIRAGE THEORY. FOR INSTANCE, I'VE LEARNED WITH DUE DILIGENCE AND OBSERVATION THAT THE MIRAGE SURVIVES OFF THE LIFE FORCE OF ITS RESPECTIVE HOST. YOU SEE, HELENA, SINCE THE DAY YOU FIRST PARTED WITH IT, ITS LIGHT HAS DIMMED BY NEARLY TWENTY PERCENT, AND IT GROWS WEAKER WITH EACH PASSING DAY. KNOW THAT THE LONGER YOU TAKE IN RETRIEVING THE ARTIFACT, THE SOONER YOUR MIRAGE WILL PERISH—AND YOU WILL NEVER KNOW FLIGHT AGAIN."

Helena's heart cracked in anguish. How long did she have before her mirage was gone for good? It had been over a month since it had been taken from her...it was possible that she had only weeks, perhaps even days before it would disappear forever...

"MAY THIS MESSAGE HELP INCENTIVIZE YOU TO FINISH THE MISSION I HAVE TASKED YOU WITH. TIME IS OF THE ESSENCE! FAIRWELL, NIGHTINGALE, AND REMEMBER—NOTHING GOOD EVER HAPPENS AFTER DARK..."

Thus concluded the Stork's message. Jimkins shuddered before he leapt to his two feet and looked to Ptero, who was still dangling Helena by the ankle. By this point, all the blood rushing to her head had made her nauseous.

"Let's scram!" Jimkins cried.

They had completed their mission in delivering the message to Helena. But before they could even think about leaving, two flashes of white descended from the heavens—Olip and Penelope had come to their rescue!

Ptero and Jimkins, however, had already perceived their arrival: Ptero's grip on Helena's ankle loosened and she fell to the ground with a grunt. The fallen avian spun around and caught Penelope midair, intercepting her silver dagger with one of his deformed hands and driving it deep into her right wing. Her eyes were two perfect black circles, mouth agape in a silent scream before she was slammed to the ground. Ptero straddled Penelope, crushing both of her wings with his monstrous feet. Olip rushed to his sister's aid, but Jimkins intercepted his path. He brandished his own dagger, all whilst belting at the top of his lungs:

*"Moonwalkers, moonwalkers, our brothers in night! Time for dinner yet? Or is breakfast the word right?"*

Olip demonstrated an uncanny reserve in combat completely unlike his typical introspective self. His feet were as light as air, and he slipped away from Jimkins' attacks as sprightly as any dancer—spinning, leaping, and twirling in the air...though he had only one arm, he executed every swipe of his long blade with swiftness and precision. Indeed, this was the signature combat style of the Nocturnal in battle: an evasive repertoire of nimble, sophisticated movements designed to outwit their opponent.

A frustrated Jimkins eventually resorted to singing a curious hymn, this time in a distinct voice: "BLACK SEED, SOWED AND SPROUTED! THE FALLEN AVIAN SHALL BIDE HIS TIME! A PROMISED RISE, A PENDING VENGEANCE, WITH HIS BLOOD THE FALLEN SHALL RISE!"

Meanwhile, Ptero's eyes lingered coldly on Penelope. "Filthy ghouls."

A glint of light appeared out of nowhere—it happened so fast Helena nearly thought she had imagined it. Penelope had taken a hidden blade and lodged it cleanly into the thigh of Ptero's giant leg. The fallen ave merely cocked his head, looked down at the dagger as if it were a mere splinter, and proceeded to yank it out without so much as a twitch of an eye. Blood pattered like rain upon Penelope's white face, and she grimaced as some of it landed in her mouth.

"Taste good?" he asked with an evil smile.

She spat at him. "I don't like pork."

In a fit of rage, Ptero lifted Penelope from the ground with one hand and beheld her dagger in the other, aiming it straight for her chest. He was about to murder one of the only two people alive who could help Helena get her hands on the artifact.

"*No!*" Helena shouted.

There was movement from the east—Phellis sprinted into the clearing bearing a jagged shard of rock. She climbed onto Ptero as nimbly as an acrobat would, swiping savagely at his face and causing him to release Penelope with a beastly cry. His massive, beefy arm swung hard against Phellis' small, slender body, sending her flying across the clearing and into a tree. The back of her bald head smacked hard against its surface, and she slumped unconscious.

With their captors otherwise occupied, Noa and Jared freed themselves from the ligatures binding their wrists and flocked to Helena's side. Before long, Ptero was upon them. Unarmed and defenseless, there was no way they could take on a monster that size...then Helena felt two fingers press against the small ridge along the nape of her neck.

"I'm going to borrow this for a minute, bird," Noa's voice sounded in her ear.

*Click.* Helena's utilitarian suit retracted from underneath her clothes and a chill came over her body. Her suit condensed into a ball in Noa's hands; he tossed it several times in the air, as if getting ready for a game of catch, before stretching it between his fingers. The U-ball instantly transformed into a staff. Fearlessly, Noa advanced towards Ptero. He swung with all his might, dragging the edge of the utilitarian staff across the nave's bleeding face, earning a groan of pain. Noa did not hesitate to take a second strike. When Noa swung the third time, however, Ptero caught the staff midair, wrenched it from his grasp, and flung it somewhere far off into the trees. Then he lunged forwards with a deathly growl. Noa shoved Helena behind him as the giant loomed over them like a great mountain. The sailor boy stood firm as the fallen avian raised his giant claw of a hand to strike them, when suddenly—

A set of strong, brown arms locked around his throat from behind—it was Jared! Ptero's wings flared and thrust wildly, propelling their combined weight ten feet into the air. But there was no way for him to shake off the determined wigeon who clung to him from behind. In a desperate bid to free himself, Ptero reversed his course and plummeted to the ground—face up—so that Jared would bear the force of the landing beneath him. It was the equivalent of having nearly three hundred pounds of weight dropped on you from the sky. The heavy impact stunned Jared, causing him to release his hold on the fallen avian at once.

Olip had nearly overtaken Jimkins when the craven nave ran off whimpering into the woods, leaving Ptero outnumbered by the entire group; despite the numbers against him, it still seemed an even match for the giant. Helena knew, however, that Ptero and Jimkins had come only as messengers. Though his bloodlust was potent enough to take a few swipes at the six who stood against him, Ptero eventually spread his wings and lifted off, disappearing into the night skies.

*"Jared!"* Helena ran to the wigeon boy who, moments ago, had been body-slammed by an eight-foot giant. His mouth was open, but no sound came out. His body spasmed from the pain and lack of oxygen flowing to his brain. "Breathe, breathe!" Helena urged.

He gasped loudly as he took the breath of life, and sweet oxygen finally flowed through his battered lungs.

"Deep breaths," Helena cooed, taking his hand firmly and guiding him to start steadying his breathing. As he focused, he squeezed Helena's hand in a wordless *thank-you*.

"I'm okay, too, in case y'all were wondering!" the obnoxious voice of Phellis called out from their left. She staggered to her feet, rubbing at the back of her bald head, and frowned to find her fingers stained red.

"Here you go, bird," Noa said afterwards, returning her U-ball and placing it in her hand. "Those lessons you gave me came in handy. Thanks."

It was the first time he had thanked her for anything. Helena only nodded and donned her utilitarian suit underneath her clothes once more, looking away to hide the fact that she was blushing.

Olip was bleeding from several places and had the imprints of teeth stamped into his neck—Jimkins had apparently taken his role as a dog much too seriously. Noa, who for the most part had come through unscathed, helped Jared to his feet. It was Penelope, however, who'd taken the hardest blow in their fight with the Nevarians: crimson blood stained her right wing, spreading further and further across her snow-white feathers. Olip wasted no time in tending to her wounds; he plucked three long feathers from his own healthy wing and, with a mortar and pestle, crushed them into a fine, pearlescent powder. He then diluted this magical feather dust with a bit of water and added a spoonful of medical ointment from his bag. The result was a shimmering white paste similar to the one Penelope had used on Jared's head injury. Olip applied this salve generously to Penelope's injured wing, and it brought her instant relief.

"The four of you did what I advised you not to do," Penelope seethed, looking from each Diurnal to the next. "You strayed from camp! What made you come to such a foolish decision? I demand an explanation!"

Jared was the only one brave enough to tell her the truth from beginning to end. Penelope listened quietly, but her face grew gradually more displeased as time went on.

"…It never crossed our minds that Krotoa might've been full of Nevarian wigeons," Jared said in conclusion. As he said it aloud, Helena realized how utterly stupid it had been of them not to even consider the possibility. "We're sorry for all the trouble we've caused."

Something in Penelope's eyes flashed. *The deal was that my brother and I would allow you to come with us in return for daylight protection!*

"Listen, we only went for a little while—" Noa protested.

Helena added, "Less than an hour, and we were back before anything bad could've happened—"

*"Time matters little!"* she thundered. "You broke our agreement the moment you left our den unguarded! Because of your stupidity, you've compromised the safety of the entire group! I took a knife to the wing because of your foolishness, which—*argh!*"

Penelope cut herself short as a sharp wave of pain overtook her wing, and she groaned.

"Look, mistakes were made," Phellis began, "but I reckon we ought to pack our things and scram before any more nightcrawlers come!"

Phellis was right—it was in their best interests to leave at once. But before they could flee, Olip wavered on his feet and uttered a strange moan. He motioned towards his sister's maimed wing…

Helena picked up his meaning at once: Penelope would not be able to fly.

"You go ahead and make sure our path is clear," Penelope told him softly. "If you get an inclination of any sort, you come down and tell me."

With a hesitant nod, Olip launched himself into the night sky, taking his place within the clouds. Phellis took the lead on the ground as the group moved with a renewed sense of urgency through the dry shrublands, and the Mountains of Alazar grew steadily larger. In a surprising turn of events, Helena was no longer the straggler of the bunch. Penelope was forced to exert a strenuous effort to keep up with the rest of the Diurnal group, requiring frequent breaks; even Helena felt bad each time the wounded Nocturnal took a minute to lean against a tree with her hands clutched to the side of her abdomen, taking stark, trembling breaths. Jared even offered his own horse for her to ride, but Penelope was far too proud a creature to accept.

Hours later, after much exhausting travel, Olip landed in front of his sister. He looked paler than usual, if that were even possible. He pointed beyond the trees and murky clouds that blocked the eastern sky, signaling towards the lightening horizon. They soon realized that they had lost track of time, and dawn was quickly approaching.

With less than an hour until sunrise, the twins raced to build a last-minute, makeshift den. They settled on a shallow overhang at the base of a rocky outcrop which was barely enough to fit one person, let alone two adults—but given the direness of the situation, they could not afford to be picky. They hurriedly stacked stones to barricade themselves inside, but Penelope had grown clumsy and weary; every time a fresh wave of pain overtook her, she fumbled with the stones and their wall crumbled.

Cautiously stepping forwards, Helena picked one stone from the ground and offered it to the Nocturnal, the first of many olive branches.

"Let us help," Helena said.

Penelope was hesitant at first. Surely this violated some obscure Nocturnal custom, or maybe, just maybe...she hadn't expected such an act of kindness from Helena and her friends. But after a long look at the glowing horizon, Penelope conceded. Together, everyone worked as one to help the siblings construct their den—Jared slugging boulders as large as his head, Noa and Phellis diligently popping pebbles to fill in tiny holes, and Helena gathering slabs of tree bark and foliage for an extra degree of protection, all while Olip and Penelope reinforced their den from within.

A crescendo grew from the belly of the wilderness as newly risen birds and insects heralded the sun. Just a little more...*there!* Noa fitted the last stone that sealed the cave just as the white sun peaked over the eastern horizon and light spilled over into the lands of Nadiir. A warmth struck Helena's skin, and she welcomed it with a smile. Sunrise.

As she turned her face to greet the morning sun, Helena's foot accidentally nudged the bottom of the barricade, triggering a miniature landslide of rocks and pebbles. Instinctively, Helena's hand reached out to mend her error, but she fumbled, and as she did, another hand from within the den reached out to fix the gaping rift in the barricade and—

*Helena caught glimpse of soft, white skin.*

*"NO!!!"*

A nightmarish scream filled the air. As Helena fell back in fear, Jared acted quickly to mend her mistake, readjusting the affected area with a dexterity only he was skilled enough to maintain under the pressure of Penelope's shrieks. Phellis cupped her hands over her ears, rocking back and forth on the floor as Noa and Helena staggered back in horror. They stood by helplessly as they listened to the panicked words exchanged between the two siblings:

"It will spread...Olip, you know what to do—"

"..."

"OH, FOR GOODNESS' SAKE, JUST DO IT!"

*Fump.*

*"—EEAAAAAAGGHHHHHHHHHHHHH!"*

# Chapter Twelve

W hat was the effect of sunlight on Nocturnal skin? How much time did they have until Helena's mirage was gone for good? What did Jimkins mean when he said that "The Fallen Avian shall bide his time?" All these questions—and more—filtered through Helena's head as a welcomed silence settled over the surrounding forest. Hours had passed since Penelope's screams had stopped, but they were still fresh in Helena's head. Noa, Phellis, and Jared had gone to try their luck fishing at a nearby creek, whilst Helena remained back at camp, sitting on a log and gazing at the Nocturnal den with sore, guilty eyes. Beams of benevolent sunlight peaked through the clouds and fell upon Helena's face. She welcomed the warmth, though it did nothing to curtail the guilt within her.

Jared was the first to come back from fishing. When he noticed Helena sulking, he set aside his catch for the day and joined her. The two dwelled together in silence until Helena spoke first:

"It was my fault," she admitted bleakly.

"It was a mistake any of us could've made."

Helena snorted. "A lethal one, at that!"

"I don't know about lethal! We still don't know what happened in there, Helena!"

"From the sounds of it, it didn't stray too far away from death."

"Well, we won't know until sunset. In the meantime, don't beat yourself over it," he said, giving Helena a cheerful pat on the shoulder.

Helena sighed. His words did leave her feeling a little better, but not by much; in truth, she hadn't heard a peep from Penelope or her brother since the incident. There was no telling what they'd find when the siblings came out of their den—*if* they ever came out.

"That nave who goes by the name of Jimkins," Helena began hesitantly, "he mentioned something strange last night. I could've sworn he was talking about the Fallen Avian..."

Jared's brows knit themselves together. "The same one Phellis was telling us stories about?"

"That's the one. Jimkins said the Fallen Avian would return to enact his vengeance, and that the fallen would rise. I don't like the sound of that one bit."

Jared paused to mull this over before saying, "We should ask ourselves, then—what exactly *are* we retrieving for the Stork?"

Helena's stomach churned with anxiety at the question. Its premise frightened her yet solidified her resolve.

"We can't just sit around and ponder any longer. The Stork himself said it won't be long until my mirage..." Helena caught herself before she could complete that thought. "...before it's too late. It's time to confront Penelope once and for all and ask her what artifact she's after."

He snorted. "With all that's happened, I wonder just how willing she'll be to cooperate...with our luck, she'll probably leave before you can ask her."

"The cards may yet be in our favor," Helena said with a wry smile. "Penelope's hurt and can't fly. There's nowhere else for her to go."

That night, the twins arose from their den as always, only now a bandage encased Penelope's right wing. Had the early morning bedlam all been an overreaction? That remained unclear, but one thing was certain: Penelope *was* injured, meaning that for the remainder of their journey, she would remain stuck on the ground with the rest of them. Helena knew she could not let this opportunity go to waste; she bided her time until she could corner Penelope when she was alone.

The Duskmuths stood shoulder to shoulder, holding up a map against the starry sky. Penelope spoke to Olip in hushed murmurs before nodding in understanding and jotting something down in that thick notebook of hers. Most of what she said went in one of Helena's ears and out the other, though she did catch a fleeting utterance of words:

"This will all be over soon," Penelope whispered to Olip, her voice weary with exhaustion. "We'll be back home, and we won't have to hide anymore..."

*Hide from what?* Helena wondered. Olip soaked these words in, gazing at the glittering skies with a painful longing. Perhaps he yearned to go home as much as Helena did. When Olip departed to hunt, leaving behind his wigeoned sister, Helena lingered behind the trees, shifting back and forth on her feet and wondering when she should present herself. Without even looking over her shoulder, Penelope spoke aloud:

"It is unwise to eavesdrop on the eavesdropper."

Helena staggered a moment, startled, before stepping into the clearing and out into the full moonlight. "I've merely come to see how the wigeon life is treating you. You seem a tad restless."

"If that isn't an understatement! My brother is out there doing the real work whilst I'm sitting here doing nothing..."

"I can't imagine the pain you're suffering," Helena said cynically. Surely, the Nocturnal would be back in the air within a few weeks' time. Meanwhile, Helena's future remained uncertain...

"Have you come to ridicule me? I'd much rather you apologized for your incompetence and insubordination, both of which combined to land me in this wretched state!"

"Listen, I'm sorry about your wing—"

"It's not my *wing* I'm angry about, Helena! Feathers, at least, can grow back."

Before Helena could make sense of the true meaning of this, the Nocturnal raised her pale left hand up into the moonlight. It wouldn't have looked like anything out of the ordinary—if it hadn't been for the absence of two things: her ring and pinky finger.

*She lost her fingers?* Unless Helena was so unobservant that she'd simply never noticed that Penelope had always been missing a few digits, she must have lost them sometime in the last several hours since sunrise...

"A long time ago," Penelope began, "someone foreordained that I, and thousands of others like me, would not live to see the sun. Not in life, not in death, not in its morning grace, nor its summer wrath…a star whose touch brings life to all—except us. We Nocturnal avians are forbidden to walk in daylight because light is to us as poison is to the body. Upon exposure, sunlight poisoning kills us, slowly but surely—if left untreated. The only solution is to remove the tainted site as quickly as possible before it can spread its corruption to the surrounding healthy tissue. Nevarians share a similar fate, only they reactively *combust* with exposure to sunlight. If there was one thing I would envy of Nevarians, it would be only this—that they, at least, get to die quickly."

Helena could not withhold her gasp of horror. *Olip had chopped off her fingers!* The price that must be paid by a Nocturnal who had exposed themselves  to sunlight was to lose or sever that part of their body forever. This revelation unleashed new and graphic imagery before Helena's eyes. She had felt guilty before, but this…this was worse than she had ever imagined…

"…Now you know, Helena, why we begin taking precautions hours before dawn. Why we build our lightproof shelters so carefully, why we purge arduously, and why we maintain our distance from Diurnals. And no matter how careful our preparations, we never truly rest. Wariness will always whisper that the walls around us could come down at any second, and that death is ever only a hairsbreadth away."

Could it have been Helena's own bias that made it seem like Penelope spoke of her life so disconsolately? She would have expected a Nocturnal to boast proudly of their nightly lifestyle! But Penelope spoke of her life as if she were living under a curse—and reasonably so! How dreadful it must be to spend your entire life running from something as pervasive as the sun…

Swallowing her pride, Helena stated meekly, "Olip is missing an arm."

"He was only a child, then," Penelope said bitterly, turning away and concealing whatever emotion might have appeared on her pale face. "A group of Diurnal bandits abducted him, exerting whatever cruelty they had stored in their pitiful little hearts, and left him for dead somewhere in the mountains. My father spent that entire night treading the snow-ridden forests, searching for him with the help of our loyal hound. He found Olip only moments before sunrise. Wrapping him in his thick winter coat, my father carried my brother back to our den, where my mother and I anxiously awaited them. I suppose Olip must have struggled or squirmed along the way, exposing a finger or two to the sunlight. By the time they arrived, the curse had already spread up to his elbow…"

Helena scrunched her brow in confusion. "But if Olip was exposed, then that means your father…"

Penelope shut her eyes briefly as she recalled a memory almost too painful to remember. "My father succumbed to sunlight poisoning four days later. Mother did not permit us to see him in his last hours, which he would have spent living in utter anguish. Olip hasn't uttered a word since that day, and remains wary of Diurnals. I was the more fortunate of the family, I suppose…"

"Penelope, I'm…I'm sorry! I had no idea sunlight poisoning was even a thing—"

"I've no interest in your excuses, Helena. Not only did you violate our agreement by abandoning our den, but you nearly cost me my life in knocking down part of our barricade."

Helena *knew* she had messed up, but felt as if she had failed a test she hadn't studied for—or even been told about, for that matter! In her eyes, it felt so *unfair* that she be held accountable for things she knew nothing about!

"Are we just supposed to tiptoe around invisible eggshells?" Helena demanded.

"We gave you clear boundaries, Helena."

"With no mention of the consequences!"

"That matters little."

Helena groaned in frustration. "This is impossible! How on earth is this group supposed to stay together when we're as different as night and day? *We know nothing about each other!*"

"That's not true."

Upon hearing Penelope's quiet statement, Helena's frustration swiftly subsided. It was almost as if the Nocturnal was afraid that someone might overhear them, though Helena assured herself there was no one who possibly could. Penelope continued:

"I know much about Avalonians. Your lot can be irrational—a bit tactless, but only because it caters to your more cluttered perception of the world, where chaos is expected, even longed for. Why else would the Murmuration be your symbol of hope?"

Helena cast a sidelong glance at Penelope. "Spontaneity is the key to life, I suppose. You make that sound like a bad thing."

The avian revealed a new expression—piqued and incendiary, quite unlike her reserved self. "You've mistaken mere observation for criticism! Murmurating is a feat of such magnitude—one I've only ever read about on the page. Imagine celebrating the magic of daybreak in such glorious fashion...what's it like flying in a Murmuration?"

Helena merely shrugged.

"You don't know?" Penelope said doubtfully. "You've flown in one and yet *you don't know?*"

"I just flew! Do you expect me to describe the thousands of faces around me? It doesn't work like that. Out there, when you're Murumurating, you can only ever think of the people closest to you. They're the only ones who matter. Focus too much on anything else, you'll be sent hurdling out like a meteor, and your flock will fall apart! That's about it. Satisfied?"

Her eyes gleamed like onyx gems. "Fascinating. Thousands of people flying at once...I once read, you know, that the smallest recorded Murmuration in history was a seven-count flock. *Seven!*"

"Yes, well, hopefully that information will come in handy one day," Helena said, stifling the urge to roll her eyes. "How do you know all this, anyway? I wouldn't have taken Diurnal rites of passage as your field of expertise."

Her smile dwindled. "It seems there are many things you have yet to know about me."

Penelope fell silent and gazed quietly up at the stars. Helena hesitated to ask Penelope a simple question, but did so anyway:

"Do you ever wish you could walk in the day?"

Helena didn't realize it at the time, but it was stupid of her to have asked such a question. Before she could think twice about it, Penelope had already burst into outrage:

*"What kind of ridiculous question is that? Of course I don't—and don't ever ask me something like that again!"*

Penelope left Helena in the woods—alone and speechless.

The next day, the Diurnal group gathered along a cool, shallow river to combat the potent effects of the hot afternoon sun. Underbelly and friends sipped water gleefully along the banks of the river. Meanwhile, Phellis kicked her stinky feet into the river's crystal clear waters, giggling mischievously as some splashed onto a sunbathing Noa, who hissed at the cold droplets suddenly touching his sandy skin. He started chasing her shortly thereafter. The sounds of girlish screams and water splashing filled the air. Jared stood nearby, ankle-deep in water with a hand held over his eyes to block out the sun's rays. He laughed as he watched Noa and Phellis chase each other around. Everyone seemed to be enjoying the hot, refreshing day—all except Helena, who preferred the cool shade of an oak tree. After some time on her own, Jared eventually joined her and sat down beside her.

"Phellis is taken with him," Helena said, nodding towards the giggling pair. Jared tilted his head thoughtfully as he considered her words.

"Noa can be quite the ladies' man when he feels like it. Though he generally likes his women with a lot more hair on their head...and a fair bit taller," he added quickly, shooting the strangest look between Helena and Noa as he did so.

Helena was unsure what Jared meant by this. Nevertheless, she watched closely as Noa caught Phellis and, in one great heave, body-slammed her into the water. *CLAP!* The sound her body made against the water was jarring, causing Helena to flinch. For reasons unbeknownst to her, she was transported back to the day of her Murmuration, when she saw the body of the ave who had died upon making a harsh impact with the water. Disturbed, Helena decided she would avoid all contact with water for the rest of the day.

After sitting together in silence for some time, Helena confessed to Jared about the conversation she'd had with Penelope the night prior. Noa and Phellis stopped their play-fighting to join in on the discussion, listening intently as Helena divulged the details about sunlight poisoning, how both Penelope and Olip were missing body parts because of it, and how their father had fallen victim to this strange, degenerative curse.

"So that's what happens when they step out into the light," Jared murmured.

Noa exclaimed, "No wonder the woman was squealing like a pig—she was being butchered!"

"I knew there was something awfully wicked about them," Phellis said to them in a hushed whisper.

"Did you ask Penelope about the artifact?" Jared asked Helena.

She hesitated before responding. "No, she stormed off before I could ask her."

Jared huffed. "Stormed off? Well, what did you say to her that made her so angry?"

Helena gave him a sheepish look. "I was so caught up with everything she was telling me that the artifact slipped from my mind and I...might've offended her by asking if she ever wanted to walk in the daylight."

"You did *what?*" Phellis cried.

"After she told you her father *died* walking in sunlight?" Jared said incredulously.

Noa heard this and threw his head back in laughter. "Gee, bird—and I took you for a gentle creature!"

Helena's cheeks burned. "I suppose it might've been insensitive, but it was a genuine question! She knows a lot about Murmurations—more so than I do, it seems, and I've flown in one. I figured she might've wondered once in her life what it's like on the other side. Pardon me for being curious!"

"Well," Jared said, giving a deep and disappointed sigh, "I guess we'll have to go yet *another* day without knowing what the artifact is...I suppose if anything, we'll know once we find it, which could be any day, now..."

Indeed, it was the day Helena had dreaded most since they formed their alliance with the Nocturnals; there was no denying that Olip and Penelope had their own reasons for wanting the artifact, and the chances of convincing them to hand it over peacefully seemed highly unlikely. *You must be willing to do the unthinkable,* the Stork's voice echoed in her head. What did he mean by *"unthinkable?" Don't be foolish*, she thought to herself, *you know exactly what he means!* Still, the question remained: just how far was Helena willing to go to fly once more?

She shook the thought out of her head. She wouldn't—she *couldn't* bring herself to consider it...

Moments later, Phellis cast a lingering gaze at Helena and said, *"You've* flown in a Murmuration before?"

"Why, yes, I have!" she said, unabashed.

Noa's eyes narrowed. "Yer kidding."

"Not at all! I had my first one earlier this year, and plan to complete many more in the years to come!"

The two wigeons shared a look of disbelief at the fact that Helena had experienced one of the most unique and magical experiences known to avian kind. Jared, not being Avalonian, was unfamiliar with the topic.

"What's a Murmuration?" he asked Helena, his eyes twinkling with curiosity.

"Once a year, Avalonians gather to celebrate the coming of spring. They come together in flocks of hundreds, even thousands of aves, all before traveling across the kingdom and making their way down to the lake at Blade's Peak and Murmurating as one."

His jaw fell open. *"Thousands?"*

"Thousands!" she confirmed.

Jared's big brown eyes filled with wonder. The concept seemed almost unfathomable to the wigeon boy.

Noa gave a dismissive snort. "All they do is just fly together and call it a day. Big deal..."

"I'll say..." muttered Phellis, shooting Helena a jealous look.

"It's more than just flying," Helena protested. "It's about celebrating new beginnings! It's about communion and dependability and flying in sync with the people who grew up alongside you. Once you're inside the flock and you find your inner circle, nothing else matters except them. And you're caught in this slipstream of thrill and adrenaline—diving and climbing, making turns left and right, feeling the force of the atmosphere press so heavily against your skull that you feel you might faint..."

Helena cut herself short when she noticed all eyes were focused on her. Phellis listened with subdued interest. Jared leaned forwards with devoted attention. Then there was Noa, who stared open-mouthed at Helena—perhaps trying to come up with some offhand comment to shoot her down, but failing miserably.

For once, he was rendered speechless.

"Go on," Jared pressed. "Tell us what it's like, flying. We're dying to know!"

Helena stiffened, her eyes glazing over in distant memory of what she loved the most. In truth, it was a question she had hardly ever considered—flying had once been an instinct to her, as much as eating or breathing was. No one ever asked what it was like chewing or inhaling—it just happened! Composing an accurate response took several moments of ponderous silence before she could finally come up with a solid answer:

"*True flight*, in its barest nature, is terrifying," she replied, her green eyes looking solemnly up at the clouds. "The moment you part with the ground, wigeonly instinct fills your belly and you're almost certain you'll fall to your death. You don't, though. Your wings thrust against air and take you higher—so swiftly you defy gravity, and in the most divine manner you conquer death."

"*Woah,*" the three wigeons said in unison.

Realizing what she had just said, Helena blushed beet-red. "I'm sorry—"

"Don't apologize," Jared said, visibly impressed. "That was great! I've never heard someone describe flying as you do..."

After witnessing her speak passionately about something he had never experienced—and likely never would—Noa gave Helena the strangest look, staring at her with a kind of potent, distant wonder that sparked a tiny Murmuration in Helena's stomach. They locked eyes; then, just like the other day, when they had talked about the splendor of wind, he granted her another firm nod of respect.

Phellis' keen eyes detected this micro-moment and flickered jealously between the two of them. Then, from out of her mouth came a catastrophic sentence that would cause them all to plunge into a painful, aching silence:

"Too bad you'll never fly again, though."

They all turned to look at Phellis, who began mindlessly digging into the dirt with her fingers. Noticing their glares, she said, "What? The Stork took her wings and likely won't give 'em back! Am I so wrong for sayin' the truth?"

"No, but that was just terrible timing," Noa said, frowning.

Helena left before they could see the tears fall. She took refuge beneath a harrowed oak tree, away from everyone else, and spent the rest of her afternoon weeping bitterly. Occasionally, a flying squirrel scurried along the branches above her, leaping from tree to tree as freely as Helena did when she lived in the Colossal Forest. Now, those memories seemed so distant. Had she ever really flown at all? Or was she always this...mundane and useless? Perhaps this truly was her reality now. Broken. Average. Condemned to forever wallow in mediocrity.

Phellis found her at sunset with droopy wing stubs and a heavy posture. She fell before Helena, a blubbering mess.

"I'm sorry, Helena. Truly, I am!"

"It's alright, Phellis."

"No! It's not alright...oh, I don't know what came over me. I guess...I guess I couldn't help but feel jealous. I've lived like this for so long, I reckon being flightless is second nature to me now, an' when I heard you talking about flying the way you did back there...it was like watching someone recall a lover, the way you spoke about it. I've never felt that way about anything."

Helena smiled sadly. "All is forgiven. I'll admit I got carried away. Sometimes, I forget I'm in this state. How to accept that something you've had all your life is gone, I still have no idea..."

Phellis sat next to her in a huff. "You get used to it, eventually."

"But it's not something I *want* to get used to. I don't *want* to stay like this..." Before she knew it, Helena crumbled before Phellis, weeping in despair. "Oh, Phellis, I had so many plans! I was supposed to travel the world and soar for hours on end! Now I'll have to take the *stairs* every day, for the rest of my life, resigned to watch others live out my dreams. My wings were what made me formidable and strong—now look at me! Insignificant! Weak! Oh, Noa was right—*who am I without my wings?*"

"Now listen here!" Phellis grabbed hold of Helena's face, a fire in her eyes. "You're not gonna sit there and pretend the best part of you were those lousy feathers. Wings grow old and useless, an' when they do, all you have left is yourself! It happens to everybody—folks like you an' I just get a head start on living it, is all. *Hmph!* You must think being a wigeon is all sorrows an' weeps, huh? You were born with legs first, Helena. There's more to life than flying, an' if you'd stop your moping an' realize how good you've got it, you'd see how much *lighter* you are on your feet—"

Leaping to her feet and raising her fists, Phellis hopped quickly from heel to heel, giving sharp kicks to the air and throwing a flurry of jabs with her hands. She then sprung towards the nearest tree and scaled its towering, crooked trunk with her nimble hands and misshapen feet. Phellis leapt from tree to tree, swinging from branch to branch as lively as an acrobat, and disappeared from Helena's view.

Then, out of nowhere, Phellis landed mere feet away from Helena, startling her. "See how easy it is to sneak up on your enemies? An' it's just as easy evadin' them! You got a nightcrawler or two on your tail? Run into the tightest forest you can find—you'll lose 'em in the blink of an eye! That's how I've managed all this time, Helena. That big bad wolf might've taken many things away from me, but he didn't take my mind, my wits, or my spirit! You can take my wings away, but then you'll just leave me, only me, an' nothing but *me.*"

That night, though much of her sorrows still persisted deep into the later hours, Helena eventually realized that Phellis was right—Helena had spent so much time wallowing in her sadness and shame that she had, in fact, failed to notice how light she felt on her feet. When examining her own quads, she was pleasantly surprised to feel lean muscle that she was certain hadn't been there before. It was bittersweet to say that Helena was slowly getting accustomed to her newfound reality —and getting stronger by the day.

It was well past sundown, and mostly everyone was fast asleep as Olip patrolled the skies above. Only two women were awake—Helena, who sat and munched on the greasy, gristly leg of a hare, and Penelope, who sat farther away against a tree, lost in that same old notebook in which she wrote like a madwoman. A faded pink color seeped through the bandages encasing her injured wing. Whilst chewing slowly, Helena shot a calculating eye at the shabby book, which looked like it was fighting for its life to keep itself together, and said:

"You write in that book like any of these days might be your last."

Penelope paused, flashed a distasteful glance at Helena, and promptly resumed her scribbles.

"That may very well be the case," she replied a few moments later, seeming faintly interested in Helena's presence.

"Why *do* you write so much?" Helena asked, before ripping another bite off her tough rabbit leg.

The pen in Penelope's hand slowed by just the tiniest bit. Eventually, Penelope heaved a hearty sigh and answered her question while still continuing to write:

"Nocturnal doctrine states our life mission plainly—*'Seek knowledge, acquire wisdom. Many seek the first and not the latter, and those who seek the latter seek not the first.'*"

Helena only gave a blank look, and Penelope rolled her eyes.

"That is why I record everything in this journal, Helena. I jot down what I see, what I think, and what I know to better understand the world around me. Knowledge, as cliché as it sounds, is power."

Helena didn't know how to respond to this. She chewed a couple more seconds before looking at the bone in her hand. Swallowing, she said, "Are rats all you guys ever eat?"

"Is this some kind of interrogation?" Penelope snapped, her pale cheeks flushing scarlet in anger.

"Easy! I'm only trying to bridge the knowledge gap between us, is all. You don't have to answer the question if you don't want to…" Helena mumbled, bitterly tossing the bone aside. It landed right next to a half-eaten, roasted rat.

Penelope leaned back against the bark behind her. For a while, she did not even write.

"We don't eat other avians, if that's what you're asking," she finally said.

"Not at all," Helena said, her brows rising. "Where did that come from?"

"There's a prevailing notion in the Upper Realm that we Nocturnals are cannibals—primarily because we're often depicted as ghouls in Diurnal legends, and because we thrive off a meat-based diet. Contrary to that belief, we eat lots of vegetables. Our dishes principally consist of hearty stews, like beef tripe and potatoes, or lamb and parsnips."

"And here I thought your kind only ever scavenged for mice and rabbits!" Helena joked.

"Hmph! You make us sound like bottom feeders! We're hunters, not *scavengers*."

"Is there really a difference?"

Penelope's head turned to Helena fiercely. "Of course there is a difference! Eating carrion of any kind is forbidden in our culture; we actively hunt for our food, which is always fresh game and *not* rotting corpses, thank you very much!"

"Noted," Helena said, grimacing once more at the fallen rat beside her. "All this talk of mice and stews is fascinating, but I'm afraid it's not truly what I wanted to ask you."

Penelope wrapped up the last couple of sentences in her notebook before shutting it with one hand. Her enormous head oriented itself to face Helena, which never failed to give her the creeps.

"What would you like to know, Helena?" she asked calmly. "I'm well aware of the efforts you've made in attempting to corner me to get information. Well, everyone's asleep, and I'm not flying away anytime soon. So, if I were you, I'd take advantage of this very moment."

Helena figured it would be easier to be direct and just say it:

"I want you to tell me what artifact you're looking for."

"A dragon egg."

Helena did not expect such a quick answer! A wad of spit lodged itself in her throat, and she started choking; eyes streaming, Helena cleared her throat and said, *"You're after a living dragon egg?"*

"Not living, per se…the dragon in question is long extinct. What we're after is more of a time capsule—inside it lies something worth more than all our lives combined."

"What's inside it?"

Penelope had the audacity to look Helena in the eyes and say, "I don't know."

"That's a lie," Helena cried, quieting quickly when Noa stirred in his sleep nearby. She resumed speaking in a lower voice, albeit a harsh one. "You're telling me you don't even have a clue what's inside the artifact you're looking for?"

"I do not lie, Helena. I may withhold certain information. I may give you my theories, which can be disproved at any time. I may even intentionally mislead you with certain bits of information, if the occasion calls for it. But never will I outwardly *lie*, and that is the truth. And it is with truth that I tell you that I cannot say with certainty what lies inside that egg, which rests in the heart of those caverns."

"You're speaking in riddles again," Helena said, rolling her eyes. "How about you tell me what you *think* resides inside that artifact?"

"A solution to the bane of my existence."

"…You're not going to tell me what you think it is, are you?"

Penelope's beady black eyes lingered on her as she said, "Why, Helena, I already have. The answer is right in front of you, and you've not a clue."

Later that night, Helena tossed and turned as she tried desperately to get some rest, but could not sleep. Penelope's vague answers troubled her. *The answer is right in front of you.* What did that mean? Helena could only think of Penelope Duskmuth's soulless eyes—two gaping pits on her face that threatened to swallow Helena whole. Eyes that had never seen the light.

Helena eventually fell into a deep sleep. She woke up the next morning feeling the warm rays of the sun against her cheeks, their light scattered into fragments upon hitting the fronds of the willow branches above. Helena's eyelids fluttered open, then closed again. The cool, soft morning breeze brushed against her skin. Had she overslept? As Helena stretched, she could not help but emit a delicious yawn. It seemed that for the first time in weeks, Helena had gotten a *full night's rest.*

Her eyes shot open. *No,* she thought. *Oh, no, no, no...*

*"Wake up!"* Helena shouted, leaping to her feet and scouring the entire camp. Jared and the others had also overslept, and her panic roused them from their deep slumber; Noa was the last to wake, sitting up from the ground and squinting at everyone running around him.

"Why all the commotion?" he grumbled, rubbing his disheveled hair.

"They're gone," Helena said. "Olip and Penelope left during the night—and they never came back."

# Chapter Thirteen

161

A<sup></sup>t the height of their panic, the group grasped at straws trying to explain the disappearance of Olip and Penelope Duskmuth. At first, they foolishly assumed that the twins had been attacked while they were out hunting or patrolling the skies. But as the sun rose higher, and reason began to wash away their panicked naivety, the Diurnal group could come to no other conclusion: the twins had simply abandoned them in the middle of the night while they were fast asleep. Their abandonment was as sudden as it was devastating to the young wigeons—even Helena found her thoughts mirroring the fiery curses that spilled out of Noa's mouth upon hearing the news. How would they ever acquire the artifact now? All seemed hopeless.

However, Jared believed that if the twins felt safe enough to leave their Diurnal watchmen behind, then that must have been a clear indicator that they were closer to the artifact than they imagined...

"Likely a day or two's flight from here," he surmised. "Maybe even less. The only problem is we don't know which direction they went."

Then, an idea occurred to Helena:

"Phellis, you can track Penelope down!"

Her silver eyes became as wide as a doe's. "M-me?"

"Yes! Penelope is likely still grounded—it would be no different than tracking any other animal. It's important we get our hands on the artifact before they do."

"B-but...why would you want such a thing?" she asked, shrinking back in fear.

"If the Stork wants to get his hands on it to do something terrible, don't you think Penelope would want the same?" she said severely. "We can't let it fall into either of their hands!"

Helena could taste the bitter hypocrisy on her own tongue. The nerve of her words, when her true intention was to retrieve that very item for the Stork! But as she gazed into the wide, glassy eyes of Phellis, Helena could only see her own reflection: a wingless girl who had been robbed of her innocence. And suddenly, everything she had endured the last few months came rushing at her in a torrent—her grief, her tears, her physical toil. Picturing the smug satisfaction it would give people like Noa if she were to remain a wigeon filled Helena with a potent, usurping rage. Then came the Stork's persecuting voice in her memory: *if you ever hope to fly again.* Nothing, absolutely nothing, could curtail Helena's insatiable desire to regain that which had slipped through her fingers—or rather, that which had been wrenched from her possession!

"You don't have to help us if you don't want to, Phellis," Jared said, keeping a watchful eye on Helena.

Phellis gulped. "I just...Penny saved my life...it'll be like I betrayed her if I helped..."

"Anybody can see plain as day that she couldn't care less about you," Noa said. "Loyalty goes both ways."

These words hurt Phellis, but she toughened up and nodded.

"Find me a lead," she said with a determined look, before setting off to search for any sign of the vanished twins. She worked light on her feet, prancing through the wilderness with the grace of a gazelle. In less than ten minutes, she found their first lead: a long, lone white feather. With Phellis leading the pack, the group embarked on their hunt for Olip and Penelope Duskmuth.

The road ahead rose in a gradual slope as they approached the Mountains of Alazar, whose giant spurs bloomed bright and green and were covered in pine trees. White cotton clouds topped each of their snow-tipped peaks, which glistened in the sunlight. Phellis' trajectory would have them diving headfirst into these mountains, which were as magnificent as they were daunting for the young wigeons.

They traveled many days and nights through the narrow valleys of the high sierra, searching for any sign of the twins. Along the way, they spotted a few abandoned watch posts jutting out from the sides of a mountain—a clear indicator that they were encroaching upon avian territory and that settlements were likely nearby. They never stuck around long enough to investigate.

The fatigue drained from Helena's limbs as a new drive had now overtaken her. Now, more than ever, she pondered obsessively about what awaited them in those caverns. Noa's bet was on something fantastical and everlasting, like a fountain of youth, but Jared believed it was likelier to be something more practical and finite—something capable of being destroyed, like a compass or a medallion. Phellis deemed all those guesses wimpy, wagering on a goblet that turned everything it touched into solid gold. Helena, however, believed that if the Stork wanted to get his hands on anything that badly, it would have to be something powerful. Something, she feared, that would bring death and ruin to all.

After much tribulation, Phellis' sharp wits ultimately led them to a flight of stairs at the foot of the rocky cliffside of a mountain; its rugged stone steps ascended steeply and sporadically along the rocky walls.

"This is where we go separate ways, my friend," she whispered to Underbelly, for she knew that past this point he could no longer accompany her. She kissed his hairy snout goodbye before heading up the stairs.

Jared and the others followed, glancing uneasily at the deadly heights at which they climbed. Eventually, the flight of stairs curved inwards, and soon they came upon a wide, grassy alcove. Its fine stonework had been overcome with the tendrils of evergreen vines, and as they got closer, an eerie hum like the buzzing of an insect thrummed at the back of Helena's ears. Her arm hairs prickled. It seemed they had encroached upon magical grounds. Within this cryptic alcove resided a massive slab of round stone etched with wispy, feather-like engravings. With a bit of teamwork, they managed to roll the slab over, revealing a mysterious entrance.

"We're going in there?" Noa said, sweat dripping down his brow as he looked up at the mountain walls looming over them. It was the first time Helena had ever seen him uncertain, if not afraid.

"Don't tell me you're afraid of a hole?" Phellis said, crossing her arms and looking at him with a curved brow.

"More like I'm afraid of being stuck in a tunnel with you."

"Well, you'd best get a grip, 'cause if you haven't got the guts to push past your fears, you'll hamstring the rest of us somethin' good."

Phellis's words may have been blunt, but the message they conveyed was still valid.

"She's right," Helena said grimly. "We're clueless as to what's inside those tunnels...all it takes is one person to hold us back. If we're going to go in there, we have to remain firm until the end...unless, of course, you'd prefer to sit this one out with the horses, Noa."

Noa seethed. "Do you take me to be so pigeon-hearted?"

"Cool it, all of you," Jared snapped, and the group fell silent. "The last thing I want is to be confined underground with the three of you squabbling like chickens. We're sticking together as a group, and that's final—so whatever you need to do to collect yourselves before going in, do it now."

With that, Jared stepped boldly into the darkened entrance. Phellis' stubs gave a determined twitch as she marched in after him. Helena threw a glance over her shoulder towards Noa, who still lingered way back.

"Coming along?"

"Needless to say!" he said stubbornly. He sent one last wary look at the wilderness behind them, knowing it would be the last true source of sunlight they would see in a long time—before stalking past Helena and into the tunnels.

Once they were all inside, the magic stone door rolled over and sealed their last connection to the mundane world, enveloping them in darkness.

*"Ouch! Watch where you're steppin'!"*

*"Yer feet are hard to miss."*

*"Quit your bickering and help me spark a flame..."*

There was hiss and a spark, then Jared raised the torch to illuminate the dark tunnel ahead. Its jagged walls were damp and cool to the touch—and for the most part, straightforward—until they sloped downwards in a long curve. Before long, they encountered a small chamber with an abandoned fire that had been reduced to ashes. The bountiful cadavers of picked-over rodents and white feathers were scattered everywhere, but the twins themselves remained unaccounted for. The group rested here a short while before moving on through the small exit at the end of the chamber. The temperature nose-dived the further they ventured into the mountain, and hints of frost soon glistened upon the ancient walls they treaded past.

Noa grew restless as he continually bumped into Helena time and time again. She was completely fed up with him by the time he crashed into her a fifth time.

"Quit it," she snarled, but Noa clutched her arm as his eyes scoured the walls with panic.

"You don't see it?"

"See *what?*"

"The tunnels," he said, licking his cracked lips, "they're getting smaller."

He was right. As they ventured further onwards, the tunnels were becoming increasingly narrow—so narrow, in fact, that they began herding the group together like sheep. To their horror, as they carefully maneuvered past the point where the tunnel's diameter spanned less than a wigeon's wingspan, they approached a wall.

"Dead end!" moaned Noa, clasping his hands behind his neck and taking stark, ragged breaths.

"Phooey," said Phellis, disappointed. "What now? We go back?"

"I'm with that!" Noa said hastily.

"No!" Helena said as she crept closer towards the dead end. "If this were a true dead end, we would've run into the twins already..."

*Drip, drip, drip.* Water patiently squeezed through a crack in the ceiling, forming a small puddle at the foot of the wall. Helena leaned closer to get a better look and saw that someone had carved three words on the face of the wall:

*The Isthmus approaches!*

"Isthmus?" inquired Noa. His forehead glistened with sweat. "What, like the Great Isthmus of Nadiir?"

Jared nodded. "An isthmus is supposed to be an extreme narrowing of some kind..."

"Fancy-schmancy word for bottleneck, I reckon," murmured Phellis as she sniffed around for more clues.

"What on earth does that mean, Red?" Noa demanded. He seemed to be growing visibly more despondent by the minute.

"It means things are going to get a lot tighter than we expected."

Noa blanched.

"But where are we supposed to go?" Helena looked around and heaved a heavy sigh in frustration. "There's no exit!"

"Well, the flockers had to go *somewhere*," Noa insisted hastily.

That answer, Helena was about to find out. At a glance, it seemed they had reached a dead end, for the only things to be seen in plain sight were the wall and a rippling puddle before it. But upon further investigation, Helena discovered the puddle was not at all a shallow collection of water; it was, in fact, a waist-deep waterway. After sticking her arm in and feeling about, she concluded that it would lead them to the other side of this dead end. Looking at the *isthmus* carved into the ancient stone, Helena's stomach brewed with apprehension for the troubles that lay ahead.

"We have to swim to get to the other side," she declared.

An audible shudder ran through Noa's body. He reclined against a wall as he struggled to bear the news.

"I know who's getting thrown into the pool first!" Phellis said rather mischievously, looming over him with a sneer.

"If you don't get yer sorry, leafless head away from my face—" he snarled at her.

"Hey," Jared said, seizing Noa by the shoulders and steadying him. "Collect yourself. We've hit a rut many times before, have we not? This one should be no different. Now, tell me—which way does the ship sail?"

Noa sucked in a breath before giving a shaky response. "Onwards."

"Very good. Keep that in mind as you follow my lead." Jared hoisted himself into the waters that reached just below his hips and took a deep breath before plunging inside and disappearing.

Seconds passed. Helena pressed her good ear against the icy wall. "Jared?"

His voice was faint. *"I'm okay!"*

"He's okay!" she reported back. "Next up, quickly!"

Phellis fearlessly leapt into the pool, and Noa shuddered as cold droplets ricocheted onto him. The wigeon girl plunged into the water without so much as a complaint, and the last thing they saw of her was her stiff little wing stubs protruding out of the water before they sank completely into the depths of the waterway. Now only two wigeons remained.

"I doubt you want to be the last one," Helena said to Noa with a weak smile.

Though he said nothing that would've admitted his fear, Noa clutched Helena's arm like a lifeline as he clambered down into the waters. On the count of three—the second count of three, to be precise—Noa plunged into the water and did not return. Finally, it was Helena's turn. Waist deep in freezing water, she drew in a sharp breath before submerging. She endured the cold's bitter bite as she crawled across the floor of the waterway before resurfacing promptly on the other side.

That first waterway was straightforward enough. By the time they reached the next waterway, however, the tunnels had progressively narrowed to the point where the group was forced to walk in a single file line with their necks craned at awkward angles. This time, when Helena's hand reached inside the waterway, she found no air pocket awaiting her on the other side. She looked at Jared in grim realization, and he immediately caught her meaning: they would have to swim until they found an air pocket—*if* they ever found one.

This time, Helena went first. The second passage was longer and far more cramped than the first, but *doable*. She gleefully resurfaced onto dry land and waited for the rest of the group to catch up. There seemed to be a delay, however. When they finally caught up with her, her friends' tardy arrival quickly erupted into a shouting match.

Jared had his arms around Phellis' waist, struggling to restrain her as her long nails swiped for Noa's face, which cowered against the wall in a shameful grimace.

"—ARE—YOU—KIDDING—"

"Let it go, Phellis!" Jared said through gritted teeth.

"What happened?" Helena demanded.

With tears in her eyes, Phellis sent an accusing finger at Noa, whose face had taken on a deathly pallor. "Why don't you ask him? He's the one who stopped for a good *two* minutes back there—*two minutes!* I nearly drowned behind him!"

The group was at their wits end...and the stakes were only getting higher; by the time they reached the next waterway, they were already crawling on their knees with the walls breathing down their necks. Oxygen was becoming so scarce that Helena was experiencing frequent episodes of lightheadedness.

Helena stifled an exclamation of horror as she looked ahead; a skeleton sat curled up against the wall, just over by the waterway which they were meant to swim through next. Its haggard jaw hung askew, and it held a pen and booklet in its hands. The booklet's pages had curled and become grimed with mold over the years, and its stiff spine gave a small whine as Helena pried it open, revealing a troubling, yet thought-provoking passage left by its owner:

*I'm but a man seeking the hoard of the dragun*
*I've no woman, no child, not a talun*
*When this suffering ends is a question of time,*
*Stop here, and the future cannot hurt me,*
*Stop here, and I cannot die.*
*I see you, Isthmus of Life,*
*Narrower of path,*
*Bearer of strife!*
*Ravel me in ambiguity,*
*Now I wonder*
*What I cannot see...*
*Is it death, disappointment?*

*Or life, thus possibility?*
*Shall I remain steadfast, like a bird?*
*That which flies onwards, never astern,*
*Shall I face you, Strangler who hinders my gait?*
*Shall I see if your grip merely tightens, or if death awaits?*

It was evident that their group was not the first to enter these caverns. Helena wondered how many before them had been successful. Her thumbs brushed over the words which her eyes lingered on: *Shall I remain steadfast, like a bird?*

"We've approached the isthmus," Helena announced to those behind. "Whoever this person was, the pressure must've gotten to them—not that I can blame them. It can't get much narrower than this…"

The waterway was so small this time, that they would have no other choice but to abandon most of their belongings, lay themselves flat, and slither themselves into this pit like eels! As Helena beheld their ultimate obstacle, it struck her that perhaps every person was a claustrophobe at heart—some were just better at disguising it.

*"I can't take this anymore!"*

Noa collapsed into inconsolability, tears running down his face; he thrashed like a bull being sent to the slaughterhouse, roaring and sending an elbow to Phellis' jaw. After a brief struggle Jared seized him, locking Noa in an iron embrace so that all he could do was curse and wail. The limited space around them amplified his cries tenfold.

"He's gone mad, he's gone mad!" Phellis cried.

"Noa, please," Helena begged, "We've come too far to give up now. We have to keep moving—"

"Can't you understand, bird? *I don't want to!* There's no end to this, and if there is, we'll likely drown long before we reach it. Let me stay! I'm tired of fighting when all it brings is disappointment…"

*If I stop here, the future cannot hurt me.* Noa would rather stay to spare himself from the dangers that lay ahead. Helena looked to Jared for reassurance, but was stunned to see his eyes were wet. Even Jared—steady, reliable Jared, seemed to have hit his breaking point. And this moved Helena to say something completely unexpected:

"You're right. There might be no merit in any of this."

Noa blinked his tears away in surprise.

"There's a strong chance that we will die no matter what choice we make here. Whether we stay here and starve, or we move on and run into a dead end, or drown trying to reach the next passageway, or the one after it—none of it changes the fact that we all die in the end. So, if it all ends the same, what does it cost you to cling to that last bit of hope deep inside you, to drag your knees across the ground, and to choose to crawl through that wormhole? *Nothing.* It costs nothing to fight for your life—to fight for that one slim chance of survival. And if we do hit a dead end, so be it! What would we lose? Nothing! That's just it, Noa! Either we lose nothing, or we gain *everything.* Because there is only one other possibility on the other side of an isthmus...if not death, life!

"That's the only option for the living: keep moving forwards, no matter how narrow things get. We must remain steadfast, despite not knowing what lies ahead. You can either stay here never knowing if you ever had a chance, or you can keep moving forwards and find out for yourself. The choice is yours."

Once again, Noa gazed up at Helena with that same speechless, bewildered look on his face. Helena, however, knew that there was no amount of words that would cause him to budge if he didn't want to—it was up to Noa to decide if he wanted to carry on or not.

Helena turned to face the next passageway and prepared to lead the way. It would be Jared behind her, followed by Phellis and, if he conceded, Noa. The plan was to crawl through those narrow tunnels, and if there was any problem whatsoever, to tap the ankle of the person in front of them three times to let them know.

"No matter what," Helena told them, "don't stop. Don't *ever* stop. If you feel like you're getting stuck, focus on the person in front of you...Jared?"

His somber, glassy eyes made it very clear that he would not be going along with the plan.

"I can't leave him," he said. "He's like my brother."

"If you stay here with him, he'll never gather the courage to do it himself."

Jared smiled sadly. "I know."

Helena took a good look at the noble young man in front of her and wondered if she would ever see him again. There was no telling whether she, or anyone else, would make it out of these tunnels alive.

"Fairwinds to you both," she said. *Fairwinds* was used to express good fortune to anyone, be they ave or wigeon, on their journey. In this case, it took the form of a bittersweet goodbye. Jared returned a grateful smile before replying:

"Fairwinds, Helena Nightingale."

With that, Helena and Phellis prepared for the isthmus, which would be their longest passage yet. Phellis looked over her shoulder several times at Noa—as if she wanted to say something, but had changed her mind at the last minute and focused her sights on what lay ahead. Helena took the deepest breath she could—who knew how long the journey would be, after all—and dove headfirst into the wormhole.

There was some squirming, worming, and occasional gliding across the slimy floor of the waterway. The first air pocket she found was generous; Helena swallowed two mouthfuls of air before moving along so Phellis could get her share. As she continued moving forwards, these air pockets became less and less frequent. Soon, Helena's chest stretched taut like leather, and her heart struck like a mallet. How could she convince herself the looming walls around her were not collapsing? She found herself overwhelmed with panic—panic that they would reach a dead end and all of this *would* be for nothing. Panic that the universe was set on crushing her just as she was about to reach the *true* isthmus, a place where both heaven and earth smothered her slender body—

Helena lost control. Her chest spasmed. Precious air bubbles spilled from her lips, floating upwards like a flock of doves, all while Phellis clawed Helena's ankles raw. Her body would give in soon. Perhaps, out of all the ways she could die, drowning here wasn't the worst way she could go...

But there are times when, impossible as it may seem, one must learn to discern the voice of hope that whispers amidst shouts of uncertainty. In

Helena's case, this voice insisted that there had to be *some* merit to this, that this passageway had to lead *somewhere,* and if she stopped here, she would never find out...

Moments later, Helena broke through the water's surface and collapsed onto solid, gloriously dry land! Phellis collapsed beside her, equally as exhausted. The world had widened, and their arms fell flat against the earth, spread-eagled to take as much space as they could, lest it all be taken away from them.

Helena had done it. She knew not how, but she had made it past the isthmus.

But they could not rest just yet. Two of their people still remained.

In a surprising turn of events, Jared exploded out of the water several minutes later, expelling murky water from his mouth and gasping for air. He came alone. Helena ran to his side to help him. His full weight fell upon her as he blabbered incoherently:

*"...He didn't want to go...we would've died back there! I told him he had to do it himself...I...I abandoned him!"*

Helena did not know what had transpired between the two boys after she and Phellis had left, but the truth was plain to see: Noa was on his own now. It might've been his darkest hour yet, but there was nothing left to do other than wait. *Please,* Helena thought to herself, *don't let him give up...*

A solid hour passed. Jared tried to go back for him, but the girls advised against it—the risk of running into Noa head-on somewhere in the middle of the one-way passage was too great...but that might've been a weak excuse. The truth was that the likelihood of Noa conquering his fears seemed slim to none, and though it pained Helena to admit it, Noa was on his own, now. They might as well have killed him themselves...

*But wait!* Something stirred in the corner of her eyes—the puddle rippled and roiled with bubbles as Noa plunged through the last barrier standing between him and sweet, sweet air! They welcomed him with open arms, cheers, and tears. Moments later, they all fell back laughing; Helena tumbled right on top of Noa, and Jared and Phellis joined in on the dogpile. As Helena pressed her ear to Noa's chest, she heard the dull thudding of his heart. There was something peculiar about the way it moved. Whereas a normal heart would beat powerfully—*Lub-dub, lub-dub*—his was a trifle weaker, almost seeming to skip a beat. *Lub-woo-dub,* it said. A tiny defect in the heart. A heart murmur.

"How did you do it?" they asked him, but Noa would not respond. Instead, he gazed up towards the ceiling in puzzling quietude. His knuckles and elbows were scraped scarlet. His dark, wet hair clung to his tan face. And when his eyes came down on Helena's, flashing like lightning, for a mere second, she could have sworn her heart danced like his.

Then Noa proceeded to puke, and the moment passed. But who could blame him? This trial would serve as nightmare fuel for years to come—though it certainly came with lifelong bragging rights attached to it, as well!

"All about the journey, *my ass!*" Jared said. He laughed, showing his pearly-white molars. Helena joined in too. As did Phellis. Noa eventually caved in and clutched his belly in laughter.

Not long afterwards, they all fell asleep.


The end of their journey came rather easily after their trial through the isthmus, and the wigeon group gushed with pride and jubilance as they paraded through the last stretch of tunnels ahead. The journey alone was enough to filter the worthy from the unworthy, and they felt as if there was nothing the world could throw at them that they couldn't handle—the residual effect of the ultra-taxing isthmus! They came to a gradual stop before a pair of great crimson doors stamped with the golden sigil of a snake-like dragon, limbless, with feathered wings curling in on itself. Its mighty mouth opened in a roar, and from the corner of her eye, Helena could've sworn the image appeared to be spinning counterclockwise...

Together, the wigeons pushed open the doors, and the image of the golden dragon parted in two. At once, they needed to raise their hands to their eyes, for the light of the room was almost too pure to behold. Once adjusted, a collective groan of wonder swelled from within the group like a tidal wave. Before their eyes lay a vision of warmth and opulence: a vault with polished granite floors and walls of solid gold; ornate tapestries with intricate inlays of crimson, gold, and indigo threading; mounds and mounds of gold and precious jewels spilling from chests like vomit, but in the most marvelous way! Noa dove into a pile of gold like it was water, tossing up coins and glistening rubies as he laughed in delight. Meanwhile, Phellis clambered her way up a mountain of treasure, a royal purple cloak wrapped around her shoulders and a scepter held in one hand:

"Behold," she roared, *"Phellicarus the Conqueror!"*

After admiring the masterful collection of preserved wines, foods, and perfumes, Helena soon found herself gaping up at a six-foot-tall, gleaming set of armor. A polished iron helmet rested upon its mannequin's proud head; he stood poised with his great sword planted between his feet.

Jared was the least interested in the abundance of wealth, instead directing his attention to the walls around them. Once Helena's eyes adjusted, and the spell of greed had worn off, she came upon a sudden realization: upon closer inspection she could see that the walls were not made of solid gold, but instead were composed of thousands of golden, egg-like globules. These globules were all stuck together, encompassing the entire vault in one giant, cohesive bubble.

"Fascinating," Jared murmured. He poked one of them, and it rippled gently from his touch, awakening the others nearby. They wiggled and morphed like a set of gooey amphibian eggs. Helena stopped before one of these globules, enraptured by the luminous silhouette within; the golden feline stirred at Helena's presence, rising from its slumber with a great stretch, before walking silkily towards her. The cat pawed patiently at the membrane to be let out.

"They're mirages!" Helena exclaimed in wonder. "Hundreds of them, maybe even thousands! What is this place?"

"They might have belonged to other avians who came before us—all the souls who never made it past the isthmus," Jared ventured.

Helena made a sound of realization. "Because upon death the bond between the ave and the mirage is severed! You're right, these all likely belonged to someone else at one point..."

"It's like walking past a graveyard," Jared said, his brown eyes shining gold as he gazed upon the mirages in wonder. "I've always wanted one of my own. I wonder what mine would look like..."

*"Guys, check this out!"* Phellis' voice beckoned them to the far end of the main vault and into a smaller—though no less elaborate—chamber with a second-story balustrade. The dimly lit chamber housed an ancient beast of mythical proportions; the prehistoric snake measured anywhere from thirty to fifty feet in length, and lay curled in a circle atop a heap of golden treasure. A fine layer of dust had accumulated over its perfectly preserved bones, and the young wigeons ventured freely in between its hundreds of ribs. Helena placed an insignificant hand against the icy surface of its skull, gazing into its gaping mouth, which she was almost certain could have swallowed her whole in its time. Given the vivid image they had seen engraved on the two entry doors, she was ever so certain that before them lay the remains of a long-dead dragon. Only one thing was missing—its wings.

The dragon's skeleton lay curled around a bed of golden coins, upon which rested a red cushion with a prominent imprint upon its velvety surface. Something of great importance was missing from this small pile of precious coins...

"Where is the artifact?" Helena's panicked voice rebounded across the chamber.

They scoured everywhere in search of the artifact, but after ten hopeless minutes, Phellis was the only one brave enough to speak Helena's fear out loud:

"I reckon Olip an' Penny beat us to it!"

"How many times have I told you, *Phellicarus*, that I do not take kindly to nicknames?"

On the balustrade above them, two slender figures emerged from the shadows, and Olip and Penelope cast their ghastly expressions upon the group. Curiously, both were wingless! *How odd*, Helena thought. They looked freakish with their skinny frames and bulging black eyes! Penelope, in particular, had an interesting expression on her face. Surprise? Maybe. Disappointment? Definitely. Penelope had likely counted on the group not making it through the isthmus.

"What happened to the pair of you?" Noa called out scornfully, referring to their newfound state of wigeonhood.

Penelope forced a smile. "The creator of these caverns did not discriminate between the winged and the wingless. These walls are enchanted so that everyone who steps foot in these caverns has an equal chance of obtaining their treasure. My mirage currently resides amidst the others of this lair, no doubt a temporary situation while we dwell here…"

Penelope spread her arms wide in a grand gesture to the dragon skeleton. "A sight to behold, is it not? The remains of a real-life dragon! I surmise this fossil must be at least a couple thousand years old…I might even wager it was alive to witness the Age of Magic…dragons were often wise, even mischievous creatures, who had an uncanny affinity for treasure. This often manifested in the form of large, underground hoards, like the one we see in this vault. Though they loved their riddles, seldom did they resort to deceit, and the paths they leave are always straightforward, albeit a bit narrow…"

"Enough talk, Penelope," Helena snapped. "Where is the artifact?"

Penelope stepped more visibly into the light and turned to reveal the stunning object in her arms—a single golden egg bigger than her own head, with precious gemstones of all sizes and colors encrusted in its magnificent shell. The artifact gleamed brightly, reflecting glorious sparks of kaleidoscopic colors amidst the dimly lit chamber. This, Helena thought greedily, was certainly the one object worthy enough to give her back her wings.

"A dragon egg!" exclaimed Jared. "That's what you've been after all this time?"

"Not quite," Penelope said. "Real dragon eggs were scaly, hot to the touch, and slightly bigger. This egg I'm holding has a shell made of pure, solid gold, forged by this dragon's fiery breath and encasing the object inside."

Helena wiped the sweat off her brow. "The egg belongs to us."

"Does it?"

"You bet your feathery ass it does!" Noa said.

"We got through the isthmus!" Phellis cried shrilly.

*Hssss!* A hiss rushed between Olip's bared teeth.

Penelope placed a reassuring hand on her brother's shoulder. "So did we, and *we* got here first. You never would have found this place if it weren't for my brother and me. The egg is rightfully ours."

"If we both got through the isthmus," Jared's voice sounded logically, "then we both have a right to reap its rewards. We can split the winnings—you two can have half of the treasure, and the rest we can split between ourselves. Same goes for the artifact."

Even Helena knew this was not a viable option. Penelope answered him at once:

"Hmph! We are not interested in worldly treasures. We came here for one thing and one thing only—and that is the artifact, which cannot be split between two parties. If you cannot accept this, then I'm afraid you leave us no choice. Olip—"

Penelope gave her brother an ominous nod, and Olip leapt over the ledge of the balustrade, landing lightly on his feet before the group. They backed away slowly as he pulled out a gleaming new sword, which he had likely acquired from the vault's depths. Light bounced off its curved white-silver blade.

"There's no need for this, Penelope," Helena said, her heart hammering against her chest as Olip backed them into a corner. "We can settle this the old-fashioned way—a duel, between you and me. Winner takes all."

Olip came to a halt mere moments before the point of his sword would have touched Helena's hammering chest.

"No!" Jared exclaimed. "Helena, you can't!"

"She'll kill you!" Phellis agreed.

"You got guts, bird," Noa said admiringly, which made Helena feel oddly giddy.

A wide, mirthless grin spread across Penelope's face when she heard this. "A surprisingly honorable move on your part, Helena...very well. If you're up for the task, and understand the implications of such a duel, then I suggest we move into the main vault and have it out there. This would be the time to exchange any last words. Olip, put your sword away. This shouldn't take long..."

Jared seized Helena by the shoulders. "Do you have any idea what you're getting yourself into? You've seen her skill in combat before—she'll kill you!"

Helena suppressed the rising apprehension in her stomach. "We need that artifact, Jared. At least this way, no one else will get hurt."

"Have you ever wielded a weapon before, bird?" Noa asked with one brow raised.

She shook her head.

"Oh, boy..." Phellis moaned. They all looked to one another in dim prospects of Helena's future.

Only then did it occur to Helena that she may not leave these caverns alive.

Swallowing her fear, she said, "I'd be more concerned if Penelope had a pair of wings to worry about, but the two of us are on equal footing now—this fight could be anyone's."

Four wigeons—including a tense Olip—stood anxiously on the sidelines as the two female contenders faced each other at the center of the treasure-ridden vault. During this brief intermission, Helena and her friends scrambled to collect a few pieces of armor they hoped would aid her in battle: a studded leather chest piece that fit her a tad too big, a pair of light leather gloves, and two iron arm bracers. Helena's weapon of choice was simple—a small dagger which fit awkwardly in the palm of her clammy hand.

Meanwhile, Penelope sat and cradled the artifact in her arms like she would a baby, staring down at it like a loving mother. She placed the golden egg down carefully on the stone floor, after which it tipped over onto its oblong side and rolled side to side in a circular path like any egg would. For many moments, the only sound Helena heard was the eerie rasp of metal crawling against stone.

Penelope drew her choice of weapon from its sheath—a long dagger with a needle-like blade, which narrowed to a tapered, pointed end. Helena mirrored her and raised her own weapon as the duel commenced. They circled each other for what felt like an eternity, each one waiting for the other to make the first move. As they did, Helena heard her peers cheer her on from afar:

"Don't take your eyes off her, Helena!" came Jared's sharp voice.

*"Oh, I can't watch this!"* Phellis cried, burrowing her face into Noa's neck. He eventually shoved her off him, never once taking his eyes off Helena.

"It doesn't have to end this way, Penelope," Helena said carefully. She remained on her highest guard as she continued moving in a circle with her dagger raised, one foot crossing over the other. "Hand over the artifact, and we can carry on as if nothing ever happened. We can both leave this place alive."

"I see no other course. I've dedicated my entire life's work to finding that artifact. I am not leaving without it."

Out of the corner of her eyes, Helena spotted one mirage across the vault that was considerably brighter than the rest. The crustacean inside dragged itself towards Penelope, waving its pincers and making sharp, sudden movements every time she passed close by; Helena identified this at once as her opponent's mirage.

"Neither am I," Helena said.

"Of course not! How else would you get back your wings?"

This caught Helena off guard. Her feet stumbled over each other, causing her to nearly tumble, and even their audience flinched.

"What, Helena? Did you take me as foolish enough not to consider that the Stork might have been extorting you and your friends?"

"What's she going on about?" Phellis sounded, looking from Helena to Jared and Noa, who fell into a dreary silence.

"You heard right, Phellicarus. Helena and her wigeon friends have been plotting with the Stork this entire time to retrieve the artifact for him. In return, he would give Helena her mirage back and grant them leave to return to Avalon. They were never interested in becoming your friend—they only sought whatever information they could get out of you. Isn't that right, Helena?"

Phellis' eyes filled with hurt upon hearing this. She broke away from the group, staggering back several feet from Noa and Jared.

Helena's face turned hot, and she replied, "How about we discuss the fact that you've always known, and yet said nothing?"

"I merely suspected, at first. Your first error was telling me that you lost your wings to him. I observed the way that you sulked. I heard your cries at night when you thought no one was listening. I realized soon enough that you would've done anything to get your wings back—any sensible being would do the same if they'd lost something so dear to them! It didn't take long to put two and two together."

"Always the keener of the litter, aren't you, Penelope?" Helena spat.

"You weren't the only one he approached with an offer," she said darkly. "When my brother and I first came down to Nadiir, the Stork sent his messengers offering us great wealth if we shared the location of the artifact. Some of us, however, aren't so easily bought out with a mere promise. Foolish, you were, Helena! How naively you bought into the Stork's words when in reality he was using your anguish to his advantage! Did it never once cross your mind that, by taking away your wings, the Stork has achieved the impossible—and for that reason, you are meant to stay as you are?"

Helena only looked at her, struggling to understand what she was getting at.

Penelope saw her expression and released a curt laugh. "Don't you see, Helena? The Stork made a promise he never intended to fulfill! Why would he? So long as you live on, you serve as a living testimony to his cruelty and innovation. You are meant to spark fear in the people around you, and only then will his legacy continue. *In other words, your one and only purpose is to become a walking tragedy case!*"

As these words sifted through Helena's ears, a burning humiliation trickled down her body. *The Stork never intended to live up to his word,* a voice shouted in her head. *I am meant to stay like this. Forever.* In an instant, the humiliation within her lurched, turning in on itself and transforming into a bitter, bitter rage that coursed hot through her veins; this potent sensation triggered an involuntary response from Helena's body, and with a sharp cry, she became the first to attack.

Helena swung the dagger madly towards Penelope with no rational thought in mind. *Just swing,* she thought savagely. *Just cut.* The Nocturnal anticipated Helena's reckless move, and her dagger came up from below and parried Helena's strike with a clash of its blade. The momentum of the blow threw Helena back onto the heels of her feet, and before she could recover, Penelope advanced with a series of three swift, agile strokes. Helena roughly dodged the first two, but the third nicked her along her leather chest plate, leaving a thin slit just above her right breast.

"Steady now, bird!" a voice shouted.

Helena leapt forwards with a heavy grunt, swinging again at Penelope, this time remaining a little more mindful of where to strike. Still, the Nocturnal evaded her easily with a short jump back, quickly countering with a lunge and strike of her own, which Helena parried with an amateur lift of her weapon. It went on like this for two whole minutes, with Penelope dodging Helena's attacks as easily as one would a child's. Eventually, Helena grew so impatient that she gave up on trying for orderly attacks and charged at the Nocturnal. Penelope swiftly spun out of the way and dragged her weapon across an exposed section of Helena's lower torso. The dagger tore through her shirt and the utilitarian layer underneath, and Helena felt the cold stroke of the blade against her skin, followed by a sharp sting.

Everyone, Helena included, drew in a sharp breath. Something warm dripped down her leg. Her hand felt along her side, just above her hip, and her fingers returned bright red.

The stakes had just risen. As Helena panted like a dog, her eyes flickered to Penelope's feet. The Nocturnal pranced on her toes like a dancer, never lingering in the same place for too long—yet she did not carry herself as confidently as she did when she had her wings. Occasionally, she leaned too much to one side as if losing her balance, or overcompensated her steps and stumbled the slightest bit. In this fleeting moment, Helena intuited Penelope must've lost at least fifty pounds since she lost possession of her wings. Helena knew from experience that losing one's wings caused temporary disequilibrium in one's coordination—a hurdle which Helena had long overcame.

The wise words of Phellis came to mind: *You'd realize how much lighter you are on your feet.* Drawing a deep breath, Helena shut her eyes and focused. She leaned ever so slightly on the balls of her feet, like a bird on the brink of take-off. Without warning, she burst into a light sprint, headed directly inbound for Penelope. She feigned a lunge to Penelope's right, causing the

Nocturnal to stagger. Helena took advantage of this momentary hesitation and rammed her shoulder into her opponent. Sprawling backwards, Penelope struggled to regain her balance. Helena came in with a dagger strike, nicking the Nocturnal's forearm and drawing fresh, crimson blood. Helena swung again, and this time her dagger collided with Penelope's so hard that both weapons were sent clanging out of reach. In one swift movement, Helena ducked and moved behind Penelope, snaking one firm arm around her neck and securing her in an armlock.

"It's difficult, isn't it," Helena asked her venomously, "fighting without wings? It's like everything is thrown off-balance. You're clumsy, and it shows."

Penelope choked out, "For me, this is temporary. *You'll stay like this forever!*"

Later, Helena would hardly be able to recall what happened next, as rage and adrenaline consumed her. Next thing she knew, her knuckles were bruised and stained scarlet. Penelope had crumpled to the floor, her face a bloody mess. Helena dashed to the gleaming artifact and took it for herself; she felt its cool metal against the flesh of her palms and raised it high above her head.

Penelope stretched out a shaky hand as she laid helplessly on the floor. *"Helena, stop! You don't know what you're doing with that—"*

*"Shut up and stay down!"* Helena shrieked at Penelope. *"If you so much as move a muscle, I'll smash this thing into a million pieces!"*

Ever so reluctantly, Penelope wiped the trickling blood from her pale, waxy face and obeyed. Her eyes were wide, black saucers, glued to Helena's every move. In her peripheral vision, Helena saw that Olip had drawn his sword to intervene, but her faithful friends Jared and Noa barred his path with a pair of wooden spears they had acquired from the vault's weapons cache.

"Why does the Stork want this?" Helena demanded. *"Answer me!"*

Penelope flinched when Helena made a sudden movement with the egg and scrambled for an explanation:

"You must understand, Helena—it is imperative that the artifact never falls into the hands of the Stork—for if it did, it would be one step closer to making the Nevarians more dangerous, and more powerful, than ever before! The fate of the universe would be set on a collision course to destruction—not just Nadiir, not just Avalon, but the entirety of both realms combined—"

Helena's eyes narrowed. "Why do *you* want this?"

"The Stork seeks power; I seek freedom. It's all I've ever wanted—"

"Freedom from what?"

*"Something your kind will never understand! I've told you enough—NOW PUT THAT DOWN—"*

In those few, few seconds, clarity alighted upon Helena's mind, and she realized that the lengths she had gone to retrieve this artifact went far beyond what the average living being should endure. She had crossed an entire continent to get here, had nearly drowned in a wormhole, and was now fighting to the death for an artifact she knew nothing about. If Helena didn't give the Stork the artifact, he'd destroy her mirage. If she did, she'd become his wingless legacy. There was no way she could win. It was a painful dawning, acknowledging the possibility that one may never fly ever again, but Helena was determined to show the Stork that his biggest mistake had been taking everything except her life.

"Then you'll both mourn your ambitions," Helena said, before lifting her arms to smash the artifact—

However, just as Helena raised the egg over her head, Penelope said something that stopped her in her tracks.

"What did you just say?" Helena whispered, her arms freezing in midair.

"It could grant you back your wings," Penelope said, sitting upright and tumbling over her own words. "There's a chance I could be mistaken...that there could be something else entirely in that artifact instead of what the Stork and I both believe there to be. And if that is the case, then there is a *chance* it could restore your wings."

"What could possibly be inside this thing that would make you say that?" Helena asked, stunned. Could it be this measly egg truly held the cure to her greatest affliction?

A series of grunts drew her attention to the sidelines. She turned her head to see Noa lift his spear just in time to block a blow from Olip's sword. But the power behind the attack was so great that it split Noa's spear in two. Phellis was teetering behind them, biting her nails and wondering what to do and who to help. Jared turned to Helena, his eyes widening as his hand reached out to her:

*"HELENA, WATCH OUT!"*

Unbeknownst to Helena, Penelope had broken the unspoken rules and had entered the duel with not one, but two weapons in her midst. As Helena held the egg high in the air, Penelope snatched a small knife hidden within her clothes and flung it towards Helena's head! The flying blade bypassed her ear by mere inches, however, and instead lodged itself in the exact spot where Penelope's mirage was.

There was a burst of light. The golden crab, now liberated, flitted to Penelope and alighted within her chest. Penelope's white wings sprouted from her back with blinding luminescence.

Penelope's mirage set off a domino effect across the entire vault as the rest of the capsules also began rupturing in a dazzling ripple, unleashing the hundreds of mirages held within them. A swarm of golden mirages rushed at Helena, blinding her. Then, a heavy force hit her right between the shoulder blades, and Helena was sent reeling. The egg was wrenched from her grasp, but she could not go after it, for the roars and cries of all the mirages bombarded her like a cascade of water. Helena swore she could even hear them *talk—*

*Help,* some seemed to say.

*Mireya, is that you?*

*Let me in, let me in!*

The mirages eventually abandoned Helena and fluttered around the cave like a flock of panicked butterflies, as if searching for a way out. A deep rumble emanated from beneath the ground, and sand rained from above as the ceiling began to crack.

In light of the impending structural collapse, Helena's friends finally came back into her view—Jared and Noa were also being harassed by a series of mirages, which left when they did not find what they were looking for.

Just behind them, Helena spotted two figures fleeing towards the far end of the vault.

*"The egg!"* she screamed. *"Don't let her have the egg!!!"*

Phellis was the only one that lay between the twins and their exit. She shrank, her eyes widening as she beheld the one person whom she undeniably feared. Her eyes flickered anxiously between her wigeon friends and Penelope.

"Step aside, Phellicarus."

A panicked determination rose in Phellis, and she lunged towards Penelope in an effort to wrestle the artifact from her grip.

*"How dare you?"* Penelope cried in outrage as the two of them struggled for possession over the golden object. It seemed she certainly didn't expect such an act of defiance from Phellis.

*"I'm not afraid of you anymore, PENNY!"*

Olip advanced towards Phellis, brandishing his sword. Before he could harm her, however, a hand latched onto his shoulder and turned him around. Noa punched Olip right smack in the face! *Craaack!* went his nose. He fell backwards with a grunt. Noa shook off the pain of his hand and kissed his reddening knuckles.

Phellis twisted so that the sharp end of her elbow struck Penelope in the jaw, and the artifact finally came loose. Taking the egg, Phellis tossed it to Jared, who caught it flawlessly. Turning, he bellowed:

*"RUN! THE ENTIRE MOUNTAIN'S COLLAPSING!!!"*

The bright flock of mirages illuminated a hidden exit at the far end of the vault. The group followed them in a bid to escape this mountain before it could collapse and crush them to death. Helena, however, stopped suddenly midway; she had spotted something in the far corner of the vault, over by a small pile of lapis lazuli. Penelope's journal lay wide open, its pages fluttering every which way as a current of mirages rushed over it. Helena wavered on her feet, hesitating, before making the split-second decision to run over and grasp as many pages as she could. Only managing to grab a handful, she shoved them in a bag and darted towards the cavern's exit.

Outside, in the middle of an unsuspecting forest, there was a golden explosion. Mirages burst forth from a small opening at the foot of the mountain and into the open wilderness, a golden current so bright that night turned into day. The wigeon group bolted deeper into the forest, following the mirages in search of safety. A tremor shook the earth beneath Helena's staggering feet, and there was a terrible, wailing moan as the entire face of the mountain gave way from underneath itself. A monstrous cloud of rock, dirt, and boulders chased after the wigeon group, who could only flee, hope, and pray they would not become a target of the boulders that toppled over the sides of the mountain. Some even flew over them like meteorites before crashing into the forest ahead in a shower of splinters and debris.

When everything had settled, the group lay panting in a small ditch, covered in dirt and dust. All of them had made it out safely, but the twins were unaccounted for. Floating mirages filled the night air, scattered amidst the innermost parts of the forest and twinkling like fireflies. After rising and dusting themselves off, Helena and her friends ascended the slope of the new mountain that had been formed. They found Penelope kneeling upon the soft ground up ahead, her soiled wings unmoving and drooping. Just feet away from her could be seen a pale hand jutting out from underneath the soil. Its lengthy fingers were stiff and outstretched, as if reaching for the sky.

Then, while everyone held their breath, a single light descended from above and planted itself upon the hand's long fingers. It was a crustacean of a different kind, similar to Penelope's but with a shapely, conch-like shell encasing the creature inside. With a mournful wave of its antennae, the hermit crab bid Olip its final goodbyes before fluttering off into the darkness of the forest, forever sentenced into exile.

Penelope did not move for many moments afterwards. Nobody could find the will, or the words, to say anything.

Then, in a flash, Penelope jumped to her feet and darted for the nearest person within her reach—Phellicarus Faye.

"Let her go!" Jared shouted as Penelope held a blade to Phellis' throat.

Helena raised her hands in surrender. "We know you're angry! Put the knife down and we can talk this out—"

*"You know nothing! Follow me, and I will not hesitate to cut her throat!"* With a feral hiss, Penelope slowly backed into the forest with Phellis in her

arms, who whimpered as she was taken away. Helena found herself following in their direction, but Jared reeled her back.

"Let me go, Jared—she'll kill her!"

"She's grieving. There's no telling what she's capable of right now, and if you chase her, you might scare her into hurting Phellis. We need a plan—"

"*Red!*" Noa's sharp voice sounded behind them.

They turned to see a razor-sharp spearhead just barely nicking Noa's throat, held by an armored, brown-winged avian with the sigil of a dragon upon his chest plate. Noa held his arms up in surrender, and Jared and Helena were too scared to move in case they startled the ave into skewering the wigeon boy.

Then, in a dazzling blizzard of brown feathers and crimson banners, a flock of twenty-plus avian warriors descended into the clearing. They wasted no time in forming a circular formation around the three wigeons. With a unanimous sound-off, the warriors all sprung into position, raising their shields and pointing their spears.

A voice, clear and powerful, sounded:

*"You stand before the Dragonback Warriors of Alazar, accused of trespassing across our lands. State your names and intentions!"*

# PART II
## THE ARTIFACT

# Chapter Fourteen

No name drew as large of a reaction as Helena Nightingale's. Many murmured questioningly to one another at the sound of it. The captain of this small host could not seem to believe it himself. He narrowed his eyes, gave Helena a once-over, and declared:

"Helena Nightingale was not described as a wigeon!"

In one breath, the Nadiirian warriors turned vigilant, raising their weapons and scanning their surroundings in case something went awry with this woman, whom they were now convinced was an imposter. *What on earth is going on,* Helena thought, bewildered. She was quite unfamiliar with these people and where they came from, yet they seemed well acquainted with her name as any old friend would be...

"She's not a true wigeon," Jared said in her defense.

Looks of confusion etched themselves upon the faces of the captain and his men, who looked to Helena to clarify his words.

Her throat threatened to collapse in on itself as she bore the weight of their distrustful stares. "My wings were stolen by a man who calls himself the Stork..."

*It begins now,* Helena thought tragically, as harsh whispers and gasps trickled across the flock. Her face burned with humiliation. The captain could not seem to grasp the true meaning of her words. He stood there with a look of utter confusion on his face, which was partly hidden behind his metal helm.

"Show us your stubs!" he demanded.

"I have none," she declared. "It was no mere act of physical removal. The Stork used magic to steal my mirage and my wings. I've been a wigeon ever since."

Chaos unleashed, with shouts and questions arising from this declaration; wings stretched and flapped, feathers flew everywhere, and the ground rumbled as they pounded the butts of their spears against the forest floor. Soon, the words *liar* and *fraud* made their way into the mouths of the men and women who glared at Helena with disbelief.

"She's telling the truth!" Noa shouted.

"Captain Rancipert!" One ave with a thick, fiery beard stepped forwards to express his thoughts—which, judging by the scowl on his face, did not hold Helena and her friends in a positive light. "Mirages are by no means a physical entity, and they only merge with us in childhood. What this girl claims—that someone confiscated her wings—defies the very Law of Attainment! For all we know, these wigeons—" He raised an accusatory finger at them. "—could be Nevarian, and this nothing more than an elaborate trap!"

This possibility sparked further outrage. What this man said couldn't have been further from the truth—but these warriors couldn't have known that for certain. And there was no way to prove their innocence until the sun came out, by which time Phellis would have been long dead or out of their reach...

"Please," Helena begged, "we're running out of time—our friend has been kidnapped! You must help us get her back or she'll be killed—"

"*Quiet,*" Captain Rancipert's voice boomed across the clearing, and the commotion subsided. "Mayghar is right. Only time will help us discern who you truly are. The three of you will not move a muscle nor speak a word until you can prove you're not Nevarian."

"But—"

"My decision is final. We wait for the sun."

The young wigeons could do nothing but endure an agonizing wait for dawn. Helena grew increasingly restless with each passing hour, mulling tirelessly over the fate of Phellis and the madwoman who had taken her captive. And with everything else that had happened over the last few hours, Helena had nearly forgotten that she was bleeding! The wound above her right hip—the scarlet slit cutting across the dark fabric of her utilitarian suit—was still fresh. Luckily, they had a spare vial of feather dust on hand, and after mixing it with a bit of water, Helena applied the salve generously to her cut; there was a sharp sting at first, but a cool, enduring relief quickly followed. Helena sighed. In less than a minute, the incision scarred over and healed completely.

Helena's eyes flickered nervously to the bag slung over Jared's shoulder. If you looked close enough, you could just see the faint, roundish outline of the golden egg inside. She dreaded the idea of their precious artifact being discovered and all their hard work going down the drain. Helena took great care to play it cool, but it was difficult to act unfazed with twenty Dragonback Warriors maintaining a smothering fixation on you for an entire night. They sharpened their spears and leered at the wigeons, as if daring them to try anything suspicious and meet the sharp ends of their polished, redwood spears...

Hours later, the soft caress of the sun woke Helena from her deep sleep.

"And up she rises!" Noa's tenor voice carried across the yard. "Now tell yer dogs to sit and lower their weapons!"

"Just because you passed the first litmus test does not mean you're off the hook," Rancipert answered brusquely. "Now, explain yourselves—what are three wigeon children doing in the outskirts of our lands?"

Jared was the first to speak. "My friends are of the Upper Realm, from the Kingdom of Avalon. They were abducted by Nevarian henchmen and sent to Nadiir, and have been stranded here ever since. They want nothing more than to return home."

"They're exiles!" Mayghar exclaimed in disgust.

"Are you deaf?" snapped Noa. "He just told you we were taken here against our will! Based on what part of that did you conclude that we were exiles?"

"Ease your tongue, wigeon," the lieutenant spat, his wings puffing indignantly. "I don't take well to insolent spitmouths like you!"

"Calm, Mayghar," Rancipert said thoughtfully. With the morning sun shining above them, the tension had lifted, and now the captain seemed more willing to listen to their testimonies. "These are just children by the looks of it, not criminals, and theirs is not the first story I've heard of the Nevarians' diabolical schemes...how long has it been since you two were taken?" he asked, directing his attention to Helena and Noa.

"It's been a few months for me," Helena responded. She nudged Noa when he was reluctant to answer.

"Five years," he said through gritted teeth.

Rancipert whistled. "By godly winds! A whole childhood, it seems...what of you, boy?" he said, looking to Jared. "You claim your friends are Avalonians, but make no clearer claim as to your own heritage."

"I am of Nadiir," he answered proudly. "I am helping my friends in the hopes that one day they will return home, and that the King of Avalon may be gracious enough to grant me safe passage into the Upper Realm."

The crowd around them burst into harsh laughter.

"Good luck with that, wigeon!" one warrior cried.

"It's been over a century since Avalon last opened its gates and offered asylum to Nadiirians," another ave said. "You'd have better luck earning your wings at your piss-poor age than *ever* making it to the Upper Realm!"

Jared never once lowered his gaze at the sound of their jeering laughter.

"Quiet, you lot!" Rancipert said, and they fell silent. "Helping foreigners is a noble pursuit, and I admire this courageous boy for going above and beyond for his friends. May the universe reward you well, Jared Pathfoot."

Rancipert then sighed. He seemed unsure of what to do with all this information. He eyed the suit poking out from underneath Helena's wigeon clothes and said, "I know an Avalonian suit when I see one, and Helena Nightingale was said to be tall, with raven hair—likely braided—and bright green eyes. You match her description almost perfectly, minus the stormy grey wings..."

He trailed off, and Helena lowered her gaze in shame.

"I suppose the only one who could confirm your identity would be Ser Ulyxes Cazador himself."

The name sent Helena's heart racing and her mind reeling. Her mind flashed back to that long-ago morning back at Mount Sulfur, when she was certain she had spotted Yulix headbirding a flock of avians whose armor matched the ones she saw here and now.

After all this time, her friend had *still* not given up on finding her.

But though she once rejoiced at the thought of reuniting with her old friend, now the prospect terrified her. Helena reckoned she would need at least a year to build up the courage to face him in the wigeon state she was in—though a decade sounded much safer!

"Captain!" protested Mayghar. "Certainly, you are not thinking of taking these wigeons in? They speak utter nonsense! Do you truly believe a Krow who goes by the silly name of the Stork is running around magically turning aves into wigeons?"

Helena hated the way these aves looked at her. Their faces were full of doubt and apprehension, and yet they still gripped their weapons tighter and looked over their own shoulders fearfully. It was as if, despite their eagerness to dismiss Helena's testimony as a farce, they suspected it still held a dark truth to it. *So long as you live on, you serve as testimony to his cruelty and innovation. You are meant to spark fear in the people around you.* Penelope's words echoed in Helena's memory.

"We Dragonbacks have never turned away a soul in search of safety," Rancipert announced finally, his voice loud and clear. "We will take them in for further questioning. Lower your weapons and send word to King Hyrax that we're headed home—we found the Nightingale!"

The courier, a young boy with white wings, took off into the pale morning sky to gain a head start on his comrades and bring word to their people. They brought forth a small, horse-drawn wagon steered by a single wigeon driver. Logistically, a host of avians had little use for wagons or horses, but when someone would become injured and be unable to fly, wagons often served as a reliable method of ground transportation. Helena and her wigeon friends would share this cramped little wagon with two other injured aves for the rest of the journey home. Before Helena entered the wagon, however, she turned to Rancipert and said—

"Our friend is still out there—Phellicarus Faye, a wigeon like us."

Rancipert looked at his warriors, who were beaten and battered from their journey, and shook his head.

"I cannot afford to risk my men and women another night."

"If you hadn't kept us prisoner until morning, we would have found the girl already!" Noa said reproachfully.

The captain replied gruffly, "We've been ambushed far too many times by Krows to take any chances...I will send word to our scouting parties to keep an eye out for your friend, but I'm afraid there's nothing we can do for her."

The captain's words were disheartening. Jared put a hand on Helena's shoulder.

"She'll be okay," he said.

"Yea," said Noa. "When have you ever seen that the wigeon girl can't fare for herself?"

But their words did not bring much assurance. After staring over at the break in the bushes from where Penelope had taken Phellis, Helena had no choice but to clamber guiltily onto the wagon and await their arrival at the kingdom.



They traveled by day through the mountains, and it was nighttime when they arrived before the small Kingdom of Alazar, home of the Dragonback Warriors. Its great wooden gates parted with a deep moan at their approach. A magnificent valley revealed itself, lush and evergreen, though the night surely dimmed most of its beauty. Still, hundreds of warm lights flickered in the distant lowlands like fireflies, illuminating the buildings and lampposts constituting the great kingdom. A deep blue river gushed through the heart of the valley and towards a grand, glistening lake at its easternmost end. Helena also counted seven great watchtowers circling the kingdom, each brandishing a red banner with the golden sigil of a dragon. The skies were mostly deserted, apart from the handful of squadrons patrolling the skies. Helena frowned at this. Rancipert explained that citizens were discouraged to stay out past sundown due to Nevarians, who had grown more numerous over the years and posed a greater risk these days than they used to.

When they finally brought the three wigeons before the king in his great pavilion, he sat crookedly upon his wooden throne; his upper body leaned to one side because he was missing an entire wing. He seemed a weary and irritable old man who took no interest in the three wigeons—that is, until Rancipert formally presented Helena.

"Your Majesty, I present to you Helena Nightingale from the precincts of Avalon and the Upper Realm. She was kidnapped by the Nevarians alongside Ulyxes Cazador, and has journeyed from Krow's Foot to seek the safety of our borders."

Helena fell to one knee and bowed her head respectfully.

"Why is it you bring a wigeon before me?" the weathered king questioned Rancipert sharply. "Surely, this is not the Helena Nightingale I've heard tirelessly about!"

"It appears so, Your Majesty...only she claims her wings have been stolen by a Nevarian who calls himself the Stork."

As the sharp crackles of the fire filled the silence, the king's mouth sank further into a frown.

"Rise, wigeon," he ordered. "Explain yourself."

Helena felt a spike of annoyance at the word *wigeon* being used to address her. It wasn't the *word* that vexed her, per se, but the contemptuous way it was used. Nevertheless, she obeyed and explained the night of her fall in great detail, including the moment she lost her wings, and described her and her friends' arduous journey through Krow's Foot and across Nadiir to the Mountains of Alazar. For obvious reasons, Helena redacted any mention of the artifact—she wasn't willing to risk having them take it away after all the work it took to get it.

King Hyrax remained silent throughout her testimony, but grew gradually more disturbed. Once Helena finished, he stretched his one prehistoric wing and dismissed his subjects with a wave of his hand.

"Leave us!" he declared. Everyone, including Noa and Jared, vacated the room until only he, Helena, and his most trusted advisor Rancipert remained.

"Do you realize the gravity of that which you claim, *wigeon*?" the king spoke with a quiet, sharp tongue. The acidic undertone in his voice suggested that he didn't believe a single word of her story.

Helena's words were clipped and icy. "I'm well aware. But the Stork stole my wings, and that is the truth."

"Am I simply supposed to take your word for it?" he demanded. "You speak of dark, dark magic, but for all I know you may be lying to instigate panic and mayhem amidst my people!"

"You must believe me!" Helena very well shouted. "Turn a blind eye, and *your own people may be next!"*

Slamming his fist upon the armrest of his throne, the king rose to his feet in a fit of anger.

"Is that a threat, wigeon?" Even this small gesture cost him significant energy, however, and he swayed back and forth upon his weak knees.

"Not a threat—a warning," she responded, this time wise enough to contain her outbursts. "I may or may not have been the first avian to have gone through this, but one thing's for certain: I will not be the last."

Scowling, he turned his head to Rancipert and said, "What do you make of all this? Speak honestly, and hold not your tongue!"

The captain began hesitantly. "Her story agrees, for the most part, with the testimony of Ser Ulyxes Cazador. As you know, there have been multiple reports of the Nevarians having already secured a connection to the Upper Realm, a portal which they use to smuggle both people and exotic goods—the Eye of Nadiir. This seems to add credibility to that…"

The king found some logic within Rancipert's reasoning and gave him the sign to continue.

"Helena also described an encounter with an avian along her journey, whom she described as a giant with two pincers for hands. It matches the description of Phi Pterodactyly, better known as *Ptero.*" His tongue lingered on the name as his gloved hand tightened into a fist. "A fallen avian infamous for his cruelty and ruthlessness. Our intel confirms he is the leader of *the Fallen Coven,* a dangerous ring of ex-Avalonian criminals with ties to the Nevarian regime. As for her grievance against the Stork…well, I cannot say for certain, but I sense there is truth in her claims, yet."

King Hyrax collapsed onto his throne with a huff. "Perhaps the Avalonian knight can help us make sense of this mess. After all, she claims he was with her prior to the moment when she lost her wings...have you any idea of his whereabouts as of late, Rancipert?"

"I've just received word that Ser Ulyxes Cazador was within several miles of the upper leg of Krow's Foot."

Helena's heart sank. "He's not here?"

"He and a squadron of warriors recently set off on an expedition to return to Avalon. They are headed south towards Krow's Foot to locate and travel through the Eye of Nadiir, which is presently the only living link between the Lower and Upper Realms. If they succeed, Ser Ulyxes Cazador would then express his grievances before the King of Avalon and urge him to take swift action against the Nevarians."

Unbelievable. Yulix had taken it upon himself to execute the very plan to get back home to Avalon that she, Noa, and Jared had discussed months ago...Helena knew, however, that even such a straightforward mission was not without its risks.

"It's a dangerous mission, to be sure," Rancipert admitted. "The Nevarians maintain a smothering surveillance over the portal. We can only hope that Ser Ulyxes Cazador and his men have the strength and resilience necessary to fight their way past their numbers."

Apprehension bubbled in Helena's stomach. Nevertheless, she raised her chin high and said:

"There is no one better suited for such a daunting task than my friend. He will get the job done."

King Hyrax's cold gaze met Helena's.

"One would certainly hope so. The day Ulyxes Cazador fell upon our doorstep, injured and in great distress, he stated his name and origin, retelling the vivid story of how the two of you fell from the Upper Realm and into Nadiir. He claimed that you were critically wounded and in need of search and rescue. I said to the knight, who was no older than my own son, 'If I send my good and honest men to help you in your time of need, what do I get in return?' The Avalonian knight said he held much favor with the king of Avalon and promised an abundance of wealth in return for our generous hospitality. But I had something much bigger in mind...'"

He leaned forwards, the shadows dancing around his aged eyes. "I agreed to help your friend on the sole condition that your king would consider forming an alliance with Alazar to help bring an end to the Nevarians once and for all. You see, my people and I have dwelled in these lands for decades, forced to coexist with these wicked demons who carry their curse on their tongues. The Nevarian race is a malicious, festering cancer that, if not dealt with, will surely grow into something beyond the scope of our control!"

"It is true," Rancipert added. "Over the years I have seen the Nevarians grow bolder and more numerous. Our scouts have seen a steady increase in late-night incidents involving them, and based off Helena's eye-witness account of Krotoa, it appears that they are usurping wigeon towns and using them as imposter colonies. The Nevarians are seeking more and more territory as we speak, and if they succeed, war is not a question of if, but of *when.*"

The old king's face darkened with greed. "And with the Eye of Nadiir under their control, they are certainly reaping the fruits of their foul labors, smuggling exotic goods and becoming richer, and more powerful, by the day. Doubtless there are many who would wage war over such a key gateway...but I digress. We can only hope that Ser Ulyxes Cazador succeeds in his mission, and that the Kingdom of Avalon accepts our alliance proposal to help curtail the Nevarians' spread of influence across the Realm of Nadiir."

It was a proposition that both alarmed Helena and instilled hope inside her. If the King of Avalon did accept this alliance, perhaps they would open a gate between both realms, and she would finally get to go home, something she longed for, now more than ever...

King Hyrax leaned back in his seat and heaved a heavy sigh. "So, wigeon, yours is a story that eludes us all! If what you claim is true, and the man who calls himself the Stork is using dark sorcery to steal innocents' wings, then there is no telling what dangers lie ahead...very well! We will send word of your arrival to Ser Ulyxes Cazador, and we shall await his pending return so that he may indeed confirm your identity. I will allow you and your friends to dwell here in Alazar, but if I get any inkling that you are up to no good and wish to stir up trouble—any at all—I will banish you from these lands! And I will make sure you never return to Avalon ever again."

The walk back to Helena's new living quarters was longer and more arduous than she would have liked, and it mortified her that Rancipert, in all his gallantry, escorted her to her cabin on foot and without complaint. Together, they trekked up a large, steep hill that overlooked a substantial part of the valley until they reached a shoddy cabin perched unobtrusively at the top. A window flickered dimly in the night, and she knew at once that Noa and Jared were awaiting her return. When they reached the front door, Helena could not help but ask:

"If I may, Captain Rancipert...many doubt me. Why don't you?"

The captain leaned in closer to Helena, spreading his great wings to provide them with a shield of confidentiality.

"Dark times are ahead, Helena. I've never seen Nevarians as numerous as they are now, and I cannot shake the feeling that they are up to something—and for the life of me, I cannot convince myself that it is anything good. Your story has only bolstered my growing suspicions."

Helena rubbed the hair that prickled along her arms as she remembered Penelope's words: *This artifact must never fall into the hands of the Stork, for if it did, it would set the entire universe on course for destruction...*

Helena buried her fretful thoughts and said, "Thank you."

He graced her with a meek smile. "We've all suffered at the hands of those Krows one way or another...if there is anything you need, anything at all, don't hesitate to ask."

The door swung open, and Helena and Rancipert jumped apart. Noa was standing at the doorway, and his face assumed a peevish expression as he took in their proximity to one another.

"Interrupting something, am I?" he said.

Rancipert clasped his hands together. "Not at all! I ought to leave you guys to settle and rest. I'd wager you all had quite the taxing journey. So long, then! I'll swing by tomorrow for introductions."

Their new living quarters were simple: paneled wooden floors, two bunk beds, a tiny writing desk with a quill and inkwell, a hearth and fireplace, a dresser, a dining table, a few wooden chairs, and two lanterns lighting up the room. It was certainly an upgrade, given their poor circumstances in the last few weeks, but quickly forgotten as Jared rushed to draw the curtains to a close. Upon the table he unveiled a new object that shined brighter than any other candle in the room. They flocked to it like moths, their mouths hanging open.

The artifact was heavy, bulbous, and nothing short of its foretold glory; it tipped back and forth on its solid gold shell, which was inlaid with sapphire gems, enamoring rubies, enchanting emeralds, and at its center, a diamond twice the size of Helena's thumb! Intricate reliefs of long, wispy feathers caressed the egg's shapely, ovular figure. Helena's eyes twinkled as she gazed at it, her stomach churning with what felt like greed. This was what the Stork desired most of all, and it was now in her possession.

"What's our next move?" asked Noa, looking from Helena to Jared.

For many moments, everyone seemed too afraid to answer. Jared was the first to break the silence.

"I believe that's up to Helena," he said, and both boys looked expectantly at the wigeon girl.

Helena found herself at yet another crossroads. Should she do what they had set out to do originally and honor the deal she made with the Stork by returning the artifact to him, knowing that there was no real guarantee he would honor his side of the bargain...or should she could keep it herself? If she did not return the egg, then by definition she would be renouncing her wings—a decision that would render this entire journey, and all their hard work, nearly pointless.

Helena rested both hands on the table and let out a lengthy sigh.

"We can't give it to the Stork," she said quietly.

Yes, even Helena's own words surprised her. After all, she'd gone through extraordinary efforts to obtain the artifact...but now, after everything Penelope had confessed to Helena, it didn't feel right to take it back to the Stork. She chose her next words deliberately:

"Penelope said this artifact is the one thing that could help the Nevarians grow more powerful than ever before. If we give it to the Stork, we don't know what kinds of terrible things could happen. I realize now that this artifact goes beyond any of our desires, and if there's truly something in there that would give the Nevarians that kind of power...then its best that we destroy it, whatever it is..."

Noa said, "But if we don't give the egg to the Krow, then that means..."

"I would be renouncing my wings for good," she concluded. "It would also erase any chance of you earning your wings, Jared. I'm sorry."

It was clear that this decision was devastating for him. After much silence, he spoke up quietly:

"Months ago, you would have done anything to get your wings back."

Helena nodded.

"Now, you have exactly what you need to do it, but suddenly it's not the right thing to do based on something Penelope said, which could very well have been a lie. What changed your mind?"

That was a great question—what *had* changed Helena's mind? She considered what Penelope told her about the artifact, way back in the dragon's lair: *It could grant back your wings.* As far as Helena knew, Penelope had confessed this to her and no one else, and it could've well been a lie. Still, Helena kept this confession to herself. If the artifact *did* have the power to grant wings, then Jared, Noa, and even Phellis, wherever she was, would want to claim the artifact for themselves—

*No.* These were scheming, even treacherous thoughts! Helena at once felt ashamed. In a desperate attempt to absolve herself, she came to the conclusion that Penelope would have done or said anything to keep her from breaking the egg. Whatever was inside this artifact could *not* bring her wings back, nothing could, and so she buried this possibility in the furthest corner of her mind...

"I simply hadn't realized how much was at stake," she said finally. "I'm truly sorry, Jared."

Helena reached out to him, but he withdrew from her touch. He turned, concealing some profound reaction as he processed what she had said. Jared could not seem to find the words to express his disappointment.

"You could earn your wings some other way," Helena started. "You don't have to confine yourself to large, impossible tasks. Most people earn their wings through simple acts of kindness. I know I did—"

"If it were as simple as an act of kindness, I would've earned them by now. Besides, I made a *vow* to you, Helena, and it rested wholeheartedly on the belief that I would help you get your wings back—if I can't do that, then there's no hope for me..."

"Well! At the very least, I'm glad yer finally coming to yer senses!" Noa said. Helena shot him a dirty look, to which he only raised his arms in defense.

"This was my one and only chance to prove myself," Jared whispered. "Maybe I'm just not worthy."

"No!" Helena cried.

"Don't do that," Noa said, groaning. "Don't make me feel like an ass! Alright, look...why don't we keep the egg until we find out what on earth is in that thing. If it's just some harmless thing the Krow's after, then we'll chuck it back at him. You'll each get what you want, we can finally go home, and we'll all live happily ever after!"

Jared sucked in a deep breath, regaining his composure. "I will honor your decision, Helena, whatever it may be. Now, if you two will excuse me—"

"Jared!" Helena cried.

He hurried out of the room and slammed the door behind him. Helena and Noa sat in silence for many moments afterwords, processing the words that had just been exchanged.

"I feel terrible," Helena said after a while. She meant it.

"Don't punish yerself, bird. He's not the only one making a sacrifice—yer giving up yer wings, too."

Noa's statement did not lighten her guilt at all. "I'm worried."

"That he'll steal the egg and give it to the Krows?"

She shrugged.

Noa looked down at his own hands and swallowed thickly. "Then you clearly don't know the man like I do. Give him time. He'll come around."

"I won't blame him if he doesn't," she said, and her face hardened. "All I want now is for the Stork to feel every bit of disappointment and rage in wanting what he can't have."

There was a sheen in Noa's eyes that suggested he was deeply intrigued by her words. It was like she and Noa were now finally on the same page—wingless, full of discontent, and determined to let the world burn for the trespasses committed against them. Something had finally bridged the distance between them, and Helena would be a liar if she said this did not elicit some excitement within her.

"You got any clue on how to open it?" he asked, nodding towards the golden egg.

"No, but I managed to snatch something that might help." Helena fetched her bag and hurried to the table. She pulled out a sizeable wad of damp and yellow paper. "Entries from Penelope's notebook."

She flattened them in an orderly fashion against the rickety table. There were anywhere from twenty to thirty pages of writing, most if not all of it blurred and smudged with muddy stains of water. Moreover, Penelope's writing was tiny and grossly inconsistent, with formless and frantic characters that suggested the author was scrawling in the mightiest rush of her life. *The only one who could truly understand the penmanship of a madwoman would be the very hand that wrote it*, Helena thought. But since the madwoman in question was not here, it would be up to her and her friends to try to decipher these pages themselves.

"It's going to take some time to read and examine these," Helena mumbled. Noa joined her side at the table, and the two of them peered down at the assemblage of papers. His right hand traced the almost hieroglyphic lettering of Penelope's writing alongside Helena's. There were several moments when his warm skin brushed against hers and goosebumps shot up her arm.

"Think there's anything worth reading in there?" he said lowly.

Helena cleared her throat and retracted her hand. "I'll wager there is. There must be something in these entries that will tell us about Penelope's true intentions for the artifact. I'll dedicate the next few days to studying them, and then maybe we can figure out how to open it."

"Aye-aye," he said, giving her a small salute. Then he frowned. "It's a shame Phellis ain't here. Fear she would've loved to kick her ugly feet up on the table..."

The thought that Phellis was still out there, likely enduring harsh weather and brutal mistreatment by her captor, was deeply disconcerting. Helena felt a wave of tremendous remorse when she recalled the look on

Phellis' face when she found out about their deal with the Stork. She likely felt used.

"Rancipert said his scouts would keep an eye out for her," she said. "Let's hope that she's okay, and that they find her soon."

"Unless the Krows find her first," he said, his face darkening.

Helena's lips pressed into a tight line. "In all likelihood, she'll find us before either of them finds her. Come on, let's rest. It's been a long journey, and I can't recall the last time I slept on a proper bed."

# Chapter Fifteen

T hat night, Helena dreamt that her bed had given way from under her, and that she fell thousands of feet until hitting the earth and going *splat.* She woke with a jolt, hands flying to her hammering heart. *Just a dream,* she thought sickly, sitting up in her bed and exhaling a sigh of relief. But then she took one look at her surroundings, and her stomach dropped. *No, it's not.* The softened face of Noa peeked over the ledge of his top bunk, mouth ajar as scandalous snores ripped through the early morning silence. This was the only time of day in which his face was not plagued with frown lines and scowls. Meanwhile, Jared slept quietly with his back facing the rest of them. Helena's heart weighed heavier at the thought of their difficult conversation last night.

Rancipert arrived at their doorstep later that morning to give the three wigeons a tour throughout the kingdom. Helena hardly recognized the captain without his helmet and fifty pounds of armor; he was a fairly attractive, well-groomed man who boasted an elastic bushel of curls for hair and kept his brows and beard trimmed to perfection. *Almost too perfect,* Helena thought to herself. *No man cares that much about his appearance. Except maybe Yulix.* Still, as handsome as Rancipert was, even he was not without flaw, for his ears were as wide as an elephant's and looked like they were continuously being pulled.

"Watch the man fly with those," Noa muttered to Helena. She dug her elbow into his ribs, and he shut up with a smirk. Helena had little evidence to account for Noa's unwarranted dislike of the avian captain, but she had a hunch it had to do with his finding her and Rancipert in such close proximity the night before. Helena wasn't too worried about this, though. Rancipert seemed fond of Helena, but she reckoned that girls in general were not his cup of tea.

First, Rancipert introduced the group to the *birdbaths,* a river system of small ponds and hot springs which citizens often visited to bathe or wash their clothes. Helena made a mental note to return here later. They visited the local blacksmith, arriving just in time to see him bent over his anvil; sparks flew as he pounded the iron sword into its predestined form. Coal dust colored his wings a full shade darker.

"Our blacksmiths provide our soldiers with the finest weaponry and armor. They could not be more essential to our cause than they are now, with the growing threat of the Nevarians from the south—and not just the south, I might add. Months ago, they ambushed our warriors just several miles east of here, near Kanyon Koli. We suspect that they've established a colony somewhere within that region."

"How many were lost?" Jared asked.

"It was a scouting group of ten," he said, his eyes glazing over. "Only one was spared to tell the tale of the horrors they witnessed. The Nevarians are a fearsome and sadistic enemy—nothing arouses them more than frightening and disorienting their prey. They surround you, and bombard you with all kinds of horrific sounds they have stored in those wicked heads of theirs, until you're certain you've gone off the deep end. Then, they kill you...if you're lucky. I've heard tales of them taking Diurnals and making them go days without sleep, using their wicked talents to emit the screeches of nails on chalkboards, the wails of widows, and other abominable sounds, until they are driven to madness."

*Keeping someone awake for days,* Helena thought, bewildered. It was a heinous thought! Something like that was sure to send someone spiraling into insanity! After traveling alongside Nocturnals, Helena knew from experience that living with little to no sleep altered a person's psyche in the most uncomfortable ways...

"Now I understand why you took such great precautions when we met," Helena said grimly.

"We've lost a lot of loved ones when we were least careful," he agreed, a pained look on his face. "My husband was one of the many scouts who didn't return. In fact, he was brutally murdered by a member of the Fallen Coven. I've been looking for the beast with the clawed hands ever since to avenge his death."

*"Ptero killed your husband?"* Helena exclaimed with a gasp.

Rancipert nodded, his face twisting in anguish.

"The beast will serve his day of reckoning," he affirmed with a tight fist.

Helena and the others shared a few uncertain glances. They had once come face-to-face with the behemoth that was Ptero, and Helena knew that slaying him would be no simple undertaking. Even outnumbered, the fallen avian had appeared invincible.

Helena had the inclination to ask, "You mentioned earlier that the Nevarian presence is growing stronger than ever...do you think there will come a day when they attack Alazar?"

Forgetting his moment of weakness, Rancipert said, "It is hard to say. For one thing, Nevarians are nocturnal—launching a military campaign would be tedious, considering that they'd have to navigate around the sun. If there's anything I've learned in my thirty-six years of life, however, it is to never underestimate your enemy. That is why our soldiers train hard every day, six days a week, running drills both on the ground and in the air. If an invasion ever happens, we'll be ready."

"I want to join," Jared suddenly burst out.

His words surprised them all—most of all Noa, who seemed to have taken this statement as nothing other than ludicrous. Even Rancipert raised his eyebrows at the young wigeon's startling outburst.

"I want to join your ranks and learn how to fight so that the day those Krows decide to invade, I'll be ready!"

"I admire your enthusiasm, Jared, but we don't have a wigeon infantry, mostly because we don't have enough wigeons to man such a thing. All our drills and training primarily take an *aerial-based* approach. I can squeeze you in for training in physical combat, though you'll be up against fully grown avians. You would be at a disadvantage. I'm not sure if you would be up for that."

Noa pulled Jared to the side before he could even respond.

"What's gotten into that head o'yers?" Noa whispered at him.

"What?" Jared asked impatiently.

Noa gripped his arm and hissed, "*You've got no place in a fighting nest! They'll tear you to pieces!*"

Jared wrenched himself away. "It's nobody's business but mine!"

Noa took this as a great slight. "Fine. Do what yer mighty big head is telling you. I'll be here to laugh when it doesn't work out..."

Noa made a strong point. Jared would be at an utter disadvantage in such a setting...after all, how would a wigeon learn to fight against a fully-fledged avian? Jared, however, wasn't just any wigeon; he was a strong, hardworking, and resilient young man capable of overcoming nearly all obstacles, including a training ground titled against him.

"If he thinks he can do it, then who are we to stop him?" Helena said, in the hopes this would make up for the night before. Jared gave her something of a rueful smile before turning to Rancipert, who'd been pretending not to weigh in on this uncomfortable conversation.

"I'll do whatever it takes," Jared said firmly, his eyes glimmering with determination. "Just please teach me to wield a sword. You won't regret it."

The resolve in Jared's words proved admirable to the young captain.

"Very well. Meet me at the Fighting's Nest tomorrow, first thing in the morning, and I will make you a steady swordsman!"


The Kingdom of Alazar bustled with citizens hustling and jostling each other on their way to work, chattering with their peers, or simply taking a leisurely stroll. The waters of the valley river were blue and surging, and a great cobblestone bridge granted passage to those who wished to access the Central Square—though it was worth noting that most avians made little use of such a thing, instead using their wings to make a short glide across the river to the other side. As the wigeon gang made their way across the bridge, Helena admired the soft, tapered brown wings of the common people. Occasionally, she spotted an avian with a set of stunning silver wings, the kind you would see in Avalon, suggesting a distant Avalonian lineage from generations past...

Helena shut her eyes and listened to the hubbub in the air: there was the slight rustle of an outstretched wing, a soft *tffft* as someone shivered and their feathers puffed, and the soft thudding of dirt as aves both landed and kicked off into the air. Helena sighed. For the first time in weeks, *Helena felt at home.*

But all her ease and contentment soon washed away. As soon as she stepped foot into the Central Square, idling avians fixed their gazes upon Helena and regarded her cautiously. They seemed most intrigued by the utilitarian suit peeking out from underneath her wigeon clothes. Many huddled closer together and soon resorted to murmurs and whispers.

*"She's Avalonian,"* they whispered to one another.

*"A Paradiser!"*

*"Not just any Paradiser! My, that's Helena Nightingale!"*

More whispers fluttered about. *How do they know who I am?* Helena wondered, as she made every effort to evade their distrustful glares.

Suddenly, a man shouted at Helena from across the square. "You there, wigeon! Is it true what they say? Did ya really lose your wings?"

Another ave nearby laughed and said, "Nonsense! You don't just lose yer wings! They ain't a pair of knickers!"

"Well, that's what they say happened to her. Stolen by the Stork, supposedly!"

Everyone looked to Helena for confirmation, but she only stared back at them with wide eyes. For a moment, she was too afraid to respond. But then Noa gave her a reassuring nod, quelling her fears.

"It's true," she said aloud. "The Stork took my wings away."

In less than a minute, her words had flitted throughout the crowded square. Many commoners gasped. Some even screamed. Soon, the news that Helena Nightingale had lost her wings to the Stork made its way out the square and across the entire kingdom. By nightfall, everyone would know of Helena's misfortune.

"It must be a lie!" she heard one mother gasp.

*"If such a thing is possible, we might be next!"*

One older avian man could not comprehend the vile, incredulous rumors that reached his ears. He raised a finger at Helena and cried, "An abomination!"

Helena felt her heart break.

"Take that back!" Noa barked at the avian, but Jared whisked him away before he would do anything reckless.

Rancipert quickly escorted them away from the chaos and back to their quarters, looking quite abashed after the spectacle.

"Please excuse them," he said. "News spreads like wildfire in these streets, and your story has taken the people by storm. They're just trying to get a sense of you."

When they got home, Helena curled up in her bed and, when no one was looking, allowed the tears to fall. Penelope was right—anywhere Helena went, people would treat her like some pariah to be feared—and if they feared Helena, then they feared the Stork. He followed her everywhere she went. There was no denying the reality that she was—and forever would be—a walking tragedy case.

Early morning when everyone was still asleep, Helena fetched a handful of Penelope's journal entries and scurried back to bed. She held up her first weather-stained piece of parchment against the light; a huge blotch of water had smeared the bottom three quarters of the page, rendering it almost entirely illegible. Still, Helena resolved to decipher what she could. After making herself comfortable in her bed, she began reading the first of many entries which was titled: _Who were the First Avians?_

_There is a general consensus amidst scholars that avian kind originated within the precincts of the Upper Realm during the Primeval Age, an estimated 100,000 years ago. It is speculated that much later, during the Age of Magic—a time when avian sorcerers opened passageways between the Upper and Lower Realms in the form of portals—an avian diaspora trickled down from the_

*Upper to the Lower Realm, promoting mass migration across both worlds. This would explain the diverse avian populations we see in Nadiir today.*

*However, apart from a few preserved historical paintings, murals, and vases, there is little available knowledge about the first avians who roamed the Upper Realm during the Primeval Age. Who were these people, and how did they live? Were they the first to wield the same abilities we later saw in the Age of Magic? Who was the first avian to have earned his wings, and how? I surmise this question invites the long-contested debate of who came first: the wigeon or the ave? Some state unequivocally that the wigeon came first and later acquired the magical ability to fly, which seems the most logical assumption, seeing as we are born wigeons first. Other groups—particularly of the more religious sectors—remain adamant that the avian came first, and that some aves eventually lost the ability to fly via divine punishment...but seeing as there's so little historical record of that time, we may never know for certain the nature of the origins of avian kind...*

"I fail to see what any of this has to do with the artifact," Helena said, after reading Penelope's intriguing thoughts aloud to both Jared and Noa. By then it was late morning, and they huddled around the transcribed piece of parchment, which Helena had laid down in the center of their cabin's dining table. Jared held a hand to his chin as he mulled over the excerpt. Noa leaned on one hip with a disinterested, even vexed expression on his face, tapping his fingernails impatiently on the table's wooden surface.

"All this talk about ancient civilizations and first avians is dreadful," he said, yawning obnoxiously, "but if you ask me, *the wigeon came first.*"

"Because you were there, obviously!" Helena quipped, with a hint of indignation.

"Don't got to time travel to know we're the blueprint," Noa replied, his finger stabbing himself in the chest at that last word. "Riddle me this, bird—are we born with wings first, or legs?"

"We don't know what happened and we never will," she said, visibly irritated. "So, let's stick to what we do know, thank you very much!"

"It's not a great deal, if you ask me."

"Penelope mentioned they were studying the origins of avian kind," Jared said after much thought. "What if whatever is inside this egg dates back to the time when the First Avians existed?"

Helena's eyes widened and fell upon the golden artifact, whose glamour seemed to light up the entire room. The idea that this egg was thousands of years old...her mind could not seem to fathom such a concept.

"We can only speculate at this point," Jared said, heaving a great sigh. "This excerpt is not much, but it's a start. We have to keep reading—there must be *something* in her writing that will tell us what's inside the artifact and how to open it. Good work, Helena," he said, before walking to his bunk and slinging a bulbous bag over his shoulder.

"Where are you headed?" Helena asked him curiously.

"I'm off to the Fighting's Nest for my first day of training."

Noa scowled bitterly. "I was hoping you'd outgrown the idea!"

Jared answered with a firm look. "I *will* learn to wield a sword, and there's nothing—and nobody—that can stop me."

"You hopeful fool," Noa said, watching him leave with a hint of a smile on his face.

"Why is he so bent on doing this all of a sudden?" Helena wondered.

"Isn't it obvious?" Noa said, turning to her. "If he can't help you get your wings back, he'll find some other way to prove his worth. He'll become the world's greatest swordsman, if he puts himself up to it. The man has always been like that...searching for different ways to prove himself. I'll admit, it's the one thing I admire most about him. If there's anyone in this world who deserves to earn his wings, it's him."

Helena opened her mouth just to close it again. It was in that moment when she realized that, just like Noa, she was rooting for Jared, too. She hoped with all her heart that by the end of this journey, Jared would have proved himself worthy and earned the wings he'd always dreamed of.

Anything else, and Helena would deem the world unjust.

# Chapter Sixteen

*I was only seventeen, reading a text I borrowed from the Bibliothek Nocturna called <u>The Magical Age of the Avian Realms: A Modern Lens on Magic and Mysticism.</u> This book described how the Age of Magic spanned a stunning 10,000 years, boasting hundreds of sorcerers, warlocks, and magical beasts at its peak. According to this text, sorcerers used their powerful magic to open gateways between the Upper and Lower Realms, allowing great intercultural exchange between both worlds. Dragons were alive and bountiful during this time, although they were sought vigorously for their scales, claws, and teeth, all of which were valuable ingredients in potions and brews. This high demand contributed to their endangerment and eventual extinction.*

*Towards the second half of the Age of Magic, we saw a gradual decline of the magical arts in the Upper Realm due to the onslaught of magical persecution. By the end of the Age of Magic, magic had dwindled and been reduced to obscure occupations such as witchcraft or divination, and dragons were believed to have become extinct. There are some, however, who speculate that some survived and withdrew into the Lower Realms, taking to remote climates and uninhabited regions away from the avian populace.*

*Dragons were keen, intelligent creatures with an eye for anything remotely lustrous or refined in taste. They were renowned hoarders, often sequestering themselves inside their dens and surrounding themselves with rare and luxurious material goods. Dragons only ever burrowed underground for two reasons: the first being to stash their precious finds, and the second being to lay their eggs, which they often left sitting upon a bed of burning coals...*

Helena read Penelope's words aloud to the only other person in the room—which was Noa; Jared was busy training at the Fighting's Nest and would not be back for some time. Noa sat languidly in a chair across the table from Helena, weary-eyed and indifferent. Listening to Penelope's inner monologue seemed the cruelest, and yet somehow drabbest, form of torture for the wigeon boy.

"Pay attention!" Helena snapped after catching him nodding off, and he woke with a start. "There might be something in this passage that could help us figure out how to open this egg…"

"Blah, blah, blah," he said, rolling his eyes. "This is all just pointless rambling, and I'll go mad if I have to listen to another second of it…"

Noa stood up abruptly from his chair, snatched the golden egg, and began knocking against its shell.

*Ding, ding, ding!*

"Would it kill you to be gentler?" Helena hissed. "It's still an egg, you know!"

Some reckless thought caused him to raise the egg up and over his head.

Helena flinched and drew a sharp gasp. "What are you doing?"

There was a wicked gleam in his eyes. "What do you say we save ourselves all this trouble and just smash this thing open?"

"Very funny, Noa. Put that down."

"I mean it, bird."

"I said put that down—*NOA, DON'T!*"

Helena's chair screeched against the wooden floor as she leapt to her feet, hand outstretched to stop him, but it was too late. The wigeon boy swung the golden egg downward with all his might.

Helena's heart might've given out at that very moment, were it not for the fact that the artifact met the floorboards with a dense *thud*. It rolled gently to and fro until it finally came to a stop, unharmed. Noa gazed open-mouthed at the golden egg, then at Helena's wide, round eyes, before doubling over in laughter.

"*Hahaha!*" He gasped for air, pointing a finger at her. "The look on yer face!"

Flustered, Helena stalked over and picked up the artifact with a huff. "I need you to take this seriously!"

His mirthful face became sober. "I am, bird! Now, we know that thing isn't as fragile as it looks. It won't take just any old thing to get it opened—there's got to be a cleverer way."

"Then what do you suggest?"

"I'll tell you, bird, and gladly, for I've heard countless tales about dragons from sailors from all parts of the Upper Realm. They were mighty, beastly things that coveted loot and treasure, and were only ever good for two things. The first is carnage. That only leaves one other thing: *fire.*"

Helena gazed down upon the heavy, golden artifact resting in the palm of her hands.

Her voice was but a whisper. "Fire?"

Noa quickly tore a piece of parchment away from one journal entry and held it in the mouth of a candle until it began to smoke. He then darted towards the hearth and dropped the flaming piece of parchment into the fireplace, where he fanned it with his breath until the light of a flame flickered. He beckoned Helena to kneel beside him, and she wordlessly obeyed. She waited patiently with the egg in her lap, watching the flames grow stronger, until they were hot and vibrant and warmed their glowing faces.

"Allow me," Noa said, taking the egg gently from her hands. Carefully, the wigeon boy placed the egg at the center of the fire, nestling it in between the smoking branches until he was sure it wouldn't tip over. A few sparks nicked Noa's wrists and arms, but he didn't even seem to notice them.

Together, they watched as the flames gradually engulfed the artifact. The flaming red tongues licked the curvatures of the egg almost seductively, and the sharp crackling of the fire filled the air. For many moments, the two wigeons huddled closely and leaned in towards the fire, entranced and waiting for some reaction from the egg...

And then, curiously, a quiver.

"Woah!" they exclaimed, eyes wide and bright like children.

"You saw that, too, didn't you?" Noa cried.

"Yes! You're brilliant, Noa! Of course it would like the heat," Helena said in wonder, taking a better seat on the floor in front of the fire and planting her butt on the wood beneath. Noa mirrored her, and for the next hour they sat there together, hoping to see another reaction like the one they had seen earlier. But it appeared that the movement was one of a kind.

"Maybe it was in our heads," Noa said sullenly.

"Not if we both saw it," Helena said, before shooting up to her feet and pacing the cabin. "We have to keep the fire burning. Maybe if we keep it going long enough, it'll open—"

"Hatch, more like," Noa said, with a lopsided grin.

They locked gazes. Noa's eyes were brimming with anticipation, while Helena's were filled with apprehension. She wondered just what resided inside this golden egg that the Stork and Penelope Duskmuth coveted so.

Only time would tell—that is, unless they found another way to pry it open first.

# CHAPTER SEVENTEEN

For the next several days, Helena and Noa worked tirelessly to keep the fire burning strongly with the egg in its midst, hauling in firewood for fuel and periodically fanning the flames with a wooden bellows to increase its intensity. They had yet had to see any movement or activity, however, like the kind they saw a few days prior, which disappointed them greatly.

Meanwhile, Jared was spending most of his free time training at the Fighting's Nest. It seemed to consume him to the point where the artifact might as well have been a slate of rotten wood, for all its failure to catch his interest; he'd return tired and worn out after a long day of training, glance curiously at the pair of wigeons sitting watchfully by the fire, brood for a bit, then fall into a heavy sleep.

"He seems troubled," Helena admitted one late morning to Noa as they made their way back from collecting that day's load of firewood. "He didn't even tell me how his training went yesterday, which makes me think it's not going well...."

"Couldn't care less about it," Noa huffed, adjusting the straps holding the hefty bundle of wood slung across his back. "He ought to know better than to sort himself with that feathered lot!"

"You're a jealous, jealous boy," she said, clutching the small load of wood in her arms even tighter.

"Get a kick out of using that word against me, don't you? What on earth makes you think I'm jealous?"

"You're bitter now that Jared's not spending all his time with you, because heavens forbid he find some fulfillment in his life without you nagging in his ear all the time!"

"Yeowch, bird. You've a serrated edge to those imaginary wings o'yers!"

Helena sighed. "I'm sorry. I know you're worried about your friend being alone in a training yard, surrounded by avian warriors...but not every person with feathers hates wigeons, you know. I didn't."

"That's hard to believe," he said wryly.

"Not at all. My own father is a wigeon."

"Is he, now?"

"Yes. So perhaps you should think twice before making assumptions about me—or other people, for that matter."

"You don't know half the life I've lived, bird! These thoughts come as an instinct. I stand before you *because* I make assumptions about people. Half the time, they're usually spot-on! It's handy in the grand scheme of things..."

"Now that you mention it, I don't think I know anything about your life." She frowned at the realization.

"It's best it stays that way."

Helena felt her heart squeeze. She could tell Noa had suffered much in the past and, in an effort to protect himself, had built walls around himself to keep others out. A strange thought floated into Helena's head, where she wondered how easy it would be to fly over those walls of his if she only had her wings...

"Caught any news of Phellis yet?" Noa said, cutting off Helena's train of thought.

She shook her head sadly. Helena badgered Rancipert about Phellis every morning in hopes that he might have some news of her, but it was to no avail. Despite scouring the entire region of the Mountains of Alazar, the scouts found no trace of Phellis or Penelope. The only positive thing to have come out of their search, it seemed, was the discovery of a friendly group of horses lingering along the southeastern precincts of the mountains. Underbelly, as it so happened, was now gorging himself on an endless supply of hay and sugar cubes here within the safe borders of Alazar!

Meanwhile, the courier had yet to return with any news of Yulix. Helena had many anxious thoughts surrounding his dangerous mission. Had he already received news of her tragedy and, in his devastation, decided he wanted nothing to do with her any longer?

"What can you tell me of this Yullox? Is he your lover?"

Noa's question came as a surprise as they clambered down a shady road. The sun was shining overhead in a clear blue sky, the fields of grass were ever so green. It seemed Helena and Noa were the only ones about to enjoy this bright, sunny day.

"His name is Yulix," she said nervously, "and he's my friend."

"Your eyes betray you," Noa said, huffing and puffing with the heavy wooden load on his back. "The way you say his name suggests something more."

Helena blushed beet-red and nearly fumbled her bundle of firewood. "I don't think it's any of your business!"

Noa gave a forced laugh. "Relax, bird! It's funny seeing you so worked up..."

They continued walking, carrying their heaps of firewood in silence, though Noa looked unsatisfied, even troubled, based on the way his thick brows knitted together in deep thought. They passed by a small, sagging well when Helena spoke up.

"Yulix and I grew up together," she said at last. "Our families hoped we would marry eventually..."

Noa's lips pressed in a tight line as sweat dripped down his face. "You say that as if it were history."

Helena's throat tightened. "He's now in line to become a knight of the King's Guard. He'll have to swear an oath of chastity eventually, so that rules out any chance of marriage. Even if he doesn't become one...after what's happened, he'll want nothing to do with me."

"Because yer a wigeon now?"

Helena said nothing, training her eyes on the gravel floor ahead and fighting the urge to cry.

It seemed Noa could not believe his ears. He grunted as he pulled taut the ropes over his shoulders, and the heap of firewood on his back groaned. "If wings are enough to turn a man, then he never felt a drop of love for you!"

"Yulix isn't like that," she defended, quickly brushing away the wetness from her cheeks. "He's noble and kind...I just don't know if I can face him after all that's happened. Or anybody back home, for that matter."

"Would you ever consider living out the rest of yer life down here?"

This question also took Helena by surprise!

"I don't think it's ever crossed my mind," she said honestly. "Forgive me, Noa, but your question gives me the impression that you're considering staying down here. Don't you *want* to return to Avalon?"

They came to a gradual stop on the road. Noa lingered several moments in silence, unsure how to answer. "You have a home to return to. I, on the other hand, have always lived my life jumping from one place to the next, never knowing where I'll end up...don't give me that look, bird. Pity is the last thing I want. I actually find this life quite fulfilling, in some respects. Now, I find myself in Nadiir, an entirely new world, largely unmapped and with countless possibilities of adventure—think about it! There's a whole set of seas just waiting to be explored!"

Helena must have been staring, for he turned a slight shade of red and gave a sheepish smile. "I know you'd rather be flying up in Paradise with yer flocker buddies, but...you'd be surprised how many things down here feel like flying."

She fixed her green eyes on him intently. "Oh, really? Like what?"

There was a fraction of a second in which his eyes flickered down to Helena's lips.

"Lots of things," he said casually, resuming his walk down the road. Helena followed. "Chugging a pint with friends, laughing until yer belly hurts...falling in love."

Again, that familiar Murmuration feeling sparked in her belly. "And I suppose you know a thing or two about love, do you?"

It was unlike Noa to give such a shy laugh. "I've met plenty of chicks in my life, yea...but most of them never paid attention to the dirty wigeon boy that was I. There was one, though, who I met in my younger years at Wigewalk...aye, a boy never forgets his first love. Theodora was her name—I called her Ted for short. We got along well, me and Ted..."

What was this strange sensation brewing in the pit of Helena's stomach? She felt sick, the palms of her hands became clammy, and her chest burned with something Helena felt rarely: *jealousy.*

"Was she pretty?" she couldn't help but ask.

"Hideous, that one!" he said, bursting into laughter, and Helena felt a little better. "I cut ties with her, eventually. Poor thing was heartbroken when I told her I wanted nothing more to do with her."

"Why did you end things with her?" she asked brusquely.

His answer was nonchalant, but the hurt in his eyes was clear as day when he said—

"The chick earned her wings."

He saw the utter disbelief in Helena's face and laughed. "Spare me the eyes, bird!"

"Well, so much for wings not turning a man!" she said disapprovingly.

He held up his hands defensively. "I'm sorry—it was fate! I just can't see myself with a flocker. It's a recipe for heartbreak."

"How so?" Helena asked, unsure why she felt the burning need to hear his response. She knew, however, given the way his dark brown eyes looked at her with sad longing, that she would not like the answer to this question.

"They always fly away and never return."

There was little reason for this conversation to have upset Helena as drastically as it did. For one thing, she was a *wigeon,* so this harsh dealbreaker of Noa's didn't technically apply to her—not that she cared! When had she ever been preoccupied with the preferences of this spiteful wigeon boy? She had only known him for a few months, and rarely did they find each other in a state that wasn't some form of grating disagreement. But the notion that Noa preferred a woman without wings troubled Helena more than she dared to admit. She became consumed by the thought that her past self—a striking image of vitality and freedom that she herself esteemed greatly—would not have been enough for him. Then, there was a second thought, an inane one. More of a whisper in the back of her mind than anything else, really—the quixotic belief that Helena would get her wings back one day...and that future version of herself would still never measure up for him.

These thoughts were absurd—undignified, even, by Helena's standards, and she was grateful they ended the moment a third party came onto the scene. A hairless wigeon man with threadbare clothing sprang from out of the tree line and crashed against Noa; they both tumbled to the ground and Noa's firewood fell with a clatter. Outraged, Noa snatched the man by the collar of his shirt and gave him a violent shake.

"Watch where yer going!" he gnashed.

The man observed at once that Noa, too, was a wigeon, and pleaded, "Please, brother! A couple guards caught me stealing a loaf for my family...I had no choice—we got nothing on the table! I gave it back, you see, but they're still after me—you must help me!"

Helena dropped everything she was carrying and inched her way around the trees in the direction from whence he came. She spotted three distant figures in the sky.

"Three aves inbound," she relayed back to Noa, who seemed torn between helping the man or sending him off to fend for himself. In a split-second decision, Noa grabbed him harshly by the neck and dragged him over to a nearby well—then hurled him over its sagging brick wall and into the deep, watery pit. There was a distant splash.

Noa leaned in and called out to him, "You'd best not make a sound, or else they'll throw you into something worse!"

By the time the three guards came swooping over the tree line, Helena and Noa had moved to a tree a little distance from the well and begun re-collecting their firewood. The small flock made a sharp, descending U-turn before coming to a running landing on the grass several yards ahead of the pair—though one slipped on a wet patch of grass and fell on his butt. Noa stifled a laugh. The guard in the middle paid no mind to his foolish friend. He was the shortest of the three, with a dark complexion and a heavy stare. His wings were as stout as he was, yet he displayed them proudly, stretching them out so that one wing even smacked his other friend on the head, which neither bothered to acknowledge. He regarded Helena and Noa coldly as he approached.

"We're looking for someone," he announced, eyeing them suspiciously. "A wigeon who we caught stealing from a hardworking avian citizen. He's bald, with rotting clothes. You see anything of the sort?"

Noa could not hide his disdain for the avian men when he answered, "Nothing that matters to the likes of you."

*Please,* Helena wanted to shout at Noa. *Please don't start. Not now.*

The guard heard his response and gave a dry chuckle. His gloved hand dropped to the leather grip of his sword, which hung at his belt. He circled around Noa and ran a scrutinizing eye over his wingless body.

"You know, it's best to take the vermin off these streets," he said cooly. His wings carelessly brushed against Noa's shoulders, which wasn't the least bit enjoyable for the wigeon boy. "The community becomes cleaner...and *safer.*"

"If we saw something, we would've told you," Helena said coldly.

He then directed his attention to her. His feathers puffed curiously as his eyes traced the navy-blue sleeves of her utilitarian suit poking out from beneath her wigeon shirt. He must have identified her immediately as an Avalonian, for he now regarded her with deep interest.

"Where are my manners? Allow me to introduce myself! My name is Timuth Greene, and you...you must be Eleanor!" He then shook his head. "No, Helena...Helena Nightingill."

"*Nightingale,*" she emphasized.

"You're quite the talk of the kingdom," he continued, overlooking her correction. He circled her this time, a hand on his chin as he examined her closely. "You know, given the way they speak about you Avalonians, one might think pure silver courses through those veins. Now that one finally stands before me, though, I must admit I am a bit underwhelmed."

Helena felt anger bubble in her stomach.

"They also claim you lost your wings to the Stork," he said, as casually as one would bring up the weather.

"You don't seem all too convinced," Helena said pleasantly, before drawing in a sudden breath—the two other guards had made their way over to the well and leaned their heads over to examine its contents. It must have been dark inside, for they squinted hard. After throwing a couple stray bricks down the well, they quickly lost interest in it and returned to Timuth's side like the loyal dogs they were.

"People will say anything these days to get their five seconds of fame," he said with an air of disinterest. "Well! I'm afraid there's only a few hours left to find that rat until the sun sets. Then he'll be fresh meat for the Krows. We'll be going, now..."

His friends took off into the sky one by one. Before Timuth followed, he threw one last look over his shoulder and said, "Oh, and if we find out the two of you were lying to protect that wigeon, we'll make sure to tar you both alongside that lowlife. So long!"

Helena and Noa watched with hardened faces as the three figures in the sky turned into specks and disappeared.

When the coast was clear, they helped the wigeon man climb out of the well with a rope, and he toppled onto the grass soaking wet. As he did, a handful of silver and copper coins spilled from his pockets. Noa grabbed the man by a handful of his shirt and forced him to meet his eye.

"Yer a pickpocket!" Noa hissed. He shook the man with ire and shoved him to the ground. "We stuck our necks out for the likes of you!"

The man looked up at the wigeon boy and blubbered on his knees. "Please! Have mercy! You've no idea what they would've done to me—"

Noa grimaced. "We've plenty idea, now..."

"He threatened to tar us—as in tar and feather?" Helena asked hesitantly.

"Aye. Back at Wigewalk, if a flocker drew too much attention to himself, they'd snatch him in the middle of the night, pluck out his feathers one by one, and pour hot tar all over his body before dousing him in his own feathers. Seems it's not that different here in Nadiir..."

Helena's keen eyes lingered on Noa, watching as his face flashed with what she perceived as guilt. She wondered if he had ever partaken in such a barbaric form of torture. He certainly disliked avians enough...Helena shook the gruesome image out of her head.

The wigeon man took a better look at Helena, and his eyes widened.

"H-Helena Nightingale!" he stuttered.

Helena's face flushed. "You've heard of me?"

"Have I! You're the Woman Made Wigeon!"

Helena's jaw fell slightly open. She was uncertain how to react or feel towards this name...

"Dare I say it, you will be the most famous wigeon of us all! Everyone will wish to meet you—and I shall live to tell the tale of this encounter! Of your benignity and of your graciousness!"

"Off you go!" Noa muttered, taking him by the shoulder and leading him away, half shoving him in the process. The wigeon man tottered away, arms swinging every which way as he looked over his shoulder towards Helena.

"My name is Abernam," he blathered to Noa. "You're a clever boy! Lean for your age, and likely a good runner. You'd make a perfect addition to our guild. We're all wigeons, you see—"

There was the slightest hesitation in Noa's step when he heard this detail, but with a grunt, he sent the man on his way.

"Yea, yea, just keep this between us," Noa called after him. "Last thing we need is that dumb flocker to know we were the ones who lent you a hand!"

"As you wish! So long, Miss Nightingale," Abernam shouted, waving his arm at her as he grew smaller and smaller further up the causeway. "I repeat—if either of you ever finds yourselves in need, do not hesitate to ask me for help. After all, us wigeons need to stick together!"

Noa stared after him, engrossed in thought. "A wigeon's guild, he said?"

"Full of pickpockets like him, no doubt," Helena said, paying careful attention to his expression. "Don't bother, Noa. He might've gotten off scot-free today, but he was lucky. Whatever he does for a living—it can't reap anything good in the long run."

Noa did not respond, but his eyes lingered on the wigeon as he disappeared into the treeline. Night would soon fall. *Food for the Krows,* Helena thought uneasily, before they made their way home.

# Chapter Eighteen

There came a point, after countless hours spent sitting by the fire and staring directly into its flames until her eyes became sore, when Helena had nearly given up hope they would ever see the egg move again. Fed up, she took a pair of iron tongs, opened them wide, and snatched a firm grip on the golden artifact to remove it. Sparks flew and embers fluttered out of the fireplace as she eased it out of the flames, and then she froze. Angling it so that she could examine its rounder end, Helena saw just the *faintest crack along its shell.*

It was a milestone of grand proportions, to be sure, considering how much she and Noa had toiled to maintain the fire, and the small payoff their efforts had earned them so far. Still, it had taken *an entire week* for a mere hairline fracture to develop! How long would it take for the mighty thing to crack itself wide open? At this rate, it would be months before they saw any significant change…Helena was not too happy about this, but decided that until a better solution came along, their best bet was to keep the fire burning strongly and maintain a close eye on the egg's progress.

Later that day, Helena paid Jared a visit at the Fighting's Nest. She dragged Noa along, who sulked the entire way there. It was a busy day at the nest; the fields were crowded with tents, soldiers, and blacksmiths. Several flocks soared through the vast and open airspace in great formations. Helena spotted a giant landing strip whose sandy floor was cratered by constant take-offs and landings. In one section, a dozen winged archers practiced steadying themselves in midair and carefully aiming their bows before letting their arrows fly. Most hit their targets in the bullseye—a feat that was far more difficult than one would think. The air stunk with sweat and feather musk as Helena and Noa bustled their way through the nest, dodging trampling warriors and aves who swooped in lowly from above.

Further away was a grassier area where soldiers sparred in midair with wooden swords. Sticks rained from the sky, often hitting unsuspecting victims on the ground. Two sets of wooden stands faced the arena so that other aves could gather to watch the ongoing duels. *Clack, clack, clack!* The collision of wooden swords sounded as one dueling pair maneuvered around in the air, exerting great energy in thrusting their wings and exchanging blows, all the while fanning the audience below with refreshing gusts of wind. Helena and Noa sat along these stands, with Helena paying close attention to their airborne techniques while Noa's head nodded as he dozed off. Once the duel ended, they touched down to make room for the next dueling pair.

Rancipert was dressed from head to toe in light leather gear, his normal elastic curls sagging with sweat. He took a wooden stick and tossed it over into a crowd of aves nearby. A brown hand reached out and caught the weapon in midair.

"Jared! You and Pekk are up next."

Jared stepped out from the crowd, dressed in taffy trousers and a loose shirt whose neckline was stained with sweat. Helena patted Noa's shoulder at the sight of their friend, drawing him out of his snooze-fest, and they watched with great interest. Jared's opponent, Pekk, was a short young man. Even his wings seemed twice his own size—and mighty things they were, pumping ever so slightly to create a rousing gust of wind that fanned the arena. As it was a central rule of swordsmanship to fight on equal footing against your opponent, the duel was set to take place on the ground.

Pekk initiated the match, striding towards Jared with a healthy strike towards the shoulder. Jared was quick to raise his sword and parry the strong blow, and the *clack* rang in Helena's ears. Again, the ave attacked, this time with a combination of three consecutive blows. One, two, three times Jared blocked them; he continued circling Pekk with his sword raised, moving one foot carefully over the other.

Jared was what they termed a *fledgling* at the Fighting's Nest, considering he was still rather new to the art of combat. Still, anyone could see the budding spirit of a quick-witted fighter. Jared skillfully used his physical shortcoming as a wigeon to his utmost advantage out in the training yard, for he was naturally gifted with light feet—a handy asset to have as a sword fighter going up against larger, more cumbersome opponents with wings. Leaping quickly from one foot to the other, Jared drove his opponent backwards with several agile strikes, until he finally landed a hard blow to the ave's ribs. In a flash, he spun forwards, ramming into his opponent and disarming him with a tough blow to the elbow. The ave's wooden sword was sent flying in midair. *Oooh,* the crowd murmured.

"The wigeon's not half bad," one ave commented.

"I told you, the boy's a natural!" Rancipert said aloud.

"Was that a sword fight, or a courting dance?" a condescending voice sounded, and a ripple of snickers coursed through the stands. "All the wigeon needs is some silks and a wig, and Pekk will have found himself a frisky mate!"

It was difficult to forget the name of the person who had threatened to burn your skin off with hot, molten tar. Timuth Greene had a careless air about him, the way he and his wings casually took up too much space. He sat with his peers at the far end of the stands, jeering and stomping their feet obnoxiously against the wooden floorboards. Helena's seat rattled and jolted at the sudden commotion. Timuth and his friends put their arms around each other and sung with all their might:

"*Wally Wigeon went a-stomp! His wings were gone, his head done wrong! Womp, womp, womp!*"

Noa grew visibly angrier as their laughter grew more obnoxious. Helena tried to ignore them, but it was difficult to act unfazed when the entire grandstand was threatening to collapse. Jared became increasingly aware of the racket sounding off in the stands, and the distraction quickly cost him his second match against Pekk.

"*Wally Wigeon went a-flop! His heart was rot, his bones were taut! Womp, womp, womp!*"

"Carry on, Jared," Rancipert ordered. He was clearly annoyed by the disruption but saw no use in intervening. After taking a deep breath and wiping the sweat off his brow, Jared continued his next bout with Pekk. Eventually, Jared landed the winning strike, prompting another onslaught of applause.

"Let's see how natural the fledgling is against a better opponent," Timuth sounded. He stepped out from his circle of peers and dashed to pick up a fallen wooden sword. "One who doesn't hold back!"

*This can't be good*, Helena thought.

"The boy's had enough training for today," Rancipert said brusquely, after Timuth entered the fighting pit.

"No," Jared said, lifting his weapon. "I can do it."

Timuth and Jared's eyes met. With a dirty smirk, Timuth spat off to the side and took his stance, waiting for Jared to make the first move.

Helena bit her nails, anxious for Jared. In combat, an avian could use their wings to briefly stun their opponent and gain the upper hand...but Pekk had not used his wings as a sign of respect for the wigeon boy. Helena knew that Timuth would be incapable of demonstrating such sportsmanship.

Jared started with a powerful overhand strike, but the ave caught it with his own wooden blade. For a moment, their blades remained locked in a cross, then Timuth shoved Jared aggressively, sending him reeling back. Raising his sword again, Jared took a deep breath and collected himself. With a fearsome cry, Timuth leapt into the air, spreading his wings menacingly before jabbing his sword at Jared's chest. Jared, however, was not intimidated by such a stunt; he nimbly leapt back and countered Timuth's strike with a strong underhand swipe that nearly sent Timuth's sword flying.

*Clack, clack, clack!* The harsh sound rattled in Helena's ears as Timuth bore down on his wigeon opponent from four feet in the air. Helena would've deemed it unfair, but even in the air Timuth could not seem to gain any real advantage over Jared, who kept nimbly evading his attacks. Timuth had no choice but to land. With the playing field now leveled, Jared pressed his weight forwards and drove Timuth closer and closer towards the edge of the arena. For a fleeting moment, panic flashed on the ave's face. He then caught one of Jared's strikes, brought his left wing over his shoulder and smacked Jared on the side of his head, sending him staggering one way.

*Oooh,* the crowd sounded.

"Foul blow!" Noa shouted nastily.

Timuth jabbed the blunt tip of his wooden sword into Jared's chest. He then whipped him on the side of his leg and forced Jared into a painful curtsy, all before disarming him with a kick to his wrist.

"That's enough. Jared, step on out!" ordered Rancipert.

But Jared wiped the sweat from his face and called, "Again!"

The dueling pair garnered a bigger crowd as people watched with growing interest. Jared advanced again towards his opponent with frightening determination, channeling his strength behind each blow of his sword. At first, Timuth blocked Jared's strikes with a smirk on his face. But Jared kept gathering momentum, driving the ave further and further backwards with every grunt and strike. In a panic, the ave swiped blindly for a hit to the throat, but Jared ducked it and countered with a bruising strike to the ribs, earning a grunt from Timuth. Jared, fueled by adrenaline, launched into a three-move combination: a strike behind the knee, a disarming smack on the forearm, and a powerful slash to the head—only the final blow never came, stopping just at the neck. Timuth had raised his arms in surrender.

A thunderous applause sounded. Jared lowered his weapon and offered his hand in an act of sportsmanship. Timuth, however, used the rigid bend of his wing to strike Jared directly in the face. A loud *crack* sounded. Timuth then spun lowly on his heel, bringing both wings around and sweeping Jared's feet out from under him. He fell to the ground with a heavy grunt. While he lay there, Timuth sauntered back to his friends, who greeted him with cheers and pats on the back.

When all this was over, Jared sulked back to the stands with a broken nose and battered dignity.

"You're hurt!" Helena cried, hastening to dab his bloody nose with a spare cloth. But he brushed her off.

"That was a real pissy sight to see," Noa said to him, fuming from the ears. "Learnt yer lesson, now, have you?"

"He's humiliated enough as it is without your petty remarks!" Helena snapped in response.

"Good! Maybe now he'll know better than to try something like this again!"

"Today, I fall," Jared said lowly, a steely sheen to his eyes. "Tomorrow, I rise all the same."

High on hubris and emboldened by his crowd of loyalists, Timuth set his sights upon the wigeon group. He spotted Helena and raised a taunting finger at her.

"Look! The woman who cried wigeon!"

Laughter ensued, and Helena's cheeks reddened as all eyes now fell on her.

Timuth flared his short wings. He looked expectantly to his audience, arms outstretched. "Does anyone here actually buy it? Certainly, I don't!"

"I don't care what you believe," Helena said, rising to her feet and struggling to keep her voice level.

"I'll tell you, anyway…" He was now in such close proximity to her that the musk of his wings reached her nose. Helena wagered it had been at least a week since he'd last preened them. "I think you're a sorry ol' wigeon who's lying for attention."

"Why would I lie about something like that?" she said as blood rushed to her head.

"Because your kind has nothing better to do than to make up stories to try to scare us real folk—"

"*Real folk?*"

"People with *mirages*. People with *souls*—"

"*I have a soul*—"

"Then why couldn't you earn your wings?"

"I earned them," she asserted, pounding her own chest. "I earned my wings, and I don't need to prove it to anyone—especially you!"

"I'll take your word for it, wigeon. The thing about your kind is that what you lack in feathers, you make up for in low self-esteem. You're bitter that the world goes on without you, so you'd say anything if it meant turning a couple of heads!"

Helena could not help the burst of laughter that erupted from her. "Men like you think you're so much better because you've got wings! Well, let me tell you something: I've seen your technique in the air, and in my day, I would've flown circles around you so fast, you'd be tossed around like a leaf!"

"That's rich, coming from a *filthy wigeon—*"

Noa came barreling past Helena with a wrathful cry and a tight fist, the latter of which he brought down upon the face of the ave who had slighted her. The two fell to the ground and wrestled with one another, howling in rage as the crowds erupted in a mixture of cheers and boos. Feathers rained about the place, and when Rancipert and Jared finally managed to pull them apart, Timuth was bleeding from the nose, and Noa was shouting, *"Say that to her again! I dare you!"*

*"YOU'LL PAY FOR THAT! ALL OF YOU!"* Timuth roared as his friends carried him off.

The three wigeons walked home in a simmering silence that afternoon. Helena could see Noa's bruised fist clenching and unclenching as he walked. His face had fallen back into that familiar, perpetual state of discontent, brooding with unresolved anger. Helena wanted to say something—perhaps thank him for coming to her defense—but her mind was still reeling from the incident, and somehow it felt wiser to not say anything at all.

"You gave him the exact reaction he wanted," Jared muttered to Noa afterwards. "You shouldn't have."

The wigeon boy kept his sights on the ground. "I didn't do it for you," he gritted through his teeth.

Helena held her chin high, despite the shame and indignation threatening to consume her from within. On their way home, they spotted a furtive figure lurking in an alleyway by the market square. A black hood concealed most of his face, though even Helena recognized the hunched and reclusive frame of Abernam. He lowered his hood to acknowledge the wigeon group with a stiff nod, and Noa returned the gesture. Helena recognized the same restless, wayward gleam in Abernam's eyes that she often saw in Noa's. It was a look that said, *wigeons must stick together*—and now, more than ever, that phrase seemed to be calling out to her friend Noa.

# CHAPTER NINETEEN

Over the next few weeks in which she spent working to both decipher Penelope's writings and crack open the golden egg, Helena experienced a predicament in which her nights grew gradually infested with nightmares. She often dreamed of Penelope Duskmuth's beady eyes; they would peer up at her through the crack of a den before the sun cast its beaming rays upon them, and they shriveled like raisins. Other times—more often than she would've preferred—Helena dreamt of the Stork. He would loom over her bed like an ominous shadow and open his mouth to speak, but worms and snakes would fall out instead. Her mother also would occasionally visit her dreams. Those were the better nights. She would leave as unexpectedly as she came, however. One particular night was the worst, when Helena dreamt of her mirage fluttering around a dark and eerie room, flickering like a dying light. There was a flash of shadow, and a hand caught the bird in midair. It belonged to the Stork, and he gave her a sinister grin as he spoke in a voice that was not his own.

"The Fallen Rise," he intoned, before his hand curled tighter into a fist, crushing the delicate white body beneath. Blood and feathers flew everywhere.

Helena woke in hysterics that night. She thrashed against her bed, pillows and blankets flying everywhere. *Leave me alone*, she would cry, wishing for an end to the torment. It would not come. Even in her dreams, Helena could not escape his keen, dark eyes, which were a haunting reminder of the night she lost everything.

Then, as Helena felt her world crumbling, two strong arms wrapped themselves around her.

"It's just a dream, bird," a gentle voice cooed, pulling her closer into his chest. "He can't hurt you here. Not on my watch."

No longer able to keep herself together, Helena wept in Noa's arms. Her outbursts had also snagged Jared out of his own dreams, as he had reached for his sword and leapt to his feet, ready to face whatever danger had posed to him and his friends...but when he saw that it was a false alarm, and that Noa had fled to Helena's side, he carefully retreated to bed.

"I dreamt about it," she confessed to Noa amidst tears. "My mirage. I...I think it's dead..."

"How can you be certain?"

"It's been so long..."

"I think you'd know if it was," he said gently. His chin rested on her head as she lay curled against his chest. This tamer side of him came unexpectedly, like a soft rise in tide. "I imagine it'd be like losing a loved one...you'd know it in yer heart."

They dwelled in silence, listening to the occasional crack of the fire. As she lay pressed against him, Helena could hear the waltz of Noa's strange heart. It soothed her, and she became more and more sleepy...

"How'd you earn it, yer mirage?" he asked quietly, breaking the silence and drawing Helena out of her doze.

They were the only ones awake at this hour. The question came across as rather unexpected and...intimate.

"With everything that's happened, I'm not sure if I can tell the story anymore. It's almost painful recalling it..." she said, drifting further into a deep sleep...

Noa understood and did not press on the subject any further, though it was plain as day that he was dying to know this small, yet significant piece of information about her life. Some part of Helena, too, yearned to share the fondest memory of her childhood with this captivating boy, but she was not ready. Not yet. Who knew if she ever would be?

Nevertheless, Noa held Helena until she fell sleep. Afterwards, she had no idea if he left as soon as she did, or if he held her the entire night...

Helena woke up the next morning alone in her bed. The cabin was stuffy, and the fire burned faintly with the egg in its midst. Another batch of wood would be soon needed to keep the fire burning strongly, but since Noa and Jared were nowhere to be found, she would have to fetch it alone. So, she stumbled off into the nearby forest to collect rotten wood and branches to lug back to the cabin.

About an hour later, Helena was making her way back from the forest with a heavy bundle of firewood slung across her back, when news of the courier's return reached her ears. She hurried to the Central Square, where a large crowd had gathered to watch the young courier kneeling before King Hyrax. The taxing journey had left his sandy hair shaggy and unkempt; grime and dirt had darkened his fair complexion, and his ruffled white wings quaked from exhaustion.

"I come bearing news of Ser Ulyxes Cazador!" he declared in a high voice.

King Hyrax said, "Rise, boy. Tell me, what news of your journey?"

The courier recounted his long and arduous journey before the king and his people:

After a long, arduous journey towards Krow's Foot, the courier located Yulix and his squadron on the sixteenth day of his travels, just hours before they commenced their high-stakes mission. They were settled upon a reliable vantage point that allowed them full surveillance of the Eye of Nadiir, which was guarded heavily by Nevarians in the sky. They planned to launch themselves headfirst towards the Eye during the day, when the Krows went into hiding. However, members of the *Fallen Coven* guarded the portal during this period—fighting and bloodshed were inevitable. Yulix and his men fought bravely against the fallen avians...but only three of them, including Yulix, surpassed them and plunged themselves into the Eye of Nadiir.

After witnessing this, the courier then journeyed back, with the Nevarians on high alert throughout the entire region. Somewhere along the way, a flock of Nevarians caught sight of the messenger and pursued him, delaying his return—just as Helena had surmised. But after enduring harsh weather and escaping the hands of the enemy, the courier had successfully made his way back to stand before the King of Alazar.

"And what had he to say concerning the claims of Helena Nightingale?" the King demanded.

Helena held her breath as she listened.

The courier hesitated. "Ser Ulyxes Cazador found the news troubling, to be sure, and said that rumors of such significance warranted an audience before the Avalonian King's Royal Court. He implores you, King Hyrax, to exercise restraint against the claimant until his swift return, whereupon he may confirm the rumors for himself."

A part of Helena wanted to take the courier by the shoulders and rattle him until he spewed out every last detail of his interaction with Yulix. What was his instinctual reaction? What were the first words that came out of his mouth? Doubtless he found the rumors absurd and worthy of dismissal—that he had used the word *claimant* meant that Yulix suspected an imposter, but perhaps the slim hope of seeing his friend alive again spurred him to urge restraint from King Hyrax. *I must see for myself.* Helena could hear his stoic words as clear as day in her head.

"Very well," the king said gruffly. "We shall await the return of Ser Ulyxes Cazador and see what his king has to say about these recent events."

"That is not all, Your Grace!" the courier said. "Along my journey, I overheard many conversations of aves and wigeons alike—and there is widespread talk of war! The Nevarians are arming themselves as we speak, and planning an excursion northwards to raid and pillage any town or village that opposes them. Though the date of their attack remains uncertain, there can be no doubt—the Nevarians are coming!"

Panic struck the crowds at this unexpected news. Helena, however, was not at all surprised; she knew the true reason behind the Nevarians' sudden rise in military activity: the Stork had finally realized that Helena abandoned her mission and took off with the artifact. Now, he was coming to take it back.

The king pounded his staff against the ground, and at once all the commotion fell to a still hush.

"Citizens of Alazar! Do not fear! We will bolster our defenses, train every man and woman capable of fighting, and the day in which the Black Plague decides to set foot on our sovereign land, we will be ready. Prepare yourselves! *For war quickly approaches.*"

From this sentence swelled an uproar, both a mix of fear and anticipation for what was to come. A familiar feeling of dread pooled in Helena's stomach, and her lower back ached—she had even forgotten she was sustaining a heavy load of firewood on her back.

It was imperative that they get the artifact opened as soon as possible.

# Chapter Twenty

T he next day, Helena took a long, tired look at the mess of pages before her and heaved a deep sigh; most of Penelope's writing was pure academic or scientific jargon—avian civilizations and their diverse physiological traits...genetic variation pertaining to wing color...varying diameters of feather shafts across populations...*yawn.*

She recalled Penelope's warning: *"It is imperative that the artifact never fall into the hands of the Stork, for if it did, it would be one step closer to making the Nevarians more dangerous, and more powerful, than ever before!"*

What resided within this egg that would enable just that? Not a single piece of Penelope's writing so far had alluded to Nevarians or their schemes for world domination! If there was any hope of finding out, Helena had to continue her tedious reading, but she was nearly fed up with the entire process...

Little did Helena know, however, as she sat alone in the cabin and began to read a new page of Penelope's journal, that this one passage would be her biggest discovery since she first found a crack in the egg's shell...

*I will admit some part of me rejoiced at the thought of flying down to Nadiir and reuniting with our lost and forgotten cousins of the night—the Nevarians. After all, we both suffer at the hands of the same curse. Perhaps, I thought foolishly, we would find some consolation in each other's plights, and together we would set aside our differences and overcome this cursed fate we share. I was wrong. Nevarians and Nocturnal avians will never get along. Even though we are both caught in the same never-ending race against the sun, the discrepancy between us lies in how we perceive our very existence: Nevarians believe that, as punishment for the deeds of their forefather, this curse was unfairly thrust upon them. My people, on the other hand, view it as a blessing, wholeheartedly insisting that living in constant refuge from the sun harbors a divine purpose—a foolish notion, indeed! There could be no benign meaning behind such a wretched way of life...in that way, I suppose I empathize with our Nevarian cousins—but even they harbor the same sentiment that us Nocturnal avians are inherently nightly, and that we cannot alter what is otherwise an accessory for our lifestyle. In other words, they believe that their curse was made to be broken—while we were simply made this way.*

Helena set the piece of parchment down as she tried to process what she had just read. *A curse,* she thought, *of course.* Nothing else could have barred Nevarians and Nocturnals from stepping out into daylight. That was clear as day. Still, this produced more questions than it answered:

If indeed it was the case that they suffered under the same curse, why did both groups have such starkly different reactions to sun exposure? Nocturnals endured a slow, painful death in which sunlight poisoning consumed their bodies. Nevarians, on the other hand, reactively combusted upon exposure, totally bursting into flames and suffering a quick death—or at least, that was what Penelope claimed, as Helena was forced to admit that she had yet to see either outcome take place. This did not, however, negate the fact that their fates remained the same: both died horrible, painful deaths at the hands of the sun. The only other conclusion, it seemed, was that both groups suffered from different variants of the same curse—though on such matters, Helena had little knowledge or authority to confirm this theory...

Then, Helena mulled tirelessly over one sentence: *Nevarians believe that, as punishment for the deeds of their forefather, this curse was thrust upon them.* What exactly was Penelope alluding to? The only thing Helena really knew about the Nevarians was that they were the direct descendants of a long line of banished Avalonians...

Helena drew a sharp gasp. "Of course! The Fallen Avian! He was the first avian exiled from Avalon and is said to be a direct ancestor of the Nevarians. Perhaps there's more to the tale that could give me greater insight. I need to find out more about it...maybe I could ask around the kingdom..."

*No,* she thought. People would start to question her interest in such dark tales. But there had to be *someone* out there who knew more about it, or who could at least point Helena in the right direction...

Then, an idea alighted upon Helena.

She put on a thick cloak, pulled its large hood over her face, and tucked the golden egg neatly into its bed of flames before making her way down to the heart of Alazar. After a great deal of walking, she wandered into an alienated, slovenly neighborhood—a place where no ave dared venture into. A handful of barefoot wigeon boys trampled past Helena, kicking a ball back and forth between themselves. Another wigeon man, surly-looking and fat, wandered into a small tavern with the green banner of a fist bearing a rock. The Wigeon's Guild.

Several heads turned towards Helena at the sound of her entrance. The air stunk of cigars, mead, and sweat. A trio of busty stewardesses eyed the young girl up and down as she made her way through the dim tavern, scanning the room for one specific person...Ah! There he was, sitting amidst a flock of wigeons who were gathered around a table and drinking without a care in the world. Helena recognized his hunched posture and shining bald head.

"Abernam," she hissed from underneath her large hood.

He squinted up at her before his eyes nearly bulged out of his head.

"Miss Nightingale, what a surprise to see you here at this late hour! Why, this is no place for a young girl such as yourself! Were you perhaps hoping to get ahold of Noa? He was here not long ago...headstrong, that boy is—always wanting things to go his way..."

Helena's face hardened. So that's what Noa was up to—he was peeking around the Wigeon's Guild, flirting with one of the stewardesses, no doubt. She did not like it one bit, but decided it was not worth questioning at the moment.

"No, I'm not here for him. I need to speak with you in private."

The two of them left the tavern and went out into a small, abandoned alley where no one would be listening.

"What does the Nightingale require?"

"You told me that if Noa and I ever found ourselves in need of help, we could count on you. Well, I need help with just this one thing; do it, and you can consider your debt paid."

"If it is in my power, I will do so gladly."

Helena lowered her voice before leaning towards him and whispering, "I need your help in understanding the enemy."

His expression hardened. "Is someone pestering you, Miss Nightingale? I can surely take care of it—"

"No," she answered quickly. She wondered what he meant by *take care of it.* "I seek information, is all. About a particular group of people that only come out at night."

Abernam's brows sunk into deep thought before a look of understanding fell upon him. "You speak of the Nadiirian Krows."

"Yes. I wish to learn more about them—how and why they came to be. It's important, Abernam—I've no one else to turn to. Tell me, what do you know of the Fallen Avian?"

A look of dark interest flashed across his eyes. "Not much, I'm afraid …but if you wish to know more about the topic of which you speak, I can point you in the right direction."

"Very well," she said.

The man looked over his shoulders—first left, then right, in case anyone was eavesdropping on their conversation—before speaking. "Myths and legends are untrustworthy because they become washed out with time. If you truly wish to learn about the Fallen Avian, there is no better way than to get it straight from the source—a Nevarian, who will have learned their creed word for word, like the parrots they are."

*"You mean I should speak with a Nevarian myself?"*

He nodded eagerly. "Not just any Nevarian. They call him the Scarekrow. It is said that his own people spurned him and cast him out into exile when he was but a boy. He is likely the only one who can provide you with the information that you seek. Follow the running river across the valley until you reach Lake Eastpoint, then head northeast along the banks until you reach the deep woodlands, and keep going until you see a spiderweb. Follow the webs, and you will find him. Go only at night."

"Abernam," she said, feeling her palms grow hot and clammy, "I'm not sure this is such a good idea…"

"Heed me carefully, Miss Nightingale. When you go to meet him, you must repeat this singular phrase: *Our kingdom is the earth.* Do this, and no harm will come to you."

"Thank you," Helena said, feeling her heart quicken.

"It is nothing, Miss Nightingale. After all, us wigeons need to stick together."

That night, the half-moon's cobalt rays streamed through the dark clouds as Helena followed the central river, which was speckled with shimmering lights from the starlit sky above. Every so often, Helena looked over each of her shoulders before adjusting her hood and continuing her way down to Lake Eastpoint. Its waters were tame at this hour, gently lapping against the shore; for a moment, Helena felt a yearning to fly just over its surface, drag a wing across the water, and feel the cool water spray against her skin…

*Nothing good ever happens after dark.* The Stork's voice echoed in her mind as she made her way along the bank and into the dark and eerie woodlands. Under the guise of the night, the trunks of the trees seemed to throw ugly grimaces at her.

Helena spotted her first cobweb nestled high above within the branches of a dark cedar tree; a spider the size of her fist reposed furtively within it. The web had been made with breathtaking composition: lacy white threads overlaid the tree branches like fine, translucent tapestry, and drops of moisture gathered along the intricacies of their designs like constellations just waiting to be deciphered. Eight beady black eyes stared back at her. Driven more by fear than by judgment, Helena hurried along until she spotted another web of similar caliber a good distance away, and continued in that direction.

Helena now approached one of the northeastern mountains, teetering along the borders of the great valley. She continued along these unfamiliar grounds with a growing sense of uneasiness and nearly tripped as a frightening notion struck her: she was about to meet face-to-face with a Nevarian—someone who had likely been raised to despise Avalonians like herself! She halted, lingering on the balls of her feet as she considered hurrying back home. *Few of 'em are decent until you cross 'em,* she recalled Phellis saying. Helena hoped that would be the case tonight. Onwards she went, the giant network of scattered webs leading her up the mountains until she reached a giant, gaping cave.

As Helena approached, a great hiss sounded—and a shadow lurched at her from within the cave! A giant arachnid with great, furry pincers came hurtling towards Helena, and she fell back with a cry.

*"Our kingdom is the earth!"* Helena cried as the arachnid pranced around her on its hairy legs, snapping its pincers and glaring down at Helena with its beady eyes. She shielded her face before the fuzzy beast could gouge her eyes out.

An airy whistle sounded from within the cave, akin to that of a bird. The arachnid withdrew at once, spinning its way up high before planting its fat body on an overhanging branch. It watched Helena intently.

A figure emerged from the darkness of the cave, and a pair of dark, sunken eyes met Helena's. The Nevarian was a wingless, gaunt figure dressed in threadbare clothing. His face was sallow; the Scarekrow appeared to have lived up to his name.

"Helena Nightingale," he said in a voice that did not suit him.

"You know who I am?" she said, not taking her eyes off the beast in the trees above them.

"The Woman Made Wigeon," he parroted, imitating the whispers of his confidants.

"The Woman Who Fell!"

"The Living Dead!"

"The Nightingale!"

Then the Scarekrow mimicked three more distinct phrases:

"Liar!"

"Attention seeker!"

"Abomination!"

Helena's body nearly crumbled from the weight of her shame—is that what everyone in the kingdom had been saying about her?

"I was told you could provide the information I'm looking for," Helena declared, swallowing her wounded pride. "I just didn't expect the Scarekrow to be a…"

There was a curious gleam in his dark eyes.

*"A WIGEON?"* he parroted, with an air of disgust.

Helena nodded.

He gave her a shrewd smile before speaking. The caliber of his *true* voice was deep and warbly, like that of a low brass instrument:

"I come from the Koli Colony, where my black-winged brothers and sisters toss you into the wilderness to die if you have not obtained your wings by eight years old. My own mother cast me out like a mutt, forcing a boy of only eight to fend for himself in the desolate Kanyons of Koli. I found my niche in this place soon enough, however, and befriended other like-minded wigeons like Abernam—the same one you helped the other day. People like us are often overlooked by common men with wings who think themselves above us. Little do they know, that though the heavens may be their sanctuary, *our* kingdom is the earth—and we hear all the rumors, secrets, and whispers that spread across these lands."

"You must've heard the rumors about me, then," Helena said, "and wonder if they truly stole my wings. Sorry to disappoint you—I have no way of proving what happened to me that night."

His dark eyes glistened curiously. "A life of wigeonhood has taught me to always believe the lesser man…how can I be of service, Nightingale?"

"I wish to know more about Nevarians—who they are, and where they come from. I was told you were the only one who could provide me with the information I need."

His eyes twinkled mischievously. "Indeed. We Nevarians are taught our history from a young age, when we first begin to mimic. We are a quipping species—and though we are certainly capable of memorizing large chunks of information, we prefer to retain our information in a manner that is far more…*digestible* to the ear."

"Like songs?" Helena guessed.

"Correct! Have you heard *The Tale of the Fallen Avian?* No? Then allow me to perform for you my people's most famous hymn." He gave a slight bow, and with a bright, melodic voice, the Krow began to sing to Helena:

> *O prince of renowned beauty!*
> *Wits of a Raven and curls of coals!*
> *Firstborn of tyrant Cerxes,*
> *And the father of our woes;*
>
> *The prince was a lowly, pitiful creature*
> *Hated, spurned, and plainly loathed*
> *Wool as dark as midnight*
> *In a flock of doves, the boy was a crow!*
>
> *Cursing the boy, the abomination,*
> *The tyrant banished him Below.*
> *An imposter's tongue as condemnation*
> *A sun never rising, a vermin's abode.*
>
> *Nameless, scorned, and all forsaken,*
> *The prince took upon himself a new*
> *name,*
> *Nevar, the First to Fall*
> *And rise from his ashes and shame.*
>
> *Black seed, sowed and sprouted!*
> *The Fallen Avian shall bide his time.*
> *A promised rise, a pending vengeance,*
> *With his blood, the Fallen Shall Rise!*

The Scarekrow concluded his performance with a bow. "That lyrical poem is an archaic work of its time, dating back exactly 267 years. We have passed it down through generations so that we never forget the pain our ancestors endured. It serves to guide us and propel us—in that way, we view our imposter's tongue as more a blessing than a curse."

Helena's brows furrowed. "267 years? That would date back to Year One, when Avalon was founded!"

"Not so coincidentally, also the year of Nevar's exile."

"Why did they banish the prince?"

"'IN A FLOCK OF DOVES, THE BOY WAS A CROW!'" he quipped. "If you were to ask any nave, they would tell you it was simply because of the color of his wings. For at that time, most Avalonians had wings as pure as snow, and dark wings were a sign of ill omen."

"But you're not just any nave," Helena observed.

He grinned. "There are others who claim the young prince dabbled in dark magic to acquire his wings, which he did not earn. Still...the cause of his exile matters little. Nevar is central to our people not because of what he did, but because of what came *after* him, because after his exile, more followed suit."

The Scarekrow then proceeded to describe the decade following Nevar's exile, known as *The Culling*. Fueled by mass hysteria and superstition, Avalon culled hundreds of Avalonians and cast them into the Lower Realms of Nadiir—they were the *original fallen avians*. But you can only throw so much away before your waste accumulates, and that's exactly what happened; after The Culling, fallen avians found solidarity in their fates, for the only comfort to the outcast is the presence of another like himself. Nevar, the first to have fallen, diligently collected their broken spirits like coins, promising them retribution in exchange for their support and loyalty. United, they would sow the foundations for a new avian empire even greater than that from which they fell. Yet two core dilemmas prohibited them from doing this, however...

Nadiir had already been inhabited by native wigeon tribes long before the arrival of the fallen avians, and it was these wigeon communities that thwarted Nevar and his plans for a greater world. Within the span of a few decades, the wigeon peoples had nearly eradicated the fallen race from the face of Nadiir—and what's more shameful than to be subverted by a race you deemed inferior due to their absence of wings? It was a colossal failure for Nevar, one he would take quite personally for the remainder of his reign and which would fuel his hatred for the wingless. Eventually, he made use of concubines to propagate his lineage, which is why most Nevarians possessed wings as dark as midnight, as the blood of their forefather ran thick through their veins.

The second dilemma, however, surpassed even the greatest of wigeon threats: the sun itself. Cerxes not only banished his own son, but cursed him as well! Because he had drifted towards darkness, Nevar was made to give up that which was entirely antithetical to it. Thus, he was condemned to live a life without light. This had generational ramifications:

"The Vespertine Curse, as we now know it, prevents anyone of Nevarian descent from treading directly in the daylight, making us slaves to the night and fugitives to the light. Because of this, we are forced to dwell in tunnels and caves like vermin," the Scarekrow said, his hand tightening into a fist.

"So that's what it's called," Helena cried. "The Vespertine Curse!"

"Indeed, any direct and prolonged exposure to sunlight results in the instantaneous death of the Nevarian ave."

"Similar to Nocturnals," she said.

*"We are not the same!"* the Scarekrow hissed, and even his pet arachnid seemed to seethe at this. "Nocturnals are nothing but a rat-munching race who *happen* to maintain a *similar* lifestyle as us—that is all. The Vespertine Curse was *inflicted* upon us Nevarians so we would all bear the sins of our forefather...a burden forced upon a group of people who did nothing but exist!"

"Forgive me," Helena said quickly, gulping as she eyed the pet arachnid. "I'm only trying to make sense of all this. You claim they inflicted a curse upon you and your people...surely, that means there must be a way to break it?"

The nave paused. "There is only one way."

Helena braced herself.

"When the tyrant Cerxes banished his son, some say he possessed the *Twilight Stone*, a medium so powerful that it bound Nevar—and anyone who bears his blood—to a lifetime of darkness."

Helena felt her sixth sense tingle. "What happened to it?"

"It is gone. Stolen, perhaps, or destroyed by some spiteful hand to ensure we can never break this curse. But there are many who believe this stone is still out there, powerful and intact. And scores of seekers have grown old trying to find this precious stone, which in itself is rarer and far more precious than gold."

"And what became of the Fallen Avian?"

"After a long reign, Nevar vanished from the face of the earth. It is likely he died of old age, for at the time of his disappearance he was but a withering frame." The nave paused, and his eyes filled with darkness as he parroted an old woman's croaky words. "SOME DARETH SAY THAT HIS SOUL ROAMS NADIIR, FOREVER IN EXILE, YEARNING TO RETURN TO AVENGE HIS PEOPLE."

Helena gulped. "Do you think the day will come when he returns?"

"You had best hope he doesn't."

"Why?"

"Because only death and misery would follow. The Fallen Avian's promise is simple: THE FALLEN WILL RISE. When they do, they will conquer the Nadiirian Realm and exterminate every wigeon or ave who seeks to oppose them. After that, they will seek to conquer the Upper Realm, which would include destroying the Kingdom of Avalon and enslaving every other avian civilization."

The look of horror on Helena's face earned a booming laugh from the Scarekrow.

"Calm yourself, Nightingale! In order to conquer the world, the Nevarians would have to work onerously to navigate around the Vespertine Curse—or to break it, which is impossible without the Twilight Stone."

Helena pondered for a moment. "There's rumors that they plan to attack Alazar, though."

"Indeed."

"How, then, do they expect to pull that off if they can only fight at night?"

"I would not underestimate the carnage that can take place within the span of a few hours...still, while it's possible for them to coordinate an invasion, it would be tricky for them to *win*. They are, after all, at an utter disadvantage."

It seemed that the sun was their greatest ally after all. Penelope's warning had been as ominous as it was vague, but now it seemed to take on an entirely new meaning: *If that artifact falls into his hands, it would be one step closer to making the Nevarians more dangerous, more powerful than ever before...*

*The Twilight Stone,* Helena thought wildly. *Could that be the key to the Nevarians' plan for world domination?*

"It is not every day that a Diurnal wigeon like yourself takes such an interest in our history," the Scarekrow murmured. "Is there a reason you are so inclined to learn about us?"

*Play it cool,* she thought.

"You must know your adversary as well as yourself. Don't you agree?"

"Keen girl," he muttered—although something about Helena's answer did not seem to satisfy him.

"Thank you for your help," she said hesitantly. "Though I find myself wondering why you would help me in the first place, considering that Nevarians hate Avalonians so much."

"Consider this a favor for helping Abernam. But if you want a true answer, I am first and foremost a wigeon. *Then* a Nevarian. The new world order that my black-winged brothers and sisters desire will never include us wigeons. If the Fallen Avian returns and his people rise, it will be the wingless who will occupy the gaps and crevices they leave vacant. You see, Nightingale, the pyramid scheme is never truly destroyed. Only...rearranged."

While the Scarekrow's words mostly assured Helena that he was not an enemy, she wondered how much this Nevarian's stance would shift if he discovered that the key to breaking the Vespertine Curse likely resided in Helena's cabin just a mile away, inside a golden egg nestled comfortably in a bed of fire.

Helena hurried back home.

# Chapter Twenty-One

"*YOU DID WHAT?*" Jared darted towards the windows of the cabin, closing the shutters and drawing the curtains before running to Helena with wide, frightful eyes. *"You met with a Krow in the middle of the night? Do you know how much danger you put yourself in?"*

"I had to find out more about Nevarians and where they came from...and it paid off. I think I finally know what's inside that egg, and the real reason why Penelope wanted it so much."

Helena walked over and knelt before the lively fire, where the golden artifact rested comfortably.

"When the Fallen Avian was banished," she began, "they condemned him and his descendants to live in darkness for eternity. More specifically, they call it the Vespertine Curse, and it's what prevents them from walking in broad daylight. Nocturnals have it, too, although it seems to affect them differently, and they seem to view it as more of a blessing than a curse..."

Noa scoffed. "So Nocturnals and Nevarians can't walk in the sun. Don't we know this already? What does any of this have to do with the egg?"

"Just listen!" she said, licking her lips as she chose her words carefully. "Since I've had the displeasure of meeting Penelope, I've gotten the odd impression that she feels...discontent with her own life."

*"Discontent?"* Jared asked, his brows furrowing. "In what way?"

"She once told me that even though they may sleep inside their dens, safe from the sun, they never *truly* rest for fear that one day their walls may collapse and the sun will kill them. She described sleeping in a den the way we might describe living in a cell...with the hope that one day she would be set free."

The two boys looked at Helena in confusion.

"Don't you see? Penelope has been searching for a way to liberate herself from her way of life! She believes that what lies inside this artifact will allow her to finally walk in sunlight!"

Jared nearly staggered back at this information. "What could possibly have the power to do such a thing?"

"It's called the *Twilight Stone,*" Helena answered, fixing her gaze back onto the egg. "It's what King Cerxes used to place the Vespertine Curse on the Fallen Avian."

Jared took a moment to process this information, pacing back and forth until he let out a sound of exclamation. "Yes, of course! Why else would both Penelope *and* the Stork want the egg, if their intention wasn't to be able to walk in the daylight?"

"They might not be on the same team, but they have the same goal," Noa concluded.

Helena hesitated. "Not exactly. Penelope once told me that she sought freedom, while the Stork sought *power*. Think about it—if the Nevarians were able to roam Nadiir without the sun keeping them at bay...all hell would break loose!"

Noa snorted. "And am I supposed to believe that Penelope only wants the stone to lay underneath sunshine and rainbows?"

Jared chuckled, but Helena found no humor in it.

"I think you're onto something," she said in deep thought.

Noa rolled his eyes. "Look, if the stone is truly in there, then our situation is a lot more precarious than we took it for. War is looming in the south, and it won't be long until the Krows are knocking on our doorstep looking to take the egg back. Same goes for Penelope. We can't twiddle our thumbs and play with firewood any longer."

Helena nodded. "We need to find a way to open the egg and destroy the stone before either of them can get their hands on it. The clock is ticking, and from the looks of it, fire isn't going to cut it. We need something more powerful to speed up the process..."

"Like what?" Jared asked.

"Magic."

Noa chuckled. "Magic, aye? I don't see any witches and warlocks around here. Do you?"

"Forget witches and warlocks. I'm talking about a tool powerful enough to crack the exterior of the egg. Something that's powerful enough to tear into anything—even the living soul."

Jared's eyes widened. "You don't mean…?"

She nodded. "The Dagger of Prince Elizar."

Noa and Jared looked at one another in grim realization.

"There's only one place I can imagine that could be," Jared said. "Back in Krow's Foot, somewhere deep within Mount Sulfur."

Noa gaped at Helena. "Yer thinking of infiltrating the mountain."

"Yes. If we could somehow manage to sneak in, we could find the dagger and get out of there before they even realize it's missing."

Jared mulled this over, a look of deep concentration on his face. He seemed to be actually considering the idea!

Noa, however, remained doubtful. "Let's just assume you *do* manage to sneak in without anyone noticing you…what if the dagger's not there? Or if the Stork has it?"

"The mission isn't without risk…but if we're lucky, they'll be in the same room, and we can do away with one while we bolt with the other."

It was probably the darkest thing Helena had ever said. Even Noa seemed impressed by her callousness.

"It won't be an easy task," he murmured, piqued by the proposition. "You'd have to fight off every damned Krow inside before you could even think of getting to the dagger. Even then, it'd be like trying to navigate yer way through a maze. It's a dead man's mission—or in yer case, a woman's."

"Well, if neither of you wants to go, I can go alone."

"I'm going with you," Jared said abruptly.

"Jared," she said in slight surprise, "this might be a one-way trip."

"I vowed to be your protector, didn't I? You need someone to help you fight off those Krows, and I've trained enough to know that I can do it."

Helena met Jared's determined gaze and nodded firmly. "We're bound for Mount Sulfur, then."

"The pair of you will do anything to leave me out," Noa said jealously, throwing his arms around them both. He flashed a wicked grin. "I'm in!"

258

# Chapter Twenty-Two

T he group spent the next week diligently preparing for their critical mission. Jared trained harder than ever before in the Fighting's Nest, and even Helena and Noa gained some hands-on practice in wielding a weapon. Helena, however, mulled tirelessly over the logistics of their mission. Noa was right—even if they *could* evade the legions of Nevarians within Mount Sulfur, how would they navigate through that maze of a mountain? Helena couldn't imagine a scenario that didn't involve the spilling of blood, or that didn't have them meandering throughout the inner workings of Mount Sulfur for eternity...

One late morning, Helena was sitting on her bed when Jared came into the cabin with an excited gleam in his eye. He took a knee by her beside and informed Helena that they were going to be going over aerial formations at the Fighting's Nest that day, and he came in hopes that Helena would join him in seeing it.

"Noa would rather watch paint dry than to go see avians fly—so I came to you! I know for a fact it would be something you enjoy...won't you come with me to see them?"

Though the premise excited Helena, she was still somewhat hesitant to go with him.

"What's holding you back, Nightingale?" he teased, tussling her hair.

She smiled sadly. "I see no point in going if there's nothing I can glean from it...I can't even fly."

Jared rolled his eyes, rising. He picked her up and carried her out of the cabin, piggyback style, despite her protests.

"You're coming with me, whether you like it or not!"

When the pair arrived at the Fighting's Nest, Rancipert greeted them with pleasant surprise.

"If it isn't my two favorite wigeons! Have you two come to join us in running air drills today?"

"Just observing," Helena said, a hint of sadness in her voice.

He frowned. "That doesn't mean you can't learn the basics of strategy; the brain's a muscle, too, you know! Come along, you two—I wish to show you something..."

Rancipert led them up a hill overlooking a mass of warriors scattered across the field. Most of them wore light leather gear, for it was a particularly sunny day. Strong winds blew in steadily from the northeast, and Helena reckoned it was the perfect day for flying. Way down, the warriors fidgeted and were anxious to begin their afternoon drills.

Helena and Jared lingered back as Rancipert climbed to the highest point of the hill. He spread his wings wide and, after puffing out his chest, the captain called his host to attention with a sharp, blaring cry that came from the base of his chest. Every soul within ear's reach of this call snapped into a stiff-necked stance of attention, frozen and unmoving. Rancipert shouted another command. In less than thirty seconds, the warriors dispersed and gathered into a more orderly formation of three giant, distinct blocks. They stood erect, wings tightly folded against their backs, and waited obediently for Rancipert's next set of commands.

Rancipert inclined his body towards Helena and Jared and said, "Can either of you name one kind of aerial formation?"

*"The V-Shape,"* Helena yelled out almost instantaneously, just as Jared was opening his mouth. He shut it with a frown.

"Excellent!" The captain stretched his long wings to their fullest potential and called out to the avian warriors at his disposal. "AVES, YOUR FIRST TASK OF THE DAY IS TO BREAK INTO V FORMATIONS. NO FLIGHT ALLOWED. RUN, DON'T WALK! YOU'VE GOT TWO MINUTES—GO!!!"

There was a moment of disarray as the blocks dissolved and the warriors hastened to shuffle into smaller groups. To Helena it looked like magic, watching the line formations come to life. The first minute hadn't even passed when sixteen individual "V" formations lined the landing strip, evenly spaced and all pointing towards the front of the field. Their diagonals were not perfect, but perfection wasn't necessary in the air, so that didn't bother Helena much. There was even one formation at the rear that only had half the members as the other formations, looking more like a checkmark than a true *V*. But that was perfectly fine, and Helena knew so.

"The most natural aerial formation for the ave is the *V-Shape,*" Rancipert explained to the two wigeons. "You may recognize it most commonly in birds. It's easy on the wings, energy-savvy, and perfect for migratory missions...ATTENTION AVES—MARCH FORWARDS!"

Helena, of course, already knew all this information. Still, that did not diminish her delight in seeing the host move forwards as one.

"CYCLE ONE!"

As they marched, they heeded Rancipert's command and, in a coordinated maneuver, each group performed a special drill. The last ave at the left leg of the *V* would run over and join the right leg, while the rest of the aves in the formation would shift up one position and to the left, leaving the formation shaped exactly the same, only with each ave in an entirely different spot.

"What are they doing?" Jared asked, raising a perplexed brow as he tried to piece together the drill.

"They're cycling!" Helena answered eagerly. "It's a basic drill vital for energy conservation, especially on long-range missions. The headbird position, being the one at the very front of the *V,* demands the most energy because they face the wind head-on. Cycling allows the formation to distribute the workload evenly across the flock, as each member shifts up a position. By the time they're finished, everyone will have had a turn at being headbird at least once!"

"It seems you've got this down, Helena!" said Rancipert, looking slightly bemused by how much she knew.

"She knows a thing or two about flying," Jared said admirably.

Helena felt herself nearly burst with a mixture of pride and nostalgia.

Rancipert turned to his warriors and shouted, "CYCLE TWO, AVES!"

"When are they going to take off?" asked Jared, a hint of impatience in his voice. He, too, yearned to see the entire mass flock up in the air.

Rancipert laughed. "That can wait! If they can't get it right on the ground, what makes you think they will in the air? What if there's rain and thunder? Or arrows flying up at them? It's critical that we get the basics down on the ground, or else there could be disastrous consequences—AVES, CYCLE THREE! CHIN UP AND EYES FORWARD. YES, I'M TALKING TO YOU, GREENE!"

Timuth Greene seemed a bit distracted as he marched with his peers, lagging in his formation as he glared up at the sight of two wigeons standing alongside Rancipert. Upon being called out, he shifted back into formation bitterly, though his eyes never left Helena. She felt a sort of smugness at the sight of him being chastised in front of everyone.

"Here's a kicker for you!" Rancipert said, turning to Helena. "Can you tell me another aerial formation—apart from this one—which would be useful during battle?"

Helena needed to exert a great deal of effort to get the cobwebbed gears in her brain cranking. After some time, she uttered a few formations: there was the *"Checkmark" formation,* a variation on the *V-shape* in which one line was a bit longer than the other; there was the *line* formation, in which they flew in a straight line, whether it be vertical or horizontal; and even a diamond-shaped formation, which was rarer than the others. All of these earned her a look of approval from Rancipert.

"I've not a single doubt that you were an exceptional flier in your time, Helena," he said, visibly impressed, but his face fell. "It's a shame what happened. That Krow should rot in Hades for what he did to you."

Helena felt a pang of anguish in her chest, but she could no longer allow herself to become consumed by grief. She accepted Rancipert's comment like a champion, reflecting on her time as an ave fondly and with nostalgia, rather than self-pity.

"It's all just teamwork, isn't it?" Helena said, looking down at the cycling formations. "Kind of like flying in a Murmuration."

Rancipert turned to her. *"You've flown in a Murmuration?"*

She nodded.

"Wow," he said, awestruck. "I've heard tales about the Avalonians and their Murmurations—it's said to be an almost supernatural experience to witness, let alone participate in. I'd say you are blessed, Helena! We don't see much Murmurating down here, apart from birds."

He turned away, slow enough for Helena to catch the jealousy on his face. "READY, HALT! AVES, I WANT EACH GROUP TO TAKE OFF AND FLY THREE LAPS AROUND THE KINGDOM, ALL WHILST MAINTAINING FORMATION AND CYCLING. LISTEN TO YOUR HEADBIRD FOR THE CYCLING COMMAND. STARTING WITH THE FIRST GROUP, AT THE FRONT—GO!"

Helena continued observing, tipping her head backwards as she watched the first formation fly over and behind them. Seconds later, another passed over.

Several black *V's* now marked the skies like bird drawings, and Helena watched wistfully as the flying figures grew more distant. It was then, while mulling over Murmurations and aerial formations, that a curious thought struck Helena.

"Rancipert," she said hesitantly, "would you consider a Murmuration to be a type of formation?"

This question seemed to catch him off guard, and he chewed on the answer for several seconds before finally responding. "A formation? Definitely. Would it be useful in battle? I'd doubt it. Keep in mind that the larger a Murmurating flock is, the slower and more cumbersome it becomes. Such a formation could serve for defensive purposes only, which is why it's become outdated in modern aerial warfare. You can't slay your enemies in a giant Murmuration!"

"But would it be possible for, say, smaller flocks to Murmurate and still coordinate offensive maneuvers?" Helena asked hopefully, recalling Penelope's words: *The smallest recorded Murmuration in history was a seven-count flock. Seven!*

Rancipert nodded, but his tone remained skeptical. "It wouldn't be impossible, but it would prove difficult. A smaller flock would require greater inertia, stamina, and teamwork to effectively Murmurate and coordinate their attacks. It would require a strong, dedicated inner circle. Skilled and unbreakable…"

"But it could work."

"In theory. What did I tell you, Helena? The brain is the greatest muscle you will ever have…move it or lose it, I always say!"

Helena watched intently as Timuth's line formation readied itself for takeoff. Moments before they burst into a sprint, Timuth turned his head and flashed Helena a wicked smile. He whispered something to his friends, who chuckled darkly to themselves. Helena had the feeling that he was still not over what had happened at the Fighting's Nest—and she would be a liar if she said the look on his face did not stir some apprehension within her…

# CHAPTER TWENTY-THREE

*What is a mirage? It is difficult to say due to the lack of physical, tangible evidence. Some say it is simply a reflection of the psyche, a manifestation of the "goodness" of our hearts. It is, after all, the mechanism through which we are bestowed our wings. Nevertheless, there remains an abundance of mystery surrounding the mirage and its origins. That begs the question—from where did the mirage originate, and at what point in history did we first acquire it and begin to fly? The answer to that question likely traces back to the time of the First Avians, of whom we know little to nothing about...*

*When the avian and the mirage become one, both parties form a permanent, magical bond, and the avian earns their wings for life. It is only upon an avian's death—the moment their heart ceases to beat, to be precise—that the bond between ave and mirage is severed, and they are parted. There are many accounts describing the moments just after an avian's death, when the widowed mirage remains and wanders in search of its previous host—how long, exactly, remains uncertain. Some accounts surmise that the mirage maintains an immortality of sorts, while others suggest the mirage remains "living" only for a finite period of time before it, too, perishes and joins their host in the afterlife.*

*But what if, in either case, the widowed mirage stumbles upon an ave who was, let's say, in the process of earning their wings? Would it be theoretically possible for that ave to claim a newly widowed mirage?*

Helena took a break from her reading to scowl at this thought. What nonsense! Claiming another's mirage? Impossible! But it only got worse...

*Better yet—can an avian claim two mirages at once? What if a living avian lost their mirage through some miraculous circumstances...would that ave be able to claim a different mirage? It's difficult to say. The mirage still harbors an abundance of magical mystery almost impossible to decipher...*

Helena simply could not continue. It was all ridiculous, pointless rambling. Of course it would be impossible for one to claim another's mirage! Such a thing sounded not just wrong, but altogether unnatural. Helena considered her own mirage, and the thought of replacing it hurt her more than she expected. Shaking the thought out of her head, Helena decided it was better to go to sleep than dwell on such absurd ideas...

*"Helena..."* The soft, ethereal voice tickled Helena's ear like the tip of a feather, stirring her from her formless dreams. But she convinced herself that her languid mind had conjured the sound and drifted back to sleep. When all was quiet, save for the crackling of the fire, a sudden chill rushed through the slightly cracked window, and *woosh!* The fire went out, casting the cabin into complete darkness.

*"Helena Nightingale..."*

She stirred once more. There remained just a trace of consciousness within Helena that allowed her to leave her bed and follow the strange voice. She paid no mind to her sleeping companions as she meandered about the room, occasionally bumping into an object and sending it clattering to the floor—but even this was not enough to rouse Helena, who continued to unconsciously search for the mysterious voice calling out to her. It beckoned her towards the unlit fireplace, where the golden egg rested comfortably amidst the ashes of its nest. Helena sank to her knees, her drowsy eyes alighting upon the artifact.

*Come to me,* it said.

The fire was out, and yet she still felt a tremendous warmth emanating from this singular, almost magical source. Yes, there was certainly an element of magic here...Helena detected a distant cadence within it. A light *thrum, thrum, thrum*—like the beating of a heart. *Or,* Helena thought, *the thrusting of wings.*

Helena had never wanted anything in her life as much as she wanted this egg. She seized it, but its metal shell was cool to the touch, despite having been blazing with heat just minutes ago. Helena mindlessly tucked it under her arms before making her way out of the cabin and into the woods.

As Helena made her way past the trees, she witnessed glorious visions of cotton candy clouds and heavenly Murmurations of birds. All the while, the artifact beat against her chest like a thudding heart. It had never occurred to Helena, until this very moment, just how *right* it felt to be so close to it. It was as if a bitter winter had befallen her, and the only source of life nearby was this here egg, like a burning fire whose warmth remedied the eternal ache in her chest...

Suddenly, two glorious wings unfurled from the golden egg, and it departed from Helena, floating away despite her protests. She chased after it, longing to be together once more. Then, a booming voice caused Helena to tremble:

*"Weary, wingless bird,"* it called to her. *"Come rest underneath the shade of my wings! Let me unburden you, and you may find yourself as light as a feather once more!"*

Oh, how she yearned to join this strange entity! One more step, and she would be bound for takeoff...

Not a moment too soon, Helena snapped out of her trance. She found herself standing along the precipice of a cliff with one foot held aloft above its edge. A single step more, and she would have fallen to her death. Crying out in dismay, she staggered backwards and fell to the ground still cradling the egg in her arms. *Incredible*, she thought, looking around at her surroundings. Had she been out wandering in the woods alone? What could have compelled her to make such a dangerous excursion? Helena then looked down at the golden artifact nestled in her arms...

*Did...did this bring me all the way out here?* She wondered as her heart raced. *No, of course not...I must have been sleepwalking...but what kind of bizarre dream was that?* Rising to her feet, Helena dusted herself off and decided it was best to leave as quickly as possible.

*Woosh, woosh, woosh!* Helena darted to the nearest tree and pressed her body up against the bark as several shadows flashed above her. The hasty propulsion of wings sounded loud and clear. *Nevarians?* Helena wondered, as she held her breath and listened to the oncoming voices.

"I swear I saw her going that way—"

"Shut up! She's going to hear us."

"Let her. I love me a hunt."

The last voice was unmistakable. Timuth and his friends had followed her into the forest, likely wanting revenge for what had happened at the Fighting's Nest. Helena looked down at the treasure in her arms. There was no telling what would happen if Timuth discovered such a valuable object in her possession. Quickly, she hugged the artifact tighter and sought refuge in the forest. She heard their voices growing steadily louder, then let out a yelp as she ran headfirst into something—

*"Hush!"* Noa urged, putting a finger to his lips.

"Noa! How did you—"

"I saw you had gotten out of bed and followed yer footprints here. Who would've taken you for a sleepwalker, bird?"

"Noa, listen to me! Timuth and his friends are out there. They can't get their hands on the artifact—"

"They *won't*. Stay quiet and follow me."

Helena followed Noa with the egg cradled in her arms as they made their way through the eerie forest, periodically dropping for cover at any sudden movements and moving again when the coast was clear. There was one instance where they were about to cross over a small stream, and two aves intersected their path at the exact point they were about to cross. Fortunately, Noa yanked Helena back just in time before they would spot her; he held her tightly against him in the shadows, and she felt his broken, erratic heartbeat against her own.

Together, they finally crossed the stream and continued making their way through the woods. Helena was panting, lost in her anxious thoughts when the sound of a twig snapping startled her. Helena came to a stumbling halt.

"What's the hold up?" called Noa from ahead.

Helena looked over her shoulder in the direction from which the sound came. She saw nothing out of the ordinary except an endless row of trees and swaying bushes. The hair on her arms stood on end. As she gazed fearfully into the deep abyss of the forest, Helena got the eerie feeling she was being watched. *Must have been an animal,* Helena reasoned, before pushing the thought away and joining Noa.

Just a little further, and Helena and Noa would be back home. They were clambering down into a small valley when they were startled by someone flying right over them. Helena's muddy foot slipped on a mossy, slimy stone, causing her to topple over with the egg in her lap. *"Oomph!"*

*"Hey, I got something!"*

"Up, bird, up!" Noa urged her, grabbing her wrist and pulling her to her feet. *"Run like yer life depends on it!"*

They burst into a sprint as a large figure overshadowed them from above the trees.

*"I found them! They're running away!"*

Soon, there were three aves on their tails. Realizing their odds, Noa dug his heels into the dirt and stopped, wrestling the egg out of Helena's possession and slugging it into a nearby bush, where it disappeared with a distant metal thud. Seconds later, three giant figures landed all around them.

There were no introductions. One ave seized Helena, twisting her arms behind her back as the others advanced at Noa. Helena watched helplessly as Timuth spread his wings aggressively and, with a powerful swing, brought his fist against Noa's face. Noa did not think twice about fighting back, but with two against one, the cowards overpowered him. Soon, Timuth was straddling Noa, looking down on him and laughing.

*"Not so tough now, are ya, wigeon?"*

"Kiss my sorry ass, flocker," Noa snarled, before spitting up at his face.

Timuth wiped the spit from his own cheek and brought his fist down upon Noa's with a vengeance.

*"You—like—that—wigeon?"* Each punch grew successively wetter and more gruesome. "Fight back!"

"Stop it!" Helena sobbed, watching helplessly as Noa's entire face ran red with blood. Timuth's maniacal laughter filled the air. *"Stop it, you're killing him!"*

"Good." Timuth staggered to his feet. Noa's head fell limply to the side, unresponsive. "Now, it's your turn."

Helena let out a cry of pain as her captor's iron grip forced her painfully to her knees.

"I said you'd all regret what happened the other day, didn't I? Do you know what we do to wigeons who lie for attention?"

They brought out two heavy buckets. One of them was full of feathers and reeked of feather musk, and the other looked like it contained a mysterious, viscous substance. Helena's stomach sank with dread. These thugs were about to tar and feather both her and Noa!

But before Timuth could pour molten tar over Helena's head, a shadow flashed down from the moonlit sky. The grip on Helena's wrists released as a terrifying creature of the night landed between Helena, Noa, and their attackers. The beast crouched and gave out a snarl, its soot-colored wings flaring and rattling as it bared its teeth at the offenders. A petrifying hiss sounded from its fanged mouth.

*"GHOUL!"* Timuth's cowardly friends cried. They took off in tears, but Timuth remained glued to his feet, gaping at the terrifying sight in front of him. Helena watched, frozen, unable to find it in herself to flee. Step by step, the ghoul of the night approached Timuth, who backed away with fright.

*"It was just a prank!"* Timuth squeaked, his hands flying up in a gesture of surrender. "We were just gonna douse her in honey, honest. No harm done, see? Please don't eat me!"

*"Leave,"* the creature hissed, its eyes glowing in the darkness. *"Leave and never come back! If you do, you'll never see the light of day again!"*

Timuth scrambled off into the night sky after his cowardly friends. Soon, only Helena, an unconscious Noa, and the ghoul remained. Helena scuffled away in fear as the creature set its grim sights upon the wigeons. Something about it was familiar under the silver light of the moon. Its wings were grimy and unkempt, and they reeked of feather musk, but even Helena could recognize the spindly nature of those feathers. Not only that, but it was missing its ring and pinky finger on one hand—

*"P-Penelope?"* Helena asked incredulously. Her eyes flickered to the Nocturnal's other hand—she was missing three more digits on that one. Had she exposed herself to the sun since the last time they had seen each other? Helena could not say. One thing that was for certain, however, was that Penelope was here; she had most likely come to collect what had been taken from her.

"Go on, then," Helena said through gritted teeth, looking her fearlessly in the eye. "The egg is right over there, Penelope! Go on and finish what you came for."

But Penelope vanished as mysteriously as she had appeared.

*"Geuuuhhhh!"* Noa stirred from his state of unconsciousness and sputtered a fountain of blood. After fetching the egg, Helena helped Noa rise painstakingly to his feet as blood continued to gush from his nose. He was incoherent, babbling and spitting past the red substance in his mouth and around his lips.

"Elenuh...Elenuh!" Tendrils of his thick black hair stuck to his blood-stained forehead.

"I'm right here," she assured him, swinging his arm over her shoulder. They staggered back home with the egg together, Helena's head swimming the whole way back. Forget Timuth and his friends—was that truly *the* Penelope Duskmuth who saved them back there? It was hard to fathom how much the esteemed and noble Penelope Duskmuth had fallen from grace! And if Helena was not mistaken, this night would mark the *second* time Penelope had saved Helena from a brutal death! But Helena could not seem to understand why. There was nothing that could have prevented her from slitting Noa's and Helena's throats and taking the artifact. Instead, she fled. Why?

Jared leapt out of bed as the pair burst through the door and into the cabin.

"Help me get him to bed," Helena ordered, grunting as she struggled with Noa's body weight. Jared hauled the beaten boy to his bed, where Noa collapsed on his back with a painful groan. Both friends rushed to tend to Noa's injuries, but between his busted lip, his broken nose, and his swelling eye, they didn't know where to start. Jared rummaged through a nearby cabinet, emerging with a vial of Feather Dust. He dumped all of it into a glass of water and, after mixing it, forced Noa to drink the elixir. The effects were instantaneous, and Noa slumped back and gave a long, wistful sigh of relief.

"It should be enough to numb the pain and combat swelling," Jared said, watching diligently as Noa's rapid panting diminished into a low, labored breathing. "How did this happen?"

When Helena explained the events that had led up to that moment, Jared's face darkened at the mention of Timuth.

"Did he touch you?"

Helena looked down at her wrists, which were bruised and scratched.

Jared shot up onto his feet—

"No!" she cried, snatching his hand before he could leave. "I'm fine! I wish I could say the same for Noa, but...Timuth left before he could hurt me, and he'll think twice before ever coming our way again..."

His eyes narrowed. "What makes you so certain of that?"

When Helena informed Jared of who they had run into that night, his eyes widened, and he pulled Helena closer.

"You're certain it was her?" he whispered intently.

"It was too dark to make out exactly what I was seeing. But that creature was missing the same fingers Penelope lost the day she got exposed to the sun—although now she appears to be missing more. I can't shake the feeling that it's her, Jared. What do we do?"

Jared turned and began pacing the room. "Be on our guards and stay indoors. I'm serious, Helena! *No one steps outside this cabin.* Penelope could come back any moment now for the egg, and we have to make sure it doesn't fall into her hands."

"I won't fight you on that, Jared," Helena said. "But if it was the egg she was after, then she could have killed me and run off with it tonight when she had the chance! She didn't, though...maybe I might've just mistaken her for some other animal..."

"Regardless, no one's leaving this cabin until the sun comes out. Whatever happened out there, let's just call it lucky that those crooks left before they could do something worse to the both of you."

Helena spent that night gingerly cleaning the blood from Noa's face with a wet cloth. Although his pain had eased, his breathing remained jagged and wheezy. When Jared wasn't looking, Helena would lean over and press her ear against Noa's labored chest, searching for his heartbeat. *Lub-woo-dub,* said his broken heart, and it was only with great effort that Helena resisted the urge to break down into tears.

Noa woke a few hours later with a jolt, sucking in a sharp intake of air. Both his eyes were black and swollen, and he grasped Helena's wrists painfully. After uttering several strained breaths, he reclined back onto his pillow and relaxed upon realizing where he was. His swollen lips parted as he tried to speak.

"F-filthy flockers!" he wheezed. "Did...did they hurt you?"

Helena smiled gently and shook her head. Her eyes then flickered to Jared, who leaned against the wall, monitoring the situation from afar. She was unsure if it was wise to inform Noa about the events that transpired, given his condition. Nevertheless, she cleared her throat and told him anyway, and when she did, he sat up on his bed, seeming to have forgotten his pain.

"I didn't quite catch ya there, bird...do you mean to say it was *Penelope* who saved us from getting tarred?"

"I don't know what I saw," she said honestly. "If it was her, she's become almost unrecognizable."

Noa uttered a rickety laugh. "I don't believe it! That would be the second time we've become indebted to that woman! And I don't like it one bit...what about the egg?"

"Safe and sound in its throne of ashes," Helena said, just as Jared came by with another glass of elixir. Noa gulped it greedily.

"Helena and I leave for Mount Sulfur in the morning," Jared said.

Noa struggled to down the last gulp of elixir. "I'm ready when you are."

"You're not coming."

The wigeon boy nearly spat out his drink. "What the devil do you mean?"

"Look at you. You can hardly breathe, and Timuth has just about remodeled your entire face!"

The feather elixir seemed to be taking its toll on Noa, for his speech became slurred, and his eyes droopy. "*Pshh!* It's only a broken nose...gimme till the break of day, an' I'll be ready..."

"Someone needs to stay and guard the artifact," Helena butted in.

He peered up at Helena in disbelief. "You...you expect me to take watch like a nanny...while the two of you go off risking yer lives at a Krow's nest?"

Helena took his hands in hers. "Noa! We can't take the egg with us and risk it falling into the Stork's hands, and you're in no condition to travel. You have to stay. Now, more than ever, is it critical that you don't take your eyes off that artifact. We need someone to guard it with their life, and that person has to be you."

Noa never did warm up to the idea. Though, after a short time, the power of the feather elixir overcame him, and he fell into far too deep a sleep to continue arguing. Even drugged, however, the resentment never left his eyes.

That night, Jared remained vigilant for any signs of Penelope's return, Noa slept as soundly as a baby, and Helena sat on the floor by his bedside in case he needed anything. As she did, she drew her knees to her chest and stared at the burning fireplace where the egg rested on its throne of ashes. *Weary, restless bird,* she recalled the voice that had beckoned her through the woods, *come rest underneath the shade of my wings!* She could recall clearly the vivid image of the egg and its mighty wings thrusting against the air. Part of Helena was unsure if she had dreamt it all, or if something inside the artifact truly had called out to her...

But she could not afford to waste any more time dwelling on dreams and visions. Right now, there was nothing more important than focusing on their mission to retrieve the dagger; tomorrow they would set off for Mount Sulfur...and so would begin another long and arduous journey. This time, at least, they would not have to babysit any Nocturnals, so Helena anticipated a much quicker arrival to Krow's Foot.

Helena glanced tenderly at Noa, who slept in pure bliss with the feather elixir coursing through his veins. By the time he woke up, she and Jared would have already taken off on their mission. Who knew if either of them would return...

Laying on the hard wooden floor with nothing but a pillow and blanket, Helena sighed and shut her eyes for just a moment. She would need all the rest she could get for the difficult weeks that were to come.

# PART III
## THE DAGGER OF PRINCE ELIZAR

# Chapter Twenty-Four

The Eye of Nadiir was a strategic gateway that allowed all sorts of exotic goods to be smuggled from Avalon into Nadiir. Such goods included—but were not limited to—jewels, spices, and nectar, all of which would be consumed by the Nevarians themselves or shipped to the southern ports of Krow's Foot for trade. Not only had the Nevarians become fabulously wealthy, guzzling nectar and gorging themselves on the fatty flesh of Avalonian hogs, but the Eye gave them a striking economic advantage over anyone else within the lower regions of Nadiir. It was only a matter of time before other nations and criminal syndicates took interest in such lucrative affairs. Caught amidst a desperate power struggle over control of the Eye, southern Nadiir soon fell into a perpetual state of regional conflict.

Krow's Foot, in particular, had grown increasingly unstable since Helena left in search of the golden egg. When she and Jared arrived on horseback, they were shocked to find the region war-torn. Conflict ravaged towns and villages across Nadiir, for the Nevarians had only hardened their resolve in pillaging and terrorizing anyone who sought to oppose them. The roads had become especially dangerous—even in the day, for the Fallen Coven also played a great role in instigating violence. These were precarious circumstances, to be certain, but Helena and Jared managed to maintain low profiles as they journeyed through Krow's Foot by day, taking great care to not draw too much attention to themselves.

It was midnight when they arrived at Mount Sulfur, and the formidable Krows' nest was under attack—an avian host had decided to attack it at full force. No greater luck could have befallen the two wigeons; with the

Nevarians preoccupied in battle, Helena hoped she and Jared would have an easier time sneaking into the nest unnoticed.

Mount Sulfur towered over them as they trekked up its slopes in search of an entrance; Helena had to tip her head all the way back to gape up at the imposing mountain, involuntarily recalling the night she stood on its peak and made her deal with the devil. As warring figures clashed in the skies, the two wigeons were especially careful to avoid falling objects from above, lest they be crushed by a body or impaled by a flying sword. The canopies of the trees shielded them well from any eyes in the sky. As they fought, Nevarians and regular avians were indistinguishable under the silver glow of the pale moon; they all dropped like flies, disappearing beneath the trees.

Nevarian archers shot arrows from within numerous pits across the northern face of the mountain, and Helena and Jared flopped onto their bellies as arrows flew over their heads. In response, a wave of archers from the opposing side ascended over the trees; their keen eyes measured their targets before letting their arrows rain upon the mountain. Four arrows flew cleanly through the opening of one pit—they must have killed however many Nevarians that were inside, for no more arrows came out of it afterwards.

"Now!" Jared cried sharply, and they sprang into action. They kept their heads low as they darted towards the pit, which was made of packed mud and stones. It had a wide enough opening to grant an archer a clear view of the enemy. Jared dove inside without a second thought.

Before Helena could even stick a foot inside, however, she heard a blaring shout from within the pit.

"Jared!" Helena cried, alarmed. As she peered inside, she could make out nothing but shadows and the glint of iron weapons. There was the sound of a sword unsheathing, and then several painful seconds of a fight ensued. She could hear Jared and a nave exchanging blows and grunts, followed by the uncanny sound of something *ripping*, spilling, and gasping for air.

Then, a chilling silence.

"Get in." Jared's voice was hoarse. Helena inched her way into the tiny niche below ground. The pit was dim, cramped, and littered with arrow shafts and canteens. Helena eyed the three bodies lying just feet away from her. All were wigeons—two had been killed by the onslaught of arrows that came from the enemy. The third, however, had been the one that Jared fought, and he lay face down with blood pooling beneath him. Blood covered Jared's sword, which quaked in his hands. Helena surmised that this had been his first genuine kill.

They had to move on quickly—there was little time to spare before someone else came crawling into this pit and discovered them. Nearby was the entrance of a long, winding tunnel that led deeper into the mountain. The Nevarians' rallying cries sounded within—so distant, and yet so blood-thirsty.

"We're diving headfirst into a Krow's nest," Jared said, an edge to his voice. "There's no way we'll make it through without them seeing us and knowing we're intruders."

Helena's eyes flickered towards the dead Nevarians. Their armor was in decent condition, despite the fine layer of mine dust overlaying their silver material.

She had an idea.

Helena and Jared stumbled from the tunnel into a much larger and draftier corridor. They were dressed from head to toe in silver armor, with the sigil of a crow upon their chests. They looked to their left, and then to their right, towards the far end of the corridor; numerous flashing shadows, lit by the flames of flickering torches, skirted along the edges of the walls. Some naves shouted orders, while others filled the echoing tunnels with the bays of hounds, the roars of lions, and the warring cries of chimpanzees to rouse their peers for battle—or, as was Helena's case, to instill a paralyzing fear into the hearts of their enemies. Helena and Jared lingered mid-corridor, debating their next move.

"If the Stork wanted to keep the dagger secure, he would want it some-place heavily guarded," Jared said to Helena in a low voice.

"And inaccessible, too," she said, out of breath. "I'll wager it's located somewhere within the deepest levels of this mountain."

"Down we go, then. Keep an eye out for any guards posted by an entrance—that's our best bet."

Their armor chinked as they hurried down the corridor. They made a good pace before turning a sharp corner, scuttling down several flights of stairs, and entering a large, drafty corridor. By that point in time, sweat drenched Helena's undergarments. *We could spend years trying to find the dagger in a maze like this*, she thought, panting as they maneuvered through several more corridors. Then, as they turned one corner, a hoard of Krows sprang at them from out of nowhere! They pulled Jared and Helena along with them like a riptide, pushing and shoving them towards battle. The two wigeons had no choice but to mimic the war-mongering cries of the naves around them. To Helena's relief, she and Jared blended beautifully into this flock of Krows. Soon enough, they managed to slink off and continue making their way through the inner workings of the mountain until they reached a great cavern.

The cavern stretched as far as the eye could see, with mineshafts and railways spanning miles across its interior. An impressive feat, for certain, by no means a natural occurrence; the Nevarians had hollowed out the entire mountain from within! Minecarts packed with coal, dirt, and raw iron sped their way across a network of intersecting railways to be received by working naves at their end. It appeared that the Nevarians had an indefinite source of fuel and weaponry in this maze! Helena peered over a nearby ledge and caught a glimpse of the abyss below. One slip, and it would be game over for the wigeon girl.

Jared and Helena shuffled their way along the narrow ledges of the cavern, which took them deeper into the mountain.

"You there, wigeons!" a voice called out from above, and they stopped dead in their tracks. Helena looked up to see a nave about four or five stories above and across from them. He puffed his black wings and glowered down at them. From his throat sounded a deathly growl—

*"Imbeciles! We're in the midst of battle! Get back to work and start delivering water and munitions to the fighters that need it!"*

Helena felt her heart thrum a thousand beats per minute.

"Had your ears torn off, the both of you? *SPEAK WHEN SPOKEN TO, MAGGOTS!*"

"Yes, sir! We'll be on our way!" Jared called back, his hearty voice bouncing off the walls of the mountain.

"So be it! Lousy, ill-born, defective creatures…" the nave muttered to himself. He turned away before coming to an abrupt stop. "That's a mighty fine sword you got there, wigeon…where did you get your filthy hands on such a fine piece of weaponry?"

Helena met Jared's soft brown eyes. They seemed to tell her exactly what she was thinking: *run.*

Just as the nave spread his wings to fly down to investigate, Helena and Jared bolted for the nearest exit.

*"Get back here, you petty thieves!"*

They fled the scene as fast as they could, escaping into the myriad of tunnels ahead. Just as Helena felt her heart nearly burst with adrenaline, the pair stumbled upon a long, decaying wooden bridge overlooking a great chasm. A giant waterfall cascaded above it and fell into the abyss below. Jared bounded across the bridge, Helena right behind him…but then a rotten plank of wood suddenly gave way underneath Helena's foot, and she fell through the wooden floor with a cry. Jared launched himself to catch Helena's outstretched hand, but it was already too late. Helena fell into the depths of the chasm, swallowed whole by the torrents of water tumbling down into the lowly abyss of the mountain. The last thing Helena heard before she plunged into ice-cold water was the echoing cry of Jared calling her name.

# Chapter Twenty-Five

Somewhere within the depths of the plunge pool, Helena lost her helmet after it took the hit from a potentially lethal corner of limestone. The current carried her a long way from the misty falls down a long channel, after which it gradually widened into a small and shallow lake. Helena dog-paddled her way back to land, coughing and sputtering as she hauled herself up over the verge of a damp and jagged shore. Here, Helena collected her scatterbrained thoughts—despite the bone-chilling temperature of the water stalling her logic and reasoning—and set off to continue her quest for the Dagger of Prince Elizar. She had no idea where Jared was now, but Helena hoped he had enough sense to use what precious time they had left to continue their mission.

Helena spent many days and nights, it seemed, stalking the humid corridors of Mount Sulfur alone—though there was no telling for sure how much time was passing this far underground. She assumed it was daytime when the tunnels were most active with Nevarians—given that they were nocturnal creatures—and spent these hours hiding in deep crevices and sleeping sparingly. At nighttime, when the tunnels were emptied and most Nevarians were out fighting in battle, Helena resumed her quest for the dagger.

*Drip, drip, drip.* Water oozed through cracks in the ceiling as Helena padded through the hallways like a prowling wolf, dodging and swatting at nettling cobwebs as she did so. She wiped off the moisture along her brow and tried to stifle her erratic breathing—these meandering paths made her feel disoriented and restless! A railway intersected her path up ahead. Helena quickly retreated into the shadows as several mine carts hurtled their way through the intersection, each of them crammed with five to seven naves apiece. Their diminishing shouts lingered in the murky corridors as they rattled away from her. *All clear,* Helena thought, before crossing the rail and continuing along her path.

Helena halted moments before turning a corner so she could peek her head around it. She glimpsed exactly what she was looking for: two armed naves at the far end of the tunnel stood guard by a metal door. Doubtless the entrance led somewhere important...but fighting her way through these guards was out of the question. Perhaps with Jared at her side, she might've stood a chance—but since that wasn't the case, Helena needed to come up with a clever way to either evade these guards or find another way in...

Any decent plan she could come up with, however, was quickly forgotten as a third party soon arrived upon the scene.

"You there, wigeon!" said a voice behind Helena, causing all the blood in her head to fall to her feet. A trio of naves appeared in the distant tunnelway, brandishing their torches in a bright ring of light as they marched towards her. "Stop there!"

Fear and adrenaline shuddered through Helena's body before she turned and made a run for it, igniting an uproar behind her:

*"After the little rat!"*

The cacophony of war cries that followed Helena up and through the tunnels struck her with a terrible fright. She raced from one corridor to the next, making left and right turns at random as her heart threatened to burst from exertion, fear, and panic. A great deal of clangor now reverberated throughout the system of tunnels, both above and below—it seemed the entire mountain was now aware of an intruder in their midst...and to Helena's dismay, she found herself utterly lost within this never-ending maze! She was convinced that if the Nevarians *didn't* find her in these tunnels—which they knew far better than she did—then she would wander these tunnels for eternity, searching for a way out! Helena couldn't decide which fate was worse.

Helena made a left and skidded to a stop—two naves patrolled the hallway some distance away, and their feathers puffed upon catching sight of her. They were onto her like hounds. Helena scrambled away in the opposite direction and fought to navigate herself through several more corridors, which seemed to grow both longer and narrower as they chased her further down into the heart of the mountain. She made another left. Far up ahead, she saw four guards. So, she took the closest right. Another right—nope, two more guards closing in on her. She went back and continued straight. This went on and on for an eternity of tortuous, panic-stricken minutes, until nearly every corridor seemed tainted with Nevarians. Helena wanted to scream. They were gaining on her, surrounding her from nearly all directions, and her options were rapidly dwindling in this endless chasm of misery. One entrance led Helena down a slippery slope and through a winding tunnel, until she finally came to a crossroads.

Helena stood at the center of a four-way intersection where each exit was as dark and cryptic as the next. It sounded like Nevarians were closing in from all sides, making it nearly impossible for her to make a choice. Did it even matter? Whether she headed straight, left, or right...all paths likely led her to her demise...

Then, Helena caught wind of a mysterious sound coming from her right. It was hard to discern amidst the growing commotion of the Nevarians closing in on her, but if Helena focused, she could just barely make out the airy laugh of a child. It rang like bells in the distant tunnels and filled Helena with hope.

*"Lena!"* it said.

Helena bolted through this exit before the Nevarians arrived, following the fairy-like voice. There was no mistaking the aura of familiarity of this voice. The scar on her chest throbbed longingly as it called to her.

To her dismay, Helena reached a dark and unpromising cul-de-sac.

"No," she moaned, groping blindly at the walls for an exit. "This can't be!"

Behind her, the voices of the Nevarians were distant, but growing steadily louder.

Just when Helena had nearly lost all hope, a pale blue light appeared in midair, just feet away from where she was standing. It was no more than a spark, at first, until it grew so bright that Helena had to raise a hand up to shield her eyes. Two white wings sprouted from this dazzling orb of light, and soon a pale white dove fluttered along the ceiling. Her mirage.

"You're alive!" Helena exclaimed, laughing in unadulterated delight. The dove mirrored her joy, flapping its wings ceremoniously and performing figure-eights and loop-de-loops over Helena's head. Still, as lively as it looked exulting itself before her, Helena's heart broke to see that it was not as bright as she remembered; there was a kink in its flight pattern where it occasionally quivered and flickered like a dying light.

"What has he done to you?" Tears welled in Helena's eyes as she stepped towards it, but the bird fluttered lamely out of her reach. Just what abominable things had this little specter of light endured since she saw it last?

"The last time I saw you, you were in the Stork's possession, thanks to that cursed dagger..." Helena's eyes widened. "Could this mean that the dagger is closer than I imagined?"

The dove looped in the air as if Helena had guessed correctly. Just then, the sound of the Nevarians closing in behind Helena drew her out of her excitement.

"Help me!" she cried to the bird. The dove shot around the edges of the cul-de-sac as if it understood her, illuminating the contents of the ragged walls around them and revealing an imperfection hidden in the far corner: a sagging section of wall that, when picked apart, revealed a small and mysterious tunnel. Impossibly small for any *normal* ave to go through—but not for a *wigeon*. The dove flew into this hole and disappeared. Helena staggered, taken aback. Did her mirage mean for her to go inside this wormhole, that was barely wider than her shoulders? There was no telling where it led, or if it even led to anywhere!

It then occurred to Helena that she had been in this position once before.

*I will remain steadfast, like a bird,* she thought. Ditching what remained of her clunky armor, Helena crawled into the wormhole. The fear and uncertainty were still there, yet despite herself, Helena knew exactly what to do. *Keep moving forwards.*

She crawled for what seemed like ages through the narrow tunnel, which eventually widened and granted Helena enough leeway to rise into a slight crouch—though she still had to crane her neck to avoid hitting her head on the low ceiling. By this point, the tumultuous sound of the pursuing

Nevarians had faded into a welcomed silence, granting Helena an immense sense of relief. She looked ahead and noticed she appeared to have accessed a giant network of secret tunnels that spread throughout the mountain. Had it not been for her faithful mirage which illuminated her path, Helena would have been doomed to lose herself in here! Onwards they went, following the bending and dipping pathways, until Helena finally reached another cul-de-sac. Built into its low ceiling was a trapdoor with a string to pull it open. But Helena refrained, for a pair of bickering voices sounded above...

The Stork's voice was cool and cunning, as Helena had always known it to be.

"...we will strike the Kingdom of Alazar in a month's time."

"And what about these adversaries constantly knocking on our doorstep? Why waste precious resources to fight on a foreign battlefield when we need those very resources to defend our homeland? We *cannot* afford to lose the Eye of Nadiir."

The Stork laughed. "Your anxieties amuse me! While you worry about these trivial clans vying for control over the Eye, I have my sights on something greater. If we succeed in overtaking Alazar, then we will have gained a critical vantage point over Northern Nadiir."

"But we are bound by daylight!" the voice hissed. "Do you think it *prudent,* my dear friend, to send an entire host of ours across the continent to attack the enemy, all whilst having to avoid the sun?"

"I've already received word that the Koli are willing to lend us their most bloodthirsty warriors for our incursion against Alazar. With our numbers, the battle will be over before dawn. Soon, the Dragonbacks will be gnashing their teeth..."

"And what you say about the egg?" the impatient voice pushed.

Helena stiffened. She pressed her ear against the wooden door to listen closely:

"It remains in the possession of the Nightingale."

"Argh! That filthy wench! The egg couldn't have fallen into worse hands! You realize that if she, of all people, manages to open it—"

"That is highly unlikely without the dagger, which is firmly in our possession! The Nightingale is merely keeping it warm until its rightful owner comes and retrieves it…"

The man sighed, then said, "It was foolish of you to have underestimated what was in that egg in the first place…your miscalculation has cost us a grand prize!"

*"I do not miscalculate,"* came the Stork's sharp reply. "Penelope Duskmuth's misjudgment simply led me astray temporarily; she believed it to be the Twilight Stone, so logically I concluded the same. I did not anticipate what truly resided inside that artifact…"

Helena's eyes widened in realization. There *wasn't* a stone inside that artifact, after all! At least, not the kind that could break the Vespertine Curse…what, then, was inside it, and what made Helena the worst candidate in their eyes to have possession of the egg?

"Yes, and neither did you anticipate the wigeon girl running off with it!" cried the man. "It seems her affinity for flight was not as strong as you surmised!"

There was something of a growl, and then a clatter.

*"Tread lightly,"* the Stork said ominously. "Have I not raised our people from the depths of misery to a position of power which we have not seen in over a century? Have my schemes not acquired us the Dagger of Prince Elizar? Were it not for my efforts alone, we would have never located the Duskmuths, the only two people who have gotten close to deciphering the true location of the Twilight Stone. Yes, it was a great disappointment to discover that the stone did not truly reside within the artifact; nevertheless, the egg remains a valuable tool for our prospective efforts. We shall wage war against Alazar and take it back, after which we shall resume our quest to find the stone—a mission, I'm afraid, that makes Miss Duskmuth invaluable to our cause…"

*He's after Penelope,* Helena suddenly thought. *I have to warn her.*

"Master Stork!" a hurried voice sounded from the other end of the room. "You're needed in the pit! On behalf of Commander Nasalik."

"We shall continue this another time." The Stork's heavy footsteps carried out of the chamber.

For a time, the unknown man lingered alone, pacing until he rushed out and slammed a door behind him. Helena was alone at last. After waiting some time to confirm that the chamber was truly empty, she tried pushing the trapdoor open from underneath. But there seemed to be some resistance on the other side, likely a rug, though it was not impossible to open without a bit of force. Eventually, Helena clambered her way inside.

These private quarters were finer than any other she'd seen in the mountain, with red, velvety walls, a crystalline chandelier that occasionally quaked and chinked, and several handsome pieces of furniture laid scattered around the room. Several portraits of what appeared to be wealthy Nevarians, both men and women, decorated the interior of the room. Helena felt uneasy looking at their eerie smiles, and their dark eyes seemed to follow her every move as she walked past them.

Then, Helena laid eyes on what she had come for: at the far end of the room, resting upon a mahogany table, sat a small ivory chest with stout legs and a golden latch. Elaborate carvings of swans, feathers, and clouds decorated all four sides of this chest. After shifting the latch, Helena pried open its hinged lid.

*The body remembers.* Helena stared down at the golden dagger with its serrated green blade. The color of envy and sickness. Her world reeled, her scar ached, and she had to resist the urge to hurl the chest across the room and flee. Even her mirage, perched atop the edge of a chair, quivered at the sight of it. What kind of object could inflict such suffering? *The destroyer of souls,* she thought disgustedly. She quickly shut the lid, for she could not bear to look at it anymore. Looking around, Helena surmised that this room either belonged to the Stork or someone much more important. Either way, they would return soon.

After taking the small chest in her arms, Helena turned to her mirage. It looked at her expectantly.

"Please! Help me find Jared so we can leave this horrid place," she said to the bird. It tipped its head at her, as if trying to understand her words. Then, with a light chirrup, the dove fluttered off the chair and into the air, spinning wayward before diving back into the tunnels from which they came.

Traversing the secret tunnel up ahead was a gaping rift in the earth, which Helena's mirage dove into and out of sight. Helena stopped at its ledge, panting and peering down at it doubtfully as sweat ran in rivulets down her face. She sat along the ledge, clutching tightly to the ivory chest. Her feet dangled over empty space. With no idea as to what awaited her, she plunged into the darkness beneath.

Helena hit the floor sooner than she expected, landing on her feet with a grunt and falling backwards in the middle of an abandoned corridor. The dagger clattered inside the velvety interior of its container, though the chest itself remained shut—and intact—thanks to Helena's grip. The corridor was dark and drafty, except for the distant flickering of a torch down the hallway. Helena was now within the active network of the mountain, but she was clueless as to how far underground she was. She had little precious time until they realized the dagger had gone absent—if they had not done so already—after which all hell would break loose. It was imperative that Helena escape Mount Sulfur as quickly as possible to minimize her risk of losing the dagger...but one thing impeded her: Jared was likely still roaming the confines of the mountain.

Up ahead, a beastly shadow with two black crests for wings loomed over the torchlit walls. Helena became paralyzed with fear as a nave made his way into the corridor. He had no helmet, and she could see his greedy grin as he locked his beady eyes upon her and growled: *"Intruder!"*

It was too late for Helena to make a run for it, as the nave swiftly lunged at her, his large black wings overtaking her field of vision. Driven by fear and instinct, Helena unsheathed her own iron dagger and, determined to protect both herself and her ivory box at all costs, swiped blindly at him. The nave, however, found this comical. With a laugh, he disarmed her with a measly kick of his leather boot, nearly breaking Helena's wrist in the process. She yelped in pain. The nave then caught her by the braids of her hair and lifted her up to his eye level; the last thing Helena would ever see would be the frightened, wide-eyed reflection of her own face in his soulless black eyes. He drew back his sword and prepared to plunge its gleaming iron right through her heart, when suddenly—

*Clank.* There was a wet, cracking noise. A substantial force had come down on the nave's head from behind. With a grunt, he slumped to his knees, his mouth fell slack, and he collapsed to the floor unconscious. The curtains of his giant wings fell to reveal the wide, silver eyes of Phellicarus Faye.

*"Phellis!"*

Soot and grime covered the wigeon girl from head to toe. Her hair had grown out since the last time Helena saw her, falling just past her ears. She looked twice as thin, and her long, sinewy limbs appeared even more vascular than usual. In truth, she looked utterly miserable, but that did not diminish Helena's joy in seeing her for the first time in so long. After Phellis helped her to her feet, Helena pulled her in for a back-breaking hug.

"Easy, now!" Phellis wheezed. "I'm not made of stone!"

Helena found herself choking up. "We thought—I thought that maybe—"

Phellis pulled away, offended. "What? That Penny did away with me? Nonsense! I reckon it'll take a lifetime for y'all to get rid of me, that's for sure!"

Helena could not help but laugh joyfully. Only now did it occur to her how much she had missed that quirky accent!

"Oh, Phellis! How I've missed you—how did you end up all the way down here?"

"Can't fit it all in a minute, Helena, but long story short, them nightcrawlers cornered me not long after Penny abandoned me in the middle of nun...I've been locked down here ever since...but these nightcrawler dungeons are a heck of a lot nicer than any of the rat's nests Penny had to offer...Anyways, I still would've been trapped in a cell if it wasn't for Jared setting me free—"

*"Jared?"*

"Yes'm! He was looking for you, too! Said he wouldn't leave this cursed mountain without you!"

It was in that instant that a great affection for the wigeon boy nearly overwhelmed Helena.

"Now, Helena, I might ask you the same thing—what brings you this deep into the heart of a Krow's nest?"

Her keen, silver eyes peered down curiously at the mysterious chest lying on the floor beside them.

"Say, what you got there?"

Helena seized it, securing it under one armpit. "There's no time to explain. We need to find Jared and get out of here as quickly as possible, before they realize the dagger is missing—where is he?"

"We split up looking for you," she mumbled, her eyes never leaving the chest in Helena's arms. "I reckon he's up a couple flights of stairs, over by the barracks..."

The two wigeon girls set off scrambling to find their friend, but not before Helena came to a sudden stop, her eyes scanning the corridor as if searching for something she had lost.

Up ahead, Phellis was anxious to get going. "What's the hold up?"

*No,* Helena thought, panicked. There was no sign of her mirage any-where! But why, if Helena was now in full possession of the dagger? For a fleeting moment, Helena wondered if she had merely imagined it all—but the ivory chest in her arms was more than enough proof that it hadn't all been a figment of her imagination. With a heavy heart, Helena carried on, with the assurance that it was alive somewhere within the mountains, and thus there remained the infinitesimal chance of reuniting once again and soaring the skies together...

They found Jared after much toil through the never-ending twists and tangles of Mount Sulfur's mines. He'd lost his helmet, too, and his iron armor had become weather-stained with water and mud. Helena, overcome with emotion, flew into his arms, which he welcomed warmly.

He pulled away and said, "I'd feared I lost you back there, Nightingale! You fell before my very eyes!"

She could not help but grin. "I may fall, but I rise all the same!"

His laugh was a light in the darkness. "No doubt about that! As relent-less as the wind, you are!"

Jared's gaze drifted towards the box in Helena's hands, and his eyes widened.

"You did it!" he cried, astounded. "How?"

Just as Helena opened her mouth to respond, Phellis' voice sounded:

"Pardon my interruption," she said, her silver eyes flickering nervously to the walls around them. "Do y'all hear that?"

A faint clangor emerged from the distant depths of the mountains. It was small and ephemeral, at first. A budding sensation of dread brewed in Helena's stomach as she listened closely; before long, the sound stretched itself into a long and wailing moan. It reverberated throughout the mountain, swelling like an impending tsunami until it became apparent to Helena that it was not a single noise she was hearing. No, it was legion of angry voices crying out at once—all of them mimicking the Stork's voice in a state of unfathomable fury.

*"Aughhhhhhhhhh! Kill them all! Bring me the Nightingale's head!"*

It was quite reasonable to assume that he had discovered their schemes!

*"Bring me the Nightingale's head!"* This bone-chilling phrase followed the three wigeons across the inner workings of the mountain. They stopped upon a high ledge overlooking another great cavern, where dozens of working Nevarians stirred with zeal and anticipation. They had heard of the transgressions committed against their leader, the Stork—and they, too, thirsted for Helena's blood.

"That's our way out!" said Jared. He pointed towards the far, western edge of the cavern, towards a glowing white tunnel. This tunnel, as it turned out, seemed to repel any neighboring Nevarians, thanks to their instinctive repulsion of the light. It was daytime—meaning that there was no better opportunity for them to escape than at that very moment!

"Follow my lead, you two. When I say run, you *run* as fast as your legs can carry you—" Jared's hand flew to the grip of his sword. "I'll distract them and fight them off as best I can!"

"*Absolutely not!*" Helena cried.

"There's too many of them!" cried Phellis. "You can't take them all on!"

"She's right, Jared," Helena pleaded. "It's too dangerous! We can find another way—"

"*There is no other way, Helena.* The longer we sit and argue about it, the sooner we risk all our efforts going to waste! Follow my lead and brace your ears—I anticipate we're about to see a lot of commotion in the next few minutes..." Jared then turned to Helena. "Whatever happens, you can't let the dagger fall back into the Stork's hands—not until after you've opened the artifact and destroyed whatever's inside of it."

*"But Jared—"*

He seized her by the shoulders. "I vowed to do everything within my power to help you get back your wings, Helena. I failed you in that respect, and for that I'm sorry. At the very least, I want to leave this life knowing I served you in some way, and if that means sacrificing myself so you can get out of this mountain alive with that dagger in hand, then I cannot imagine a more honorable death! Now, you must promise me you'll do whatever it takes to get back home and open that artifact. *Promise me, Helena!*"

Helena could not fight back the tears any longer. She embraced him fiercely.

"I promise! You did anything but fail me, my dear friend. If this truly means goodbye, then I bid you Fairwinds!"

The two wigeon girls followed Jared's lead, shuffling down the treacherous ledges of the cavern. They'd just stepped upon solid, plain-level ground when an eagle eye from above caught sight of them at last. The nave let loose a harrowing cry, alerting the entire chamber to the intruders in their midst.

*"Run!"* shouted Jared, and they burst into the sprint of their lives.

*"RUN! R-RUN! R-R-R-UN, RUN!"* the Krows parroted as they chased after them. Helena and Phellis ran ahead, with Jared guarding their rear with his sword raised. A Krow landed just beside Phellis and swung down on her with his sword, but Jared blocked the blow and pressed the nave tightly with his own blade. After several strikes, the Nevarian was down, and they kept going. One after another, Jared was forced to fight off Nevarians who swooped in on them. But he rendered them all either disarmed or injured.

The tunnel ahead grew closer. Behind them, Krows poured out from every tunnel, nook, and crevice and came together in one giant flock that bubbled over itself like a viscous black potion. It lurched its way forwards, looming over them like a vengeful face which shouted, *"BRING ME THE NIGHTINGALE'S HEAD!"*

At last, they made it inside the tunnel! Their path lay straight ahead—but it was a long way until they reached the outside world, and the Nevarians had amassed a flock of massive proportions. It was clear that, unless something deterred them, the group would not make it out alive.

That was when Helena realized that Jared had stopped some distance behind them.

*"Jared!"*

*"Go,"* he cried, beckoning them away. "I'll hold them off while I still can—*GO!*"

Helena and Phellis had no choice but to leave their beloved friend behind. Tears streaming down her face, Helena hurried onwards with the chest secured tightly in her arms, before looking over her shoulder to catch one last glimpse of Jared. He was putting up a good fight, his sword glinting in the distance as he hacked at his enemies. Although his efforts had bought them several precious seconds of time, the cancerous black mass eventually overtook him and surged through the tunnels after Helena and Phellis.

The Nevarians could not fly much in these narrow tunnels, though they still gave Helena and Phellis a run for their money as they chased after them on foot, snarling as they gained on them. The road was long, though Helena could just make out the mountain wilderness emerging from the blinding light ahead. Any closer, and Helena felt her eyes would burst into flames. *Almost there,* she thought...yes! She could smell the grass outside! Just a little further, and they would be free...

Phellis launched herself headfirst into the refuge of the sun. But moments before Helena could break out into the frontier of light, a nave sprang onto her from behind. Tackling her at full momentum, the two of them burst forth from the cool depths of the mountains and toppled out into the blinding, unyielding fortress of daylight.

*"Helena!"* shrieked Phellis.

The nave's rough hands closed around Helena's throat, sinking his nails into her flesh and preventing any air from reaching her lungs—but he let go of her soon enough.

The sun ascended over the mountain, and its hot morning breath beat down upon them with an almost divine wrath. Exposed to raw sunlight, the nave collapsed beside Helena, writhing as the rays seared his skin; his face broke out in boils which burst and spewed scalding pus everywhere. Helena scrambled away from the blazing inferno that was the Nevarian. His flesh sizzled like a slab of juicy meat pressed against a hot iron grill, and Helena gagged at the stench. His agonizing screams were almost unbearable. As the fire consumed him, the Nevarian was driven by some Krowly instinct to recite the most primal noises his mind could unearth—howling cats, roaring lions, and a kind of high-pitched, demonic shrieking that he had likely pulled from the depths of Hades itself. Twenty long, life-spanning seconds passed until his cries dwindled away into nothingness. *The Vespertine Curse,* Helena observed. Penelope's chilling voice sounded in her head: *They, at least, get to die quickly.*

As the screaming dwindled, the hundreds of naves who had been pursuing them through the great tunnel came to a halt just before reaching the blazing light. They watched with impotent, vengeful faces as the flames engulfed the corpse of one of their own.

Not a single Nevarian dared venture out into the light, for the Vespertine Curse was sure to kill them. Helena and Phellis staggered to their feet and clutched to one another. They turned to face the hordes of naves who were rendered powerless by the merest sunbeam. With newfound valor, Helena dug her heels into the dirt and proclaimed fearlessly to the dark audience before her—for though he was nowhere to be seen, she knew her words would be carried to the Stork verbatim:

"The dagger and the artifact are mine. If you want either of them, you're going to have to come and take them from my bare hands. Gather your men, Stork, and meet me at the Kingdom of Alazar, as you intend to do. I'll be waiting for you. And remember—*time is of the essence.*"

# Chapter Twenty-Six

The journey home was long and dreary, and the heavy stench of loss lingered in the air. Helena spent many nights weeping for Jared, and she often found herself wondering if the cursed dagger would be worth the price they paid for it in the end. When she and Phellis stopped to camp for the night, they trembled at every sound, every owl's hoot, each coyote's howl from off in the distance, in fear that they were Nevarians sneaking up to exert the Stork's wrath upon them. They never came, however. *The worst is yet to come,* Helena thought, for she was certain the Stork and his men would soon strike Alazar with ten times the power...

In the weeks they spent on the road together, Helena noticed something odd about Phellis. Yes, she was leaner, and her hair was longer and more disheveled...but she was different than she used to be. Once a glimmering silver, her eyes now had a dull, vacant look about them. Whereas there was a time when the wigeon girl would talk an earful, now Phellis seemed lost in her own troubled thoughts, often curling into a ball and going hours without saying a word. Helena suspected it had a lot to do with what happened after Penelope took her hostage.

"Phellis," Helena pressed as they sat by a fire to eat dinner, "what happened after Penelope took you?"

Phellis tore a piece of bread with her bare teeth, staring blankly into the flames. Eventually, she swallowed with great difficulty and mustered the courage to recount the horrible events that transpired after she and the group were separated.

That night, Penelope marched Phellis at knifepoint through the dark and desolate woodlands of the Mountains of Alazar. After much distance the Nocturnal, wrought with grief, tied Phellis to the thick trunk of a tree; the wigeon girl could do no more afterwards but watch Penelope build her den. Unlike before, however, Penelope refrained from using raw building materials and instead spent an entire hour burrowing into the ground with her bare hands until her nails bled, after which she crawled into the hole and did not leave it for days at a time. Phellis said she was forced to listen to the Nocturnal's inane ramblings as she hibernated throughout the day.

The only thing to eat was what the Nocturnal could spare—namely rats. Phellis wept a little upon describing this and preferred not to go into detail. However, that was not the worst she endured during this time, for there were days when Penelope, for reasons unbeknownst to any sane, rational mind, would stick her hand out of the burrow so that light would strike the tips of her fingers. She would then retract her hand, allowing the curse to spread what little it could through her fingers before biting them off. It was Phellis' fate to overhear the entire ordeal.

Helena listened to this, horror-struck, as she recalled her recent encounter with Penelope and how the Nocturnal had been missing more digits than usual. It appeared that upon the death of her own brother, she had gone mad to the point of biting off her own fingers! Phellis claimed that Penelope grew madder by the day, to the point where she began scheming...

*"The egg,"* she moaned, *"the egg is the only thing that can help me break these chains of darkness...I must find her. Yes! I must find Helena Nightingale before the Stork does, because she has the egg—my egg! Nothing would make her happier than to see me forever bound by this wretched curse...I will find her, and when I do, I will kill her! Yes! I will end her life for daring to take away my freedom..."*

The Nocturnal soon abandoned Phellis as she set out to fulfill the vow she had set upon herself to end Helena's life. It shocked Phellis to know that the night Penelope found Helena, the Nocturnal had not killed her, but *saved her.*

"That don't sound right," Phellis said, her eyes narrowing in disbelief. "Why would she just leave the egg after all she's done to try an' get it?"

"I can't say for certain," Helena mumbled in deep thought.

"Something ought to have changed her mind that night," Phellis surmised, a strange look in her eye.

Helena recalled the Stork's conversation that she overheard at Mount Sulfur: *She believed it to be the Twilight Stone, so logically I concluded the same. I did not anticipate what truly resided inside that artifact.* Penelope, however, had long confessed her doubts to Helena about the artifact. Something must have happened the night Helena sleepwalked with the egg that made Penelope only certain of it...Helena could not bring herself to remember much of that night, however, only her bizarre dreams and her brief skirmish with Timuth.

The question remained: *what truly resided inside that artifact?* If not the Twilight Stone, then what could possibly be inside that, according to Penelope, could restore Helena's wings, as she once claimed?

"It wasn't long after she left 'fore a horde of them nightcrawlers found me," Phellis said in conclusion. "Before I knew it, I was in Mount Sulfur, an' they kept me in a dungeon there for weeks in the darkness! I reckon I didn't know night from day. It felt like I was rotting down there for years...until the Stork came down to see me."

Phellis gulped, looking at Helena with wide eyes. "All them rumors of him are true, ain't they? My goodness, isn't he handsome...but he's got a look in his eye that'll turn you into stone, if you look long enough. I reckon my heart might've given out the moment he walked into my cell."

"Did he do anything to you?" Helena asked intently, and when Phellis didn't answer, she seized her by the shoulders and gave her a firm shake. "I mean it, Phellis! *Did he touch you?*"

She gulped and shook her head. "He didn't lay a finger on me...but he said all sorts of terrible things..."

"That's what he does, Phellis!" Helena said gravely. "The Stork does whatever he can to get inside your head and make you doubt yourself. None of what he says is ever true!"

"But he told me you guys used me to get to the artifact...that part was true, wasn't it? You ran off with the egg the first chance you got an' left me to die!"

"You're mistaken, Phellis! We tried going after you, but there was only so much we could do without scaring Penelope into hurting you...and we soon got caught up and couldn't go after you. But we looked everywhere for you—" Helena pulled her in for a tight hug. "I'm sorry if you felt used. I won't lie and say that I didn't grow desperate to find the artifact. I was only doing what I thought was necessary to get my wings back at the time...not that any of that matters anymore."

Phellis pulled away and raised a brow. "From the looks of it, you don't seem so hell-bent on it, now!"

"I renounced my wings the moment I ran off with the artifact, Phellis."

A curious gleam shone in her eyes upon hearing this. "What changed your mind?"

"I realized it would be a grave mistake to give it to the Stork."

"You gave up the chance of a lifetime," Phellis burst out, her face contorting in disbelief. "Don't you realize you'll stay like this *forever?*"

This took Helena slightly by surprise. "I suppose it...wouldn't be so bad. It feels like wigeonhood has already become second nature to me, now. After all, wasn't it you who said there was more to life than flying?"

Phellis crossed her arms and turned her back on Helena, revealing her short little wing stubs. They wriggled as she said, "I don't remember saying that."

"Yes, you did! That day when—"

"Goodnight, Helena," Phellis said, before going to bed. Helena found this brief exchange odd, though she eventually concluded that the last few weeks had been rough on all of them. She wondered, however, if the Stork had said anything else to Phellis during her time at Mount Sulfur that might've stuck with her ever since...

Several long weeks had passed when Helena and Phellis finally arrived at the Kingdom of Alazar. As they climbed up towards their cabin, Noa greeted them midway, clambering down the big hill to meet them. The last time Helena had seen the boy, he had hardly been recognizable. But in the weeks since she had been gone, the swelling around his eyes and nose had reduced considerably, and the face that Helena had grown to admire was finally returning to its handsome, rascally disposition. He stopped before the two wigeon girls, and his eyes flickered doubtfully to the chest in Helena's arms.

Something twinkled in Phellis' eyes as she laid her gaze on Noa, for it was long known that she harbored special feelings for the wigeon boy. She extended her arms out wide in invitation of a great hug.

"Well! Did you miss me?"

Noa did not acknowledge Phellis—not even a twitch of a smile. She dropped her arms, evidently annoyed that he had paid her no mind and instead fixed his gaze upon Helena.

"Where is he?"

Helena didn't need to ask who he referred to, and it seemed Noa himself anticipated the answer to his own question. She lowered her gaze and swallowed guiltily before saying:

"They have him."

Helena reckoned she had not fully processed the scope of their loss until the moment she recounted the events leading up to Jared's capture. Its effects were devastating and predictable, for both girls found it necessary to restrain Noa and keep him from traveling all the way to Mount Sulfur himself.

*"Let me go!"* he shouted as they grappled with him.

"Does that thick head of yours think you'll be able to just march in and save him?" Helena yelled.

"We saw firsthand the works of those demons," Phellis cried. "You'll never make it back alive!"

*"I don't care! I won't abandon him, not after all he's done for me..."*

Helena took his head in her hands and forced him to meet her eyes. "Listen to me! It pains me as much as it pains you, but we need to focus on what's at hand! We have the dagger and the artifact, now—"

He lurched away from her touch. "You've done well in pissing off the hive, bird! Do you know what will happen now that they have him in their midst? That damned Krow will make a spectacle out of Red just to spite all of us! He'll torture him—make his life a living hell!"

"Don't you think I know that?" Helena roared back at him. "What would you have me do, Noa? Walk right back to Krow's Foot and offer up both artifacts in exchange for Jared? Do you think the Stork is so forgiving that he'd let all of us walk free after such a slight? We've passed the point of no return! All that's left now is to open the egg and destroy whatever is inside before the Stork comes for it—it's what Jared wanted!"

The wigeon boy appeared to be wrestling with a myriad of thoughts and emotions, and Helena was willing to wager at least one of them blamed her for the capture of his best friend. Though he never uttered such a thought out loud, Helena secretly wished that he would, for she grappled with the fact that Jared would still be here if she had never suggested to retrieve the dagger in the first place.

"I should have gone with you," Noa said afterwards, his face twisted in anguish.

Helena bowed her head. "There was nothing you could've done. If it hadn't been for his sacrifice, we would never have acquired the dagger. We let his efforts go to waste."

Noa looked away, a pained expression on his face.

"Stay with me," Helena pleaded, her voice soft. "I can't afford to lose you both."

Something in her words doused Noa's ire, and his harsh features softened. After a long silence, he said, "Show me the dagger."

They convened inside the cabin at the table, upon which Helena placed the white chest. Noa moved to collect the egg from the fire with a pair of iron tongs, and after a shower of sparks and embers, he let it cool before placing it on the table next to the chest. The two objects immediately repelled from one another, the golden egg rolling off the table as if fleeing from the dagger. Noa caught it just before it hit the floor.

It was as Helena expected—she was not sure how these two artifacts were connected, but it was clear they had a powerful effect on each other. She wondered what would happen if she were to strike the egg's shell with the end of the dagger's blade...

"How did you even manage to find the dagger, bird? It seems impossible to maneuver through that maze of a mountain, even for you," Noa said skeptically.

At first, Helena considered it wiser to keep her serendipitous encounter with her mirage to herself. But she knew it was a detail of too great a significance to withhold. When she revealed to her friends that her mirage had led her to the dagger, they were wrought with disbelief. Noa, especially, seemed thrown off by the tale of this encounter.

"Yer mirage is a dove?" he asked, his voice faint.

Helena nodded, suddenly feeling very shy. She had never truly told him how she earned her wings, but now he knew with certainty that it had to do with a dove.

Phellis cast an annoyed glance at Helena and snorted. "You mean to say this magical dove appeared out of nowhere an' led you directly to that cursed blade?"

"I believe her," Noa said cooly.

"You do?" Helena asked, her eyes wide and blinking at the handsome sailor boy who had once doubted her every word. He seemed to hold her in a different light now from when their adventure first began, and he nodded at her intently.

"Tell me, bird, what of your mirage? What happened to it?"

Helena lowered her gaze. "It disappeared not long after I caught hold of the dagger—which is strange, considering the Stork used its magic to hold it hostage. But now that I have the dagger—it's nowhere to be found."

She said this quite melancholically.

Noa pondered this a moment. "Maybe the Krow did not have as much control over your mirage as he originally let on."

"Maybe," Helena said, her mind wrapped in deep thought. "I just can't shake the feeling that something bad must have happened in the time the Stork had a hold of it...something grave that might've severed the magical bond between my mirage and the dagger. I guess there's no proper way of finding out..."

Helena wondered how much time was left until her mirage withered away, almost certain that she would remain wingless forever...

Phellis' silver eyes glimmered as they fixed themselves on the precious golden egg. "Anybody got any idea what's inside this here egg?"

Helena took a deep breath before she began. "Originally, we thought the artifact contained the Twilight Stone, which would help Penelope and the Stork break the Vespertine Curse and allow them to finally walk in the daylight…"

Helena trailed off.

Phellis flashed her a doubtful look. "You don't look too sure of that, now."

"What's the matter, bird?" Noa wondered as he, too, noticed her hesitancy.

"When I was at Mount Sulfur, I overheard a conversation between the Stork and someone else. He didn't want to admit it, but he had miscalculated about what truly resided inside the artifact. Since Penelope believed it to be the Twilight Stone, he came to the same conclusion. However, Penelope had long confessed to me that there was a chance something else could lie inside it instead…"

*Something that could grant my wings back,* Helena added internally, though for some reason she decided not to say this part aloud.

"What are we waiting for?" Phellis said impatiently. "Let's pop this sucker open an' find out!"

"It'd be my pleasure to finally crack the bloody thing open—" Noa said. He darted towards the white chest, but Phellis snatched it away and hogged the dagger for herself.

"Hey, now! What if I want to open it?"

"You'd sooner eat what's inside the egg than tell us what it is," he said. "Give it here!"

He moved to take it, but she pulled away from him. "It's mine!"

They wrestled the chest between them for some time before Helena's voice finally interrupted their antics.

"It's neither of your guy's calling. It's mine."

Noa heard this and let slip the chest from his fingers. It fell into the arms of Phellis, who clutched it possessively and regarded Helena with a jealous sheen in her eyes.

"Why's it gotta be you?" she asked pointedly.

"We don't know what the effects of using that dagger might be, and I'm not willing to risk either of you touching it. I'm the only one in this group who's felt the bite of its blade; there's no one else who could open it but me."

Noa raised his hands in surrender and backed away. Meanwhile, Phellis placed the chest back on the table ever so reluctantly. Then, driven by some impulse, she unlatched the ivory chest's golden clasp and lifted the box's lid.

The air instantly became three times heavier as the enchanted weapon came into view. Helena's breath hitched as she drank in the sight of the dagger. Vivid memories of the pain and suffering it had inflicted upon her flashed before her eyes.

*"Woah,"* came a sound of wonder from both Phellis and Noa. Neither dared to touch it, though the handsome dagger possessed an undeniable appeal, the way its emerald-like blade glistened beautifully in the firelight...it seemed to beckon them closer until they were looming over it with greedy eyes and slack mouths. Whatever its effects were on Noa and Phellis, Helena experienced the complete opposite sensation—when she looked at the dagger, her scar throbbed painfully, and as she gazed at it longer, she swore she could hear voices talking...no, *screaming*. Could it be the cries of all the souls this wretched blade had butchered?

"Oh!" Helena suffered a moment of fragility, and she gasped and covered her ears.

"Put the cursed thing away," spat Noa, and Phellis quickly shut the lid. The screaming stopped, and Helena emitted a sigh of relief.

"You sure yer up for this, bird?" Noa asked her after noting her reaction.

She nodded, regaining her composure. "If I spend the rest of my life running from what happened that night, I'll never live in peace. The moment I take this weapon into my hands is the moment it ceases to have control over me. I need to do it. I know I can, I just...I just need time."

"Well, from the looks of it, we don't got much of that around here," said Phellis irritably. "The Stork knows we have the egg *and* the dagger. I reckon he'll be here any day now to claim what's rightfully his."

Unbeknownst to Noa, Helena's eyes had flickered instinctively towards the wigeon girl over her use of those three words: *What's rightfully his.*

"Tomorrow morning," Helena said slowly, keeping a close eye on Phellis, "I will open the artifact."

Noa met her gaze, his eyes somber and full of remorse. "For Red."

She nodded firmly. "For Jared."

It was settled, then. Come dawn, the group would finally uncover the mystery of what lay inside the artifact. That night, Helena went to bed troubled, wondering what was to come in the days ahead. She laid her head on her pillow, brooding at the flickering fireplace. Jared drifted into her thoughts often, and her heart became heavy. The vivid image of her mirage came to mind as well, and she wondered if it was out there fluttering in the cold, yearning to be reunited with Helena as much as she did...

The last thing Helena saw was the striking image of the golden artifact wreathed in flames, before she fell into a long, overdue sleep.

# Chapter Twenty-Seven

Helena had been flying amidst fluffy, fuchsia clouds when a distant ringing interrupted her dreams. There remained a little while still until daybreak—why would they ring the bells this early? Half irritated, she dismissed the nettling noise and tried to fall back asleep. The ringing, however, grew more frequent, more *urgent*—a clattering noise that made Helena's stomach pool with dread. Her eyes flickered open. She concentrated on the sound as it progressed into a jarring, percussionist racket. *A celebration, maybe*, she thought, *or perhaps an early morning ceremony*. That's when the screaming started. Helena shot out of her bed at the same time Phellis did. They scuttled towards the window, stirring Noa from his sleep as they did so, and peered through the curtains.

"What's all the mighty racket for?" Noa mumbled, swinging his legs over the high ledge of his bunk and rubbing his tired eyes.

Helena's chin lay atop Phellis' head as their eyes fought to discern what was happening through the misty morning fog which blanketed the entire valley. It was difficult to see, given what little light was available—although a dim halo permeated the backdrop of the eastern mountains, meaning the sun would rise shortly. Helena trained her eyes upon the nebulous haze, troubled by the continuous commotion taking place within the kingdom.

*What is going on?* she wondered as goosebumps trailed along her arms.

Then, in the foggy distance, several avian citizens shot out of the haze and into the sky, fleeing west towards Helena's cabin. Mirroring them, a crowd of wigeons emerged from the fog and bolted for the hills as they fled from something in the east. As they ran, they looked fearfully over their shoulders, some tripping over their own feet and getting left behind, for it was every man and woman for themselves—but exactly *what* they were fleeing from, however, remained unclear.

"They're running from something!" Helena exclaimed, straightening up.

*"The Krows have come to kill us all!"* Phellis cried.

"Relax," Noa said, jumping from his bunk and landing on the floor with a dull *thud.* "This close to morning? I think not."

"It might be the Fallen Coven, or another Diurnal clan they've struck alliances with," Helena said grimly. "We might be getting attacked at this very moment! Noa, get the dagger!"

*"Aye!"*

"I'll get the egg!" cried Phellis, moving to fetch the tongs to take the egg out of the fire, but the wigeon girl came to a jarring halt when Helena beat her to it and practically ripped the iron tool out of her hands.

"The egg goes with me," Helena said stiffly.

Phellis stared at Helena in bewilderment before her face quickly gave way to cold indignation. "Fine."

The group left their cabin and hurried down the hill. The egg was stuffed safely in the bag slung over Helena's shoulder, while Noa secured the chest in his arms. They made their way down towards the nearest greenwood, where dozens of citizens had gathered and huddled in fear. Funnily enough, most of them had not a clue what they were running from, but had merely followed the crowd and fled from suspected danger.

One young ave, however, gathered a sizable crowd as she sat on the edge of a fallen log. She wept unconsolably, and no one could fish any bit of information out of her that didn't have them scratching their heads anxiously. She sobbed and cried—*"I looked at her! I didn't know what I was looking at—she looked so normal. I am cursed!"*

Helena, Noa, and Phellis looked at one another in grim doubt. Slipping away from the murmuring crowds, they headed east towards the heart of the kingdom to investigate. As other aves and wigeons flocked past them, fleeing from the unknown threat, the group wondered if they should join the herd, too. But they carried on regardless, the morning fog diminishing as they did so, and the vast stretch of valley became more visible. The skies were a clear blue and free from any smoke. There was no clanging of swords, or war cries, or ululations of any sort—only the songs of the morning birds. Helena spotted nothing out of the ordinary, apart from the occasional stragglers who fled past them and the glorious crown of the sun peeking over the eastern mountains.

But as the impending threat beckoned them further eastwards, Helena realized it wasn't an *army* they were fleeing from, but a *woman*. The sun had risen, and its warmth came down upon her pale frame with a wrathful grace. It seemed so clear, now, why the common folk fled at the sight of her. Nothing could have prepared Helena for what she was about to see.

Penelope Duskmuth was walking in broad daylight.

It was a jarring experience, laying your eyes upon a daywalker—it was a wonder the world did not implode! Penelope was the same as always, stiff-necked and bumptious to a vexing degree, but those eyes...all the light in the world could not change the haunting nature of those beady eyes. Still, there was an unearthly beauty to the daywalker that Helena could not help but marvel at: Penelope's skin, which had always looked cold and macabre, had now acquired a kind of translucence. Her long hair, once a dark and nightly shade, was now a pleasant brown highlighted with streaks of gold. She stretched the lengths of her white wings open to their fullest potential just as streams of benevolent light descended upon her...and the moment in which light struck feather, they flourished like two blinding, incandescent fronds. All of these features which had never revealed themselves in the dark were now illuminated in unrestrained sunlight...including the freest of smiles.

Penelope had never looked as beautiful as she did in the sunlight.

*"NO!!!"* Phellis covered her eyes and ran the opposite way. *"I DIDN'T LOOK, I DIDN'T LOOK..."*

As easy as it could have been for Helena to give in to cowardly superstition, she remained where she was—as did Noa, who struggled to understand the scene playing out before his eyes.

"I can't believe she did it..." Helena said, at a near loss for words.

"She's just walking," Noa said, unimpressed. "Why isn't she screaming like she did the first time her finger got caught in the light? Bleated like a dying goat, she did!"

Penelope set her eerie sights on them and approached them.

Helena drew out her iron dagger from her belt and shouted, *"Keep your distance, daywalker!"*

Penelope came to a slow halt. "You remain wary of me."

"It's no surprise, given everything you've done," spat Helena.

"Still, you do not flee like the rest. Why is it that you two stand before me, without so much as a care in the world that you behold a walking contradiction? A daywalking Nocturnal! Are you not worried I'll bind you to a lifetime of misfortune?"

Noa snorted. "With the life I've led, I'm afraid my Creator already beat you to it!"

Penelope gave him a rueful smile. "That, we have in common."

"Well, if you're here for the artifact, you're out of luck," Helena declared, raising her dagger. "It's ours now, and we won't let you take it without a fight! This time I'll make sure that you'll never get the chance to take it from me again!"

"There's no need, Helena. I have no further interest in the matter."

"You expect us to believe that after you tried to kill us in those caverns for it?" Noa's indignant voice sounded.

Penelope's stiff-necked gaze locked onto Helena. "If I still wanted the egg, I would have killed the both of you that night in the forest, and you very well know it."

"Why didn't you?" Helena demanded.

Something of a faint, mournful humor appeared on Penelope's face. "Believe me, I wanted nothing more at the time. I spent my entire life searching for a way to break this Vespertine Curse...and when I located the artifact, I believed I had finally found the Twilight Stone. But then you ripped it from my hands, Helena! I was determined to hunt you down and take it back, even if that meant taking your life in the process. That night, I found you sleepwalking through the forest with the egg cradled in your arms. I was determined to cut your throat, toss your body in a river, and get it over with...until I saw the full moon cast its silver beams upon the egg, and in an event so magical I could barely comprehend it, the artifact revealed itself to you."

Helena sucked in a sharp breath. *So, it wasn't just a dream after all,* she thought.

"Truly a magical, eye-opening sight, indeed—it confirmed the remaining suspicions I had of what truly resided within that artifact..." Penelope saw their looks of confusion and laughed. "Is it not ever so clear to you both that what lies inside that artifact is not a stone, but a *mirage?*"

In an instant, Helena felt her world stop spinning.

*"What did you just say?"* she whispered in disbelief.

"Not just any mirage," Penelope continued, choosing her words deliberately. "A perfectly preserved fragment of a soul predating us by thousands of years."

It was a bombshell of a revelation. In a matter of seconds, Helena's center of gravity shifted entirely. Now more than ever, she became hyperaware of the golden artifact in the bag slung across her back, which seemed to have almost doubled in weight.

"You're lying," Helena growled, all while her heart raced.

"Of course she is!" Noa snarled. "It's all her kind knows!"

"I've since abandoned the need for deceit."

"Fine. If there is such a thing as a mirage in that egg...*who* does it belong to?" demanded Helena.

"If my assumptions are correct, it may have belonged to a powerful individual—one of the *first avians* who roamed the Upper Realm hundreds of thousands of years ago, or a descendant, at least. Perhaps someone who lived to see magic and dragons in their prime..."

Helena's mind reeled. She thought back to Penelope's journal and everything she had written about the First Avians, dragons, sorcerers and mirages...

"...but such a theory could only be confirmed by opening the artifact and claiming the mirage for oneself," Penelope said.

This time, it was Helena's turn to laugh. "How absurd! As if it'd be possible for an ave to claim a mirage that was not their own! All my life I was taught that every mirage is unique to each person and only ever belongs to them! I've never heard of an ave *claiming* another ave's mirage..."

"It is not to say you have been taught *wrong*, Helena, merely that we've yet to fully understand the complexities and nuances of the avian mirage. When we speak of an avian claiming another mirage, the statement may be unheard of, but that is not to say that such a thing would be altogether impossible. The only criteria I would expect is that the person in question must not have a mirage—which, given your present situation, is a condition aptly met."

"No!" Helena said, shaking her head stubbornly. "I can't accept it! Putting together an avian and a mirage that isn't theirs sounds wrong...it would be like trying to jam two mismatched puzzle pieces together—it would never work!"

"Some puzzle pieces can still go together, even if they are not a perfect fit."

"What you're saying," Helena said warily, "is that, given the right circumstances, anyone could claim the mirage inside that artifact?"

"Theoretically, even Noa would have a chance to claim it, if he were up for the task—"

"Not a chance!" he snarled. "Do you think me so weak-minded as to take it? I'm no sellout!"

"I didn't think so," Penelope said with a grim smile. "Regardless, it is neither mine nor yours to claim—that is a fate entirely reserved for Helena."

"*Me?*"

"What's this got to do with her?" demanded Noa.

"She must be the one to take the mirage when it opens," Penelope said, staring right into Helena's wide eyes. "The mirage revealed itself to you and no one else. Do you think it mere coincidence that you, whose tragic fate involved the loss of their mirage, ended up in the possession of another mirage? It is, dare I say it, *Fate.* And it is nobody's but your own."

"You speak nonsense!" cried Noa. "You expect us to take yer word for all this?"

"He's right," said Helena, though her hands were now trembling. "For all we know, there might not even be a mirage inside that egg. You could simply be trying to mislead us again!"

"Might I remind you that this artifact was found within a dragon's lair which contained hundreds—perhaps even thousands—of mirages? The concept of a single mirage is awesome enough, let alone a hundred thousand mirages clustered into one room! Given that information, does it seem so improbable to you that there may be a mirage inside that egg? It would do you well, Helena, to recall the moment in our duel when you threatened to break the egg, and I flung my knife at your head—everybody knows my aim is anything but poor, and if I wished to lodge a knife cleanly through the back of your eye socket, then I would have! I purposefully aimed the knife at my own mirage to set it free—but what happened afterwards was an occurrence that left me pondering for nights on end! Every single mirage in that chamber flocked to you like an angry flock of sparrows. Might you do us the courtesy, Helena, of sharing the supernatural experience of being swarmed by the purest matter known to avian kind?"

"I didn't see much," Helena admitted reluctantly. "I was blinded—it was like looking directly at the sun. I did, however, hear the voices of many strangers whom I had never met; they seemed desperate, as if they were searching for something..."

"Not something—*someone.* Those mirages were looking for their original hosts—people who never made it past the isthmus and thus departed from their mirages upon death. Since they were nowhere to be found, the mirages flocked to the closest living thing that would have given them shelter—which was you, Helena. They were drawn to you because they sensed the absence of your own mirage."

"If that's the case, then why didn't any of them try to claim me as their host? Or Noa, or Jared, or Phellis?"

"I surmise there is some degree of compatibility that comes into play when claiming a mirage. They likely left when they realized they were incompatible with any of you...in your case, Helena, perhaps they had realized you were already destined for the mirage inside the artifact..."

Penelope hesitated before continuing. "There's one more thing that may be of interest to you, Helena. In the chance that you may prove compatible with this mirage, it is possible that it could grant you your wings back."

It was the moment of truth Helena had been waiting for. In the long, devastating months that had followed the night of her fall, Helena had made a strenuous effort to break her own heart—to convince herself that she had lost her wings for good and would never fly again. But only hope could flourish in despair, and this was the case for Helena; she had always held out a sliver of hope, a tiny spark, that no one—not even herself—could put out. She had known from the beginning, whether she was conscious of it or not, that one day she would soar the skies once more.

"I could fly again?" Helena whispered, awestruck. But the words came out more as a realization than as a question.

Penelope confirmed this with a single nod.

"Yer not actually believing her, are you, bird?" Noa's hasty voice came from Helena's left. "You said it yerself—what she speaks is impossible!"

Noa's outburst had piqued Penelope's interest, and she eyed him watchfully. "Helena's case is unique for one reason, and one reason alone: her mirage was stolen from her, leaving a vacancy inside her that yearns to be occupied. Is it such a coincidence that Helena finds herself so drawn to the egg that she actually sleepwalks with it? Such a thing could only indicate that whatever is inside the egg has chosen her..."

"What would become of me if I took the mirage?" Helena asked Penelope quietly.

"Bird!" Noa cried in dismay.

"I only want to know what would happen in the case that I do," she snapped, to which Noa scoffed and looked away, clearly upset. Helena gave Penelope the sign to continue.

"I will confess that a shroud of mystery lies over the process, so we can only speculate given the limited knowledge that we have. More than likely, the moment you lay claim to the mirage inside the artifact would be the moment you renounce all claims to the mirage of your past, severing the bond with the old and in turn forging a bond with the new."

"I would be renouncing my own mirage," Helena stated, her heart tightening at the thought of the flickering dove.

"It would erase any chance of reunion, certainly—if it hasn't already perished."

"And then what?"

"Well, if you and the mirage do, in fact, prove compatible, then logically it would be safe to assume that this new mirage might grant you a new pair of wings. However, we must also take into account the Law of Attainment, which states that all aves must earn their wings. I'd wager you *would* have to earn your new wings in some way—though *how*, exactly, I cannot say with certainty."

"But they wouldn't truly be mine," Helena argued. "They would have belonged to someone else."

Penelope shrugged. "Beggars can't be choosers."

"Enough of this!" Noa spat. "Yer filling her head with half-truths and impossibilities—for all we know, yer rushing her headfirst into something that could kill her! But you would like that, wouldn't you? Since the day we met, you've harbored nothing but ill will for the bird—I'm sure nothing would bring you greater joy than to see her demise!"

Penelope chuckled softly at this. "I assure you, Noa, this matter goes as far beyond my personal dislike for Helena as it does your affections for her. There is only one person alive who has the highest potential claim to that mirage, and it's Helena; and if she waits too long to stake that claim, then there will be no stopping the Stork from stealing back the dagger and creating someone else suitable for the job! Are any of us eager to see Ptero the Bloodthirsty become the next candidate?"

Nobody objected to this. The thought of Ptero claiming this mirage was enough to send chills down Helena's spine.

"All the same, it is neither up to you, Noa, nor me to decide if Helena is to claim that mirage. She must decide for herself. I have given you all the information necessary to know what awaits you if you decide to take the mirage. As for me—I'm afraid our time together is coming to an end."

Helena looked at her, confused, until the true meaning of Penelope's words settled in. She gasped—

"You've stepped completely into the light! You've crossed the threshold...that means you'll die!"

The Nocturnal looked somber when she said, "The curse has been set in motion. I shall soon meet my fate."

*"Why? Why would you do that?"*

"The Stork will soon resume his quest for the Twilight Stone, of which I will not partake in. He and his spies in the Upper Realm spent years tracking my brother and me, who have gathered mountains of evidence pertaining to the stone's existence. Much of it would have aided the Stork in his quest to find the stone, but I've ensured he will not get his hands on our work in two ways: first, before my brother and I set off to Nadiir, we burned all evidence, every document or text that we found that might prove useful to his efforts. Secondly...well, the answer is standing right in front of you. By stepping out into the sun, I have assured that by the time the Stork gets his hands on me, I will be rendered either incognizant or dead. Either way, he will never obtain any information from me that could aid his nefarious cause, either by way of torture or compliance."

"But now all those years you've spent looking for the Twilight Stone, all that hard work...it will all be for nothing?"

"That is correct."

For reasons unbeknownst to Helena, she was overcome with mixed feelings of anger and sadness. It was a decision she simply couldn't fathom. It seemed too futile...too defeatist...as if some deep recess inside Helena's complicated heart actually hoped that Penelope would live on and someday find absolution in her troubled existence...but Penelope had already sealed her fate the moment she stepped out into the light.

"Cheer up, Helena. Would there be any use in trying to rectify what has already been written in stone? I've wasted years trying to change the inevitable...for all I know, the Twilight Stone has either been destroyed, or lies at the bottom of the sea by now—and after the loss of my brother..." A thick tear caressed her gossamer white cheek, leaving behind a glittering trail. "Why seek glory if you have none to share it with? Olip was my soul companion—we did everything together, but now he is long past, as are my mother and father...

"My dear father...he was the one who planted the seeds of daylight in my mind, long before his death. Every night before bed, he filled my head with descriptions of wonders he could've only gleaned from the hundreds of books he had read in his life—Murmurations, rainbows, sunsets. Pale skies, cotton clouds, and bright summer days…all those things which your kind readily takes for granted! And so it was written that my father, a man who spent his entire life locked within the confines of this miserable, wretched darkness, would die basking in that which he spent his entire life pining for—and in that way, I am my father's daughter…"

Penelope let out a cry of dismay. "No cure for this curse could ever surmount the loss of my family! I will grieve their deaths until my last breath, and while I could not fulfill the dreams we created together, I will spend the remainder of my days enjoying the splendor of the sun in their honor. If I am lucky…I may even get to witness a true Murmuration before I pass. Fairwinds, Helena Nightingale! Perhaps in another life, under different circumstances, you and I might have been friends…for you see, you and I are not so different. We are kindred spirits that yearn to be free—whether it be by flying amidst the clouds or simply walking in sunlight without constraint…I came before you today to reveal the contents of the artifact, in the hopes that you might achieve the freedom you so desperately desire. As for myself, well…is it not ever so clear that I already have?"

Penelope turned and made her last venture across the sunlit valley, laughing joyously as she called out:

*"Death! Death! I am no longer afraid of you! There is nothing sweeter than the newborn breath of the sun. Belly-warming and rich, like nectar. Harken, the endarkened! What is life without light?"*

# Chapter Twenty-Eight

With rumors of a ghoul stalking the kingdom spreading like wildfire, no one dared step foot outside their houses, and an eerie chill fell upon the streets, which were left desolate. The superstitious believed that to lay sights on such a creature was an ill omen. Phellis, for instance, believed it would lead to a life of misfortune and an untimely death. As she and Noa watched Phellis crying hysterically underneath her blankets, even Helena could not deny the small amount of anxiety she felt over the infinitesimal chance of all this talk harboring some truth.

*"She's cursed us all!"* Phellis sobbed.

"Please! You really think the three of us will die 'cause we saw someone *walk?"* Noa asked incredulously.

"My great-great-grandpaw had a cousin whose friend knew a guy whose sister laid her eyes upon one o'em daywalkers. She caught a cold the next day and *boom!* Keeled over dead as a doornail! Don't tell me it's all just some kinda coinkydink!"

Though Noa's instinctual response was to roll his eyes at this, a look of uncertainty eventually flashed across his face.

"Got to admit Penelope *has* gone off the deep end, hasn't she?" he said warily.

"Grief will do that to you, I suppose," Helena said in agreement. "She's got nothing more to lose."

Phellis was still sniffling under her covers when Noa made a harsh sound of dissent—

"*Chh!* That's why I'm sure she was speaking nothing but farces! What lunacy she was on about, talking about sunsets and rainbows and mirages ..."

Phellis stopped sniffling at the word *mirages.*

"I don't think she was lying when she said there was a mirage inside that artifact," Helena said gravely. Their eyes fell upon the gleaming token of gold sitting upon a bundle of clothes on the table.

Phellis uncovered herself, revealing her puffy face. "What are you guys talking about?"

After explaining what Penelope had revealed about the artifact, Phellis cast an enraptured gaze upon the egg, seemingly forgetting that she had ever shed a tear. She sat up and swung her bare feet over the edge of her bed.

"You're saying this here egg can give you a pair of wings?"

"It's not that simple," Helena answered, "but theoretically, if the mirage and I were compatible...then yes, it could grant me back my wings."

"*Your* wings?" Something flashed in Phellis' silver eyes and she stood up. "Since when did we decide *you'd* be the one takin' it?"

Helena reeled slightly from this response, thrown off by its scathing tone. She chose her response deliberately, though she made no effort to conceal her irritation:

"I only assumed it would be mine to claim since I would also be the one to open it. And, well...my wings were taken from me, which is what sparked all these events in the first place. Penelope herself said I should be the one to take it, and she seemed certain that once I do it'll grant me my wings back. It's rightfully mine."

"Well, what if I want *my* wings back?"

The air shifted, and Noa stirred uncomfortably as the two wigeon girls fell into a deadlock. In truth, Helena had felt Phellis had grown a lot more distant since their return from Mount Sulfur—the dynamic between them had changed, and it was ever so obvious given the way the coin eyes of Phellis regarded Helena so coldly.

"You lost your wings a long time ago, Phellis," Helena said stiffly. "Mine were stolen only recently."

"Mine were taken all the same! And wasn't it you who told me you'd given up on getting yer wings back?"

"Things have changed."

"Oh, really? What about your mirage?"

"It's gone and will most likely perish any one of these days." Helena played this off as if it didn't hurt her so terribly to say it aloud. "My only remaining option is to take the egg."

Phellis huffed. "Well, why's it gotta be *you*, of all people? Who's to say Noa doesn't want wings, too?"

"Don't drag me into this," he said to her warningly. "I want no part of this."

"Jared wanted his wings, too! It's all he's ever wanted! What if he were standing here today—"

"He isn't," Noa snapped. "So, keep his name out yer mouth! As for me—I've long made peace with who I am. For I was born a wigeon and a wigeon I shall stay!"

Phellis crossed her arms. "*Hmph!* All I'm saying is it's not fair that *Queen Helena* gets to claim the mirage above everyone else, an' we're all expected to just go along with it all willy-nilly—"

A wave of anger rushed over Helena, and she could hold her tongue no longer. "Why can't you understand that I'm the only one with a legitimate claim to that mirage? The artifact *chose* me because my mirage was taken from me. Yes, you lost your wings, but that doesn't mean you lost your mirage, too. Technically, you still have one, and you can't claim a new mirage when you already have one—"

"I'll remove it with the dagger, then!"

"Oh, don't be ridiculous!"

"*But why not?*"

"Because I said so!" Helena snapped, her face flushed in anger. "You're treading dark waters, Phellis. Living without a mirage is a lowly life I wouldn't wish upon anybody, not even my worst enemy...but enough! I won't spend a minute more debating this with you. *I'm* taking the mirage, and there's nothing you or anyone else can do about it!"

"*Oh, it's not fair!*" Phellis cried, before marching out the door and slamming it behind her. Her sobs sounded loudly, even from afar. Helena only stared at the door, taking deep breaths in an effort to control her breathing. Noa seemed indifferent, even annoyed by the entire ordeal, yet he offered no criticism of Helena's selfish decision. *Yes,* Helena thought. *Selfish. That's what I am. It's selfish of me to take the egg for myself...*

But there was no other way.

"So, it's settled, then?" Noa asked Helena afterwards. "Yer claiming the mirage?"

Something in his expression shifted. A look of doubt, perhaps even hurt showed on his face. Helena's memory flashed back to a conversation they had shared some time ago:

*I just can't see myself with a flocker,* she recalled him saying.

*Why?* she demanded.

*It's a recipe for a broken heart. They always fly away and never return.*

"Nothing is set in stone," she said at last, and Noa turned to look at her hopefully. "Let's say that, by *some* miracle, I do manage to bond with that mirage...it would erase any chances of me reuniting with my true mirage. Though I would earn my wings, they still wouldn't be *mine.*"

Helena decided that she would need peace and quiet to contemplate the decision she was about to make.

Somewhere deep within the woodlands, surrounded by endless columns of shady oakwood trees and honeysuckle bushes, Helena found ample time to think. Noa eventually joined her, though he looked anxious as he sat down next to her. They sat in silence for many moments until Helena finally broke it.

"Do you believe in the saying that those we love never truly leave us?"

When Noa heard this he chuckled to himself, though his eyes harbored little humor.

"Yer asking the wrong person, bird—all my loved ones left before I could walk and never came back."

Helena frowned. "I had no idea you were so young at the time."

He shrugged, playing off the hurt on his face. "Yea, the scummy woman who birthed me dumped me on some doorstep with only a name tag that read *Oskar.*"

*"Your real name is Oskar?"*

He laughed. "I reckon it's hard going by a name given by someone you never met! I ditched it not long after I left the orphanage. In efforts to start anew, I chose Noa after the biggest ship I knew at the time—*The Noadine.* It was my dream to board her and sail the world…

"Well, if you want a real answer to your question," Noa said after a while, "It's my belief that you'll meet tens of thousands of people in yer life, but only few ever mark you, inside and out. Blood's got nothing to do with it," he said firmly, and Helena knew that Jared passed through his mind at that instant.

"…the best kind of people never leave. Even if they do, they'll never cease to exist in yer mind, even after they die. That only happens when you forget them—which, in most cases, is impossible…why the somber question, bird?"

Helena mulled over his answer for a good long while before she answered.

"My mother died shortly after I turned five."

"My condolences," Noa said with a frown. "Do you remember what she looked like?"

Helena shook her head. "Hardly. I can, however, recall what it felt like to lose her. I was a child, then, barely old enough to understand the concept of death, yet wise enough to know that her absence had left a rift in my life which I had no idea how to mend. My father never fails to mention how I was a talkative child. Spunky, outgoing, and even humorous—like him." Helena smiled sadly. "Things changed after my mother's death. I became quiet and lonely. Often left to my own thoughts."

"Yer mother's departure changed you," he said.

Helena nodded. "Things became easier after I got my wings, which was about a year after her death. Before long, the clouds and I were inseparable. Flying helped take my mind off things, you see. I suppose you could say it became an obsession at some point…but it was the only thing that made things bearable. When I was flying, I wasn't grieving. I wasn't angry…I just *was*. With every wingstroke, my thoughts and troubles carried off into the wind. I suppose that's why the loss of my wings hit me so hard—it was the first time I felt true grief since the death of my mother. And this time, I felt everything, and all at once—with no ability to escape."

Her face was wet now. "I was told that the things we love always have a way of returning to us, even if in a different form. For me, my mirage was my mother's way of coming back to me. When I flew, it was as if she had never really left me. And my father...well, he was there the day I earned my wings. He always says it was one of the happiest days of his life, second only to the day I was born. He's just as much a part of my mirage as my mother is...if I claimed someone else's mirage, it would be like trading in the memory of my parents. For good."

Driven by a sudden impulse, Noa took Helena's hands in his.

"Come with me!"

Helena stuttered, "W-what?"

*"Leave it all behind.* Rid yourself of that rotten egg and forget you ever had anything to do with it! We both know it's unlikely you'll find yer true mirage in time, and it doesn't look like your heart's fully committed to claiming this new one—so just forget all of it and come with me! Listen...there's talk at the Wigeon's Guild of a ship at the Western Coves that's preparing to explore the Nadiirian seas. Come with me, and we could set sail across the New World together! We can start anew, you and me, as wigeons!"

"Sail to the New World?" she asked hesitantly.

He nodded eagerly. "Sailing is just like flying—you said so yerself. Doesn't it sound exciting?"

"Yes, but..."

His smile fell. Leaning back, he crossed his arms and huffed, "If I didn't know any better, I'd say yer scared!"

"Of what?" she asked, scowling.

"Of staying a wigeon."

She stammered, "I-it's not that! Penelope said the artifact chose me! If I turn it down, it might have disastrous consequences..."

"That's a mighty poor excuse, bird, and you know it!" Noa seized her by the shoulders so that he was looking right into her eyes. "I've known you less than a year, bird, and I can tell clear as day that yer terrified. You spent yer entire life tossing and turning in the air, and now you tremble at the thought of staying grounded forever. Why? Is it 'cause of what others would think of you? Do you think you wouldn't be enough?"

"You don't understand how hard this decision is for me, Noa," she cried, tears leaking from the corners of her eyes. "I had a whole life before all this. I used to soar so high, I could almost touch the sun—the night you found me fallen...well, that was the lowest I'd ever been!"

He shook his head firmly. "I don't see it that way. I wasn't there to see you in yer prime, as you say, but this—" He gestured to her from head to toe. "—is the only person I've ever known, and that's okay. You don't need a pair of wings for me to accept you. You can just be yerself. That's more than enough for me."

Helena could not formulate a response to this and could only look down in shame. When Noa saw her expression, he softened a bit. He released her and leaned back with a sigh.

"I won't force you to do anything you don't want to, bird. It's yer choice, and yers only. As for me...there's nothing left for me here, or in Avalon. Red's likely dead, and I've got no living kin. If things don't work out, my next course will be for the Western Coves. I won't press anymore on the subject, but I want you to think about it, bird, and think on it hard. The offer remains on the table."

Noa rose to his feet and offered his hand to her. "Come. I want to show you something."

"Where are we going?" she asked, taking it hesitantly.

"It's a surprise."

Noa led Helena through the deepest woodlands of the valley. Helena was clueless as to where he was taking her.

"Do you remember way back in those caverns, when we reached the isthmus?" he started as they crossed a stream. "That night, you helped me when I needed it most."

Helena snorted. "Yes, by abandoning you!"

"Sometimes the greatest thing you can do for someone is putting them on their own two feet. But that's not what I'm referring to...something else happened to me in those caverns. Something that I never had the courage to share with you...until now."

Helena tilted her head curiously. "What are you talking about?"

"That night in the caverns, when we reached the isthmus...I felt I was done for. I had no fight in me. I would've died in those tunnels, if it weren't for you. Yer words moved me, and when you left, and then Red left, only me and that cursed waterway remained. I swear something called to me. I don't know what it was, but I mustered the courage to slip into the water and crawl my way through the tunnels. It wasn't long until I felt fear creep around me like a python. I felt the air flee from my lips...

"I knew I had come a long way, but I still had a long way left to go. I felt my future dim. I stopped, my body shuddering with fear. I knew it was the end—until I saw it: a bright light at the far end of the tunnel. Stay with me, now, bird. I know I sound like a lunatic...but it called to me. So, with the remaining strength I had in my limbs, I crawled through that waterway and followed the light. The closer I got, the more I could see it. It...it was a dove leading my way through the tunnels."

"A dove?" Helena stuttered, her heart fluttering. "You mean to say you saw my mirage? But that's impossible!"

"I don't know what I saw. I just know that the closer I got to this light, the more it filled me with...with hope. And when it called to me, it was yer voice I heard. You carried me through those tunnels, Helena."

The sound of her name coming through his mouth sparked a flurry of butterflies in Helena's stomach.

"Noa, I—"

"You needn't say anything. I only tell you this because...well, you mean more to me than what I usually let on. I'm just glad we met that fateful night, bird."

"I am, too," she gushed.

They reached a hill overlooking the great valley, which was aglow with amber rays of light as the sun prepared to set.

"Close yer eyes," Noa asked, and Helena did as he said. He led her up the steep hill, and though she felt a tad uncomfortable trekking blindly up the slope, she trusted that Noa wouldn't let her stumble. When they reached the top of the hill, they were struck by a cool breeze, and Helena sighed, basking in the wind as she always had.

"Don't open them yet," he said in her ear, sending shivers down her spine. "Just listen."

Helena trained her senses on a strange, yet somehow familiar noise. At first, it was but a distant murmur. Rolling...crashing...like indecisive waves against a shore. Helena imagined herself burying her toes in the fine sand. As she inched herself closer, the sound of gentle tides rose in a deafening crescendo! A million voices hurled themselves at her, and she could no longer keep her eyes shut.

The sky was no more. Hundreds, if not thousands, of starling birds surrounded them, emblazoned spirits crying out as one as they relished the magic of their own Murmuration. Oh! How to decipher which feeling was more prevalent—longing or gratitude—she could not determine. It seemed so long since she was back home, flying amongst the clouds. Helena's heart yearned for home, for her father, and for the freedom that had slipped from the palm of her hand like smoke...how she yearned to fly once more!

And yet, she was so moved that this boy whom she had known for only a brief span of time had gone to such great lengths to show her this. By what cause had he the inclination to show Helena a Murmuration—the symbol of her people, the pinnacle of her notion of freedom—all as she faced uncertainty?

Then, amidst all this emotional turmoil, Noa turned to Helena and made one request:

"Tell me how you earned yer wings."

The request was as sudden as it was invoking. Her heart swelled so impossibly big that it threatened to explode! That fateful evening, Helena decided to reveal her deepest secret to the heart that resonated with hers the most. She pressed her lips against his ear and whispered the five words that would forever define her life, and would, for that moment, be lost within that small window of time.

# Chapter Twenty-Nine

Something had shifted between Helena and Noa as they strolled through the streets later that evening, though Helena was unsure how to label their new dynamic. Friends did not walk the streets laughing with their hands brushing against each other, their fingers occasionally intertwining and sparking trails of sensation up each other's arms. Had Noa been just a friend, he would not have leant so dangerously close to Helena that she could see the lightning streaks of caramel in his dark, impish eyes, before they would flicker playfully down to her lips and then back up to meet her green eyes again. Never once did he take the risk to kiss Helena, however, which she found odd. She didn't take him for the courteous type. Part of her surmised that he was waiting for *her* to initiate the kiss, which Helena was grateful for, given her novice experience in such matters.

As their interlinked hands swung back and forth between them, Noa said, "Abernam tells me *The Late Duchess* sets sail within the next month."

The momentum of their hands fell to a slow rock as this news threw Helena slightly aback.

"So soon?" she said, her eyelids fluttering.

"Of course! I heard she is aglow, her panels polished and sails crisply woven with the finest hemp fibers. She'll have no problem catapulting us headfirst into the New World," he said with an enthusiastic grin.

Helena felt an immense wave of guilt. Though this was the fondest she had ever been of the wigeon boy, Helena never recalled distinctly agreeing to accompany him on his endeavor to explore the Nadiirian seas! It seemed that the tenderhearted moment they shared had convinced Noa that she would choose a life of wigeonhood with him...when in actuality, it had only solidified Helena's resolve to taste flight again as she had known it once before.

"Have you ever considered how dangerous it is to set sail upon uncharted territory?" Helena said, a tad nervous. "I suppose there's no telling what you'll find out there. Storms, pirates, sea monsters...who's to say you won't fall over the edge of the world?"

Their walk came to a gradual stop. He paused, glancing at their interlocked hands before saying, "Yer not getting cold feet, are you, bird?"

In that instant, a spine-tingling noise blared across the valley. It shook the earth and trees, striking fear into the hearts of all who heard it. All eyes looked to the sky as a golden beam parted the clouds and touched down upon the center of the great valley. Three flashing lights fell along this beam like falling stars before they touched the Nadiirian floor. In a wisp, the beam was gone, and only silence remained.

Nearly every citizen who had seen this marvelous scene unravel flocked to the heart of the kingdom. Hand in hand, Helena and Noa ran to see what all the commotion was about. They met a great crowd surrounding a trio of silver-winged knights dressed in gleaming iron suits. They boasted silky black banners displaying a flock of seven silver birds—the sigil of the Kingdom of Avalon! The knights stood before King Hyrax, Rancipert, and a handful of other military officials who acknowledged the Avalonians with a stiff salute. One of Avalon's knights towered over the rest, with black, flowy hair and enormous gold-speckled wings...

*"Yulix!"* Helena exclaimed, releasing Noa's hand.

"Behold! A message from the King of Avalon, His Majesty King Haeron IV!" Yulix declared.

Helena fought her way through the thick crowds as Noa called out after her, but she did not seem to hear him—she was too busy fighting to get a better look at her old friend. She could only glimpse his wings and the back of his head, though she had no problem hearing his bright, trumpeting voice.

As the king rose to acknowledge his guest, Yulix knelt and bowed his head.

"We meet again, Ser Ulyxes Cazador," King Hyrax said, his face as grim and uninviting as ever. "I have heard brave tales of your journey back to Paradise."

"It was not without sacrifice," Yulix responded, his head still bowed. "I would not be here if it weren't for the honorable men you stationed at my side, three of whom remain in Avalon, the rest of which died bravely in our endeavor to cross the Nadiirian Plate."

"I expect, then, that these men did not die in vain, and that you come bearing promising news?"

Rising to his feet, Yulix removed the silver wax seal of the scroll in his hands, unraveling it completely until it was the length of his entire torso. With a voice that was clear and bright, he declared the following before the king and his people:

"Whereas His Majesty King Haeron IV has duly taken into consideration the crimes committed by the Nevarian race against His subjects, as well as the rapid spread of their influence across the Lower Realm, and as a courtesy for the generosity and hospice that the people of Alazar demonstrated for Ser Ulyxes Cazador, a prospective member of His Majesty's King's Guard, His Majesty doth think it prudent that the two great Kingdoms of Avalon and Alazar enjoin their efforts against a common foe and make common cause to mutually aid each other as good and faithful allies, which shall include the granting of military aid to help curtail the growing threat of the Nevarian regime. Avalon shall henceforth open a gateway between the Upper and Lower Realms to allow the proper flow of military aid, as well as to grant the women and children of Alazar asylum within the Kingdom of Avalon if they so choose. Long Live the King!"

"The Kingdom of Avalon is opening its gates!" a citizen exclaimed.

"We are saved from those demons!" another cried.

"Mama, does this mean we may yet go to Paradise?" a young boy asked his mother.

"Hope willing, dear!" she replied.

With a proud, diplomatic disposition, Yulix approached the Nadiirian king and handed him the scroll, along with a shining, silver-feathered quill.

"With your signature agreeing to the terms provided within the treaty, we shall henceforth honor the alliance between Alazar and the Kingdom of Avalon."

King Hyrax, however, remained skeptical, one brow pointedly raised as he read over the contents of the treaty.

"Your promise of military aid—what does it amount to?"

"By courtesy of His everlasting grace, His Majesty has promised a host of two hundred soldiers, all well-seasoned in combat."

"Two hundred? Hmph! A small lot, if ever I found one..."

"I assure you that one seasoned Avalonian soldier is worth ten of those Nevarian Krows. You shall find yourself well equipped."

"Explain to me, then, what we should expect on the day of their arrival."

"In a week's time, by command of the King, a portal shall henceforth be opened between both Realms. By then, a host of two hundred men and women will be waiting for the order to touch down on Nadiirian soil. Once they have done so, the Gate will remain open for a finite amount of time to allow women, children, and the elderly safe passage into the Upper Realm."

"What does 'finite' mean, in measured terms?"

"From the time it opens until the time it closes, the portal shall remain active for no longer than twenty minutes total."

"A narrow window, I might say!"

"His Majesty acts with haste to reduce the number of hostiles who would seek to cross over into the Upper Realm. Thus, he encourages all citizens of Alazar who would seek passage to make their due preparations—for once the Gate closes, they will not be granted a second opportunity to do so."

"I see. So, Ulyxes Cazador! You grant us military aid and asylum, but what does *His Majesty* expect from us in return?"

"In light of our shared interests in these lands, His Majesty requests full access to your natural resources, including iron ore deposits, gold, timber, and coal, all of which shall be used in service of our efforts to curtail the enemy."

By the looks of it, the Nadiirian king was none too taken with this condition...but the prospect of aid and asylum was still too good an offer to refuse.

"Very well," he said at last. He raised his silver quill. "May this day mark the first alliance between the heavens and the earth!"

The people of Alazar rejoiced upon the news that a gate would be opened to Paradise, where they would live safely and soundly away from the clutches of the wicked Nevarians. One young boy with white wings shot off and struck the bells in celebration. *We're going home!* he cried, repeating it to unsuspecting passersby who ran to spread the news. Helena, however, could not find it in her to mirror their joy just yet, for she had pending matters still in Nadiir—which included reuniting with an old friend.

Helena found Yulix in his private pavilion tent that same evening. He was sitting at his desk, yawning and stretching his tired wings after a long day. Helena didn't think twice before bursting into the tent and calling his name brightly, with the same notes of familiarity she had only ever used with her childhood friend. He was the same as always, though his dark hair ran a bit longer past his ears now, and dark stubble ran untamed along his jaw and neck, which was rare for the dapper young man. Still, the knight's amber eyes burned as brightly as they always had, shining like two golden coins in the dimness of the room as they saw Helena for the first time in months.

"Lena!" he exclaimed, drawing in a sharp breath and leaping to his feet. His noble face broke into an impassioned smile at the sight of his long-lost friend. It was a most joyful reception indeed—but to Helena's dismay, their rejoicing was short-lived. As he registered Helena's wingless appearance, his smile fell first; Helena's quickly followed upon noting his reaction.

His voice was but a horrified whisper: *"What have they done to you?"*

Helena had entirely forgotten that she was now a wigeon. No longer able to conceal her anguish, Helena gasped and cried out, *"Oh, Yulix! You could've at least pretended to be glad to see me!"*

"How could I, when you're in such a state?" he said sharply. He averted his gaze, for he could not bring himself to look at her. It was humiliating, to be certain. Still yet, Helena found it strangely cathartic watching the disbelief, denial, anger, and woeful acceptance—all in that order—flash across Yulix's face as he processed the misdeed that had been committed against his friend. Yulix was the first person to have physically mirrored the complex emotions that Helena herself had felt since the night of her fall. The truth was that neither Noa nor Jared could ever fully grasp the changes Helena had undergone after losing her wings—they had no else to compare her to! Imagine comparing the tired, defeated Helena they knew now to the Helena who had conquered the skies only months before! They found her fallen, but Yulix was the first one to have seen her *fall*.

"I didn't want to believe it, at first..." he said, his voice laden with remorse. "I hadn't heard of you in months, Lena. I thought you were dead! Then I received the news that you were alive, and what this so-called Stork had done to you...I had been hoping it was all some sick misunderstanding...then, as I began considering the possibility, I thought to myself: *she was better off dead!*"

Helena wept at this. Yulix walked over and pulled her pitiful frame into an embrace, and they grieved her fate together. Helena felt smaller than ever, held in his sturdy arms beneath his great wings, which enveloped her like a great cocoon. The tears came harder as she breathed in his pinewood scent, which reminded her so much of home. Once they had both exhausted themselves of their sorrows, Yulix pulled away, his face wrought with pain.

"This is all my fault," he said. "I let you out of my sight, Lena."

She lifted her hand to his cheek. "There was nothing you could have done."

He seemed not to hear her. "To think you were once a proud sight in the sky, a force to be reckoned with...and now...no worse tragedy could have befallen you. What was done to you is unforgivable, and may the vile, *wretched* hand that played a part in it never find rest! I cannot fathom the grief you endured that fateful night, let alone the last few months...if it were up to me, I would have been the one who lost my wings that night, not you!"

"What happened to me was fate, Yulix. It's taken me months to reconcile with it. I won't lie to you and say the process has been easy—in fact, I'd rather not relive it. I just...I just want to know how *he's* doing."

His eyes softened, and he bowed his head. "Your father is worried sick, Lena. Not a day goes by that he doesn't ask about you."

This thought struck Helena like a dagger to the chest.

"Utterly clueless, the old man, isn't he? About everything that's happened to me?"

"For his sake, yes."

"Good. Let it stay that way until I return..." *If I return,* Helena wanted to add. "Now, Yulix...you don't know the lengths I've gone to get ahold of you—what happened to you after we got separated?"

"That fateful night, I turned and saw the shower of white splinters and blood that rained after a Nevarian brought his morningstar against you. You were gone before I could stop you from falling to your death, and a mob of Nevarians nearly overtook me. Outnumbered, armorless, and with only a sword in my possession, I managed to slay two enemies before one hacked their silver battleaxe into my right shoulder. I nearly lost an arm that night. I fled—not out of cowardice, but because I knew you were in grave danger. So, with what little luck I had left, I narrowly evaded the hands of the swarming naves and swept across Krow's Foot in search of you. I found the blood trail from your broken wing the next day, which led me to a nest of your feathers, but there was no sign of you after that. I suspected, then, that those devilish fiends had apprehended you, and I knew if I had any hopes of getting you back, I would need to return with reinforcements...

"I knew I had a better chance of getting help if I flew north of Nadiir to other avian settlements. I flew many days and nights without rest, and most nations turned me away. I carried on, however, until I encountered the Kingdom of Alazar. After explaining my situation, Hyrax hesitantly agreed to equip me with seven of his strongest warriors to help get you back...I won't even bother telling you how tedious that exchange was. Nevertheless, we were able to launch an expedition towards Mount Sulfur to search for you—which resulted in another failed attempt."

"I was there at Mount Sulfur when you were looking for me," Helena said. "I saw you! You just couldn't hear me...had you just looked a little longer..."

"A shame we hadn't," he said regrettably. "After that, I wrestled with the possibility of your death, Lena. I had slim hopes that if I could somehow return to Avalon and express my grievances before the King of Avalon himself, he would be gracious enough to authorize a rescue mission for you. It was only after I set off on my third and final mission to return to Avalon when a Dragonback messenger informed me that you were still alive—for which my heart was glad, of course. But he also revealed to me what had become of you. I was devastated. At first, I refused to come to terms with your fate...to lose one's wings in such barbaric fashion...but I knew at once it was an allegation grave enough to warrant investigation from the Crown.

"I carried on with my objective to return to Avalon and fought my way into the Eye of Nadiir. Crossing the Nadiirian Plate was as strange as I remembered it to be—there is a moment when you are suspended in nothingness, and there is neither up nor down. Before I knew it, I shot out of the lake at Blade's Peak—and I was back in the Upper Realm, in Avalon! I then journeyed to the Aeriodome and stood before His Majesty the King, whereupon I described in great detail the events that had transpired since the night of our fall..."

"And what happened? What did he say?"

"Oh, it caused a great deal of chaos. A rift formed among the king's court—some called for intervention, others objected vehemently to the notion of meddling in the affairs of a foreign land, let alone a place historically used as a wasteland for Avalon's criminals! They would have dismissed my case altogether...if it hadn't been for you."

"*Me?*"

"Indeed. As I anticipated, your fate roused the Crown's suspicions that the Nevarians had acquired some dark and powerful magic...tell me, Lena, what do you recall of the night you lost your wings? How did it happen?"

Helena could not forget the cursed night even if she wanted to. She recounted the details of the Stork's crime and his use of an enchanted dagger, and Yulix's face turned grave.

"It's as we feared," he said to himself. "The Stork is in possession of the Dagger of Prince Elizar!"

This was no longer true, as the dagger now belonged to Helena, yet she still found herself thrown off by his response. "You're familiar with the weapon?"

"It is a wretched artifact that has long evaded destruction. It is believed to be cursed, often falling into the hands of the righteous and corrupting their hearts—as seen in the case of Prince Elizar. Its origins, however, stretch back even further into the Age of Magic, where it was likely forged with dark sorcery."

Helena's mind lingered on the words, *corrupting their hearts.* She wondered just what that meant for her as someone who had fallen victim to the cursed dagger's touch.

"And it so happened that, after thousands of years, it fell into the hands of the worst man alive," she said bleakly.

"How it ended up in the hands of the Nevarians is beyond me," he said bitterly. "But it was ultimately your fate that persuaded the King at last to draft a declaration that Avalon would solidify an interest in the political affairs of the Lower Realms of Nadiir. The seed to such an endeavor, of course, would begin with an alliance with the Kingdom of Alazar."

Helena reeled from this abundance of information and pressed her hand to her forehead. "By godly winds, Yulix, it seems you've been through Hades and back...if they don't bestow your seventh golden feather upon you for your bravery these last few months, I'll be convinced the world's gone mad!"

His gaze softened. "It was never about the golden feather. I had to see you again, Lena. I made a vow to your father that I would protect you. If you perished on my watch, I would never forgive myself..." Taking her hands in his, he pulled her in slightly closer. "All this time not knowing if you were alive, I wracked myself thinking about how foolish I was to pursue a course towards the King's Guard. I thought that maybe if I got the chance to see you again, I could renounce it all, and there would come a day when you and I could live our lives together..."

His words reminded Helena too much of Noa's similar declaration, and she pulled away.

"Oh, please!" she said, huffing.

Yulix blinked at her, bewildered by her response.

Helena crossed her arms. "It took my presumed death for you to realize that you wanted to spend your life with me?"

"I-I only meant that your disappearance made me contemplate many things," he stuttered, blushing beet-red.

"It made me rethink many things, as well! And after everything that's happened, the last thing on my mind is commitment! Besides, Yulix...you've worked far too hard the last decade of your life to become a Knight of the King's Guard just to give it all up for *love.*"

He only stared at her, his mouth falling ajar in speechlessness.

Noa's face flashed in Helena's mind, and she gave a sad smile. "Sometimes, my dear friend, Destiny calls one way while the heart calls another...I should be careful knowing which path leads where, and if the heart leads me someplace where I'm not myself, then Destiny it is."

He frowned. "You've grown so much in the time we've spent apart, it's almost frightening."

"Nothing more than hard-won wisdom, after all that I've endured. With that being said, it's time I tell you what I've witnessed since the night of my fall, and everything I've learned. There are dark powers at play, Yulix."

His face turned grave. "What do you mean?"

"The Nevarians seek revenge against Avalon for banishing their ancestors long ago. Apart from sending victims down to Nadiir, the Stork has been searching for the Twilight Stone to break the Vespertine Curse, which is what keeps them at bay in the darkness. If he were to succeed, there would be no stopping them from conquering both Realms!"

Yulix's eyes narrowed. "How do you know all this, Lena?"

The truth came spilling out of Helena like a torrent of water—her deal with the Stork and how she played into his schemes, her journey to find the golden egg, as well as her expedition to Mount Sulfur to acquire the dagger.

*"I'm sorry, Yulix!"* she couldn't help but burst, overcome with shame and remorse. "I didn't want to do his bidding, but he had my mirage, and I felt I had no other choice..."

He seized her. "He will pay for what he put you through! I will make sure of it. But first you must tell me, Lena, where you've put those two artifacts. It's imperative we secure them in a safe place so the Nevarians cannot get a hold of them!"

She pulled away from him, hesitating before answering.

"I can't tell you."

Yulix regarded her skeptically. "Don't be ridiculous, Lena! Those artifacts must be turned in and kept under strict supervision, with at least twenty guards on duty to protect them. You must tell me at once!"

"I would gladly do so if I had a choice...but I can't risk losing the egg after learning what's inside it."

Yulix reared back in slight surprise. "What are you talking about?"

"There's a mirage inside that artifact, Yulix."

His amber eyes filled with disbelief. "What makes you come to such an unlikely conclusion?"

"Penelope Duskmuth," Helena answered. "The name may not ring any bells with you, but trust me when I say that the evidence she's gathered points to an ancient mirage residing inside that egg. There are no adequate words that will help me convince you, Yulix, but...it's like I'm drawn to it every time I'm near it. And I think it might be because it's the one thing my soul is missing..."

He released her with a snort and said, with an air of sarcasm, "And I suppose you think it's yours for the taking!"

Her agreeable silence prompted him to utter a sound of disbelief.

*"Helena, there's no possible way you believe you can lay claim to that artifact!"*

"I'm the only one who could! I don't have a mirage anymore, and if there's truly one inside that golden egg, then there's a chance I can claim it. Would you rather the Stork get his hands on it? Besides, in the slim chance that we prove compatible...it would mean I get my wings back."

"You speak of a transplant of the soul! Do not fool yourself, Lena. Such a thing could never be yours. It would violate nature's most sacred laws...it would be an abomination!"

"I already am!" she cried with watery eyes. "Haven't you heard yet what they say about me? I'm a walking abomination after what the Stork did to me..."

"To Hades what they think of you!" he roared. "I promised your father I would look after you, and I'll be damned if I allow you to ruin yourself in this manner!"

"It's not your decision to make. It's my duty to claim the mirage—*I'm taking it, and that's final.*"

"*...Yer taking it?*"

Unbeknownst to Helena, Noa had followed her and eavesdropped on their entire conversation. Helena's cheeks burned at the thought of Noa weighing in on her and Yulix's intimate moment, but that did not compare to the utter shock and devastation of knowing that he had overheard her decision to claim the mirage. He burst into the room with a face that expressed anger, disappointment, and, most importantly...betrayal.

"Noa, I wanted to tell you, but—Noa!" Helena reached out to touch him, but he jerked away, turning his wingless back on her. The outline of his spine imposed harshly upon the back of his shirt. His shoulders rose up and down raggedly, as if he were trying to control his breathing.

"Lena," Yulix sounded, a sharp edge to his voice. A shadow cast itself over his face as he took in their unexpected visitor from head to toe. He stretched his wings and puffed his feathers alarmingly.

"Give us a minute in private," she said to him. Helena's request nettled Yulix, but after reading the tension in the room, he reluctantly did as Helena wished.

"This matter remains unsettled," Yulix said to her as he made his way out of the pavilion. He did not shy away from sending a distrustful glance towards the wigeon boy, who still had his back to them.

Noa's quiet voice sounded as soon as they were alone.

"After everything we've been through?"

"Noa, I—"

"*I thought you'd accepted yer wigeonhood!*"

"That was before I knew what was inside that artifact," she said regretfully. "If there's truly a mirage inside that artifact, then that leaves nothing more than for me to take it. I can't help but think I was destined for this, Noa...would you please turn around and look at me?"

Fists clenched, Noa ever so slowly turned around, but his brown eyes looked anywhere but at her. A series of conflicting emotions flashed across his hairy face.

"If you take that mirage," he said, "then all of our suffering would have been for nothing."

Both guilt and indignation swelled inside Helena. *"Our* suffering? You weren't the one who lost their wings and had to grieve their livelihood—that was *me.*"

*"Yes, but I was there alongside you!"* His outburst made her flinch, and it crushed Helena to see that when he did look at her, his eyes were wet. "I was there when you lost them. I was at yer side when you were at yer lowest. Sure, we might've butted heads at the beginning, but we grew alongside each other. What we went through, all the time we spent together...did that mean nothing to you?"

"Of course not," Helena said, taking his hands in hers. She was glad he did not pull away. "I'll treasure those moments until my last day...but I have a responsibility to claim that mirage, Noa, and I can't refuse to take it simply because you want me to stay like this all my life."

He turned his head the other way, his face pained. Helena squeezed his hands and pulled herself closer.

"You know deep in your heart that this was bound to happen," she said gently. "Flying is my sole purpose in life. I can't imagine myself any other way. It's what I love most."

"Even more than me?"

Her heart skipped a beat. "What?"

There was a fleeting moment in which Noa's eyes betrayed him and revealed a tenderness that only a lover could possess. But then he tore himself from her and put his boney back between them once more. In seconds, Noa had reduced himself to what Helena had always known him as—a belligerent flame that scorched anyone who wandered too close.

"Yer a sellout," he said coldly. "I should've known yer all the same, you flockers. I never want to see you again."

And without even a glance at her, Noa stormed out of the tent, granting Helena the freedom to weep quietly—and alone—inside it.

# CHAPTER THIRTY

There was no more time to waste. Helena wiped her tears and slipped out of the pavilion to head back home and open the artifact. Some distance behind her, Yulix realized she was gone and, recalling what she had set out to do, took off into the evening sky to look for her. Helena knew he would try to put a stop to her efforts to claim the mirage inside the egg. She watched furtively from behind a tree as he circled the skies like a hawk. Helena did well in evading him, though admittedly it was costly in time. Eventually, she arrived at the cabin and barged into the room, where she was met by a wide-eyed and panic-stricken Phellis. Upon laying eyes on Helena, Phellis ran up to her and uttered all kinds of nonsense that Helena couldn't understand—

"Calm down, Phellis!" Helena said, grabbing her by the shoulders and steadying her. "Take a deep breath and then tell me what's happened."

Phellis collected her thoughts and expressed her sentiments more clearly:

"Noa was here not too long ago—he was so upset—said you were bent on taking the egg for yourself an' that he wasn't gonna let you do it. He tried to take the dagger, but I wouldn't let him, see, so he took the egg instead an' said he would take it to the Stork to trade it for Jared—oh, Helena! I tried to stop him, I really did! But he ran off with it, an' I couldn't do a thing about it—"

Helena bolted straight to the fireplace and saw, to her horror, that the egg was missing. At once, her heart sank deeper than it ever had before. Helena knew she had disappointed Noa in taking the egg, but she had not considered him capable of such betrayal! She thought herself foolish in failing to anticipate it. Still...as much as it hurt to know that Noa had willingly gone behind her back to steal the egg, Helena could not find it in herself to harbor a single feeling of ill will for the wigeon boy who had become so dear to her in such little time.

Helena whirled around to face Phellis.

"We have to go after him," Helena said urgently. "Did he tell you where he's headed?"

"No, but I can track him. Follow me."

Together, the two girls ventured into the dark wilderness, with Phellis leading the way. Helena ran blindly after her, the white chest secured in her arms, as she was too afraid to leave it behind. Noa's words tumbled over and over inside her head. *Yer a sellout,* his voice shouted at her. *I never want to see you again!*

It was much too dark for Helena to see where they headed. Before long, the two wigeon girls arrived at the edge of a dim clearing in the woods, far off and secluded from the rest of the kingdom. Almost immediately, Helena once again felt that familiar premonition of disaster, the gut feeling that told her something was not right.

"It all ends here," said Phellis. "Look."

She raised her finger towards a glimmering object in the center of the clearing. Helena, after shooting a look askance at Phellis, walked onwards. The moon was full and bright, and its powerful beams bounced off the shell of the egg in cool flashes of light. As Helena drew closer, the air buzzed with energy, as if the moment of truth was quickly approaching. She carefully knelt before it, her heart racing. Keeping her firm sights on the egg, Helena said aloud:

"Noa must have been a fool to leave this out here."

"Yeah, he must have been."

Ever so slowly, Helena placed the chest in front of her next to the egg. They did not repel one another as they once did. She lifted the lid of the chest just enough to peek inside and saw that, sure enough, the dagger was missing. Withholding a sharp breath, Helena gently closed the chest and rose to her feet.

"Why did you lead me all the way out here, Phellis?"

There was no answer. Helena turned to see the wigeon girl standing with the dagger in her left hand.

"You lied about Noa stealing the egg so you could get me all alone—were you planning to get rid of me so you could have the egg for yourself? Is your lust for wings so bad, Phellis, that you would kill a friend in cold blood just for the small chance to fly again?"

"I was ten," Phellis said, a single tear running down her cheek. "I reckon I didn't even have my wings a full year before I lost them. It wasn't fair."

"No child should have to go through what you went through," Helena said carefully. "I'm sorry, Phellis, I truly am—but this is absurd, even for you...after all, weren't you the one who told me that day in the woods, *'Take away my wings, leave me, only me, and nothin' but me?'*"

Phellis gripped the dagger tighter, her breath becoming more ragged. "You think it's easy living like this? Having to wake up every single day with these hideous stumps on my back? At least you don't have to deal with the physical reminder that your wings were taken away!"

"You're mistaken, Phellis." Helena said, licking her cracked lips. "I have a scar that will last a lifetime. Every night, I relive the moment when the Stork cut me open."

"An' every night I remember the sound of my bones crunching under teeth." Phellis wiped her tears. "None of it matters, anyway. I'm going to get my wings back, one way or another—even if it means taking you out of the picture."

"Very well," Helena said cooly, ignoring the way her heart faltered at these words. Her green eyes flickered towards the artifact and then back to Phellis. "Do what you feel is right, but before you do, answer me one question...did the Stork put you up to this?"

Her silence was telling, and Helena felt her heart sink.

"I knew it," she said, devastated. "I didn't want to admit it, but...it's clear the Stork has had you under his wing this entire time!"

"You're wrong!" Phellis' breathing became labored, as if admitting this cost her a great effort. "You guys were my friends! I would have never abandoned y'all the way y'all abandoned me...but then they locked me up in a dirty ol' cellar, an' he saw my *stubs*. He knew how much I hated them, an' he told me if I retrieved the artifact for him, he'd take them away an' grant me a new pair of wings—"

"And you believed him?"

"Now I do! If there's a mirage inside that egg, an' I do as he says, then he'll keep his promise an' reward me for helping him."

Helena couldn't help the dark chuckle that escaped her mouth. "He told me the exact same thing months ago! I played into his game, too, until I realized that he never intended to give me back my wings. He manipulated me and used my grief to his advantage—the same way he's doing to you. He's a liar and a manipulator."

This seemed to agitate Phellis considerably. With both hands she raised the dagger at Helena, who flinched—

"The Stork has shown me nothing but mercy. He could've killed me, starved me, even tortured me after what our Avalonian ancestors did to his people. But he fed me, clothed me, an' mentored me better than Papa ever could. The Stork never hit me. The Stork never belittled me an' made me feel like some worthless thing. He promised me that once I got my wings, I would be the one to help him forge a new empire n' the new era that will begin once the Fallen Avian returns."

Helena stiffened. "What are you talking about?"

"Haven't you heard? The Fallen Avian will return to enact his revenge upon all those who wronged him—an' once he does, he'll kill every last Avalonian until there's none left. Only then will the fallen rise up an' take their place." She took one look at Helena's horrified expression and laughed a high, piercing laugh. "Hasn't your time as a wigeon opened your eyes, Helena? All this time we've been so busy fearing Nevarians that we've failed to realize who the real enemy is. It's Avalon! Our entire lives we've been told that they were the good guys, that their world is one meant for fellowship. If that's the case, why does it toss its own people out like filth so they can suffer in Nadiir while those flockers enjoy their paradise up in the sky? If Avalon is such a great kingdom, why do they treat us wigeons so badly? We writhe in their slums like worms; we toil in their harbors like slaves. They exclude us, demean us, an' hate us because we don't have wings, an' yet they can't live without us! The truth is, no matter what we do, those flockers will always see us wigeons as soulless monsters—they will *never* accept us as their own."

"You fool!" Helena cried. "Do you honestly believe the Stork is on your side? He's a Nevarian, and what's more, a Nevarian with *wings*. He couldn't care less about wigeons like you and me! Who do you think will take their place once the fallen rise? The Stork is only using you to do his dirty work while he hides away in the shadows. Once you've exhausted your use and brought him the artifact, he'll discard you—you can't trust a thing the Stork says!"

*"The Stork is true to his word an' will reward us if an' only if we do as he says,"* she said, but it wasn't Phellis who was speaking anymore. Her once silver eyes glistened like rubies, and a dark, dark shadow had been cast over her youthful and innocent face.

*"He told me you would say that, you know—he said that you were nothing but a liar an' instigator, an' that sooner or later you would have killed me to have both Noa an' the egg for yourself—don't give me that look! Yes, I see the way you look at Noa...you want to get rid of me so you can have him all to yourself—isn't that right? I don't know how you managed to get him so smitten with you...you must have him under a spell! You're a witch! Well, you can't hide behind that sweet, honorable persona any longer, Helena! I see right through you!"*

"Phellis," Helena said, frightened at the sight before her, "this isn't you! The dagger is making you think things—*see* things that aren't real! Nobody needs to get hurt. Set the dagger aside and we can talk this out—"

"SHUT UP!" Phellis' face twisted in anger, and she swiped out with the cursed dagger, causing Helena to stagger back. "I'M ONLY DOING WHAT YOU WOULD'VE DONE IF IT MEANT FLYING ONCE AGAIN...ONLY YOU WERE TOO MUCH OF A COWARD TO GO THE DISTANCE! YOU WERE TOO SCARED TO KILL PENELOPE IN THE DRAGON'S LAIR, AN' AFTERWARDS YOU WERE TOO SCARED TO CONTINUE FIGHTING FOR YOUR MIRAGE. BUT I AIN'T SCARED! I'M WILLING TO CROSS THE FARTHEST LINE TO GET MY WINGS BACK, EVEN IF IT MEANS ENDING YOUR LIFE RIGHT HERE, RIGHT NOW."

Phellis was too far gone. There was a glint of light as she brandished the dagger and lunged forwards, swiping savagely at Helena. In a rush of adrenaline, Helena dodged the attack and advanced towards Phellis, tackling her head-on. They fell to the floor amidst screeches and howls, grappling for control of the dagger. Phellis, however, was nimble—not to mention a pathetic scratcher—and it wasn't long before she managed to gain the upper hand and straddle her opponent. She then grabbed the dagger and thrust it down towards Helena's chest, at which point Helena could only keep it at bay with her bare hands. Phellis, with a red sheen in her eyes, pressed the dagger further and further down, until just the tip of its green blade pierced Helena's skin—right where her scar was. In an instant, Helena became ignited with an agony that consumed her body and soul. Her shrieks carried off into the night as Phellis, little by little, drove the blade further into her chest...

A flash of silver flew in from the right and struck Phellis from the side, sending her flying face-first into a tree, where she collapsed to the floor with a grunt. The dagger fell to a clatter beside Helena. Breathless, she looked up to see Yulix in the air, circling back. She looked to the left and saw Noa, who now had Phellis locked in an iron embrace as the wigeon girl struggled to set herself free.

*"Let me go,"* Phellis shrieked. *"My wings! She's going to take my wings!"*

Driven by impulse, Helena leapt to her feet and snatched the dagger from the ground. As soon as her skin made contact with the weapon's cool metal, white-hot fire coursed throughout her body and threatened to consume her entirely...but Helena had already felt the kiss of its blade once before, and the sensation was familiar enough to her now that she was able to push past the excruciating pain and rush towards the golden egg.

*"HELENA!"* sounded a voice from above. Yulix angled his trajectory down towards Helena to stop her, but he knew it was already too late. "Stop her!" he cried to Noa, but the wigeon boy made no attempt to do so.

Helena brought the dagger down with all her might and struck the golden shell with its blade. There was an explosion of light, and then darkness, and all else was forgotten.

# Part IV

## The Prophecy

# CHAPTER THIRTY-ONE

Helena recalled little of what she experienced after opening the artifact. Waking up was like rising out of a thousand-year slumber, and she stretched her stiff limbs, giving a great yawn. She rubbed her tired eyes, opened them, and gazed up at the shimmering stars above. She traced each constellation with a single finger. *The stars,* she thought. *Hello, old friends.* When she sat up, she found herself sitting in the same old clearing she last recalled herself to be in. Still, there was something different about the world around her which she could not adequately put into words. *This place,* Helena thought, *I recognize it, but I could've sworn I was someplace else just now.*

Noa was the first person she laid eyes on after waking up. He gaped at her, his mouth parted slightly in awe.

"Why are you looking at me like that?" she said, almost dreamily.

He shut his mouth, swallowing deeply, and remained speechless. It wasn't until after staggering to her feet and swaying side to side that Helena immediately felt her equilibrium was off. Every muscle that ran down the length of her back felt taut and tense. Too afraid to look, Helena's eyes flickered to the ground before her, where the silver moonlight cast her shadow across the floor, and saw a pair of magnificent black crests jutting out from her silhouette.

Helena brandished her massive wings on either side of her, stretching them out and taking as much space as she possibly could. They seemed to be much bigger and darker than her previous pair; they boasted an impressive ten-foot wingspan, and unlike her old wings—which were a stormy silver—this new set came in a beautiful array of feathers as dark as midnight.

Every now and then, when the moonlight struck them at just the right angle, they glimmered like emeralds. Helena stretched and retracted her new wings—slowly and amateurishly at first, as if learning to control her wings for the first time—before opening and closing them faster and faster, causing an invigorating gust of wind that fanned Noa's shaggy hair away and revealed the look of wonder on his face.

As Helena approached him, there was a taller, prouder quality about her that Noa had never seen until this moment.

"So, this is the real you, bird."

Helena nodded, bracing herself for the worst of his reaction...but it never came.

"Yer striking," he said at last, and she beamed.

*"Lena."*

Helena's smile died as she turned and saw the towering figure of Yulix in the darkness of the night. He stopped in his tracks as he took in her appearance from head to toe, as if refusing to believe it was her—and when the reality set in, his face contorted in disgust.

"Look at you," he hissed, his eyes scouring the length of her wings. "Your wings...they're black!"

"Come, now, Yulix...they're only a shade darker than before, and weren't you the one who always admired the darker nature of my old pair?"

"Yes, but this is different. It's like you're one of *them,* now...you've ruined yourself!"

Yulix's wounding words made even the sharpest of blades obsolete; they slashed and tore at her chest as a crippling shame overcame her.

*"Easy, now,"* a warning voice sounded. To Helena's surprise, it was Noa who came to her defense. There was a jealous sheen in Yulix's eyes as they flickered dubiously between the two of them, before finally falling upon Noa in quiet, abject loathing.

"You allowed this to happen," he said icily to the wigeon boy. "You could have stopped her, but you didn't. Whatever affections you held for her are now meaningless—that is, if you ever held them at all!"

"I let her choose her own way," Noa retorted. "It was an act of love."

*"Love?"* The word came rather disingenuously to Yulix, who seemed to regard it with a dark humor, his forced chuckles failing to conceal the mask of jealousy on his face. At last, he buried his callous thoughts within himself before forcing himself to look at Helena once more.

"This is the life you chose for yourself, then? A life of ill omen, all for the sake of flying once more?"

"The truth is, old friend," she answered sadly, "I could've chosen to remain a wigeon the rest of my life, and that still would not have changed the look of pity you have on your face right now."

Yulix turned to leave, then paused to cast one last glance over his shoulder at Helena. She could see, even in the nighttime dimness, that his amber eyes were glistening.

"I've failed your father, and I've failed you. For that, I am sorry."

Without another word, Yulix took off into the night sky, flying further and further away until he was but a speck against the pale moon. Helena did not move from her spot for a long time, her eyes still fixed upon her friend in the distance. A part of her longed to weep, but the tears would not come. Helena reckoned she had shed enough tears in the last few months.

Only Noa and Helena remained. They lingered for many moments in silence. She wondered if he was still angry with her. Surely, after earning a new pair of wings, he would want nothing to do with her now...

"Where is Phellis?" she asked hesitantly, recalling the events that had taken place just prior to her opening the egg.

"The lunatic left soon after you got yer wings—a real mess, she was. Always knew she had it out for you."

"And the dagger?" she asked, looking frantically around for the weapon.

"She took it with her, I'm afraid. I expect it won't be long until the Stork gets his hands on it again," he said, scowling.

Helena was greatly disappointed to hear this. But as much as it pained her to know the Stork would have possession of the dagger again, she was satisfied knowing that they had completed their objective in opening the artifact.

"Phellis lied to me. She told me you were the one who had stolen the egg," she confessed. "I'm sorry—I should have known better than to believe her."

The thought of Phellis painting him out to be a traitor did not please Noa in the slightest.

"That mangy ol' mutt! I had only just come to the cabin when she raced up to me muttering all sorts of nonsense about you and the egg. But I told her I didn't want anything to do with that rotten egg or cursed dagger any longer...so I left! That's all!"

"Why, then, did you come back? I thought you said you didn't want anything to do with me..."

"I didn't plan on returning," he admitted bleakly. "I was angry at you for choosing this route. I would've abandoned this kingdom entirely and set sail across the Nadiirian seas if it meant never crossing paths with you again."

This hurt Helena a lot more than she dared to admit. "What stopped you?"

"Yer knight friend found me not long after I left—wanted to know what business I had with you. I told him to shove off, that whatever happened between us was over now, though it had hardly ever began. He said if there was one thing we had in common—apart from our affections for you—it was that neither of us wanted you to take the egg, and if I truly cared for you, then I would help him stop you from claiming whatever was inside it. I agreed, though it was a miracle that we found you before the traitor did away with you! In the end, though...I just couldn't bring myself to intervene. Yer friend was right—I *could've* stopped you from claiming the egg, but I didn't. I don't know if that makes me a terrible person."

"On the contrary," she said, "it was one of the greatest acts of kindness anyone's ever done for me." Or, as Noa had so casually put it, an *act of love.* "Thank you."

He gave her a sad smile. "That's not the true reason I came back, though."

Helena looked up to see a fire in his eyes that she had never seen before.

"I can't stay away from you," he said, unabashed. "I realized that as much as I could try to flee, as much distance as I could try to put between the both of us, you'll always be at the back of my mind, and I'll always find a way to come back to you. You've marked me since the night I first laid eyes on you, Helena Nightingale. I would follow you anywhere, even if it meant running barefoot across the earth as you soar the skies."

Helena felt as if she would burst any moment now with the multitude of emotions all flowing through her at once. She moved in for an embrace, but Noa backed away, shaking his head. Helena sent him a look of confusion and hurt, but Noa smiled sadly and stepped aside, gesturing towards the skies.

"Now go and do what you love most."

# Chapter Thirty-Two

For the next several days, Helena voyaged across Northern Nadiir with no particular destination in mind. Her only goal was to soar to her heart's content. If she had died in the time she spent soaring amongst the clouds, she would have died the happiest girl in Nadiir. Flying once again was like drinking a frosty glass of water after traveling forty days and forty nights through a seemingly insurmountable desert—and she savored every drop. Helena spent days exploring the towering Mountains of Alazar, whose spurs and snow-tipped peaks once posed a formidable endeavor for the wigeoned girl. Now that she had wings again, those same mountains had been reduced to mere anthills from the heights at which she soared! She counted the rivers, valleys, and streams; she marked her initials on the highest summit overlooking all of Nadiir; and on the rare occasions when she wasn't flying—when she was forced to focus on such mundane tasks such as gathering food for sustenance or drinking water from a mountain spring—Helena spent her time mourning the person she once was.

And so, she had succeeded in getting the one thing she had wanted so desperately, which was to fly again...but at what cost? Helena had renounced her own mirage, and if there was the slightest chance that it still remained alive, then there could be no chance of reconciliation. Her suffering was not entirely forgotten, either; all of the sorrows, the hardships, and afflictions she had endured throughout this journey would forever remain a dark stain upon her psyche. Even if she had not claimed this new mirage, she was certain she would never be the Helena Nightingale that existed prior to the night of her fall. She was permanently and irrevocably changed.

Throughout her voyage, the Stork maintained a looming presence in the back of Helena's mind. Who knew if Phellis had already delivered to him the dagger, along with news of Helena's success in opening the artifact and claiming the mirage inside it. Doubtless the Stork would be coming soon to exert his vengeance upon Helena for spoiling his plans. It was only a matter of time...

Still, after claiming this new mirage, Helena was ashamed to acknowledge her own disappointment. She had gone to the ends of Nadiir and back to acquire this artifact, open it, and claim the mirage inside it—which Penelope believed might've belonged to someone who had lived thousands of years ago—and yet the only real difference Helena noted was the color of her wings, which otherwise worked as well as her old pair! The Law of Attainment stated unequivocally that *all avians must earn their wings,* but Helena had been granted these wings almost gratuitously! Or that was what it seemed like, at least. What kind of miraculous, powerful gift comes so easily to a person? Doubtless there would be a cost to be paid for such a thing...

What that cost was, or how great its scale would be, Helena could not say. She suspected, however, that it would reveal itself to her of its own accord—and soon.

It was on the sixth night of her voyage when a squadron of Dragonback Warriors ambushed Helena as she nested along the ridges of a small mountain, just miles from the southern borders of Alazar. She was sitting before a campfire, cupping her black wings around the smoke and flames to warm them on that chilly night, when a half dozen warriors descended upon her, casting a great net over her wings and reeling her in like some wild animal. *Krow,* they called her, despite her protests that she was anything but. The sight of her silky black wings, however, convinced these warriors that she was a child of darkness. They tossed her inside a cramped metal cage and airlifted her to the Kingdom of Alazar, where they locked Helena inside a pitch-black cellar that reeked of urine and rat feces.

Hours had crawled by when they finally came to fetch Helena from that putrid cellar. No matter how much she cried out that she was not Nevarian, they would not hear her pleas; they simply shoved her inside yet another cage, which they shrouded with a thick cloth before shipping her off to a destination unknown to her.

The wheels of the wagon squeaked with exhaustion just as the presence of a murmuring crowd loomed in the distance. As they came to a stop, Helena could hear the ramblings of the common people, the giggles of children, and the occasional puff of wings of the many avian citizens who had gathered to wonder what mystery lay inside the cage, unaware that it was Helena inside it. It was not long until King Hyrax's sharp-tongued voice carried over the crowds:

"Citzens of Alazar!" the king declared. "News of the enemy has at last arrived! Scouts have reported witnessing a *Black Wave* crossing the Great Isthmus of Nadiir just a week ago; a host of Nevarian warriors are making their way north towards us as we speak!"

This announcement instilled fear in the hearts of the crowd.

"The Black Wave is said to be accompanied by the *Fallen Coven,* head-birded by none other than Ptero the Bloodthirsty! Rumors of the colony in the Kanyons of Koli mobilizing stir in the east, but there are fewer convincing reports of this. For now, there is no greater threat than the Nevarians to the south! Their host is expected to arrive sometime within the next twenty to forty-eight hours!"

A chill fell upon Helena. *He's coming for me,* she thought. She was horrified at the thought that these innocent people would pay for her trans-gressions against the Stork.

"We will bolster our defenses. All seven of the fortified watchtowers along this great valley are to light their torches and arm themselves with our finest bowmen. We must brace ourselves for a long and arduous battle!"

"What of Avalon?" a concerned citizen called out. "Did they not vow to send soldiers to protect us from those wicked demons?"

An angry chorus of voices shouted in agreement. There was a brief pause before Helena heard Yulix's dignified voice address the crowd.

"Avalon *will* open its gates, under the sole directive of King Haeron IV—"

"The Krows will have run us into the dirt by the time your king pulls up his trousers and flies down here," cried one ave, who began pushing through the crowds. "I'm leaving before those demons arrive, and I'm taking my children with me. I won't risk their lives waiting for something that'll never come!"

"Those of you who wish to stay until Avalon arrives may do so," announced King Hyrax. "Those who are in doubt and wish to flee are also free to do so. As for me and my men, we will stay to defend our homeland and await the Kingdom of the Heavens! And for you naysayers who doubt the claims of an impending invasion, here in this very cage lies a creature who we caught lurking along the borders of the valley. Behold! *The devil of the night!*"

They tore the tarp from Helena's cage, exposing her in a rush of wind, and she shielded her eyes from the blinding light of the torches around her. Once they had adjusted, Helena could see it was nighttime. They had brought her outside in the middle of the Central Square. King Hyrax stood high above on a wooden platform, overlooking a great and murmuring crowd. Captain Rancipert stood on the king's righthand side, while Yulix stood opposite of him on the left. There was a unanimous gasp as the crowd laid their eyes on Helena and her sleek black feathers.

"*A Krow!*" someone shouted.

"*Wings of death!*" shouted another.

"*Kill her!*"

"*Out of my way!*" sounded a voice. Noa shoved his way to front of the crowd to get a better look at the girl in the cage. When he realized it was Helena, he lunged forwards in an attempt to save her. A team of guards, however, drew their spears and blocked his path.

"Let her go!" he snarled. "You dirty flockers, let her go!"

"*Silence, wigeon!*" cried one guard, pressing the tip of his spear against his throat and cutting him off.

"*Lena!*" Yulix said, distraught.

"Step aside!" Captain Rancipert said as he descended the wooden platform to inspect the cage. There was no denying the impressive set of black wings folded neatly against Helena's back, and when his eyes fell upon her familiar face, he reeled back and gasped.

"Impossible...it's...it's Helena Nightingale!"

This didn't quite register with the crowd.

*"Helena Nightingale?"* someone asked.

"I thought she was a wigeon!"

"She was!" cried another voice. "I saw her only weeks ago!"

*"Do my eyes deceive me?"* King Hyrax's face contorted with disbelief as he recognized Helena. "When I first laid eyes on you, you were but a wigeon! Now you come before me winged and bearing the mark of a Krow..." His disbelief quickly morphed into outrage. "You're a witch! A shapeshifter who can change her appearance at will!"

The crowd erupted in outrage.

"I am neither of those things," Helena declared, despite her fear.

"Then explain how you have wings when weeks ago you did not!"

"Since then, I have claimed another mirage which has granted me a new pair of wings—these which you see here and now!"

It was an outrageous claim that both baffled and horrified the citizens of Alazar, who levied vile claims of fraud, witchcraft, and other assorted forms of wickedness towards Helena. She struggled to make her voice heard amidst the growing unrest of the crowd who sought to tear her asunder.

"It is true!" came the commanding voice of Yulix, and at once the commotion subsided. Helena felt a mixture of affection and guilt stir within her as her old friend stepped up to defend her.

"I vouch for Helena Nightingale," he declared, though he could not meet her eyes. "That which she speaks of...I didn't think it possible for one ave to claim another's mirage, until many nights ago I witnessed it myself. Helena Nightingale is the only case I know in which an ave has successfully claimed the mirage of another, one who has long been deceased."

Yulix's testimony did little to quell their reactions; there was an immediate explosion of mayhem in which the people surged forwards and began hurling both insults and food at Helena, who at last had the wings to shield herself from their attacks.

Upon the order of the king, the crowd fell into a chilling silence. He looked upon Helena with sheer disgust and loathing, just as he always had when she was a wigeon.

"These are the fruits of dark sorcery! What innocent soul did you sacrifice to acquire those wings? I want no part of this dark magic, witch! An abomination like yourself could only bring misfortune and chaos to our people! Guards—seize her, and cast her into the Desert of Daveed, where she is to remain an exile for the rest of her days! Away with you, witch, and return only at your mortal peril!"

"*No!*" cried Noa as they took Helena away. She clutched at the iron bars of her cage, trying to see past the crowds as she rolled further and further away. Noa lost himself amidst the sea of bodies. Helena could just barely see Yulix having an intense argument with King Hyrax, who appeared resolute in his decision and did not regard the Avalonian knight in the slightest.

And just that like that, Helena was whisked away to spend the rest of her days lost amidst the Desert of Daveed...


The horse-drawn wagon traveled through the mountains, leaving behind Alazar. The Black Wave would likely descend that very night over the kingdom. An eerie silence carried in the wind, occasionally ruptured by the distant howls of coyotes. She felt especially anxious being this far out, knowing the probability of encountering Nevarians at this hour was at an all-time high...

Later on, the distant sounds of murmuring, shouts, and occasional laughter stirred Helena from her troubled sleep. It startled her to see countless crescent shadows against the starry sky. Dozens of avian families, presumably fleeing the carnage that was about to take place within the kingdom, took to the peaks of the mountains, perching upon the ridges and huddling to combat the lethal temperatures. Helena could not help but think back to the wigeons in the kingdom who did not have the means to escape so easily—children, especially, who would be forced to flee on foot. She thought about the elderly whose wings were too great a burden for them to use. Most of all, she thought about Noa, who would never flee in the face of danger and instead face it head on. Her heart squeezed at the thought of him.

When Helena least expected it, the horses at the front of the wagon screeched and made a jarring turn. The wagon then veered off the main path, and Helena was briefly suspended in midair before she was flung harshly across the interior of her cage as the wagon crashed against the ground. Battered and dazed from the accident, Helena clambered her way out of the broken cage, which lay in bent pieces along the length of a river teeming with boulders. The horses had run off, whining and squealing as they did so. It was unclear just *what* had struck fear in them as to cause them to stray off course. The wigeon driver was nowhere in sight.

The hairs along Helena's arms and neck prickled and she stiffened, training her keen senses on her surroundings...but she heard nothing more than the gentle trickling of water and the distant howl of a wolf. *Something's off,* she thought at once.

Then, there was a breach in the silence. Somewhere in the distance, a melodic *TWEEEE* sounded.

Helena's shoulders relaxed. *Only a nosey bird,* she thought. Probably nestling in its tree before it went to sleep. *TWEEEE,* another bird went, this one coming from another direction. Suddenly, a series of trills sounded through the night air, their sweet notes echoing throughout the mountains. Their sweetness quickly turned tart, however, after transforming into an unsettling, ear-piercing hymn that rattled Helena to the bones. Those were not *true* birds making those noises.

There was movement down south—dozens of Nevarians spewed out from within a cave resting high above along the rocky ledges of the mountain, rising into the air before raining downwards upon Helena.

She was up in the air before they could catch her. Soon, Helena raced across the mountains of Alazar with twenty Krows nipping at her heels and calling for her blood. *"BRING ME THE NIGHTINGALE'S HEAD,"* they said. Helena, however, evaded one nave after the next, scaling up the lengths of the tall mountain walls, diving steeply, looping, banking left and right, and outmaneuvering them with barrel rolls as they pursued her. Helena was so clever and cunning in the air, in fact, that they simply could not seem to pin her down. It would have made for a thrilling experience had the ordeal not been so terrifying.

Then, just as Helena swooped down, skimming just above a cluster of trees, a nave popped out from beneath and tackled her. The two of them crashed to the ground.

In an instant, the vultures of the night circled Helena and closed in, ensnaring her in a vortex of merciless cacophony—teakettles, blazing elephants, the wails of widows, all these sounds and more were hurled at her like raining bombshells. Helena recalled the day that Rancipert had described the Nevarian method of attack—how they tormented you and violated your ears before going in for the kill…but he failed to mention the worst part, which was when they *knew* you and used your loved ones against you.

A familiar voice echoed throughout the forest:

"HELENA!"

"Jared?" she cried, disoriented. His voice was so full of anguish that Helena could come to no other conclusion other than that he was being tortured.

"HELENAHELENAHELENAHELENAHELENAHELENAHELENA—"

And with that, the wicked smiles of beady-eyed Nevarians descended upon her. They clawed at her arms and thighs while bombarding her with Jared's tortured cries. It was a nightmare that Helena would not impose on anybody, the way the sounds swirled around her and threatened to engulf her whole. Helena couldn't even tell when it stopped, for hearing everything at once was the same as hearing nothing at all. She covered her ringing ears with her hands and crawled into a ball.

But the crowd of Krows soon parted in a flash of silver light! Ulyxes Cazador descended upon them, bearing his gleaming white sword. Alone, he slayed the cruel creatures of darkness, who hissed and fled at the sight of the mighty Avalonian knight. Those brave enough to face him met his great wrath. Yulix took on five challengers at once, bearing down with his longsword, which flashed in midair like a bolt of lightning. One by one, they fell at his feet, until all that remained was him, Helena, and the fallen bodies of his enemies. Approaching Helena, Yulix offered his hand and pulled her to her feet.

"Yulix—"

"There's no time," he said, wiping away her tears. "The Black Wave has fallen upon the kingdom. The battle has already begun."

Helena's heart quickened at this grave news. "Where is Noa? Is he alive?"

Hurt filled his eyes when she asked this, but Yulix swallowed his wounded pride and nodded.

"He's safe. I tasked the boy with rounding up the weak and elderly and taking them to Lake Eastpoint."

She could not withhold a breath of relief. "What other news do you bring me?"

"Our future remains uncertain," he stated darkly. "We underestimated their numbers, and the Nevarians are a fiercer opponent than we anticipated. Captain Rancipert, however, is confident we can hold them off until Avalon sends reinforcements. The King of Avalon should open the gateway any moment, now—but it will only last a sparing moment of time. It is imperative, Helena, that you get through this gate the moment it opens—for once it closes, you may never be granted the opportunity to cross again!"

"What about you?"

"I have a duty to join the battle and help fight against the enemy."

"Then I will join the fight!"

"Don't be ridiculous, Lena! Your only job is to take shelter until Avalon opens its gates. Your father awaits your return!"

"None of this would be happening if it weren't for me! I will not burrow away like some...coward whilst innocent people suffer and die for my transgressions. Please, Yulix. If I can't fight alongside you, then the least I could do is help round up the weak and wounded and get them to a safe place!"

"Very well," he muttered, knowing it was useless to try to change her mind. "But the moment you see the gate open, you must make every effort to cross that threshold and get back home, do you understand me? Don't be a hero, Lena."

*Don't be a hero.* Helena's thoughts lingered on these words before she nodded and said, "I'll do my best to get home."

# Chapter Thirty-Three

Darkness fell over Alazar like a black mist as Yulix and Helena flew back to aid in the fight against the Nevarians. As the pair reached the northern borders of the kingdom, they exchanged lasting looks before parting ways—Yulix heading straight towards the battling masses, and Helena zooming down towards the valley floor in search of Noa.

Hundreds of warring figures filled the skies. *Clang! Clang! Clang!* Above, Dragonback warriors in crimson armor brought their swords down upon their black-winged rivals in powerful swings. Helena made a landing run just beside the central river. She hurried through the hectic streets, dodging citizens left and right as they made their last-minute attempts to flee.

*"Noa!"* Helena called, cupping her hands around her mouth. *"Noa, where are you?"*

She had no luck in finding him.

*Thump!* Helena cried out as the body of a Nevarian hit the ground mere feet away from her, a sword lodged deep into his chest. *Thud—SMACK!* Two dead Dragonback Warriors smashed into the ground just behind her—*oh!* Helena skidded to a stop, slipping and falling as another nave landed headfirst in front of her, his body snapping into a fatal *"C"* position. *Crunch,* went his spine.

Helena turned a corner just in time to see Captain Rancipert, high up in the air, driving his sword through the heart of a Krow. The two of them fell; the latter fell dead to the ground with a dull *smack,* while Captain Rancipert landed harshly on his knees, his brown wings trembling and exhausted. He clutched at his left shoulder, and for a second it seemed he could go on no longer.

"Rancipert!" Helena cried. She rushed to his side but immediately regretted it as he swung his sword at her. Were it not for Helena's keen reflexes to jump back just in time, he would have lopped her entire head off! She fell back with a yell, and Rancipert blinked several times as he realized that it was not a Nevarian he had swung at, but Helena.

"Goodness, Helena!" he said breathlessly, pulling her up with one hand. "Forgive me—with those wings, I mistook you for a Krow! What are you doing here? I had been certain you'd been sent into exile!"

"I came back to help," she said, still a bit shaken. "To aid the effort against the Stork any way that I can...Rancipert, you're hurt!"

Helena helped bring him under the shelter of a tree, away from the chaos, and reclined him against its trunk. As she carefully removed the iron pauldron from his left shoulder, Rancipert leaned his head against the tree with a labored sigh. It horrified Helena to see that someone had cut deep into Rancipert's flesh, in the nook just between his neck and shoulder, leaving a wide, gaping red cut. Blood seeped through his undergarments. Rancipert's normally tan face had turned sallow. When Helena retracted her hands, she found them stained with crimson.

"You're bleeding out. We have to get you to a medic—"

"No, Helena..." he said, baring his teeth in a silent hiss as he was gripped by a wave of pain. "...my time has come."

A wave of panic rushed over her at those words, and she cried, "No, don't say that, Rancipert! Good men like you can't die! The world needs more of you—"

"And so there shall be many more to come. As one good man falls, another rises. And if I am to die, I wish to do so bravely and honorably in battle. I am comforted by the thought of reuniting with my loved ones...especially Adam."

Farther up ahead, Ptero the Bloodthirsty touched down from the sky, landing so heavily that it made the earth tremble. His monstrous grey wings cast a great shadow over the earth as the armored giant made his way towards them. Even Helena found herself wondering just how many ingots of iron were consumed in the forging of this beast's iron armor. Something flashed across Rancipert's eyes as he looked upon the fallen avian who had slaughtered his lover; his pupils dilated, and all the warmth washed from his face.

He cried out, "Have you come to serve your day of reckoning, beast?"

But Ptero had little interest in Rancipert, for he was there for only one other reason:

"Helena Nightingale," he growled.

Helena's heart raced, and she quaked with fear.

"If you want her, you will first have to go through me." Clambering to his feet, Rancipert puffed his shining feathers and stretched them out on either side of him in one powerful motion. He lifted his sword and brandished it in the bright rays of the moon. Ptero merely cocked his head to the side and grinned wickedly.

Rancipert looked at Helena and said, "Fairwinds, Helena! This may be the last time you and I will ever see each other. If it is, I am glad you have your wings back. Go now."

There was nothing Helena could say to convince Rancipert not to take on the beast that was Ptero. She made the motion to run and take off into the air, but could not help but send one last look over her shoulder at the pair.

"Fallen avian!" Rancipert cried, pointing his long iron sword at him. "Your time of cruelty is at an end! You shall pay for all the innocent lives you have taken, including the life of my beloved!"

Helena was in the air before she could see the outcome of this deadly duel. Wishing Rancipert luck from the depths of her heart, Helena carried on looking for Noa.


Helena swept over Alazar, taking great care to stick close to the rooftops and keep her distance from the fighting above. She dodged countless falling bodies, both Nevarian and Dragonback. Only when she risked flying up higher could she catch a wider glimpse of the kingdom, and her keen eyes spotted a migrating group of wigeons making their way towards Lake Eastpoint. They cried out in terror as Helena swooped in, made a harsh landing run and tackled Noa at full momentum. Together, they barreled over into a ditch.

Noa groaned in pain as Helena lay on top of him, wings and all. The fall seemed to have knocked the wind out of both of them. Breathless, Noa squirmed under Helena's weight until she clamped her hands over his mouth and looked directly into his eyes.

"It's me!" she said urgently.

His bushy brows shot up in disbelief before relaxing. Rolling his eyes, he took her hands off his mouth and gave her a big, toothy laugh. "You've got a knack for bizarre entrances, bird, I'll give you that!"

She grinned. "I like to leave lasting impressions."

"And last, they will!"

*"A nave's got 'im!"* a distant voice shouted. Several wigeons came bounding over with daggers and cleavers in their hands, ready to defend Noa from the likes of Helena, whom they had mistaken for a Krow. Abernam was the first of them to arrive at the scene, and he stopped dead at the sight of her. His eyes ran enviously over Helena's sleek, dark feathers.

"It appears the rumors are true," he said icily, as Helena rose to her feet and dusted herself off. The hurt and indignation were amply visible on his face. *"You're a flocker!"*

"Look, Abernam," Helena began, "I had my reasons for taking these wings, but there's no use arguing about it now. We must get these people to safety...so let's set aside our differences for now, and work together against the Nevarian invaders."

A myriad of emotions passed across Abernam's face, and his gaze angrily flickered from Helena back to Noa until it diminished to cold resignation.

"Yes, indeed," he said. There was an odd gleam in his eye. "Let us work together."

Helena's feathers puffed slightly as a wave of apprehension stirred within her. For a reason unbeknownst to her, she felt she could no longer trust this man.

Noa sounded off to her right. "There are dozens of decrepit wigeons who were left for dead by their flocker family members...and if that isn't the scummiest thing you can do, I don't know what is. I've already got a crowd of them sitting nice and warm by the lake—the battle hasn't touched that side of the kingdom. Yet."

When they arrived at Lake Eastpoint, a crowd of thirty or more gathered by the shore. Friends held one another a little closer, and wigeon mothers hugged their children tighter as they watched the battle from a distance. Noa was right—most of the fighting was taking place along the southern front of the kingdom, leaving this area relatively untouched. For now, they were safe...

The battle endured. Helena sat huddled with the others, counting down the hours until sunrise. They had received no sign of Avalon's arrival, which seemed the only viable thing that could save them from the hands of the Nevarians. Helena hoped that help would arrive before it was too late...

Helena suddenly felt the cool edge of a blade press against the small of her back. Someone's hot breath ran down the length of her neck as he whispered a message in her ear.

"START WALKING," the Stork's voice said, "AND DON'T MAKE A SOUND. IF YOU RESIST, WE WILL SLAUGHTER EVERY MAN, WOMAN, AND CHILD YOU SEE BEFORE YOU. YOU'RE SURROUNDED."

All the blood in Helena's body fell straight to her feet. Ever so slowly, she dragged her eyes over just a short distance away, where Abernam had Noa pinned against a tree with a dagger to his throat. Abernam met eyes with Helena and raised a silent finger to his sneering lips. Her instincts about this man had been right. Meanwhile, the Nevarian wigeon who had gotten a hold of Helena now urged her to get a move on. Reluctantly, the two of them complied and headed into the woods.

Rugged wigeons and Nevarians alike escorted Helena and Noa through the woodlands like prisoners. Before long, a furtive, skeletal figure emerged in the darkness ahead; he leaned against the tree, arms crossed, with a wicked grin on his face as he beheld their arrival. The Scarekrow cast an enraptured gaze upon Helena, for it was the first time he had seen her since the night she had sought him out.

"It appears that the rumors are true—the Nightingale has become one with the night. WINGS OF DEATH! SHAPESHIFTER! WITCH!"

Helena regarded him coldly. "The sight of you does not surprise me, though I'll admit it does disappoint me. It appears you've switched teams."

"I am inclined to favor my own kind."

"After they cast you out and abandoned you?"

His eerie smile fell. "The Stork has offered us a promised ascension; he is adamant that there will come a day when our curse is broken, and we Nevarians will one day be as free as you are to roam the day. As our Lord Nevar declared: THE FALLEN WILL RISE."

"It was you who told me the Fallen would never build a world where wigeons like you would be accepted."

"Indeed, it was! Then I learned that the Stork could turn ave into wigeon, and wigeon into ave! Just look at those feathers! I've never seen a pair of wings with such an emerald sheen to them...my, my, aren't they a sweet sight to behold..."

The manner in which he lusted after her wings revolted Helena, and she retracted them when he had the audacity to attempt to stroke them.

"I suppose it's my fault for taking the fickle word of a Krow," she snapped. "The Stork does not have as much power as you think—even if he did, you'd be foolish to believe he would grant wings to just anybody!"

A sly grin. "Of that, we shall see in time. You'd be interested to know that he's requested your presence and awaits you ahead. Until next time, Nightingale...I should not think this the last time we encounter one another."

That was the last Helena saw of the furtive Krow, for the time being. The Nevarians ushered Helena and Noa further through the forest until they reached a large clearing. There were about twenty to thirty Nevarians present; many of them perched upon the top branches of the trees and glowered down upon the scene, their eyes glittering like onyx gems in the shadows.

Helena's eyes fell upon the mountainous figure of Ptero, whose presence only confirmed her fear that Rancipert no longer lived among them. She was heartbroken, to say the least. Only once she realized that Ptero was missing an entire hand—a wound which he had been forced to cauterize to stop it from bleeding—did she find some solace in Rancipert's death. There was no doubt that the Dragonback Warrior had fought valiantly until the end.

As Helena and Noa approached the scene, the strange sound of soft, gurgling moans carried over into the night.

"Dear Penelope!" a cold, familiar voice cried out. "Have you lost your train of thought so soon?"

Helena registered two figures in front of her: the first was Penelope, who lay groveling on the floor. She looked like she had been deteriorating for years since Helena had last seen her: her skin was waxy and sallow, her eyes were sunken deep into her skull, and her feathers were lined with stress bars and fell off by the dozen. Third-degree burns scarred her entire body. This, Helena surmised, was the work of the Vespertine Curse, and she knew Penelope had little time left before she finally succumbed to sunlight poisoning. The Nocturnal writhed and wormed, growling and gasping like a zombie at nothing in particular...

The second person hovered over Penelope's stirring figure, chuckling as he looked down upon her.

"Once an esteemed genius in your own circle of daywalking heretics...but now you are nothing, Penelope—nothing but a vegetable rotting from the inside out..."

Though his back was to her, Helena had grown to recognize the narrow frame of the Stork's wings. He looked the same as she had always known him—handsome, cunning, with a secretive gleam in his eye that suggested he always had something up his sleeve. The only difference now, however, was the gleaming half-silver mask that clung to the entire right side of his face. It was an accessory that Helena had never seen until now, and was quite unexpected for someone with such a charming and enrapturing disposition...

Whatever business he had with the Nocturnal, the Stork set it aside the moment he became aware of his new company. The moment he laid eyes on her, a sudden and petrifying fear struck Helena, and she found she could not flee, as much as she wanted to. His one keen and visible eye ran over her wings, then flashed with fury upon realizing these were the wings that she had stolen from him.

"The wings of death become you, Nightingale!" he announced, but there was no hint of approval in his words. "I always said your wings were the stormier of the litter—now, it seems you've embraced the look of the true Nevarian! A shame that your mirage is not alive to have seen you discard it so easily!"

Noa cast a worried glance at her, for she trembled like a leaf and could not bring herself to respond. The air had caught in her throat, her head felt lighter than usual, and the familiar ache of the scar on her chest began to throb once more. Meanwhile, the Stork seemed to enjoy Helena's instinctual reaction to his presence.

Helena's eyes flickered towards Penelope, who still lay gurgling on the ground. The Stork followed Helena's gaze to the Nocturnal's withering frame and gave a disingenuous look of pity. He spread his wings wider, taking up even more space than usual, and circled Penelope, who only reached out feebly to him.

"A shame, truly. Her mind has regressed to that of a toddler and her motor skills have suffered immensely. She bears no recognition of you or anyone else. I suspect she has but a few hours left before her organs shut down completely and she wanes away into nothingness..."

Helena looked upon Penelope with a face full of pity. This was, she believed, the final stretch of a daywalker's life. The price to be paid for a fleeting moment of freedom. *Perhaps in another life,* Helena recalled Penelope's cool voice, *you and I might have been friends.*

"You spied on her all these years, just like you did me," Helena choked out.

"Indeed! Although I had more incentive to spy on Penelope and her dead brother. It so happens that over the course of their brief lives, the Duskmuth siblings had dedicated themselves to the same cause as I—to find the Twilight Stone and break the Vespertine Curse which has kept us from walking freely in broad daylight. Before long, they acquired a codex revealing the location of an ancient artifact in Nadiir which potentially housed the stone, and flew down to Nadiir to retrieve it."

The Stork stopped just feet away from Penelope, who now crawled towards him.

"I submitted my offer to her—bottomless wealth in exchange for acquiring the artifact. But Nocturnals are self-important creatures! They do not accept any sort of material offer unless it involves an abundance of knowledge—even then, they take every bit of information with a grain of salt, wondering if they could gain some sort of *wisdom* from it!"

He laughed obnoxiously as Penelope gnawed on his leather shoes. "As if wisdom buys you eternal life or glory! The men of kingdoms past did not rely on *wisdom* to rule their worlds, nor did conquerors use it to take entire continents—it is *power* that enabled them to do so. Raw, unadulterated *power*."

"And you believed that the artifact possessed the one thing that would give you that power?"

"The Twilight Stone would have set us free from the Vespertine Curse—it would have made the scope of our world domination limitless."

"But there wasn't a stone inside the artifact. There was a mirage. You were *wrong.*"

The Stork's wings stirred in agitation. Helena continued—

"And the worst part is, the only person who had acquired a lifetime of information on the whereabouts of the Twilight Stone stepped into the light to render herself incognizant before you could get your hands on her! Penelope Duskmuth made sure that, no matter what, you could never access the knowledge she's gathered to break your curse...a rotting vegetable out-smarted you!"

Helena knew at once that she had said too much.

*"Ptero,"* came the Stork's sharp voice. Before she could even think about running away, Ptero hastened across the clearing and used his hand—his only hand, to be specific—to strike Helena across the face. She saw stars. Her knees gave way underneath her, and she hit the floor.

*"No!"* cried Noa. He lunged towards Ptero, furious at the incident that had just occured, but another Nevarian caught the wigeon boy and subdued him in an arm lock. Even then, Noa thrashed like a madman. *"You dirty Krow! I'll tear off all yer feathers myself!"*

Helena tasted blood as she held a hand to her throbbing cheek. The Stork approached her, crouching down to her level.

"All this time without wings has not diminished your pluck, Nightin-gale," he murmured softly, admiring the trail of blood that now trickled from her mouth. His silver mask glittered under the moonlight. "But from here on out, I would advise you to choose your words carefully. The next time you anger me, I shall not be so lenient."

The Stork rose and dusted himself off before he began circling Helena. "'The dagger and the artifact are mine. If you want either of

THEM, YOU'RE GOING TO HAVE TO COME AND TAKE THEM FROM MY BARE HANDS...' Are these not the words you had purposefully sent out to me, Nightingale?"

Yes, Helena had spoken those words in hopes they would reach him after their escape from Mount Sulfur. Truly, she hadn't imagined ever hearing them again, even less while at his dubious mercy...

"Well, here I am!" he announced, raising both his arms and wings on either side of him. "You have something that belongs to me, Nightingale, and I have come to collect what is rightfully mine. Now, you may have already *claimed* the mirage inside the artifact, but that does not mean *I cannot take it back—*"

As if out of thin air, the Stork revealed the Dagger of Prince Elizar, the moonlight reflecting blindingly off its warped emerald blade. "This is what I first used to take your wings away, and it is with this that I shall take them from you once more! You gave me quite the surprise that night at Mount Sulfur when I discovered it missing, my dear. I will see to it that you are aptly punished for such a slight. But I digress! I wouldn't be standing here today, with this dagger in my midst, if it weren't for a charming little helper who brought it back for me...Phellis, dear, don't be shy!"

A nimble shadow fell from amidst the high branches of a tree; Phellis landed before all of them on her two dirty feet. With her head held high, she marched across the clearing, bypassing Helena and Noa. The two of them only watched in silent outrage. She kneeled before the Stork and, though Helena could not see her treacherous face, she could still see the pitiful outline of her wing stubs, ashen and droopy despite her otherwise proud disposition.

"Phellicarus Faye! You and I had agreed that if you successfully brought me both artifacts, you would be one of the first candidates chosen for the opportunity to claim the mirage inside the golden egg...after we have retrieved it from Helena, of course. You have proved yourself ever so worthy in returning this dagger to me..."

Phellis looked up with great hope at the Stork, her silver eyes gleaming.

"I commend you for your service, even if you only brought me one of two objects I assigned to you. Your name shall henceforth be added to the top of the list…and because I find myself in a more *generous* mood than usual, I shall grant you one wish—anything you so desire! Gold, jewelry…" The Stork caught Noa's reproachful look and smiled. "…even a slave, if you wish. Name it, and it shall be given to you."

Phellis quickly stowed away her frivolous affections for Noa and bowed her head in a sign of utmost submission to the Stork.

"I wish to join you," she said. "I wish to serve the Fallen Avian to the best of my abilities, if you'll have me!"

*"You hairless, double-crossing mutt!"* Noa roared.

"Phellis!" Helena could not help but cry out in dismay. "You can't do this!"

Phellis kept her stubbed back to them as she said, "I can, and I *will.*"

"Please think this through, Phellis! He'll discard you the moment you cease to be of any use to him—"

"It's no use, bird," Noa said bitterly, a look of pure loathing on his face. "That traitor made up her mind a long time ago."

As much as it enraged Helena, seeing Phellis resolved in her decision to cross over to a life of darkness…she found she could not bring herself to hate the child. That's what she was, after all—a child. Someone who, in light of her worst tragedy, had been preyed upon by a monster of a man—yet *another* thing the two girls had in common. Perhaps, under a completely different set of circumstances—in a world where Helena had not been consumed by spite to ruin the Stork, nor influenced by the goodness of her friends—maybe, just maybe, Helena would have been the one to kneel before the Stork as Phellis did that very moment.

With a conflicted heart, Helena relinquished any hold she had of her old friend Phellis—the sweet, brazen girl who once comforted Helena in her darkest moments. *Take my wings away, leave me, only me, and nothin' but me.* Helena would continue to treasure those words, even if she no longer recognized the person who had said them.

"Very well, Phellicarus! If that is your wish, then the fallen welcome you with open arms! For certain, your resourcefulness, endurance, and cunning may prove a valuable asset to our cause."

"I should have known from the first you weren't to be trusted!" Noa spat at Phellis. "Yer a filthy sellout!"

His reaction seemed to have touched a rather sensitive nerve of the wigeon girl. As Phellis rose to her feet, tears filled her eyes. She raised an accusing finger at Helena and cried, "She's the one who sold herself for a pair of wings—*she's the sellout, not me!*"

"The bird didn't sell out to the enemy—that was *you!*"

"It's alright, Noa," Helena said, rising to her feet. "She can join their cause. But wings or not, she'll spend the rest of her life knowing that she'll never belong there, and they will never truly accept her as their own."

"*YOU JUST SHUT UP,*" Phellis shrieked. "*SHUT UP, SHUT UP, SHUT UP!!!!*"

"Now, now, Phellicarus..." the Stork began, draping an arm around her and tucking her tightly under his wing. "You must not let their meaningless words affect you in such a manner, for that would only mean you still hold some affection for them. If you are to learn the ways of the fallen, you must relinquish whatever fondness and amity you hold for these people! Learn to let go. Only then can you achieve greatness as I have."

Helena's eyes narrowed at the way he kept Phellis close to him; her doe eyes looked up at him as only a daughter's would, absorbing his every word like a sponge. It reminded Helena of the night of her fall and how the Stork had captivated Helena with a mere look...

"I think," Helena began quietly, "I've finally figured you out."

The Stork's feathers puffed inquisitively. "Would you care to elaborate?"

"You target vulnerable, malleable children who can hardly tell the difference between right from wrong, especially wigeons, and you manipulate them so they see no other choice but to join you. Every now and then, however, you encounter someone you *can't* convince or brainwash. So you extort them, like you did me."

"*I'm not brainwashed,*" seethed Phellis.

"Calm, Phellicarus—let her spill her poison. It is true—for years I've rescued the inept from Avalon's bosom, taking them under my wing and teaching them to see your kind for what they really are: selfish, exclusive, and wasteful beings who never bother to look below their own feet. A corrupt civilization that thinks it is immune to the threats of the Lower Realm just because supernatural borders protect it. Little do they know that this era of invincibility will soon come to an end—and when it does, Avalon shall cease to be a beacon of glory and soon become a destination of ruin and despair."

He turned to his crowd of devoted followers. *"It is time for the fallen to rise and destroy the empire from which we fell, and raise a new one from its ashes!"*

Phellis and the Nevarians raised their weapons with bared teeth and cheered: *"THE FALLEN WILL RISE!"*

When all the uproar had subsided, that was the Stork's cue to turn around and face Helena.

"Ptero," he said, twirling the dagger in his hands, "hold her down."

Helena tried to run, but Ptero took her by the wrists and forced her to her knees. He turned to his Nevarian audience, arms spreading wide, silver mask flashing like a stage light. "Behold! Witness the true power of the Stork!"

*"Please! Have mercy!"*

The Stork approached Helena and raised the dagger high in the air—but there was movement to their right. Noa had escaped and thrust himself in between Helena and the dagger! He and the Stork wrestled for control over the dagger before the Stork thrust himself forwards and plunged its emerald blade deep into Noa's chest. There was an explosion of light...

Noa's agonizing screams cut cleanly to the bone. Helena had been in his place once before and could just imagine the searing, inescapable pain coursing through his body that very moment. As the Stork carved away at Noa's soul, a strange phenomenon occurred, and images flickered before them. Helena soon realized that these were memories of all the people he had met in his life, and the vile things they had said to him. The Stork raced through them like pages in a pamphlet:

*"'...dirty wigeon! Get your cursed feet off my property—'"*

*"'...I heard his mama left him as a babe 'cause he came from bad blood. His father was a wigeon, see, and she was afraid his son would grow up to be just like his daddy...'"*

The pretty face of a girl with blonde hair and baby blue eyes material-ized, and her bottom lip trembled.

*"'…but why don't you want to see me anymore? Don't you like my wings, Noadine?'"*

The memory was gone in a flash. Then, Helena's vivid green eyes ap-peared, and fragments of all the conversations she and Noa had ever shared played out before their very eyes:

*"'…you've never flown in your life, and it probably kills you inside to know that while there's still some slim chance of me getting my wings back, you'll stay stuck like this forever!'"*

*"'…your wings thrust against air and take you higher—so swiftly you defy gravity, and in the most divine manner, you conquer death.'"*

*"'…I set free a dove. That's how I earned my wings.'"*

The connection ended and Noa collapsed to the ground, seizing. The Stork admired the dagger in his hand, well-satisfied with his own work.

*"Noa!"* Helena ran to his side. He convulsed as if pulses of electricity coursed through his veins. There was a gaping rip in his shirt, and what remained of the dagger's touch had left a gruesome scar upon his chest.

"I'm so sorry," Helena said to the wigeon boy, tears streaming from her eyes. "This is all my fault…"

The Stork looked down at the squirming boy with distaste.

"Oskar Noa," he said darkly. "The traitorous Blood Feather who was foolish enough to throw a rock at me in a vain attempt to protect Helena Nightingale. That youthful bravado of yours does nothing to hide the fact that you are full of spite and self-loathing…" His eyes sparkled as a realization struck him, and he looked to Helena. "And yet, how interesting to see that your soul is centered on this girl…yes, fascinating, indeed! This wigeon boy is in *love* with Helena Nightingale!"

A great chorus of laughter erupted, as if the concept of love seemed so trivial, so *foreign* to these demons of the night that they felt no other obligation than to resort to mockery. Noa could not seem to look at Helena.

"…but she does not seem to love the wigeon boy in return."

"That's not true," Helena snapped bitterly.

The Stork grinned evilly. "In that case, be my guest and tell the boy you love him! Go on!"

Noa's face was deathly pale as his eyes finally fell upon hers. Helena wanted to say it, but her tongue was uncooperative.

"Her silence is telling! Don't you see, Noa? Helena Nightingale is incapable of loving anyone because she will always love flight above all else. You saw the lengths she was willing to go to get her wings back. You cling to her now in the hopes that one day she may reciprocate your feelings, but do you truly think she would ever consider being with a lowlife such as yourself? Helena is, by definition, out of your reach! Let us be optimistic and say that perhaps one day she may grant you a once-in-a-lifetime opportunity to win her favor...how, then, do you plan to meet Helena's rather...*high* expectations? Doubtless there will come a day when she will grow tired of you. When she will want to go a mile further and you—being the wigeon that you are—will only hold her back. When that day comes, as it inevitably will, she will turn her back on you and find another who can journey with her all the way."

The Stork's words were cruel, and Noa's eyes glazed over with hurt.

"Don't listen to him, Noa!" Helena cried, angry tears leaking from her eyes. "I care about you—far, far more than this man is letting on. You're...you're my *friend! I would never turn my back on you—*"

"Caring is not the same as *loving,*" the Stork said with a sly grin.

"What do you gain in toying with his head?" she snarled back at him.

"I speak nothing that hasn't already passed through his mind. Such thoughts can be rather sticky and linger for quite some time...in any case, let us stop this madness. I want what I came for."

He looked into Helena's eyes with an intensity that paralyzed her with fear. "We had a deal, Nightingale. Bring me the artifact, and with it you would have bought both your wings and your freedom...but you turned on me the moment you got cold feet. Now, you and your friends shall suffer greatly from the consequences of your actions. If you thought that Jared Pathfoot would be dead by now, you'd be unfortunately mistaken. He is alive and kicking...so to speak. As well as one could be after suffering as many beatings as he has...and the same fate awaits your wigeon lover."

"I will kill your friends one by one. Slowly. Painfully. I will take them apart piece by piece, until their last words are whispered pleas for mercy they know well will never come. You, I will save for last. I will carve you up from the inside out with this very dagger—I will tear up your soul like a piece of silk, until nothing but a few frayed strands remain. By the time I am done with you, your soul will be so disfigured that you will have become but a shadow of a living being. It is the price you will pay for ever daring to defy me."

"Go on, then," Helena choked out, stifling her fear. "Do it. Finish what you should have done the night you first laid eyes on me."

But the Stork never completed his promise. At that moment, a flock of Dragonback Warriors descended upon them all. Phellis screamed and cowered away into the forest. Ptero lurched off the ground to take on two soldiers in the air—and Yulix slammed shoulder-first into the Stork, knocking the dagger out of his hands and spiraling off to the side. Yulix, in all his glory, raised his sword proudly and planted his feet firmly between the Stork and Helena.

"Villain!" Yulix bellowed, his voice carrying across the clearing. "You shall regret ever laying your hands on her!"

An icy rage overcame the Stork. *"KILL THEM ALL!"*

Looking back and forth between Yulix and the dagger, the Stork knew he had no chance of retrieving it without meeting Yulix's blade. With a hiss, the Stork leapt upwards into the sky and disappeared into the clouds before Yulix could do anything else. Yulix hurried to Helena's side and hoisted her up onto her own feet.

"Are you well?" he asked her, concerned. When she nodded, he asked, "Where is the dagger?"

"Over here!"

Helena turned and saw Noa placing the dagger back within its white chest, using a large leaf to avoid touching it directly. He limped over and handed it to Yulix, who did not seem to take well to the wigeon boy. Nevertheless, he gave him a curt nod of respect.

"Cornelius!" Yulix shouted. One of the two Avalonians who had accompanied him to Nadiir landed with a great thud against the earth.

"Sir."

He handed him the white box. "Take this and guard it with your life. It is now the property of the Avalonian Crown. We shall take it in for further examination."

"Yes, sir!" Cornelius said with a salute.

Meanwhile, Helena had flocked to Noa's side, utterly disconcerted by the sight of the gruesome mark on his chest almost identical to her own. She stifled a sob at the realization that the worst thing she had ever endured—that is, being impaled by the cursed dagger—had been committed against someone so dear to her. Both of them were now forever marked by the dagger's touch.

"Are you okay?" she asked frantically, but Noa waved her away.

"I'm fine, bird." His eyes were distant.

"Noa...about what he said back there..."

"I said I'm fine," he snapped.

He wasn't—Helena knew that all too well. Something had shifted in the way he looked at her; though the affection he felt for her was indisputable, there was now a trace of doubt in his eyes every time he ran them over her tall, dark wings. Helena had the Stork to thank for that. *She will grow tired of you,* Helena could almost hear the Stork's words echoing in Noa's mind. *She will want to go a mile further and you—being the wigeon that you are—will only hold her back.* She could tell that Noa would never forget them. Neither would she.

As if things could not get any grimmer, the blaring cry of a war horn reverberated across the valley. Goosebumps shot up along Helena's arms. Both Yulix and Helena kicked themselves off the ground and flew up higher to investigate. It turned out that the sound originated from a Dragonback watchtower located along the eastern borders of the kingdom. The Dragonback Warriors were trying to warn the people of a danger approaching from the east.

"It is the Koli," Yulix said sharply. "The Nevarians have sent reinforcements! The battle yet continues!"

# Chapter Thirty-Four

A second Black Wave emerged from the east, and in response, a hundred Dragonback Warriors rose into the air to meet the enemy head-on, ascending into the sky like a flying red serpent. Helena held her breath as she watched the second Black Wave and the Red Dragon collide. The two parties became indistinguishable at this late hour...

"What's going on?" Noa demanded as soon as Yulix and Helena landed.

"The Nevarians have sent reinforcements from the east," Yulix said gravely. "I estimate this second wave to be at least two hundred naves strong..."

"I don't like that look on your face, Yulix," Helena confessed.

He sucked in a sharp breath. "Earlier, I believed our numbers would be enough to hold them off. But we lost a lot of good men and women on the battlefield, and our numbers have been reduced significantly...the scales have tipped. We are now outnumbered. We might not live through the night."

"And what of Avalon?" Noa demanded. "Did the king not promise to open a portal and send reinforcements?"

"The king's word is law," Yulix snapped. He hesitated, then added, "but there's been some sort of delay...our only hope is that they arrive within the next hour. Otherwise, our future remains grim."

Yulix was right. At a glance, the Nevarians outnumbered them two to one—which wasn't the worst set of odds they could have faced, but definitely a cause for concern. As Helena surveyed the eastern horizon, her keen eyes caught sight of a light disturbance up ahead—several birds fluttered out of a tree in one cohesive flock, zooming up and around the top of its branches before steep diving and soaring away...

An idea dawned on Helena.

She met quiet, discerning eyes with Yulix. "I have an idea."

He must have recognized that same clever, ambitious gleam in her eyes that he had grown to love over the years, and he did not seem to like it one bit. "What is it, Lena?"

Helena had considered it once before, when talking aerial formations with Rancipert—may his soul soar free. Yes, it was an ambitious plan. Ludicrous, even. That is why, when she revealed it to Yulix, it was as divisive as it was brilliant.

"You're suggesting we *Murmurate?*"

Helena's face broke into a miraculous grin. "Yes!"

"*You speak madness!* We've only ever been taught the Murmuration as a form of ceremony, not a combat formation! Besides, most of these people are not Avalonian; they have never flown a Murmuration in their lives—"

"Because they never had the *chance* to fly in one, Yulix! If we give them that chance, we might be surprised at the results!"

Yulix rolled his eyes and huffed. "Even then, there may be less than a hundred of us left. Unless you can magically pull a thousand aves out of thin air, what makes you think we can even pull off such a wild stunt?"

"The smallest recorded Murmuration in history consisted of only seven aves," she said. "So, it's not impossible! Listen to me, Yulix…giant Murmurations are great for defense, but their size greatly limits the scope of their mobility. The smaller the flock, the more agility it possesses to move around—thus granting the flock the ability to go on the *offensive.* All we need is five other aves to pull it off. Just five! If we built up enough speed and momentum, not even the Nevarians could deter an offensive Murmuration!"

Yulix looked conflicted as he gazed up at the massive black cloud that grew closer every minute. He must have known that they needed some sort of trick up their sleeves if they were to have even a slim chance of winning this battle.

"It would be an onerous task," he admitted, though the look in his eye suggested he was considering the idea. "I imagine maneuvering an offensive Murmuration would be twice as taxing as a ceremonial one…"

Yulix was right—a giant Murmuration was a cumbersome thing that tended towards wider, slower movements because of its mass. Quite manageable, in Helena's opinion. You really had to *try* to fail at it. A primitive Murmuration, however, would be far more demanding than anything Helena had ever experienced, both physically and emotionally.

"That is why such a thing would require a dedicated inner circle," she responded. "Skilled and unbreakable."

When Yulix caught the *true* meaning of her words, he blanched.

"No," he said at once, shaking his head. "No, I won't allow it!"

"But Yulix—"

"I will *not* allow you to fly out into battle, Helena!" he bellowed. "I promised your father I would protect you! If I let you fly out there, you could get gravely injured, or worse—you could be *killed*!"

Noa, who had been listening furtively to this conversation, now raised his head to look at her, and his eyes widened at this new possibility.

"You and I both know that I'm one of very few fliers skilled enough to pull off such an aerial maneuver," Helena insisted. "You *need* me out there, Yulix—same as I need you. I can't do this alone. Fly with me. Please."

Perhaps with the direness of their situation, Helena's idea seemed the only option that offered a sliver of hope—for Yulix knew as well as she did that there was nothing Helena did better than flying. His gaze fell, and he took Helena's hands in his. He swallowed deeply before those striking amber eyes shot up to meet hers.

"As I always have, Lena."

They had their first two, but in order to effectively coordinate an offensive maneuver against the incoming Nevarians, they would need more numbers; Helena and Yulix succeeded in finding five more aves and convincing them to join them, which included one knight who went by the name of Ser Ramsey Quellstone, an Avalonian who had accompanied Yulix to Nadiir. Together, the seven of them would form a primitive Murmuration. Yulix and the rest were armed with their reliable swords, while Helena—unwilling to take any lives just yet—armed herself with a big, burly branch certain to knock any unsuspecting nave unconscious.

With everyone armed and ready, the only thing left to do was to spark the Murmuration. As Matcher, Helena braced herself to take flight, but a hand stopped her.

"Where are you going?" Noa demanded.

"I have to help spark the Murmuration," she said.

He tried to rein her back in to him, and they struggled. *"You can't go out there!"*

"I have to do this, Noa—you have to let me go!"

"But if I do that, you might not return—" Pulling her in closer, he cupped her face with his hands and looked into her green eyes imploringly. "Don't go, please. I've never begged for anything in my sorry life, but if something happens to you out there...I wouldn't know what to do with myself..."

For the first time, Helena saw true fear in Noa's eyes. By now, they were standing so close their noses were touching...just a little closer and his bashful mouth would be on hers...

*"Stay with me,"* he whispered.

Helena smiled sadly, placing her hand on his left cheek. She traced the faint mark of his scar softly with her thumb. "If I die today, then let it be doing what I love most."

Helena would never know what crossed Noa's mind at that moment. Perhaps the Stork's words echoed in his mind, whispering that he would only ever hold Helena back. Or perhaps some innate part of Noa knew that the things we love most always find a way to return to us.

He pulled her in for a last embrace, this time wrapping his lean arms around her waist, and Helena's arms instinctively reached to encircle his neck. They lingered like that for several moments, with Noa's crooked heart beating against her chest. Helena was afraid to let go, as if this was the last time they would ever see one another.

"Come back to me," he muttered in her ear.

Something had become lodged in Helena's throat. "I will. In the meantime, promise me you'll take care of yourself, Noa."

He didn't answer.

"Promise me!" she pressed.

"...I promise."

"Good. Then watch me soar."

He pressed his warm lips against her ear. "Fairwinds, Helena Nightingale."

Passion overwhelmed Helena and caused her to do the unthinkable; taking Noa's face with both hands, she pulled him in and kissed him. Even Helena was startled by her own pluck as she held Noa's lips to hers. They were much softer and warmer than she'd expected, and they moved against hers with an urgency that sent shockwaves of electricity coursing throughout her body. Their kiss was fleeting, as were many good things in this short life, but it was just enough to spark the flame within her and ignite the inspiration for the ambitious task she was about to take on...

Yulix observed this passionate exchange from a distance. There was a stoney look upon his face when Helena joined him, breathless, yet invigorated by the kiss. He said nothing, though she could tell it bothered him. But Helena knew there were greater things at hand. After giving Yulix a determined nod, Helena leapt into the air and got to work.

Helena felt a shift in the air to her immediate right—Yulix had joined her side. There was another shift to her left as Ser Ramsey Quellstone joined the flock. Then another joined on her right posterior, then another on her left, and so on and so forth until they formed a solid septuplet with Helena as headbird at the center of the flock.

A curious phenomenon took place as soon as the seventh avian locked into formation. There was something inherently magical about Murmurating with your peers—there was no doubt about that—but this was another matter entirely. Helena felt, for lack of better words, *not herself.* In a most inexplicable manner, a foreign presence overtook her mind, her senses, and her limbs. The rushing wind seemed to breathe life into her wings, which grew longer, firmer, and much more vibrant than before; their green iridescence seemed to take on a stark nature now, glowing vividly in the dreary setting of the night. They glowed so brightly, in fact, that a green halo permeated the air around Helena, enveloping both her and her flock—whether Yulix and the others noticed what was happening, there was no true way of knowing. All Helena knew was that she was no longer *Helena,* but something else, and at one point she was looking *at* herself and all six of her flockmates, as if watching from someone else's eyes.

It wasn't long before the glowing Murmuration soared above the great Kingdom of Alazar.


The second Black Wave had fallen upon Lake Eastpoint, and the crowds of women, children, and elderly who had gathered there dispersed in cries of dismay as the enemy descended upon them. With the ranks of the Dragonback Warriors reduced by at least half, the Nevarians overcame them like a dark storm, unleashing their cruelty upon anybody unfortunate enough to cross their path. Many cried out for Avalon to come and save them, and when their pleas for help went unanswered, it seemed all hope was lost...until they spotted something peculiar in the distance.

A strong glow emerged along the western horizon. For a moment, these civilians weighed against their natural instincts and mistook it for the setting sun, even though the sun had set hours ago! *No, it couldn't be*, they thought. It had to be a comet, the way it shot across the sky—a flaming green streak, its tail burning golden. Even the Nevarians warring along the shoreline paused a moment from their fighting, stupefied at the phenomenon unraveling in the distance...and then—

*Whoosh!* The Murmuration swept across the lake in a blazing blur. It whirred upwards, high above the lake waters, before coming down on their unsuspecting enemies like a flaming meteor! Helena braced herself as her squadron hurtled towards a congregation of Krows—*WHAM!* Yulix, at the forefront of the flock, drove his sword cleanly across the throat of one unlucky Krow and sent him sprawling to the ground. Ramsey rammed into another Nevarian shoulder-first, sending the nave reeling in mid-air across the lake. Losing momentum, the flock circled around and regained enough speed to head towards their next targets, who were so stupefied by the startling sight of the Murmuration that they were knocked several feet into the air and rendered unconscious before they even realized what hit them.

Helena and her flockmates glided across the skies like flying daggers—accelerating and turning, rising one moment and steep diving the next. Her peers instinctively responded to every one of Helena's movements—if she inclined slightly upwards or downwards, or veered to the left or right, they did the same. The forces of gravity pressed harder against Helena's skull the higher they went; there were many moments when she became lightheaded and nearly lost consciousness—a dangerous possibility this high in the air. Nevertheless, the group made strenuous efforts to cycle positions, each of them shifting and taking turns being headbird in the middle, which was considered the most energy-consuming position. At the rate at which they were gaining speed, it was a miracle that a flock of such small proportions did not fall apart!

Helena and her peers, however, had learned to fight against this inclination towards disorder, and they pressed tightly against one another as they flew higher in the air. Helena even had the pleasure of hitting one nave smack up the jaw with her wooden club, and she very much enjoyed the sound of his teeth clashing together.

Down the Nevarians went! Helena's plan worked better than she had anticipated. Soon, the number of enemies fell to half of what they were originally—though she certainly felt her energy depleted after such an endeavor...no matter! Helena sucked in a sharp breath and continued working with her peers, flying higher and higher into the skies...

As for Penelope Duskmuth, her time had finally run out. The Nocturnal avian slumped against a tree with her black eyes wide open, the lake within her view. Helena liked to think that, in her last moments, Penelope's dream had finally come true—that she had realized that a *true* Murmuration, driven by pure instinct and synergy, was taking place before her. Perhaps there had remained a sliver of reason in her mind that said that however much you suffered for it, freedom was well worth the cost.

The fight carried itself high above the clouds, where the winds were fierce and unmerciful. Helena's Murmuration continued plowing through the remaining flocks of Krows. By this point, the flock had cycled positions many times, Helena's back muscles were weak and aching, and the Murmuration had depleted much of her energy reserves. She was at the forefront of the flock when a bellowing voice drew her attention. Three figures rose from the depths of the clouds, and upon realizing who they were, Helena's blood went cold.

"It's a diversion," Yulix cried, as if sensing what she was about to do. "Keep formation, aves, or we will lose this battle!"

*Do it,* a foreign voice said in her mind. *Save your friend, at whatever cost.*

Without warning, Helena heeded this voice and made a jarringly sharp turn, diverting from her flock's trajectory. Leaving her inner circle was like pushing against an elastic band to its limits—and when it finally ruptured, the Murmuration instantly collapsed, sending Yulix and her peers spiraling out into the winds as Helena made her way towards the horrifying sight:

Two Nevarians had Jared suspended in midair by two long chains and were raising the wigeon boy higher and higher into the air. It was the first time Helena had laid eyes on Jared since Mount Sulfur. Though she did not want to admit it, she had taken him for dead. It would've been a far better fate than what he must have went through since then, for the wigeon boy was hardly recognizable. His usually warm, brown face had been beaten to a black and bloody pulp; lacerations ran down the lengths of his thighs, shins, and arms, and his body periodically shuddered with a series of dirty, wet coughs that sent blood spattering every which way. The worst part about this punishment, Helena realized, was that there were no shackles or cuffs binding Jared to the chains which suspended him thousands of feet in the air—it was only his own dying grip which kept him from plummeting to his death. One slip, and he was done for. Helena was not unfamiliar with this barbaric punishment—the *Avian Death Grip*, they called it.

"Jared!" she cried, her heart shattering at the sight of him. *It just wasn't fair.*

His head lifted at the sound of her voice. He could barely open his swollen eyes, though when he saw it was Helena who was flying in front of him, his body shuddered, and from his lips came a sputtering moan.

*"Helena...your wings...I knew it..."*

The Stork suddenly burst forth through the clouds, thrusting his narrow wings as he maneuvered himself in between Jared and Helena. There was a cold fury on his face, laced with the satisfaction that he held greater leverage over Helena, now, more than ever.

"Release my friend!" she demanded, her voice carrying over the harrowing winds.

The Stork grinned. "Why, I am not keeping the wigeon boy against his will! He's free to leave whenever he pleases—though it would be imprudent to do so at these heights! Did you know that hitting the water from these heights would be the equivalent of *SPLAT...*" He clapped his hands together. "...hitting solid ground? In that case, I suggest the boy hold on for dear life!"

"*Gah!!!*" Jared cried out in anguish as the two naves on either side of him drifted further apart, pulling his arm muscles taut, and his grip slipped an inch down the chains on either side of him. Helena sucked in a tense breath as her black wings fought against the violent gales. She squinted down to where the misty clouds obscured the shrunken lake below, and a dizzying rush came over her—if Jared were to fall, even the best flier could not be sure to catch him in time under these conditions...

"*Helena!*" A panicked voice echoed somewhere beneath the clouds. Yulix was still searching for her. "*Helena, where are you? ARGH!!!*"

Helena could only guess from the cries and commotions below that the enemy had overwhelmed her flock. She could've sworn she sank an inch in the air from the weight of her guilt.

The Stork's bitter voice sounded. "You've outdone yourself, Nightingale! An offensive Murmuration? Why, even I am impressed that you conceived such a resourceful strategy at the last minute! At the height of its momentum, there are very few things that can stop an offensive Murmuration in its path...add weapons to the mix, and soon you have a fearsome, nearly invincible opponent. You could've succeeded in laying waste to every last Nevarian solely with the power of inertia and flight! And yet you deserted your own flock for the likes of *this...*" He pointed to Jared, who kicked his feet as he looked at the abyss below. "...a mere wigeon boy?"

"Does it bother you," Helena declared furiously, "to know that I'm not willing to risk my friend's life for a speck of glory?"

"Glory is fleeting, perhaps, but reputation is everlasting!"

"And I suppose that is the reason why you stole my wings and ruined my life," she cried. "For some pitiful attempt at infamy?"

*"PITIFUL?"* he bellowed in laughter. *"I AM THE STORK!* The man who turns ave into wigeon! The people of Nadiir now shrink and quiver at the sound of my name, and when they see my shadow loom, they fall to their knees and beg for my mercy! Soon, my name will overtake the entirety of both Realms! But you are overlooking the true reason why I confiscated your wings that fateful night…"

The Stork's energy shifted dramatically. "I took your wings because *I enjoyed it!* You fell into the palm of my hand that night, helpless and injured…yet so pure. I knew from the first moment I laid eyes on you that you came from a place where you were *loved*. So, I cut you open, and watching your face contort in pain as I carved you from the inside out gave me a thrill that no mind-altering substance or pleasure of the flesh could ever bring me—"

Helena covered her ears. *"Stop it, stop talking—"*

"I watched how you earned your wings. I saw firsthand the love you had for that stupid little bird and your foolish father—I saw and felt the purest part of your soul, Lena! And that will remain a bond between you and me until the end of our days!"

*"STOP IT!"* Helena shrieked. *"WHY MUST YOU TORMENT ME THIS WAY?"*

Jared seemed to stir at the sound of Helena's agony, lifting his head ever so slightly to look at her, before it fell back down. Meanwhile, every tear that Helena shed seemed to breathe more life into the Stork—he seemed to grow bigger, and his wings thrust harder.

"I never asked for any of this," she said through gritted teeth.

"A common grievance made against the workings of Fate," the Stork observed. "But all of this is nothing more than a consequence of your insubordination, Nightingale! Had you simply done as I asked, you would have already received your reward and flown back to Avalon by now, as you desired. Instead, you allowed your mind to be corrupted by covetousness and spite! Yes, when they informed me that you had run off with the artifact—*my* artifact—I was overcome with a grizzly rage, along with an arid thirst for revenge. I planned to destroy your mirage once and for all, in the most brutal way possible, using the Dagger of Prince Elizar…"

The Stork trailed off.

"Why didn't you?" Helena asked. She felt disconcerted by his hesitance; the Stork *never* hesitated.

His expression darkened. "I tried to—of that there is no doubt…the instant the blade made contact with your mirage, the reaction was instantaneous. There was an explosion of light, and as I sunk the blade deeper into the fabric of your soul…there came the voice of a woman."

Helena stiffened. "A woman? I don't understand…whose voice was it you heard?"

"That, I cannot say for certain," he snapped irritably, "but before I knew it, the magic had rebounded, scalding me like the kiss of a flame! Your mirage escaped into the depths of the mountain before I could lay eyes on it again, all while leaving me maimed and forever disfigured…" His hand rose to the mask which concealed half of his face, which curled into a snarl. "I would give anything to have it here now, and to feel it crush between my fingers."

Helena swallowed thickly. "Well, there's no use in holding grudges—my mirage is dead. You've had your revenge."

"Have I?"

Several aching moans diverted their attention back to Jared, who stirred once more, groaning as the Nevarians stretched his arms further and further apart…

"Jared Pathfoot! The boy who wanted wings!" the Stork announced. "You accompanied Helena on this long journey to get her wings back in the foolish hopes that it would prove you worthy enough to grant you your own…but now we see that not even going to the ends of the earth to aid a friend is enough to do that for you. It seems that even after all your hard work, Helena was the one who was worthy enough to acquire her wings, not you! How does it feel, Jared, to know that after all this time and effort, you are *still* unworthy?"

"You're wrong," Helena called sharply. "Jared is a fierce and loyal friend, and he has all the noblest qualities a man could ever hope for. He's noble, and kind, and just…and it only took me the first few seconds within meeting him to recognize it. He doesn't need wings to be a good person, nor does he need to hurt other people to prove it. Jared is the man you could never be."

In an instant, the Stork's face was as furious as the war-torn skies around them. "Why, Nightingale, you seem to have acquired a bit of affection for this wigeon boy! Just months ago you couldn't have cared less about him, or the other wigeon he hangs around with...you yourself said, 'JUST SO WE'RE CLEAR, THEY'RE MERELY STRANGERS I MET THE OTHER NIGHT, IS ALL.' Is that not so?"

Jared's face twisted in hurt upon hearing this, and in that moment there was nothing Helena despised in the entire world more than the Stork. She hated the sound of her own words and wondered if they would be the last thing Jared heard before he fell to his death...

Then, overcome by some impulse, the Stork brandished his sword, and in one great swipe he cleanly severed one of the two chains that Jared held on to, sending the wigeon boy reeling. Jared cried out fearfully, swinging back on the only chain which remained intact. The Nevarian holding holding onto it now struggled with the added weight, and he and Jared both began to sink. Helena cried out in dismay, reaching out a hand towards him, but the other Nevarian now held her at bay with his sword.

"Please," Helena begged the Stork, her heart racing as she watched Jared struggle to maintain his grip on the single chain which was keeping him from falling to his death. "I'm the one who ran off with the artifact—Jared had nothing to do with any of it! Leave him out of this—"

A greedy grin broke out on the Stork's face. *"Please.* That's the magic word! What are you willing to give me in exchange for this boy's freedom?"

"...anything."

"Very well," he said darkly. "I will spare the boy's life on one condition."

This time, Helena and Jared both looked up to see a dark, hungry look on the Stork's face.

"Join me, Nightingale. It's time you grew past the childish need to depend on some measly flock and become a woman of her own name—the woman you were always *meant* to become. Leave it all behind—every person, every flock, every false thing you've been taught about the world—and pledge yourself to me."

*"No!"* Jared yelled, thrashing in midair. *"Don't do it, Helena! Forget about me and save yourself!"*

Helena felt her throat tighten. "Just moments ago, you wanted me dead."

"Indeed, I did…until I witnessed your supernatural performance in that Murmuration you led just now. You are talented in the air, my dear, but even I know that talent alone cannot reproduce what we all witnessed with our own eyes—that was not just *any* Murmuration. It was laced with *magic*, fueled by a power unseen in all my years of searching. I suspect there is a power hidden in those wings that will prove invaluable to my endeavors."

"…and if I say yes?"

"I'll let the boy go. You'll have my word for yours," the Stork said.

*"Don't listen to him! He's a trickster—a trickster, Helena!!!"*

Helena sent Jared one last look of utter regret before she said, "I'll do it. I'll join you—not for you, but for *him*."

Fearsome tears filled Jared' eyes. *"No, you can't!"*

The Stork's face lit up with a victorious grin. "Excellent! I expected nothing less from you, Nightingale! Well, that leaves nothing more for me but to honor this newly forged alliance and fulfill my end of the bargain! I told you if you'd join me, I would let the boy go…"

Helena's stomach dropped upon grasping the true meaning of his words.

Without warning, the Stork took one final, powerful swing at the chain which Jared clung to, breaking it in two. With a harrowing cry, Jared fell.

*"No!"* Helena yelled, nosediving to catch him as an icy wind cut against her tear-stained cheeks.

For Helena Nightingale, nothing mattered except getting to her friend in time. She shoved her instinctual fears of death to the back of her mind, ignoring the shouts of her old flock as they were slain by Nevarians. As she had on that fateful night, Helena fell, only this time with purpose. And though the wind conspired against her body, she narrowed herself and her wings to the likeness of an arrow to gain the speed she needed to catch Jared before he hit the water below. As Helena reached out, her fingers just inches away from him, a fleeting thought occurred to her: *Hitting water from these heights is like hitting concrete.*

Helena caught Jared just feet above the surface of the lake. There was just enough time for her to curl her wings over his delicate frame before making harsh contact with the water and breaking her neck.

And with that, her world ended.

# Chapter Thirty-Five

They say the *penultimate moment* is the critical point in time, just before diving into water, in which the avian's fate lies uncertain. In this instant, the ave must act precisely, for even a split-second's hesitation can mean the difference between life and death. In the case of life, this moment is nothing more than a brief, exhilarating brush with death. What most don't know, however, is that in the case of *death*, the penultimate moment is the moment when your life flashes before your eyes. And in that moment before Helena Nightingale's death, the memory that presented itself to her was the day she earned her wings:

It had been a year since Helena's mother had passed, and on that particular day, she felt most melancholy. So, Raphael decided to take Helena on a tour through the Colossal Gardens in hopes of raising her spirits. The Colossal Gardens boasted a magnificent arena of flowers, crystal-clear streams, and short, breezy trees. It also happened to be a playground for many curious creatures, three of which Helena had been admiring; as a green hummingbird hovered nearby, basking in the rich nectar of a red rose, two electric blue caterpillars inched their way up the leaf of a tall shrub. They were fuzzy, rotund, and lively, and Helena observed them devotedly.

Then, there was a skirmish amidst the branches. *Kraaaw, krawww!* A crow's bitter call sounded, and something white fell smack onto the cobblestone path before Helena. It was a bird with crimson streaks staining its creamy wings. The culprit, a black crow with a wicked gleam in its eye, perched high above. It took one good look at the fallen white bird, then at Helena, before it gave an intellectual cock of the head and took off into the shadows.

"A dove," Raphael said, as he cradled the milky fluff in his arms. "She is fallen, and her wing is hurt. What do you say we help her get back in the air?"

It was hard for the six-year-old girl to discern her feelings for such a creature, especially one found in such terrifying circumstances of pain and blood. Nevertheless, Helena felt a dire need to *help* the poor thing. That day, her father took the tiny fluff home with them. At first, little Helena observed the curious creature only from a distance, but eventually she came around and helped her father mend the little dove's wings.

Weeks later, the day of its release was upon them. Both father and daughter stood upon Blade's Peak, the dove cradled in Helena's arms, ready to be set free. It was a great day for the bird...much more so than it was for Helena. It turns out that in caring for the little creature—in feeding it, and helping it bathe, and soothing its pained little cries—Helena had become extremely fond of the dove, and it had never crossed her simple mind that the time would come when she must part with it until that fateful day. When it did, it devastated Helena's precious little heart. Raphael had also developed a particular attachment for this bird, for it reminded him greatly of Helena's late mother, Efevra. He had always claimed that Helena's mother flew with as much grace as a dove flocking over a funeral—which, given their recent loss, seemed to take on a much different meaning, now.

"Papa, I wish to keep it," Helena said.

"But it is time for her to fly home, Lena."

A few tears trickled down her rosy cheeks. "Do you think she will return, Papa? Oh, won't she come back to visit me?"

Raphael looked to the horizon, regarding her words with thoughtful consideration.

"There are many things that will come and go in our lives, my dear. Sometimes, it can be a good thing if they don't come back. Take this dove, for example; any dove's destination is where there is life, so if she doesn't return, it would mean that she has found her home elsewhere. Isn't that great?"

Something in his eyes shimmered upon hearing his own words, and it was clear that he was thinking of Helena's mother. "Her absence will serve as a testimony to the living world beyond our reach. Do not fret, Lena, for what we love always has a manner of returning, even if in a different form."

Only with time would Helena gain a greater understanding of her father's words. In the meantime, Helena had enough sense to approach the ledge of the cliff and hold the bird out with her own two hands. The dove sat fat on her palms, momentarily giving little Helena the false hope that it didn't want to leave her after all. But eventually, it stretched its stiff wings and fluttered out of her hands and up into the air. Helena watched with tear-stained cheeks as the dove became a tiny speck in the orange sky, before eventually flying out of sight.

Before long, a seed of light sprouted from high above her. Helena gaped up at it in wonder as the light grew gradually bigger, illuminating the entire scene. From this ball of light two white wings appeared with a flourish, and soon a magnificent white dove fluttered above them. Raphael released a joyous laugh as he watched his daughter chase after the dove.

"Oh, my dear Lena! Do you know what this is?" he asked, beaming. He held his hand out, and the dove fluttered down to perch on his finger.

Helena shook her head, gazing up at the bird.

"This is your mirage! It is what grants you your wings, which you have so dutifully earned! I told you that what we love has a way of returning, didn't I? Now, this dove lives within you forever, a memory that shall always remind you of the beauty of life and its dire need for hope! Cherish it, Lena, for in your darkest times, this memory shall be your light."

Helena's mirage fluttered out of his reach and alighted upon her, diving into her chest. From within, a strange iciness spread throughout her body, down her back, and to her feet. Before she knew it, a pair of delicate, snow-white wings hung from her small back.

Helena Nightingale earned her first pair of wings that day. But there is a gentle technicality that defines this milestone of her life; while caring for the bird was an act of service worthy enough to have granted anyone their wings, it was ultimately the *act of setting the bird free* which granted Helena *her* wings. For to love something and clutch to it is *easy*—anyone can do it, without question. But to set aside one's own desires, to say farewell to that which you love for the sake of its own happiness...such a sacrifice requires the strongest of wills, and is undoubtedly one of the greatest acts of kindness one person can demonstrate for another. At just six years old, Helena Nightingale accomplished what even most adults could not bring themselves to do.

The memory trickled away like running water, and Helena found herself back at Lake Eastpoint. The lake waters were still, except for its gentle lapping against the shores. The skies were empty. Helena wished to take a vantage point up in the air but found she could not fly—her wings were missing. How odd. She wandered for several more minutes along the shore, searching for any sign of life.

A halo of light in the distance beckoned Helena towards the center of the lake—it hovered just inches above the tepid waters. She walked across the surface of the lake and, to her surprise, did not sink. As she did, Helena found it difficult to tell what was ahead of her. At first, the light was indiscernible. Then, as she inched closer, it began to take on the faint outline of a dove—like her mirage! When the light became too bright for Helena to bear, she stopped. Squinting her eyes, she could just barely make out the faint outline of a woman.

"Lena," said a kind voice, with a tenderness only a mother could possess.

*"Mother?"* she asked.

"I've been waiting a long time for this moment, my dear."

"*You're* my mirage?" Helena asked, holding up a hand to partly shield her eyes from the light. "But...but my mirage takes the form of a dove!"

"I take many forms, but I prefer the image of the dove. It reminds me so much of you."

It was then that the tears came readily. Oh, how Helena wished to run up to the golden figure and hug her! But the light was so bright that she could not step any closer without being blinded. It was then that Helena became small again, her voice meager and afraid, like it had been those many years ago when she had called out for her mother, but she would not come.

Her bottom lip trembled. "You've no idea how much I've missed you..."

"As have I, my dear Lena. But the truth is you can only miss that which goes away, and I never truly left. I've been flying alongside you all these years, and I have watched you blossom into the beautiful young woman that you are today! Words cannot express the joy I feel in seeing you now...only it shatters my heart to know that our reunion came so soon, and under such tragic circumstances..."

It is said that an avian only sees their mirage twice in life—the first time on the day they earn their wings, and the second when they die. Helena looked down to their right and gasped! A body floated along the surface of the lake, drifting aimlessly with the current. It was an avian girl in the prime of her youth; her black wings were soggy and limp, her neck was skewed at an unnatural angle, and her green eyes were dull and lifeless.

"I'm dead!" Helena cried.

"Yes," her mother said, drawing in a sharp breath, "the force when you hit the water was enough to snap your neck, and you died on impact. But you accomplished what you were set on doing—which was saving your friend from an untimely death."

Up ahead, a figure emerged from the depths of the lake, exploding out of the water with a gasp. Jared sputtered and flailed for many moments, looking everywhere for Helena, until he spotted her body bobbing along the shallow waters near the shore. He raced towards her, his arms slicing through the water until he reached her broken body and dragged it ashore.

He laid her on the cool, crumbly sand. Helena's eyes were fixed upon the starlit sky, and her large black wings had turned stiff. Jared knelt beside her, his swollen eyes blinking down at her pale face. He tapped her cheek gently. When he received no response, he placed his hands against her chest and pumped a half-dozen times before putting his lips to hers and breathing air into her lungs. But it was of no use. After many failed attempts to resuscitate Helena, and with a heavy heart, Jared closed her eyes so that she could rest. His head hung low, and his body quivered with short, stifled sobs.

"He is a noble young man," Helena's mother said with an air of sadness. "He protected you when I couldn't. There is not a person in all the Realms who deserves their wings more than Jared Pathfoot."

*"Then why didn't he get them?"* Helena found herself yelling. "He's proved himself more than worthy these last few months! It's not fair!"

"It is not for me to say why someone does or does not earn their wings," her mother replied. "Perhaps Jared is meant for something greater…"

Noa came bounding down the shore not long after, and the scene that followed was one of the most agonizing things Helena ever had to witness. He fell to his knees before his friends, struggling to piece together the scene in front of him: Jared, who sat with his head in his hands, and Helena, who lay on the sand with a look of utter peace on her face, as if she were asleep. But then Noa reached for her hand, whose touch was as cold as ice, and he let out a cry of anguish. He sat himself upon the sand and pulled Helena's pale frame into his arms, rocking back and forth as he caressed her paper-white cheeks. His brown eyes searched for any trace of life on her waxy face. They found none.

*"I told you to stay, bird! Why didn't you listen to me?"* Though Noa's words were angry, he cradled her face and body. When Helena did not respond, Noa pressed his lips against her forehead and held her close.

"Fairwinds, Helena Nightingale," he said, tears streaming down his face. "Today, we part. May we reunite in another life…"

As Helena watched her friends weep over her dead body, she wished so desperately to take their sorrow away. She wanted nothing more than to throw the two of them over her shoulder and fly back home with them!

"I don't want it to be this way," she whispered. "I can't part with them. I can't!"

"You must," her mother said. "As the Law of Attainment states, *all avians must earn their wings.*"

"I…I don't understand…are you saying I had to *die* to earn my wings?"

"It is more than that, Lena. You gave up your own life to save your friend's. There is no greater love than that. Now, you must depart from that which you love most dearly, as it is the only way to consummate your sacrifice…but don't worry—that which you love always has a way of returning. And if it doesn't, well, it must mean they found their home elsewhere. Isn't that wonderful?"

"Not to me…*I love them!*"

"Yes, indeed! You love them! And are you not so certain in your gossamer little heart, after seeing them mourn you, that they truly feel the same for you?"

Upon hearing this, Helena wept.

A deafening noise blared from above, as if a thousand horns played all at once. Jared and Noa looked to the skies just in time to see a golden lightning bolt shoot down from the heavens, striking the earth. A fearsome explosion sent powerful gusts across the lands. The ground quaked, and the lake waters trembled. There, in the furthest remote corner of the valley, a gateway of massive proportions emerged. Even the Eye of Nadiir could not compare to such things, for the portal thrummed with a magic unforeseen to the average mind, and it stretched wide across the earth in a grand archway. Beyond it resided the Kingdom of Avalon. It was daytime on the other side, and light pierced the darkness of Nadiir like a great, golden sword; Nevarians nearby shrieked and cowered as rays of light scorched their cursed skin.

"Avalon has opened its gates!" cried Jared.

A single war horn sounded from the other side of the gateway. Before long, a host of Avalonian soldiers streamed from the Upper Realm and into Nadiir! It shimmered like a gleaming silver ribbon as it soared over the vast precincts of the kingdom. At the head of the host was a knight with armor of solid gold, and a massive sword in his hand that shone like a beacon in the darkness. It was a Knight of the King's Guard. Beside him were two lesser knights, each holding a banner of Avalon with the sigil of seven Murmurating birds.

As he held Helena's limp body in his arms, Noa waved his fist at the Avalonian army soaring above—

*"Curse you, mighty Avalon, for not coming a moment sooner!"*

The Gate Portal burned like a flame in the darkness and drew hundreds, if not thousands, of avians from across Nadiir; they flocked towards the gate like moths, willing to do whatever it took to cross over into Paradise...

A horse-drawn wagon came barreling past the lake not far from Noa and Jared. It came to a sudden stop, its horses releasing an ear-piercing neigh. The wigeon driver cupped his hands over his mouth and shouted over to them:

"*OY!* You two best jump aboard—once that portal closes, you'll be stuck down here forever! It's our only chance to get to Paradise!"

Noa and Jared shared startled looks before staring down dolefully at Helena's body.

"She deserves a proper burial," Noa choked out.

"And there would be no better place to have one than her home, with her father," Jared said.

Noa did not argue. Together, they hauled Helena's body towards the wagon. There was barely enough room for the three of them; the wagon was packed heavy with trunks, parcels, and miscellaneous paraphernalia that the handful of passengers on board had decided to take with them to Paradise. One of these passengers was Timuth Greene who, in an ironic turn of events, had lost his left wing in battle. He was now a halfwigeon. Noa and Jared swaddled Helena in a white cloth before laying her gently upon the wagon's wooden platform. Timuth said nothing to the two wigeons; he only looked askance at Helena's dead body.

Jared moved forwards to board the wagon, looked over his shoulder, and noticed that Noa had made no attempt to follow him.

"What are you doing back there, Noa?"

"I'm staying."

A look of hurt flashed across Jared's battered face.

"I've already lost one friend tonight," he said dolefully. "Don't make me lose another. This might be your one and only chance of returning home."

"With her gone, there is nothing left for me up there. This is my true home, now."

"Get on with it!" shouted the driver. "The gate won't stay open forever, you know!"

Jared looked between Noa and the gate and knew there was no use in trying to change his friend's mind. He pulled Noa in for a fierce embrace, and the two muttered their final words to each other before Jared boarded the wagon. The driver gave a sharp crack of his whip, and the horses burst into a fast gait, launching the wagon towards the glowing halo in the distance. Noa waved at his dear friend in farewell.

"Fairwinds, Cap'n!" he bellowed. "I expect to see you in them tufts of feathers, next time I see you!"

Noa couldn't tell from this far, but a single tear ran down Jared's cheek as the wagon drew further away. It would be the last they saw of each other for a long, long time.

Noa lingered by the lake long after the Gate Portal had closed, dwelling in the mournful silence that prevailed. Most would have deemed him a fool, turning down the chance to go to Paradise, but he knew he didn't belong there. He belonged in Nadiir now, where he would be free to pursue his two greatest desires—freedom and adventure.

Time was running out. The portal grew smaller and smaller, and countless stragglers, including Jared and his wigeon peers, were in the mightiest race of their lives to reach Paradise.

*"Yah, yah!"* the driver yelled, snapping his reins harder, and the horses exerted all the power they could to pull the wagon faster. Up ahead, countless other wigeons congested the main road with their own modes of transportation—caravans, oxes, mules, all laden with their personal belongings as they journeyed to the Upper Realm. Jared knew that the fastest way to get to the portal would be to divert from the main road and cut across the murky and treacherous grounds of the woodland forest.

*"Brace yourselves!"* the driver cried. The wagon veered off the road; Jared held on for dear life as it launched itself headfirst into rough and uneven terrain. He also kept a firm hold of Helena's body.

"It's too far," cried one wigeon. "We're not going to make it!"

"Whip those horses like your life depends on it!" snapped another wigeon to the driver.

"They've hit their limit," the driver bit back. "We're going as fast as we can!"

"Unladen her!"

Everyone, including Jared, turned to gawk at Timuth, who had a mad look in his eye.

"Don't you all want to make it to Paradise?" he said sharply. "Throw out everything—every ounce of unnecessary weight, and we'll go faster. What are you waiting for? *Do it!*"

The few wigeons on board heaved a trunk off the moving wagon, and it fell to the ground with a crash, shattering to pieces. At once, they picked up speed. They tossed overboard every bulky item they could find—trunks, briefcases, parcels. Soon, the wagon was flying across the fields, making significantly more progress than before. But it was not fast enough.

Then, Timuth laid his sights upon the swaddled object beside Jared.

"*NO!*" Jared roared as the halfwigeon stepped towards Helena's body. They clashed, grappling with one another like warring grizzly bears.

"*Don't you touch her!*"

"*She's dead weight! We've got to toss her—*"

"*You'll have to get through me, first!*"

"*Suit yourself.*"

Timuth used the bend of his remaining wing to strike Jared upside the chin, stunning him briefly, before bearing down his fist against the side of Jared's face. *SMACK!* Weakened by the many beatings he had already suffered at the hands of the Stork's men, Jared collapsed to the wooden floor of the wagon, unconscious and unable to stop Timuth from hoisting the body up and tossing it overboard. Helena flew one last time before making her final landing, smacking hard against the earth so that her white cover fell off. Her limp body went tumbling past the trees, across the rocky ground, until it finally rolled to a stop.

Helena was quickly forgotten as the wagon hurtled towards the Gate Portal, picking up more speed than it ever had before. Hundreds of Nadiirians, aves and wigeons alike, also hurried to make it across. Just a little further, and they would all be in Paradise...wait for it...almost there...the portal had now shrunk to the size of a small cottage...

Jared's wagon was the last to bound across the portal into Paradise, just seconds before it shut completely and cast the Realm of Nadiir into darkness once more.

Many succeeded in crossing over. Many more did not. It was not long until the chilling silence was replaced by the wails of those who had been left behind.

Somewhere deep within the woodlands, Helena Nightingale's body lay alone amidst dead leaves and stones. She faced upwards, her eyes eternally fixed upon the clouds, as they always had been. It was a tragic outcome, indeed: Noa had left with the assumption that Helena would be returned to Avalon, while Jared, who had succeeded in crossing over, remained unconscious and unaware that she had been left behind. Neither boy had the slightest clue that she lay in a strange forest, in the dead of night, alone. So terribly alone.

The one who did eventually find Helena was Underbelly. He must have escaped his stable amidst all the chaos. Nevertheless, the noble steed approached her and let loose a mournful whine as he pawed at her lifeless frame.

Helena's mother uttered a cry of dismay, drawing her attention away from the tragic events unfolding. The bright silhouette of her mother staggered, clutching at her chest as if wounded. She flickered like a dying light.

"What's wrong?" Helena asked, her heart racing.

"I don't want it to end this way," she said, suddenly sounding a great deal more distant. "I shouldn't be here, but I had to come and bid you farewell! I had to see you before it's too late…"

"What do you mean?" Helena looked around frantically. "What's happening? Why can't I see you anymore?"

"You're dying, Lena. This is where we part ways—"

"What? *No!* You can't leave—we're supposed to leave this life together!"

"I must go. You must stay."

*"I can't lose you again! Stay, mother, please!"*

"I cannot! *He's* here, and he does not welcome me very much…"

"Who are you talking about?"

"I must go! Remember, Lena—that which you love always has a way of returning!"

Out in the still forest, a glowing mirage descended from above and perched itself on Helena's unmoving chest. It searched for a heartbeat, for some sign of life, but found none. And so the dove, with a weeping coo, finally parted ways with Helena Nightingale and fluttered off to seek solace in the darkness of the forest, whose silence was riddled with loss and grief.

When Helena opened her eyes again, she was still in Nadiir. Not much had changed, only the sun had risen, and all seemed well; the skies were clear, the oceans a pleasant blue, and the lands lush with green forests and hills. As Helena looked to the skies, however, this period of peace came to an end. A fissure of incomprehensible proportions split the skies of Nadiir, and a deafening groan reverberated across the lands as the rift grew bigger. The sky fell apart, raining fire and earth. It was as if the magical boundaries between the Upper Realm and Lower Realm were slowly beginning to dissolve; mountains from high above toppled over like defeated chess pieces, cliffs ruptured and crumbled like dust, and lakes and rivers spilled into Nadiir. Tsunamis soon ravaged the lands. That was when a universal cry of anguish pierced Helena's ears; hundreds of Nadiirian aves took to the air, fleeing the destruction, leaving wigeon men, women, and children behind to be swallowed by the encroaching waters. From the Upper Realm, hundreds of thousands of wigeons fell into Nadiir, plunging to their deaths. In a vision so horrifying as to defy belief, the Upper and Lower Realms appeared to be colliding into one another.

The terrible vision ended, and an even more abominable sight revealed itself to Helena. There was a great mountain, thrice the size of Mount Sulfur, and at its summit stood an abomination: an avian with leather wings and scaled skin like that of a reptile. Beneath its taloned feet stood not a mountain made of earth and stone, but of hundreds of thousands of bodies—wigeons and avians alike, piled high atop one another. The Fallen Avian perched high upon this mountain like a conqueror, raising his sword and crying out, *"The Fallen Rise!"*

Helena, frightened sick by this vision, had no words. When everything faded, something approached her from behind; this entity, it seemed, possessed a gravity that seemed to bend the very fabric of space and time itself. When she was too afraid to turn around and face it head-on, a mighty, usurping force took hold of Helena and forced her to turn around. All she saw was light. She could not scream, though she so desperately wanted to.

"Helena Nightingale," said a voice which seemed to penetrate her very soul. "I've come to deliver the prophecy. Hearken! For I shall only recite it once."

*The Era of Convergence approaches!*
*The Fallen will soon rise.*
*His is the hand that will sow fear and*
*hatred.*
*His is the hand that will reap chaos*
*and destruction.*
*He shall devastate the balance of the*
*two realms*
*Until no distinction remains.*
*There will be no above, nor below.*
*There will be neither heavens nor*
*earth.*
*Whosoever shall take me as their mas-*
*ter,*
*will be the one to destroy the Fallen*
*Avian,*
*and restore balance between the two*
*realms.*

"I don't understand," she cried. "What does this have to do with me?"

"It is you, Helena Nightingale, who must work to counter the forces of evil at play. You must be the one to defeat the Fallen Avian."

*"But I am just one girl!"* she cried. "How can you expect me to achieve such a thing—and alone?"

"The prophecy has been delivered. Make haste, for time runs short, and many will seek to tear you asunder. The fate of all that is good remains in your hands, Helena."

*"Wait!"* she cried. "Don't leave, please! I have so many questions and I'm...*I'm scared of the dark!*"

The vision went as quickly as it came, however, and Helena was overcome by that which she had grown to fear...

Darkness.

# CHAPTER THIRTY-SIX

The Nevarian Regime almost certainly would have declared a night of victory, were it not for the late arrival of the Avalonian army. As promised by the King of Avalon, a host of two hundred Avalonian soldiers touched down upon Nadiirian soil, and they fought valiantly against the Nevarians. The battle was over before sunrise, and the Nevarians were left with no choice but to retreat shamefully to their nearest colony—the Kanyons of Koli, where thousands of their own kind resided amidst the great crevices of the dry river-valley. There they took their dead and wounded, bringing back wagonfuls of dead bodies in the hopes that their corpses might be repurposed in some way—to have their flesh given over to feed their hounds, or their bones brewed for use in dark potions, or whatever else they saw fit to fulfill their sick desires.

Back at the Koli Colony, naves sulked their way through the cracking valleys with broken wings, burnt skin, and missing limbs. One Nevarian stood alone before a great mound of dead bodies, sorting them into a series of smaller piles. He grunted and groaned as he picked up and tossed corpse after corpse; he was just about to toss one body onto the pile designated for the hounds, until—

"Not that one," a voice commanded.

The nave reeled from this sudden order and turned to bow before the narrow-winged figure who stood behind him. Approaching the mound which reeked of death, the Stork's dark eyes lingered curiously on the body, which was quite unlike the rest. Its black wings had grown stiff and curled inwards around its body like an onyx cocoon, as if in a final attempt to protect it from the world—which it must have been, for if any depraved soul in those last war-torn hours had come across the beautiful and youthful face that resided beneath those wings, they certainly would have taken advantage of such a sick and serendipitous opportunity. It took a bit of force to pry the wings open, and even then, they only budged just enough to reveal the pale face of a girl—a face which must have certainly been beautiful in its prime, but which now lay waxy and rigid. When the Stork leaned down and pried open her eyes, they were a vivid green, as he had always known them.

"I want this one preserved," the Stork said. "Take great precaution not to leave anyone alone with the body. No one is to lay a finger on her until she wakes."

There was a split-second's worth of hesitation as the nave's dumb face blinked stupidly at his master's strange words. He looked questioningly from his master to the stiffened corpse—but the Stork was not one to be questioned.

"O-of course, Sire! I shall set this one apart from the rest."

The Stork watched in contentment while the nave did as he asked. As the night wind swayed the black feathers on his wings, a mysterious figure appeared from the shadows. He wore a thick black cloak covering his wingless body, as well as a thick hood that shadowed his ugly face. He took his place by the Stork's side, accompanying him as they watched the nave delicately place the body on a wagon to be taken elsewhere. When the man spoke, it was like hearing the grating of metal against concrete.

"You're certain she is to wake?"

"I have never been so certain as I am now."

"How soon?" the cloaked wigeon prodded impatiently.

"Ease yourself, Nevar. We shall not rush the process. For the fallen, all that is left to do is rise. When she does, she will cease to be Helena and shall become known by her new name: *The Elusive Nightingale.*"

"A poor choice of moniker, I'd say…"

"Really? I think it's rather fitting. The Nightingale eludes us all…"

417

*TO BE CONTINUED.*

# ACKNOWLEDGEMENTS

In efforts to formally recognize those who helped me in my pursuit of publishing this work—whether you contributed directly to the creative process, or simply expressed support for my endeavor to become an author—I offer my sincerest gratitude to the following individuals:

*Matthew Ross,* who provided both a developmental and copy edit of TFA Volume I. You were one of the first people to have believed in Helena Nightingale and have outdone yourself as both an editor and a friend. *Taylor Ostendorf,* for providing a thorough proofread of this work—you're the best! My beloved beta readers: *Erandi Macias, Jasenia Arambula, and Nora Kim.* Your feedback and support were instrumental in making this novel what it is today. A special shout-out to *Jasenia* (@sokosgraphics | IG) for gifting me my first ever fan-art, which I will treasure for life—you are an extraordinary artist! A huge thank you to *Patrick Zapata* (@coliurrs_dx | IG) for creating the first official character design for Helena Nightingale. A round of applause for *J.N Ignacio* (@_sushinori_ | IG), the talented artist behind this book's one-of-a-kind cover.

Gracias a mi familia: mis padres, hermanas, sobrinas y sobrinos, Arturo, mi tios...les agradezco a todos desde el fondo de mi corazón por su apoyo. *To my family: my parents, my sisters, my nieces and nephews, Arturo, my aunts and uncles...from the bottom of my heart, I thank you for all your support.*

Last, but certainly not the least, I offer a heartfelt thanks to the person reading this, for deciding to give this novel a warm spot on your bookshelves. I hope to have given you something to daydream about in your day-to-day lives.

# About the Author

Xochil América, like most authors, developed a passion for reading and storytelling at a very young age, almost as soon as she picked up her first book. At the blooming age of twelve, she conceived the idea of *The Fallen Avian*, only to stow away the rough draft on her computer and forget about it...

It wasn't until almost a decade later, when the COVID-19 Pandemic struck—a time of great uncertainty—that she gained the sudden inspiration to continue Helena Nightingale's story after being locked in her room all day.

When she's not writing, Xochil enjoys cozying up and reading enthralling literary works like *The Hobbit, Game of Thrones,* and *Wuthering Heights.* Some of her favorite pastimes include pottery and playing the saxophone (though, these days she wishes she had more time to dedicate to them...) Xochil also likes to spend her free time binge watching T.V. shows like *Game of Thrones, The Walking Dead,* and *Demon Slayer,* her all-time favorite anime.

Xochil enjoys a private life in her Southern California hometown with her friends, pets, and loved ones, cherishing every minute with them.